*Stifling Folds of Love*

# Stifling Folds of Love

An Aliette Nouvelle Mystery

# John Brooke

Signature
EDITIONS

© 2011, John Brooke

All rights reserved. No part of this book may be reproduced, for any reason, by any means, without the permission of the publisher.

Cover design by Terry Gallagher/Doowah Design.
Photograph of John Brooke by René De Carufel.
Printed and bound in Canada by Hignell Printing.

Acknowledgements
'Verse of the Maid of Nagara' is from *The Three-Cornered World* by Sōseki, translated by Alan Turney and Peter Owen, Perigree Books; excerpt from 'The Motive for Metaphor' by Wallace Stevens is from *Wallace Stevens, The Palm at the End of the Mind: Selected Poems and a Play*, Vintage Books; lyrics excerpted from 'Frou-Frou' were written by Monréal and Blondeau, music by Chatau.

We acknowledge the support of The Canada Council for the Arts and the Manitoba Arts Council for our publishing program.

**Library and Archives Canada Cataloguing in Publication**

Brooke, John, 1951–
    Stifling folds of love / John Brooke.

ISBN 978-1-897109-57-1

    I. Title.

PS8553.R6542S75 2011        C813'.54        C2011-907599-7

Signature Editions, P.O. Box 206, RPO Corydon
Winnipeg, Manitoba, R3M 3S7
www.signature-editions.com

for Annie
…for love
without the folds

# Prologue

They were keeping a close eye on Inspector Nouvelle that spring. The way she'd been smiling lately. Had she finally found someone? Everyone in the third-floor *Police Judiciaire* detachment at Rue des Bons Enfants was attentive to the investigator's every move. PJ Commissaire Claude Néon nodded knowingly. Monique Sparr, Claude's secretary, was positive she saw something. Which meant that everyone was catching snippets of surmising as they filtered down to Commissaire Duque's busy City Police station occupying the second and first. Cops of all description beamed their curiosity when they encountered the inspector on the stairs. Pathologist Raphaele Petrucci observed her carefully whenever she came down to his basement morgue to view a body. Forensics specialists Charles Léger and Jean-Marc Pouliot of *Identité Judiciaire* were both sure they'd spotted traces of a blooming passion.

For her part, Aliette had to wonder, Does it really show when you're in love? Because in fact she was. Or hoped so. Still early days, one moves cautiously. There'd been no talk of anyone moving in. My place? Your place? It depended on the night. But it had been a beautiful change in her life since New Year's Eve and it was still going strong in April when the problem of Pearl Serein arose. A gentle, unseasonably warm spring was a perfect time for love and the inspector was enjoying it. She just didn't broadcast it. It was private. Love had not affected her professional abilities — as her results showed clearly. *Au contraire*, she told herself, being in love helped her do her work. They could speculate till they dropped. Aliette Nouvelle stayed mum and carried on.

She could not have cared less about Pearl Serein and her fabulous life. Stardom was the last thing she needed. It went counter to her style. But the problem touched her: Love. Work. The basic virtues. A question of the well-tuned heart. Pearl's life threw Aliette's into turmoil.

Because it was a time of confessional display. We French call it *le déballage*—literally, the unwrapping. Thus the verb *déballer*, in the figurative sense: to spill your most intimate secrets in the public square. Everywhere you looked someone was baring his heart. And everyone gleefully enjoyed a piece. The Pearl effect? It seemed Pearl Serein created a murky nexus wherein deeply private notions of romance converged, and each citizen was a separate entry point to the mystery.

Our city is really very small. If nothing else, Pearl Serein proved that.

Pearl Serein was a fantasy and nothing more. But this fantasy gripped us and revealed us. All of us. It started on a Friday, a Friday evening in our unusually gentle spring when three men died—each of them a leader in his field, three of our very best. Banker Jerôme Duteil was discovered first. Normally it would've been ruled a heart attack—because it was—and that would have been the end of it. But these weren't normal times. There was a disturbing coincidence clouding the death of Monsieur Duteil. Popular radio personality Jean-Guy Gagnon also died that night. Then noted documentary filmmaker Pierre Angulaire was found on his office floor. Three within twenty-four hours, and in much the same manner, according to pathologist Petrucci's preliminary prognostics. But it wasn't the hearts. It was Pearl Serein.

Commissaire Claude Néon latched onto this apparent fact.

Although Inspector Nouvelle and Commissaire Néon worked closely together, their approach to the mystery was fundamentally different and diverged from there—dangerously, all things considered.

And Pearl herself was nothing if not problematic to the process of ensuring justice for the dead.

# Part I

She was the focal point of light at which the totality of things converged.

— Gustave Flaubert, *A Sentimental Education*

## — I —
## The Pearl effect

Saturday. Inspector Aliette Nouvelle had a major operation planned for the checkpoint at the Swiss border that afternoon and had come in to the office to finalize details. A certain car would be stopped and searched as it tried to enter Switzerland, its ultimate destination a town on the Dalmatian Coast. A well-connected car, where it came to Turkish drug channels. She had been working on this one all winter. Her counterparts in Switzerland, Austria, Italy and various jurisdictions along the shores of the former Yugoslavia and Greece were expecting big things. Commissaire Claude Néon too. Her bust, Claude's feather. So he was in that morning, working the phone confirming Swiss actions—and non-actions, composing final memos, signing forms. Which meant Monique had to be there too, to ensure letter-perfect presentation. Junior Inspector Bernadette Milhau was also in, on Duty Desk, because weekend duty is a right of passage. The four were gathered in Monique's office, taking a break, sipping coffee. Monique was all aflutter. The news was too late for *Le Cri du Matin,* but the deaths of Jerôme Duteil and Jean-Guy Gagnon were all over the morning broadcasts. All reports mentioned the common link to Pearl Serein.

Inspector Nouvelle wondered, 'But who is Pearl Serein?'

'Never heard of her,' replied Commissaire Néon.

So much for the *Police Judiciaire*'s two top investigators and their knowledge of the local social scene.

'She's always in Tommi's column,' Monique explained, 'going to parties, falling in and out of love with interesting men. She was with both these guys, but then she dumped them.'

Aliette remained in the dark. 'And who's Tommi?'

'*Le Vrai Tommi.*' Monique poured more coffee. 'Celeb gossip guy in *Le Cri du Matin*?'

'Oh yes.' At the back with the birds and the gardening. Aliette had never really read it.

Claude asked, 'With them at the same time?'

'Our Pearl could do it,' Monique replied, vicarious pride suffusing her voice. 'She's amazing!'

The discussion was interrupted by a call from the city police dispatch desk downstairs. They'd just heard from the beat cops who responded to a call from an east end building. One Pierre Angulaire had been found dead in his office. Someone from PJ should come and have a look.

Bernadette Milhau said fine, drained her coffee and bustled out.

Claude asked, 'Pierre Angulaire — isn't he some film guy?'

Monique gasped, 'Yes! And he was with her too.' With this Pearl Serein.

Aliette and Claude got back to work. When Inspector Milhau called an hour later saying she needed a second opinion, Claude was happy to oblige. The view from his office window showed a clear morning in Alsace. The temperature had dropped to more normal seasonal levels overnight. Sparse clouds were running quick on a fresh nor'westerly, the Vosges mountains had assumed a splendid green, the vines along the Wine Road were taking leaf. The invigorating air was a good enough reason for the commissaire to decide to personally lend his experience to his rookie's uncertainty. He could sign international documents just as boldly in the back of a cab.

He turned to his senior inspector. 'Care to come along?'

'Why not?' Everything was pretty well in order for the afternoon's operation.

They joined Inspector Milhau, two uniformed beat cops and two SAMU (Services d'Aide Médicale d'Urgence) ambulance medics in the scarred and threadbare hallway on the low-rent east side. The tarnished brass plaque on the door read *Les Productions Angulaires*. Directly inside the cluttered but obviously low-rent office, a medic carefully lifted a blanket to reveal the victim rigid on the floor. His death-misted eyes were wide open. His arms hugged his chest as if he had just heard a great joke. Adding to the effect, the curve on his lips was hauntingly glib for a man stone dead where he lay. It looked like a heart attack. But this Pearl woman, the two others found last night: Claude called Dr. Raphaele Petrucci and requested that he come. Saturday or not, in a small prefecture the pathologist is also *Légiste*, the medical expert whose role it is to liaise with physicians and police in determining criminal cause in both the living and the dead.

A too-thin woman in cowboy boots had been crying but was now collected. Nanette. She had been with the deceased for a dozen years. With an exasperated sigh, Nanette explained, 'It's very near what he looked like when he was getting rid of someone.'

'Anyone in particular?' Aliette asked.

'Everyone? He was so stressed and depressed lately, not a lot of patience. If someone wasn't on the same page for whatever reason, Pierre's eyes would roll up like that — like: Oh God, why do I have to put up with such fools? And he'd tell them to get out. He was alienating a lot of people.'

'What was he working on?'

'Nothing much. We kept it going on little pieces for the regional news, regular enough thanks to his track record, but still hand-to-mouth. Mostly he was in perpetual pre-production on his Pearl project.' Nanette reprised her large sigh. 'Not that anyone in their right mind would ever license two hours on Pearl Serein. But he was beyond listening. It was getting embarrassing. Poor Pierre.'

'His Pearl project. Meaning a film?'

'A doc. Pierre only did documentary. He said he could easily deliver two hours.'

'What about?'

'*B'en*, Pearl Serein.' *Obviously* was implied; same presumptive tone as Monique's. 'Pierre was an expert. A broken-hearted expert.'

Claude asked, 'What he did say about her?'

Nanette shook her head, glum, mystified. 'Almost nothing. That's what's sad. He'd say, Nanette, this Pearl thing has so many layers! And he'd sit there for a week and think and think, make a few notes, then throw them away. He'd come out of it to earn some money stringing for the news, then sink straight back into his obsession. I talked to his last ex-wife once or twice, trying to find out if she had any idea…' Nanette was still shaking her head.

'Was she angry, his last ex-wife? How many did he have?'

'Four. Everyone who loved him was angry! It was a waste of a man and his talent.'

'I meant was she angry at this Pearl Serein.'

'Not really. It's like, well, she's really just some schoolteacher, if you know what I mean.' Nanette's eyes were focused on Aliette — not Claude. 'I think Pierre did it to himself.'

Aliette understood. A woman knows which rival is deserving of real scorn. Or worse.

'I think they all do,' added Nanette.

Claude asked, 'Who?'

'All Pearl's sad ex-loves.' Again Nanette's response was pointed, as if Claude should know.

Raphaele arrived with another uniformed cop wielding a camera. All present were quiet as the pathologist perused the body and the officer took pictures. 'Get his face and eyes,' requested Raphaele. The officer obeyed. 'I mean very close.' The officer adjusted, moved close.

Aliette thought, Dead eyes are merely dead. It's the body posture that gives effect. She noted that Pierre Angulaire had been a good looking man: six feet tall, full head of curly black hair, clean teeth, strong jaw. But the way he was lying there was daunting. As if he had answered a knock at the door, listened to an offer that made him laugh — then died. Wham: straight back on the floor.

She sniffed him. Sometimes smell is the key. She smelled a third-day shirt. And death.

Nanette asked the pathologist, 'What do you think happened?'

'Can't say yet,' replied Claude on Raphaele's behalf.

Nanette reached to touch the victim. Raphaele intercepted her hand. And smiled. 'You mustn't.' Nanette returned the smile. She watched with overly polite interest as Raphaele set about exchanging and signing various official forms with the uniforms and SAMU people. Aliette thought the woman far too thin and perhaps as impetuous as the far-too-impetuous Petrucci. But though the inspector sensed something odd at this scene — maybe murder — she could not sense a murderess.

Nor could Claude. After providing coordinates, Nanette was free to go.

At first glance, Raphaele estimated the time of death at sometime the previous evening, which fit with Nanette's description of her day's activities, having left Pierre alone at six. Claude noted it was within the same reported frame as the other two men who had loved this Pearl Serein. He made another call, this time to Jean-Marc Pouliot of *Identité Judiciaire*, requesting his presence.

'We need to have a look at this,' Claude said in an official way. 'Someone came calling.'

The two uniforms were told to secure the site and canvass the building's occupants, pending the arrival of IJ. The beat cops knew the PJ Commissaire had no right to ask for such a service, not without a mandate. They worked for Commissaire Duque, not Néon, and they'd both heard the légiste muttering 'heart attack' after the deceased's assistant had left the scene. It wasn't even suicide. But they obeyed. As did the SAMU medics when Claude told them to deliver Pierre Angulaire to the police morgue.

Raphaele Petrucci was less acquiescent. Every aspect of police work costs money. Claude had leeway with his own time and that of his inspectors, but in ordering these extra services he was getting ahead of himself. Raphaele, though impetuous where it came to women, was ultra cautious when it touched on his career. He was openly dubious when Claude ordered him to make calls requesting that the bodies of Duteil and Gagnon be re-routed through his shop.

'Weird eyes? Think Gérard will go for weird eyes?'

He meant Chief Investigating Magistrate Gérard Richand. Also called the instructing judge, he or she weighs initial police reports and recommends charges to be laid by the *procureur* (public prosecutor), then assigns mandates and budgets relating to subsequent police investigations.

'Just do it. Please.' Waving off the doctor's caution.

Petrucci obeyed. Claude announced he was on his way to the other two scenes: Jerôme Duteil's flat in the boutique district, and Jean-Guy Gagnon's warehouse condo by the docks.

It was almost noon. Inspector Nouvelle had her operation at the Swiss checkpoint to attend to. She would ride back to the office with Bernadette Milhau, then head down to Basel. Before going their separate ways, the inspector asked her commissaire, 'Are you sure?' Because Claude was being impetuous too.

'This is interesting,' said Claude. 'You heard him. Those eyes: something not right. And three in one night? And the same woman? We should check it.'

Aliette agreed, 'Yes, it's interesting.' Later, she'd be wishing that she hadn't.

Like that, Claude got a bee in his bonnet. The Pearl effect had started.

## — 2 —

## Three broken hearts

The bust at the border went perfectly, a rich vein was opened and before the day was over there were searches being conducted and arrests being made in a dozen different jurisdictions. But the prize for strategic brilliance is always more paperwork. Aliette Nouvelle knew she was hereby condemned to the better part of the next two weeks at her desk. And she would be required to assist in the interview process. Well, that could mean a trip to the sunny Adriatic—where she had never been. As for a police action *per se*, the inspector's part had been enacted quietly and cleanly. She got home in time to go for a run in the park and respond to a message from the man she thought she might love suggesting an early film. 'Yes.' They had a rendezvous at Cinema Luxe. An action movie from America—his choice tonight. She had no problem with that.

The day had warmed. Aliette sat on her third-floor apartment balcony and sipped a beer. Piaf, ancient and dirty white, ate his cat food. The park spread out beyond Madame Camus' garden was green and in full blossom, filled with people enjoying their weekend freedom.

Then she changed into something nice for Saturday night.

Cut to darkness: Aliette felt no particular attraction to the hero on the screen: another overly sculpted, wooden-voiced star. Yet she felt the adrenaline surge inside her as she absorbed the heroic hyper movement. A literal rush. The Americans knew how to create this effect better than anyone. More intriguing was how she sensed that the man beside her might actually *want* to be the man up on the screen. She felt him warming. She could smell it, *feel* it as he rolled with the choreographed blows and breathed in perfect rhythm with the stoked-up energy. He clenched a fist and whispered, 'Bastards!' He pumped said fist when the hero finally (inevitably) won. Aliette didn't hold it against him. Men respond differently to the heat of action. Simulated action too.

Later that night, in a deeper darkness, in the heat of the action, Aliette breathed, 'Let's roll.'

*(On roule;* because even a star saving the universe must be dubbed into French.)

She couldn't know this quick line would become historic. She only knew he liked to hear her say it. Because he picked up the pace — which she liked too. *Mais oui.* Hyper movement. Heat. Afterward she patted his back. He nestled on her breast, placid. Very stock, this little love scene. Our French films work the same, but on different impulses. It's a matter of taste. Aliette tasted the salty residue of sweat on his neck before they slept. She remembered it Sunday morning as they went for a walk by the river. Against all odds and logic, she was enjoying being with this man.

—

Sunday afternoon the inspector joined Claude Néon in Raphaele Petrucci's morgue. The three deceased lay on metal pallets. Their hearts had been removed and waited in metal bowls. Claude had visited the scenes. He admitted there was nothing untoward to be found in either the banker's elegant living room or the morning man's sand-blasted bedroom — no sign of illegal entry, struggle, missing property. But the windows: 'Wide open. Interestingly, both are five floors up.'

'It was a lovely evening, Claude.'

'Even so.' Claude had directed IJ, whose tiny, drastically under-funded forensics lab was across the hall from Raphaele's equally under-funded morgue, to have a look.

There were no photos of Duteil or Gagnon. Heart attacks don't call for this procedure. But Claude had taken notes: Dr. Mercier, a physician in Duteil's building, had been summoned from his breakfast by a neighbor alerted by a distraught housekeeper and had monitored the scene till the police and SAMU arrived. The banker had been sitting at the time of death, enjoying a glass apparently. He was found with his dead eyes gazing in the direction of the open window. Not unusual, and to the best of the doctor's knowledge and experience it had seemed an obvious heart attack and thus no need for forensic examination. As for the radio host, Jean-Guy Gagnon's producer had come looking for his star when he failed to show up for a Saturday morning PR appearance at a local Renault agent. He'd given Claude more or less the same picture: a man in bed with a book, staring toward his open bedroom window. Suddenly dead. 'His producer said he was looking pained in death.'

'Heart attacks hurt,' Raphaele said.

Aliette asked, 'What book?'

Claude had noted it. 'That new bestseller from America about evolutionary psychology.'

'An ironic time to die,' offered Aliette. Had Jean-Guy been contemplating the precepts of evolutionary psychology, trying to determine exactly where *he* fit in with the fittest of the fit? Her eyes moved from Jean-Guy Gagnon…to Jerôme Duteil…to Pierre Angulaire, so surreal with his rictus smile. They had nothing in common physically, these three ex-lovers. What had Pearl Serein been seeking? Turning to Raphaele: 'No drugs or poison? Prussic acid?' One of a growing menu of deadly items leaking out of military labs and into the criminal world. Aliette had been waiting for her first prussic acid case.

Raphaele Petrucci knew the inspector was only half-teasing and he had to be careful. 'Needs more time for an absolute no on that, I'm afraid.' The previous summer Raphaele had completely missed the home-made hallucinogen at the root of the Mari Morgan murders.

Aliette knew Raphaele's tendency to be circumspect, and persisted, 'No Viagra or the like?' Nodding at Duteil: 'What? Seventy-two?' Implying that a Pearl Serein would likely exact yeoman service and the penis proper-uppers were known to have adverse effects on ageing hearts.

'If he was, not lately.' Raphaele checked the information sent along by Duteil's physician. 'Seventy-two and counting. Birthday coming up in July. Pretty good shape, I'd say. They say he was quite the tennis champ.'

'Who says?' Claude asked.

'Tommi Bonneau.'

Aliette was amused to hear it. 'I would never have marked you for a gossip column fan.'

Raphaele Petrucci dismissed this little barb, blowing air through his lips — '*pleu*' — the way all French do, your basic camel fart, and shrugged. 'I like to stay informed, Inspector.'

'I think they were murdered,' repeated Claude.

The inspector asked the pathologist, 'Do you?'

Raphaele's dark Tuscan eyes rolled ceilingward. The last thing he wanted was to be caught in another power game between Néon and Nouvelle. 'I say heart attacks.'

'Someone was there,' said Claude. 'Both places. In through the window.'

'Five floors up?' Aliette had to ask her commissaire, 'How could anyone get there?'

'Climb?' Claude shrugged. 'We'll be looking at the roofs, wall surface. I mean, if we can get a budget. I mean, if we can just find a touch more indication.' He meant physical evidence, whether on the person or the premises, which would allow for a valid mandate. Because it would cost a fortune to do a forensic exam of roofs and walls. 'And of course a comb through our film guy's building.' Claude dropped the bizarre death shots of Pierre Angulaire on the table. 'Look at him: on the floor dead square to his door. A visitor! Had to be. Someone came in, something made their hearts stop. We'll see what IJ says, then…' Commissaire Claude Néon trailed off, scratching his nose, fighting uncertainty, but unable to dismiss his hunch.

*Our* film guy? Claude was already assuming ownership. It's a psychological thing: you have to embrace your hunch wholeheartedly. Aliette had been there. She could see it happening to Claude. It was why she suspended judgement and remained sympathetic. For the moment. Because you've got science, legal logic, physical evidence. But hunches are basic to the job: One woman called Pearl Serein; three high-profile boyfriends, dead. Almost impossible to resist the suspicion of murder. 'I'd be more concerned about what Gérard says,' she advised.

No budget, no investigation.

Claude's eyes said, Please don't bother me with Gérard Richand!

OK. Fine. In response to Claude's stated reason for her presence in the morgue that day, she turned to the three bodies and confirmed, 'No, never dealt with any of them.'

'No links to any of your usuals?'

'I doubt it.' Considering it, thinking back, thinking sideways, but nope, 'Not really the type for my usual crowd.' Her usual crowd crossed borders. Could a respected banker be an impeccable front for a tax-dodge cash-stream to a bank in Basel? Possible. Or to launder drug money? Bankers *were* known to launder money. Radio and film types were known to like drugs. It *was* mostly drugs, her work these days. Zurich was an easy two hours down the road and in the process of struggling with its transformation into a kind of Swiss Amsterdam. Spillover into nearby Basel and our quiet burg was inevitable. 'Of course it's always possible. I'll ask around the street.'

Claude nodded. Good.

Turning back to Raphaele, she asked, 'So — heart attacks? That your final word?'

'That's it.' Raphaele would not endorse the possibility of murder.

Aliette pushed him. 'How do you induce a heart attack?'

The pathologist screwed up his handsome face, as if to ask: Why can't you accept the facts here? But he knew she wanted an answer. 'You could scare someone to death,' he ventured. 'People have dropped dead of fright at their own surprise birthday parties. There's also what they call voodoo death — like when a witch doctor literally scares a person to death with his spells and such — but that's pretty primitive.' Raphaele shrugged. 'Basically, if you can get a person stressed enough, the huge flow of adrenaline can be toxic. Boom. Gone. It happens. As for inducing it deliberately, well, you'd need to know the victim — I mean like that witch doctor who personally knows the guy in his tribe who's getting all the pins stuck in his effigy. And vice-versa. It couldn't work any other way. I mean to say, inducement starts in the mind, no?'

But there were no signs of any birthday parties at any of the three sites. No signs of anyone but the victims at the time. Two open windows five floors up. An open office door.

The two cops looked to their pathologist: Does it make sense to you?

Looking like he knew he'd regret it, Raphaele elaborated. 'There's heart attack: wham, bump, bump, good-bye, we call it cardiac arrest. A first look at some very messy blood flow traces seems to indicate these three hearts got confused, struggled to re-establish a normal rhythm, but, um…' he paused, trying to formulate something reasonable and more definite—what they would need in order to have a legal starting point. He spread the photos of Angulaire across the countertop like tarot cards. 'These images, and your notes, they make it appear these three men knew something was happening. But it looks and sounds as though they didn't believe it. What I mean is, there's a difference between being afraid—that is, scared to death—and not believing.' Raphaele stared at the late Pierre Angulaire. 'It's like a gesture, as if he's in the process of communicating something before falling back dead on his floor. The other two? No struggle or panic apparent in the way they were found. Just sitting, looking out the window. Or at it. And the fact that it *is* three of them. But…' The pathologist concluded with one of his trademark noncommittal shrugs: Sorry, I just don't know.

Aliette spoke first. 'If someone did come in, they must have known him.'

'Yes,' affirmed Claude.

Raphaele sniffed, 'Your witch doctor?'

Claude ignored the skeptical scientist. 'Medically weird, compounded by coincidence. It's like a mark. A killer's mark, you know? And there's this woman. Pearl Serein.'

'I'd like to meet her,' said Raphaele, adding, 'They say she's quite something.'

'So would I,' said Claude. But although you can fiddle your budget and squeeze out extra forensics, you cannot go hauling in ex-lovers for interrogation when people die of apparent heart attacks. Claude told Raphaele Petrucci, 'Before we do, I'll need my medical expert to give me more substance, won't I?…There has to be something inside these hearts.'

Raphaele blustered. 'Look, I'm interested! Who wouldn't be? But—'

Claude cut him off. 'Bill the damn time on a consultant's scale if that's what you need to do. I'll handle that. You just find me something that I can take to Gérard Richard.'

'Heart attacks,' Petrucci replied, now snide and sullen.

'More!'
Which brought an impasse in the morgue.
'*Bon*,' said Aliette. 'Is that all?'
Claude said, 'I might need some help.'
She knew he would. 'You know I'm available if you need me.'
Claude only nodded, *merci*. He indicated that the meeting was over.

Aliette Nouvelle returned to her office with the potted shamrock in the window, the view of the Vosges beyond. She sat at her desk and got to work. All that paperwork attached to yesterday's success. May as well get a leg up on it, seeing that she was here.

Last night was fun, this morning was peaceful, but the better part of Sunday was gone.

## — 3 —
## A SULLIED STORY

Monday. The left side of the Entertainment page in *Le Cri du Matin* noted the passing of a local star: *Film community loses a leader: Acclaimed local cinéaste Pierre Angulaire died suddenly Friday evening, the victim of heart failure. The filmmaker was found dead at his office early Saturday morning. He had lately been preparing a documentary about socialite Pearl Serein, with whom he had been romantically linked in the past. According to colleague Nanette Roufach, the project had become his raison d'être. Monsieur Angulaire, who once stated his working motto as 'reality is magic,' rose to prominence a decade ago on the strength of a series of documentary television productions conceived and shot in this region, where he was born and raised and to which he returned after apprenticing in the film industry in Paris...* There followed a resume of Pierre's accomplishments, the suggestion that his career had stalled somewhat, but the piece concluded with kind words on the part of Madame Roufach and other colleagues. Because *Le Cri* does not publish on Sunday, radio personality Jean-Guy Gagnon received much the same treatment on the right side of the same page. An appreciation of Jerôme Duteil's life and role as a mainstay of our financial community appeared on the front page of the Business section.

In a column on page two of the front section, *Le Cri* crime specialist Serge Phaneuf could not resist reporting: *Police Note Coincidental Deaths. While police attended the discovery of Pierre Angulaire's death, there is yet to be a statement issued regarding any suspected malfeasance concerning three coincidental and apparently similar deaths in a single day of three men all known to have been romantically involved with local socialite Pearl Serein in the recent past. All requests to police headquarters for related information were referred* to Police Judiciaire. Monique Sparr, spokeswoman for PJ Commissaire Claude Néon's office, said, 'The coincidence has been noted, but as you know, we do not act until directed accordingly by the court.' Madame Serein had not responded to a reporter's calls concerning the three deaths.

Speculative flame fanning of this sort is normal. Claude Néon was undeterred. He was locked away in his office with his hunch, busily drafting out a report. Instructing Judge Gérard Richard could and would quash a hunch without a second thought. On the other hand, the *procureurs* who direct instructing judges tend to be political animals — Michel Souviron certainly was — and journalists stirred the muck that released political scent. A hunch could gain momentum, if not legal credibility. Claude's best hope was there.

The Angulaire family had not questioned the police department's need to keep their loved one for an autopsy. The elderly mother of morning man J-G Gagnon had long ago moved in a second marriage to a suburb of Paris and had not yet responded to the sad notice she'd been sent.

The family of Jerôme Duteil was another matter. Around mid-morning Inspector Nouvelle was deep in her Swiss checkpoint operation reports when Monique buzzed — could she meet Claude in the basement? Something about moral support. The banker's son had come to claim his father's body. Aliette went down to find the two men at the foot of the stairs outside the morgue, Commissaire Néon decidedly on the defensive in responding to the man's queries as to why his papa had been detained. 'Look, please, I don't want to worry you at a time like this.'

'It's too late for that!' snapped the visitor. Another high-ranking banker, Duteil Jr. was impeccably turned out, and clearly accustomed to being obeyed. He had no time for diversionary nonsense. 'What happened?'

The harsh tone raised color in Néon's cheeks. 'Monsieur, it was a heart attack.'

'We know this! Tell me why you kept him.'

Strictly speaking, Commissaire Néon should have offered nothing but a sincere apology. Sorry, just a mistake, everybody makes them, even the police. But most citizens do not have an in-depth understanding of the rules, and some cops (Claude) find it existentially impossible to let go of a hunch without at least a look. Running interference, Aliette gently told the distressed man, 'We need to know what happened between your father and a woman called Pearl Serein.'

'Oh, god!' Duteil Jr. was aggrieved just to hear the name. The tables were instantly turned. He seemed to sense the inevitable dynamics of the situation. His bluster took on a whiny tone. 'Why do you need to know? It was in the paper. It was the only mistake he ever really made.'

Mistake? Claude's eyes narrowed. 'It didn't hurt his business any.'

'No, just his life. And my mother's.' Duteil expressed a sigh of disdain for a sullied story.

'Was it a volatile thing? Did he…did he do something to make this woman angry?'

'No. He said he loved her.'

'He told you that?'

'He had to explain himself. I mean, he just upped and left poor Mama.'

Aliette jumped in. 'Could he say why he would be so rash? Unhappy at home?'

The banker's son addressed her. 'It wasn't about my mother. It was only about *her*. Papa said she was the most elusive of pearls.' The son's face contorted to reflect the low-quality metaphor, visibly revolted by a sophisticated father's maudlin descent into the fog of a doomed passion. 'He lost control, was saying lots of things like that. Some kind of fantasy. It was the only time I was ever ashamed of him.'

'But then she left him,' continued Claude.

'*B'en*, she leaves everyone,' replied Duteil. Like Monique. Like Nanette. As if *everyone* knew.

Aliette blurted, 'And you follow her adventures?' It seemed everyone did but her. And Claude.

The man's eyes turned condescending: Adventures? 'My father's good name was part of it. It would be foolish not to know what they were saying.'

The inspector nodded, Yes, I would too… '*Le Vrai Tommi?*'

'No, that's garbage.'

'Oh? Then where?'

'Rose.'

'Rose?'

'I forgot, you're a cop — you only read *Le Cri du Matin*.' Curling a dismissive lip. 'Rose Saxe — in *Le Soir*?' The local competition. 'She's friends with my mother. Comes to all the parties.'

'Nice job,' the inspector responded.

'But,' Claude asked, 'your father wouldn't have been after Pearl Serein? To settle the score?'

Condescension was transformed to incredulity: What kind of question was *that*? 'No!'

'Your mother?' wondered Aliette. 'Would *she* have some grudge she needed to — '

'No!'

'But your mother didn't forgive him,' Claude suggested.

'No,' the banker's son agreed. 'How could she?'

'Nor could you,' Aliette added. Yes, a romantic link creates many suspects.

'We have standards in our family,' he stated, unapologetic. But, feeling two cops watching, waiting, Duteil Jr. duly reconsidered. 'If it had been one of her friends…what I mean, my mother can get jealous like anyone. But Pearl Serein? Who is she?' he asked, and followed directly with the answer. 'No one.' Ergo, no one to be jealous of.

Neither cop replied to that. Claude asked, 'How did they meet?'

'That filmmaker, Pierre Angulaire, he brought her to lunch with him one day when he was trying to get money out of my father for one of his films.'

'Did he get the money?'

'He got a promise, contingent on other promises. My father believed in supporting the arts.'

'But Pierre lost the girl,' Aliette noted. 'Was he bitter? Threatening?'

'Not that we heard about. I heard he fell apart.'

Exactly as that Nanette had claimed. 'Then she left your father for Jean-Guy Gagnon?'

'No, she left my father for Pugh, the lawyer. So what?' Duteil Jr. was now watching the police with something like fear.

Claude asked, 'What was your father's relation to Jean-Guy Gagnon?'

'Papa sued him for defamation. He called Papa one morning, you know the way he does?'

'Yes, I know the way he does.' *This Is Your Wake-Up Call* had been a popular item on Jean-Guy's show. He'd called Claude early one morning about a year ago, waking him, gleefully demanding that a sleepy Claude explain to his listeners why he should be the new PJ Commissaire. Claude thought Jean-Guy Gagnon was a total ass and would not miss his celebrated voice at all.

'It had to do with that hateful rumor about giving money to a local *Front National* group.'

The far-right: on the upswing. Which was interesting, but getting off track. Love. Love was the nexus of Claude's hunch. 'So she took up with Georges Pugh next — not Gagnon.'

'Pugh was defending Gagnon's station against my father's suit.'

'Did they know each other, Georges and your father?'

Two PJ inspectors certainly knew Georges Pugh. Brash, a publicity hound, he knew a lot of bad people — had made his fortune and name defending them. Could Maître Georges Pugh have arranged for three rivals in love to be killed? He had the money, the right connections.

Duteil shrugged. 'A little. From the club. The Quarter Racquets Club? They were never friends. We can't be friends with someone like that, not with the company he keeps.'

Claude returned to the basic, most logical motif in this unspooling chain. 'But was your father bitter? Did he talk about revenge on Pugh?'

'No.' Whining again, in pain and having it rubbed raw by these insinuations. 'And he never could have. When she left, it was as if the life went out of him. It was if he *wanted* to die.'

'Like Pierre Angulaire,' Aliette noted. At least according to the picture she was getting.

Claude asked, 'But then how does Pearl Serein end up with Jean-Guy Gagnon?'

'I have no idea! I don't care!' Jerôme Duteil's son stood there, scandalized — and now afraid.

They watched him, the way cops will.

The banker's son cottoned on. Looking toward the morgue. 'They're both in there?'

'*And* Monsieur Angulaire,' Claude confided. 'Your father and the other two died identical suspicious deaths on the same day and they shared the same obsession. This woman. Pearl Serein.'

'Obsession. You got the right word.' Duteil let his confused eyes tell them he had no explanation. He took a breath. 'You think he was killed?...*they*, I mean — all three of them? How?'

'Don't know,' Claude replied. 'At the moment I'm trying to get a sense of this woman,' patting the man's shoulder, professionally sympathetic. 'I'm sorry to add distress to your pain but the coincidence is too much to ignore. We're releasing the body. Of course we'll let you know when something more concrete develops. *Bon courage, monsieur.*'

With that, Claude headed back up the stairs, leaving the bereaved to sign Raphaele's forms.

Aliette lingered on the landing. 'Did you meet her? Pearl Serein?'

'Not really. She was there that time I went to confront him — she didn't say a word. She was reading a book. She got up and left the room. Almost like I wasn't there.'

'What did you do?'

'I said my piece and left.'

'I see,' she said. Which meant nothing — a simple ploy, hoping he'd speak further.

But Raphaele appeared at the morgue door and beckoned the man to come along.

Monsieur Duteil shrugged glumly and went in to sign for his dad.

Aliette returned to her large stack of Euro Union paperwork.

Claude's report and request for a mandate regarding an investigation into three suspicious deaths constellating around a woman named Pearl Serein were his responsibility and problem.

– 4 –
## Clippings

Monique's desk was cluttered with news clippings. Research for Claude.

Somewhere in a previous life, Aliette Nouvelle had possessed a mean top-spin on her forehand stroke. And so she was immediately drawn to the action shot of 'The practicing woman' (*Femme qui s'entrain*), as dubbed in the cutline below a photo depicting Pearl Serein hitting a ball against a wall—on the practice court at her club, apparently. Pearl had been perfectly captured at the apogee of an elegant and forceful stroke; sunny legs taut, almost air-borne; slim mid-body torqueing surely through her swing, tan arms parallel in follow-through, shoulder-length *châtain* tied in a flying ponytail, a dead-on intensity in her eyes. A portrait of excellent form.

'Good concentration,' commented the inspector.

Monique glanced over. 'That was after Georges Pugh…last autumn.'

'Who comes after Jerôme Duteil, yes?' In the line of loves.

Monique indicated this was correct. 'We think she was probably sleeping with Raymond Tuche by that point, but Raymond's not a tennis player, although he *is* a member of the club.'

'Probably?'

'Pretty sure, but not absolutely.'

'When was Jean-Guy Gagnon?'

'After Raymond Tuche.'

'Did he play tennis?'

'Not that we know of…J-G started in early autumn and went to just after New Year's.' After tennis season.

'And then?'

'Then she ran away to Bruno Martel's spiritual farm.'

'A spiritual farm?' The police miss out on all the fun things.

'Healer—very mystical. Has this high-end spa-cum-meditation place up in the mountains.'

'I see. Not a club member then?'

'Oh, he probably is when he's in town. They all are. I mean, if you want to be in the right circles, you almost have to be. Can't see him playing tennis though. A bit large.'

'And then?'

Monique shook her head. 'That one ended on Valentine's Day. She's been quiet ever since.'

'So: Pierre, Jerôme, Georges, Raymond, Jean-Guy and Bruno. Six boyfriends—in how long?'

'About three years, maybe less. Seven of them, actually. It started with Didi Belfort.'

'That noble...the architect?' Half-German blueblood; known to consume a lot of speed. She had heard the name in closing down a lab posing as a rowing club at the south end of the docklands.

'Didi gave her the magnificent penthouse on top of his father's apartment building. Pierre charmed her away when he was making his movie about Didi's work.'

'Yes, and then Jerôme charmed her away from Pierre...And this Bruno guy? He's the last?'

'So far.' Monique left that open-ended. Because a new tennis season was just now starting.

The line under the picture of the practicing woman asked, 'Can no one match her?' Aliette placed a finger on it. 'Is this the work of that Tommi person?'

'Of course. Tommi's our main source.' Monique handed over a clipping. *Le Vrai Tommi*. The photo beside the column showed Pearl gripping a shopping bag in each hand, staring at the camera. The cutline below it read, 'Shopping around again?' In the body of the column, following news from Rome concerning Mussolini's right-leaning granddaughter and her penchant for push-up brassieres, was an item under the subhead: **Local Scene**

*Pearl Serein has been shopping alone since splitting from artist Raymond Tuche. Pearl is not reported to have run to anybody. She just ran, leaving Ray in a sorry state, according to a source who assures us the sculptor will surely transform his melancholy into another masterpiece. How romantic. But not, it seems, romantic enough for our Pearl, who continues to blaze a trail through the lives of some of this city's most eligible men. The fascinating problem for each of us to consider as we watch the broken-hearted parade is, Why? What happened, Ray?*

*All we can do is wonder, Has no one got the stuff to make her happy?*

Aliette accepted a cup of coffee from Monique. 'Our Pearl?'

Monique assured the inspector, 'She's incredible.' Lifting the page from Aliette's fingers, she found its proper spot in her larger pile. 'The boss said be careful of chronological order.'

'Right.' The inspector was quietly rueful. She felt her respect for Monique fall a notch. Respect was suddenly contingent. It was wrong to judge like this, but she could not suppress the surge of scorn. Was Monique's life really so empty? Was Raphaele Petrucci's? Aliette Nouvelle was no fan of celebrity gossip. It seemed premised on the notion that the lives of a magical few were meant to provide benchmarks, both the high and the low. She had never felt the need of those benchmarks. Not for love and happiness. Or *un*happiness, come to that — which it often did.

No thanks, my own little life will do fine.

She was bemusedly perusing Monique's collected clippings when Claude came out of his office in a rush. 'In the mood for a funeral?' Jerôme Duteil's was set for eleven at Notre Dame de Bons Secours. Claude straightened his tie as he directed Monique to a file in the computer, commanding her to spell-check, read for grammar, then print and send attn. Procureur Souviron, cc. Chief Magistrate Richard. 'Thanks... Back by one, if anyone's looking.'

Aliette followed Claude along the hall to the stairs. 'Did Raphaele find something?'

'He's still working on it.'

'You don't mean to tell me that gossip garbage is the basis of your case for Gérard?'

'Of course not. I've been running searches on all of them.'

'All of who?'

'Pearl's boys. Gérard will see it.'

'See what? ...Claude?'

When someone is caught in the act by police it is termed *flagrant délit*. There *is* a case; but not until the police bring the information and materials to the *procureur*, who examines it, decides on the charge and appropriate legal action, then passes the file along to the judge of instruction. When it's obvious, the judge opens a rogatory enquiry and begins to build the case, interviewing people, collecting evidence and facts to be put before the court. When circumstances are less clear—when the police *think* there is case, or *want* a case—the judge, upon receiving the proc's opinion, will initiate a preliminary enquiry. The case has to be established. The police sniff around, trying to determine if a crime exists, collecting pertinent facts to be presented to the judge…to be offered back to the *procureur*, who decides on the charge and the ensuing legal action. A preliminary gets considerably less attention (and budget) than a rogatory. But in either situation it is the judge of instruction, a referee of sorts, operating impartially and independent of the court, who monitors the activities of the police and controls the development of the case. Or its closing.

In this sense, the police work for the judge. We have eight in our prefecture. They occupy the offices at the shady end of the top floor at the courthouse. (The proc's team gets the sunny end.) When PJ Commissaire Néon took the lead in a matter, it usually meant Gérard Richand, chief of the eight, would be instructing. And they did not like each other much.

And Claude had nothing. Inspector Nouvelle ran back for her coat, suddenly very worried for her commissaire's professional credibility.

The church was packed, attesting to the banker's large career and wide circle of influence. Claude pointed out *Le Soir* society columnist Rose Saxe in the second row next to the deceased's estranged wife, her good friend, according to the deceased's son. From where she sat, Aliette felt the society scribe may have overdone it with her lipstick. Looking around… Ah. There she was. Pearl Serein had found a place at the back. She appeared so ordinary. She remained alone and unnoticed.

They all hushed as the casket was wheeled in.

And when the service was done and the casket wheeled back out and the congregation had shuffled along behind it, Pearl Serein left without a word to anyone. The two cops watched her as they made their way through the throng of mourners milling quietly on the church step. They saw Pearl walking away from her banker's final moment without glancing back.

There was a man leaning against a '58 Citroen Deux Chevaux, beige with black fenders and trim, a bona fide French classic. He was wielding a camera decked out with a flash attachment for a cloudy day. As Pearl Serein turned up the city stairs to Rue Victor Hugo, he raised it to his eye and flashed off some pictures. Pearl Serein *must* have known she was being photographed — the way the unnatural shimmer of green-white light spread, momentarily enclosing her in a halo before diffusing into the overcast air. But she held her stride, kept moving up the stairs and disappeared.

They approached Tomas Bonneau. *Le Vrai Tommi* (The Real Tommi), as his readers knew him, was tall, willowy, in that nebulous thirty-five to forty-six age bracket. Tommi's face was never shown at the top of his column, at least never in full. The editors of *Le Cri du Matin* reduced the image to a pair of probing eyes. An allusive touch. Aliette now saw that the face Tommi hid from his readers showed the beginnings of jowls, which tend to make a willowy man look sad. Adding to this effect, his gaze, so steady in the morning paper, was tired in person, cloudy. In fact he did not look well. There was an orangey tint to the rings under his pale green eyes.

'Getting anything good?' Claude asked with an intrusive cop insolence that usually provokes.

'Not yet.' Nonchalant, looking the two of them up and down. 'And who are you: friends of the family or fans of the story?' Bonneau's voice had an oddly high pitch, boyish, with a smirky edge.

'We're from the police,' Aliette said.

'Oh, good.' Bonneau aimed, focused and flashed a shot before either cop could react.

'Hey!' A blinking Aliette turned away, focusing on the church spire till the world held steady.

Claude Néon was not amused. 'What the hell do you think you're doing?'

'My job. Is there some crime connected to this? I saw Serge Phaneuf's note yesterday. That would be perfect.' Dutiful reporter, he pulled a writing pad from his pocket. 'Names?'

'Put it away,' Aliette said, implying he'd better.

'Inspector Aliette Nouvelle, right?'

'Put it away,' repeated Claude.

Tommi Bonneau complied. Then he extended a large hand to Aliette, tired eyes suddenly lit in a playful mode, as if daring her to accept it. 'I am thrilled.'

She shook his hand, but warned, 'I don't want to see my name in your space, monsieur.'

Claude asked, 'What's so special about Pearl Serein?'

Tommi Bonneau began to dismantle his camera and flash. 'Everyone wants her.'

'Yes, but why?'

'*B'en*, because everyone wants her.' This was well known and understood.

Claude persisted, 'But *why*? There has to be something.'

'You'd be surprised.' Now methodically packing his stuff into a battered old schoolboy-type leather satchel. 'She's got the basics: looks good enough, she can dance, plays decent tennis. Amazing apartment, apparently. More than that?' A shrug to indicate nothing special.

'But still, they all love her?'

'These things have a way of snowballing.'

'Which things?'

'These Pearl things, *les femmes très recherchées*, they tend to go up in value.'

'How high?'

'The be-all and the end-all? That one today, Duteil: he gave her half his bank, apparently.'

'Ah.' Claude nodded knowingly. Lots of people kill for money.

Aliette, choking on scorn, echoed the operative word. 'Apparently?'

'Ask her,' countered Tommi. 'They all give her everything. Didi Belfort gave her his penthouse. Pierre Angulaire made her into the project of his career. Crazy Ray Tuche has renamed all his pieces for the love of Pearl. Georges Pugh changed the name of his boat to Pearl, which any sailor will tell you is asking for disaster. Gagnon called her up while he was on-air to see what Pearl was eating for breakfast... Martel gave her free therapy. It's absurd, but that's love for you. No?'

The inspector asked, 'What did *she* give?'

'Good question.' Tommi thought about it. 'She gave up her position at the primary school to someone who needed it, an admirable thing to do, we have to grant.'

'I don't get it.' Claude shrugged, staring at the empty city stairs.

'It's the sex.' The inspector said it. She said it on behalf of the police.

Tommi Bonneau signaled negative. 'Sex can only take you so far, then you're an outcast, a whore or a rock star, usually both. Our Pearl's not like that.' A snide chuckle. 'Then again, you never know till you're there, do you?'

'*Our* Pearl?' Did they own her?

'Pearl has something for every heart, Inspector. And never forget: *the great Faith is Love*!'

Aliette Nouvelle had heard this. Where?... 'Rimbaud?'

'Very good.' Tommi was impressed. 'I'll bet no one in that church today could get that.' Another dry and cynical sniffy laugh. 'Least of all poor old Jerôme Duteil.'

'What about her — does she know that?'

'I don't know what she knows.' Tommi smiled. 'Our investigation is ongoing.'

Aliette searched his tired eyes. 'Just a schoolteacher then?'

'Ex. But still the epitome of feminine virtue.' Lifting his bag into the backseat of his car, he climbed in behind the wheel. 'It's still all about passion, Inspector. Or the lack.'

'Thanks for the information.'

'Any time. By the way, who's your boyfriend?'

Aliette ignored that. She turned and walked away.

Claude advised Tommi Bonneau, 'Not a word about our chat. That clear?'

With a shrug and a nod, Bonneau pulled away, falling into place at the rear of the long cortège accompanying Jerôme Duteil to his final rest. Ten minutes later, climbing the steps to the Commissariat door, the two cops paused to watch a woman coming up the street.

Pearl Serein was approaching, uncertain, reading the numbers and signs along Rue des Bons Enfants. Seeing she was at the Hôtel de Police, she cautiously mounted the first step. Looking from Aliette to Claude, then back again to Aliette, she asked, 'Would you know if this is where they're keeping the body of Jean-Guy Gagnon?'

'This is the place.'

'I've come to claim it. To send him home.'

Aliette held the door for Pearl as she climbed the steps, eyes worried, trying to see inside.

## – 5 –
## Pearl's burden

Monique was so proud to meet her! They went through to Claude's office and shut the door.

Pearl's eyes wavered as she handed over a letter. 'From his mama.'

Claude reached for it — but she handed it to Aliette.

Posted from a suburb north of Paris: *Madame. You may or may not have ruined my son's life. Along with the tragic news which has made me turn my radio off forever, I have learned from certain of his colleagues that my Jean-Guy seemed to lose control of his beautiful talent after his involvement with you. I am too heartsick to come and face you with my grief, indeed, too weak to bring the poor boy home. I ask you to do the decent thing and take care of this business for me. He told me he would give you everything. Now it appears he did just that. Do this for him, and for me, and I will do my best to forget you. And pray for him, if you can. With regret…*

'That's quite a load,' said Aliette.

Pearl Serein, lips pursed tight, nodded to agree.

Face to face, she was stylishly thin but hadn't been starving herself, with skin that was brown for April. A lean, English-seeming nose, well-defined cheekbones. A healthy look. But indeed, beyond these basics, as Tommi Bonneau had put it, Aliette saw nothing special. OK, she was much more attractive in person than in print.

Claude snatched the page and had a look. He made a face and laughed.

Aliette had always believed the police should be polite. 'You find it funny?'

'He's supposed to be this big, ballsy radio journalist.' J-G's mama had given the act away.

Aliette said, 'That's not the issue.'

'No.' Claude agreed. Turning to their guest, proffering the letter. 'Is this accusation justified?'

'No,' said Pearl.

'No?'

'No.'

Claude smiled at her, waiting to hear more.

The woman seemed to search his smile—and decided to remain silent.

'You were involved with him,' Aliette prompted.

'Yes, I was. But I wasn't when he died.'

'Maybe he still loved you,' the inspector suggested.

'Maybe. What could I do about it?'

'Hearts are fragile things,' commented Claude.

Pearl did not respond or even look at him—she remained focused on Aliette. But a grimace broke the stolid mask. Her umber eyes tightened, as if she were struggling to maintain her patience. Aliette couldn't blame her. It was not a useful thing for Claude to say.

For his part, Claude turned automatic. The queries came rolling on, as if he held a shopping list: when, where, how long, arguments or insults either way, jealousy, provocation? Fights with fists? Pearl responded to his tone in kind. No, no, no, no…

Claude persisted. 'Did you love him?'

This one, she paused at. 'I don't know. Maybe. For a bit.'

'Maybe for a bit?' The answer made Claude increase the pressure. 'Did you hate him? Were you mad at him?' Then waving the letter at her, 'Were you mad at his mother? Eh? What is *a bit*?'…till he had practically shoved the letter in her face. 'Give me *some*thing, madame.'

Pearl squeezed her eyes shut in the face of this barrage.

'Claude!' snapped Aliette.

'Well, how am I supposed to get anything done if she sits there mute like a nine-year-old?'

Aliette did not respond.

Perhaps realizing she had an ally, Pearl asked, 'If it had been his mother instead of me, would she have had to go through all this?' Claude only stared, petulant. 'I'm not here because I feel guilty, monsieur. I'm here because nobody else has come and his mother wants him home. I don't know what you could want from me. I haven't seen Jean-Guy for months. Since early January. We broke off at New Year's. I never met his mother. Why are you asking me all these questions?'

Suddenly Claude was embarrassed, like his brain had just now returned to his head. 'I'm sorry,' he stammered, 'it's, it's…Well, you see, madame, the death of Monsieur Gagnon and the deaths of Messieurs Duteil and Angulaire, with both of whom I've been led to believe you were also involved, yes?…' smiling, contrite, 'There seems to be a connection that might concern us.'

'And you,' added Aliette.

Pearl said, 'I heard it was a heart attack. All three of them.'

Claude was being an ass and he deserved to be embarrassed. It was Aliette who accompanied Pearl Serein downstairs, where Raphaele could not stop looking at her. But the woman knew how to ignore it and the inspector stayed quiet.

The papers duly signed on behalf of the morning man's mama, a forwarding address for the body copied out, Pearl murmured, 'Merci,' before slipping back into the street.

Claude was gazing out his office window when Aliette returned. She joined him. They could see Pearl Serein walking away, northbound, out of the quarter. 'Looks to me like she has a secret,' Claude muttered.

'She looks alone,' Aliette responded. 'A woman very much alone.'

That observation made him sigh. 'Fine. But do you think she's part of something?'

'Which part, Claude?'

He heard the bite. 'What's your problem?'

*My* problem? She repeated it. 'Which part?'

'Instigator…Or object — a decoy of sorts.' This was posed as a suggestion.

Aliette Nouvelle mustered a smile. 'Given the situation, I would think your instincts would be more attuned than mine.' Gently arch. And actually quite interested to know.

'She's not too bad to look at,' the commissaire admitted, 'but,' wrinkling his brow, 'she doesn't really feel like either, does she?'

Either an object or an instigator? Aliette stayed mum. Let Claude mull this essential question.

He returned to his desk and sat. 'She contrives to meet them. She takes what she needs from them, moves on to the next one. But they're pestering her, maybe worse, so she has them killed. Three for the price of one. Clean sweep.'

A murderous ball-breaker? 'Do you really get the sense she's that kind of woman?'

'You never know!' he blurted, ears going red. He could hear professional disdain.

'You'd *better* know!' she volleyed, letting her voice rise with his. 'The way you lost it there, you're going to blow this thing before you even open a new docket—*if* the judge lets you open a new docket. You'd better get her right, monsieur.'

Perhaps Claude Néon saw that she was trying to work with him. To make him think. He cooled down. He tried to re-assess. 'No. She's not. She's not like that at all. She was lost…Wasn't she?'

Aliette confirmed this perception.

'And a bit desperate.'

'Possibly.'

'But tough too, for that matter… She thought I was being an ass. I'm not blind.'

'But,' asked Aliette, 'why did you get mad? Why did she *have* to tell you something? Why did you assume she would have something to tell?'

'They were in love with her. The mother's letter. The filmmaker's assistant. That banker's snobby son… You heard what they said. That Bonneau's a ridiculous fool, but he's not lying.'

'But you heard what *she* said. She didn't know if she loved them. It's not always a two-way street, is it?'

'No.' Claude's sallow cheeks regained their blush as he granted this essential point.

'And there's no law that says she had to.'

'No,' he agreed again. 'There's no law.'

'So?'

'So what do you see, monsieur: innocent schoolteacher or femme fatale?'

Claude rubbed his chin. Picked at a tooth. Pearl had disappeared from view.

Aliette gave him her opinion. 'I would agree with the banker's son and the director's assistant, and even that radio star's bitter mother: it's *their* problem, not hers. Some kind of obsession. As for her: I would take away lost — although, sure, a bit desperate under sudden bombardment from some totally rude policeman — and I'd replace it with a woman who's probably not that tough but who does have a sense of her own dignity. And who has no interest in killing anyone.' Feeling obliged to remind him that they were still only speculating, she added, 'If they were in fact killed.'

Aliette watched her commissaire looking out at the afternoon sky, vexed by her reasonable doubts. 'Claude, if you have something here, it starts with the lovers, not the beloved.'

## – 6 –
## Gazing up

*Le Soir*'s editorial stance is geared to appeal to a more discriminating demographic, and all its components, from obituaries to film reviews, build on this perspective. What people read should fit their way of thinking, no? Since the man she thought she might love was working late, Inspector Aliette Nouvelle sipped beer and (taking a cue from Duteil Jr.) perused the evening paper.

The block-long Duteil funeral cortège merited a front-page photo. Society columnist Rose Saxe's report was extensive.

### Society Notes

*A pillar of the community was bid adieu today at Notre Dame de Bons Secours. A packed chapel heard Monseigneur Artaud Détu describe Jerôme Duteil as 'an honest and energetic man dedicated to serving people.' The bishop went on to wonder just how many of the loyal friends seated before him were living in houses and pursuing careers or enterprises backed by the confidence of Monsieur Duteil. Several friends and colleagues also eulogized Jerôme Duteil, painting a picture of a passionate man who was tough but fair and possessed 'one hell of a back-hand!' Though sad, the funeral of Jerôme Duteil was cathartic in the true meaning of the word: one was imbued with a sense of life in all its color. Watching Nippy, the banker's cherished poodle, lead the family out of the chapel behind the casket, a reporter had to fight back tears. Nicolette du Marnes-Duteil, estranged wife of the banker, had mixed emotions. 'That he was a great man, no one can argue. As you know, however, he had recently brought a great deal of pain upon me and my children. There is, assuredly, a time to forgive, but I am not so sure that this is it,' commented the widow, referring to the deceased's much publicized romance with former nursery-schoolteacher*

*Pearl Serein. Madame du Marnes-Duteil did not sit in the front pew with her children…*

Names of the nobles present were listed first amongst the mourners. They were followed by those of other bankers and financiers and their spouses or companions, then professionals, mostly from the financial and legal communities, then came a scattered grouping of arts and media people, a construction mogul, a favorite chef; and then the banker's staff, which included his tellers and his chauffeur. Lastly: friends, neighbors…his tennis partners. It was indeed a pageant. Rose Saxe must have left the reception early in order to make her deadline.

Two questions: Had Madame Saxe a tape recorder hidden in her hankie?

Why was the name Pearl Serein only a reference and not a part of the list?

The city lights began to twinkle. Aliette fetched herself a second beer and came out onto her balcony, where she stood at the rail in the warm night air gazing up, Piaf circling her ankles.

Thanks to Monique, she now knew that she and Pearl were neighbors. More or less. That is, inasmuch as a society queen's luxury penthouse atop a ten-story apartment building can be said to occupy common space with a single-working-girl's third-floor flat. Aliette sipped beer. Oh hell, sure they were. They shared the park. Pearl could look down at Aliette; she could gaze up at Pearl. The city was small, but the world was smaller. The inspector had spent close to nine years in her modest place beside the park, many lonely evenings staring empty-headed at the lights across the way. But she had never heard of Pearl Serein. No idea Pearl had moved in, somehow got the place (did she own it?) from a half-German noble who had designed and built it, and that lately the most interesting love affairs in the city had been going on up there. How could there have been no sign of it? 'Eh, Piaf?' You'd think the evening sky above Pearl might show a different color. Aliette could hardly see the fabled penthouse—a hedge protected it from telescopes. All she could see was the top end of a ladder with a diving board attached. Obviously over a pool. From Aliette's low vantage, it appeared to be hanging suspended in the sky. She imagined the unseen pool. No doubt it glittered. She hoped Pearl would emerge tonight, go climbing up the tower ladder, step out under the starry night, do a swan dive…

Gazing up: There is, from one moment to the next, the ineffable notion of separate lives, unequal fates. Not much point in dwelling on it. Still, Aliette supposed Pearl was alone in her bed this night. If Pearl were not alone, everyone would know. How intolerable would that be? The inspector mused on the lot of the most sought-after girl in town. The physical thing: Would it really be better making love to Pearl Serein up there than, say…to Aliette Nouvelle, down here? Did pure height raise a man's lust factor, induce a deeper passion, a more committed heart?

Gazing up: There was the notion of angels. Was Pearl Serein a modern angel, burnished by fame and affluence, aloft in rarefied air? These days so many people seemed to need to believe in their existence. (Monique!) In meeting Pearl, Aliette had marked an isolated woman with worry in her eyes, no hint of the passionate heart. But Aliette was a woman too and the thing she saw in Pearl was obviously mirror-like. She saw natural restraint, that innate sense of privacy. Then again, a police station was not very romantic, not like a private pool high above the world. It was clear Claude Néon saw Pearl differently. Aliette had to deduce Pearl's tragically smitten loves had too. Tommi Bonneau had evoked a mundane snowball syndrome: one boy wants her so the next does too. She deduced that men felt Pearl's presence in a way she could question, criticize, but never feel.

Gazing up: Was it strictly male generated? And did Pearl nurture the mystique, creating her own exclusive solitude? Wilfully? Or instinctively? Might angel-hood be a kind of purgatory, locked in by that incessant question: Why can I not choose a man? Because it is instinctive to choose *right*. What impedes it? Lack of choice? That was not Pearl's problem. The pressure to *make* a choice, then, to choose someone and get on with life? Public pressure. Private orgasms. Aliette gazed up, wondering about Pearl's choices. Pearl's joy. Pearl's luck? She had to admit the story of Pearl and its effect presented the mysteries of love writ large — *large* being the problematic word.

Aliette felt her own choice was more of an inevitable meeting of souls. Clumsy, diffident souls. In finally finding each other, their separate bodies had been surprised, delighted, and continued to be. A bit of a miracle after all that time alone under the scrutiny of curious eyes. The inspector had made it quite clear to this possible other half that they would live their nascent love away from expectations, unknown. (She hadn't even told her mother). *We are not a story, monsieur.* If the private chemistry of love takes, their hearts will merge. That was the hope. The silent hope. But it would take time and you had to let it. The inspector deduced that Pearl hoped silently as well.

Aliette gazed up. Seven high-profile boyfriends in three years? No, she did not envy Pearl Serein.

## – 7 –
## Total fan

Elsewhere that night Willem van Hoogstraten, proprietor of the Rembrandt Café, had locked up early as was his custom—he had no wish or need to compete with the clubs or the brasseries. Brandishing a bottle of Ricard, he invited his two remaining guests to join him. A slinky, thirty-something, poodle-tressed street girl known only as Anne-Marie and an elderly-but-still-very-statuesque, silver-maned artist's model named Georgette Duguay followed Willem up the stairs. A makeshift rooftop terrace attached to Willem's apartment was a perfect vantage point on this balmy April evening. Below, the streets of the old quarter teemed with a happy urgency that made you feel alive. But it was Pearl Serein and death that dominated the talk.

'It would be impossible to live after Pearl,' mused Willem. 'I'd definitely want to die.'

'Risky.' Anne-Marie speculated on who'd be next to dare to prove himself in Pearl's bed. She was positive it would be the lead singer of a local band that was on the rise—the guy was luscious, how could Pearl resist? Willem was betting on the famous chef who'd recently divorced. Willem had heard the man was learning tennis. Everyone knew Pearl loved tennis.

Georgette banged her glass down, righteously fed up with Pearl. 'Why do you waste your time with such useless things?'

'But she's fabulous!' gushed Anne-Marie.

'Oh, stop!' Georgette demanded.

In the distance, north toward the Parc de la République, you could see the protective garden hedge surrounding the 11$^{th}$-floor penthouse perched at the top of the city's most exclusive building, the lonely diving tower etched against an indigo sky, the evening star just now twinkling into position directly above it. Though a loyal member of Georgette's drawing group, Willem was staunchly with Anne-Marie. He refilled their drinks. 'She's my inspiration. I've created this dessert. I'm calling it Pearl's Kiss.' Willem beamed. The dour waiter guise was his protective shield — only his friends were privy to the sensitive romantic underneath.

'Yes, and we women are inspired too,' added Anne-Marie.

Georgette protested bitterly. 'It's absurd. It's demeaning and ridiculous.'

'You're just jealous,' reposted Anne-Marie, blithely dismissive.

Georgette was insulted. 'I resent that. I do not believe in this silly story.' She stood, threatening to leave. Willem pleaded with her to stay. Please. For the sake of a beautiful evening.

Now a solitary light could be seen at Pearl's. The highest point. The most romantic.

Anne-Marie left instead. Pearl was affecting their friendship. Too bad, but she was in no mood for Georgette's gloomy bitching. She was in the mood for love — or at least some sex. She climbed in the old Westfalia van, a street girl's home on wheels, and pointed it downtown.

Club Diabolik shook hideously. Anne-Marie was sipping pastis, blending comfortably with the sounds of the Lonely Blue & Sad Times Band, watching a couple dancing by the stage. The music was hyperactive, hyper loud, but they were barely moving. The guy was a lanky beanpole with unkempt blond locks falling over his ears and collar, ruddy cheeks pulled taut around a weakly formed jaw, his small mouth opened wide in a painful, almost indecent ecstasy as he held his partner tight. She was a tiny thing, barely half his size. Her velvet arms circled his shapeless bum. Her face, buried under extravagant red curls, was pressed against his navel. He looked like an oversized boy dancing with a doll. Anne-Marie loved indecent ecstasy. *Allez-y!...* Go for it! She grooved coolly to the bass line and cheered the lovers on.

Happy. All she ever really needed was pastis, music, the occasional man...

Like magic, a man sat down beside her.

He was busy loading up his camera, half an eye intently fixed on those two immodest lovers. The waiter left pastis and water. He ignored it, busy peering through his view-finder, adjusting his lens. He was not a pretty man. Anne-Marie studied the baggy eyes, waxy skin, fleshy lips. She liked his mouth. All his defects came together around that mouth. She sensed a fellow traveler. Waiting to be noticed, Anne-Marie was aware of her heart beating double-time.

The next tune exploded. The tall blond man and his red-haired doll continued their deep slow dance, drifting closer to Anne-Marie's table, oblivious, turning, clinging to each other. The guy beside her with the camera was lining them up, waiting for his moment. Into the first chorus, the band pushed the music up another notch. A series of flashes created a greenish halo around the two lost dancers, streaks of white brilliance pulsed into their dumbfounded eyes.

Arms raised in front of their faces, they ran for cover on the far side of the room.

Sitting back, the camera guy tasted his drink. And found the time to give a hovering table-mate some attention. He had horrible bloodshot eyes. Anne-Marie returned his gaze.

Their eye contact ended with the music. Break time. The band promised to return.

'*Alors?*' she breathed, casual as she could make it — what's your excuse?

'Working...always working.'

The moment did not last long. The tall blond guy was standing there and did not look happy. His milky fingers worked non-stop, smoothing his wrinkled shirt. Anne-Marie knew he was far gone on something. 'I'm warning you. I won't have my dignity trashed again in your slimy column.' A squeaky voice, smoke-caked, breaking apart like his chaotic hair and ravaged face.

The man beside her wasn't worried. He responded, laconic, 'But Didi, I believe in love.'

Didi? Where had she heard that name?...and, a double take: working? With his camera.

No! Like most of his readers, Anne-Marie had only ever seen the penetrating eyes at the top of Tommi's space. Yes... Now *le vrai Tommi* was sitting beside her in Diabolik. Unbelievable! Cosmic?

She would have another look at that day's horoscope when she got back to the van.

The blond guy called Didi said, 'You are grotesque, Bonneau. Unspeakably low.'

Tommi Bonneau just laughed. '*Me*, grotesque? You're the one who's out dancing with his cousin. She *is* your cousin, eh, Didi? I heard half-sister.' He took a pad and pencil from his pocket, peering at the diminutive woman hunched in the far corner. 'What was her name again? Charlotte?'

'She's none of your business.' Didi's spindly fingers were going crazy up and down the front of his shirt.

'Let's say first cousin,' Tommi said, making a note, sipping his Ricard, adding water, sipping again. So casual. Anne-Marie, no stranger to the violence that went on between men, admired his mode of attack. The street girl who loved brinkmanship and grace under pressure knew immediately that Tommi Bonneau lived in a special kind of pain. She observed, eyes wide, as Tommi told his enemy, 'It's sad, but it must be wonderful if you can get past all the rules. Your own flesh and blood. An innate understanding of each other's needs. There's a purity in that, when you think about it.' Then Tommi intoned, '*O fangeuse grandeur! sublime ignominie!* ... Remember that, Didi? Do you remember your Baudelaire?'

*Oh filthy splendour, ineffable shame!*

Baudelaire. Anne-Marie was no poetry fan but she knew *that* name.

The man called Didi sputtered, 'If you say anything untoward, make any of your shitty insinuations or publish any of this, I promise I will put you and your paper out of business.'

Tommi raised his glass in a toast. 'But you're gorgeous, Didi. Scintillating!' Patting his camera, he surmised, 'I can sell these in Paris for ten times more than any judge would ever award you. They love cousin acts in Paris. *Especially* nobs with German connections. Mm?' Tasting more pastis, Tommi asked, seriously now—Anne-Marie could feel how deeply serious Tommi was in broaching this moment, 'Is a first cousin the only thing you could bear to touch after touching Pearl? *The only way to a woman's heart is along the path of torment.* There's a bit of de Sade, if you don't want Baudelaire. Eh,

Didi? From Pearl Serein to cousin Charlotte? I mean, is this logical? Inevitable? Speak, man! My readers need to know.'

Anne-Marie clued in. 'You're Didier Belfort.' She put an excited hand on Tommi's sinewy forearm. 'I read all about this.' Pearl Serein tested men and put them through the wringer.

Ignoring her, Belfort pointed a trembling finger. 'You're warned. I know where to find you.'

In a not ungentle voice, Tommi prodded, 'Tell us about your heart, Didi. And Pearl's. Does she even have one? This is the most important thing and Tommi's gentle readers want to know.' Now Tommi turned to Anne-Marie. 'They *need* to know. Right?'

Anne-Marie knew she should have paused to think more deeply. But Diabolik was not a place for thinking. Staring at the noble's stricken eyes, she nodded to confirm, Yes: we need to know.

Tommi sipped pastis and made a proposition. 'I'll trade you tonight's negatives for an exclusive confession.' The noble swayed as if punched, utterly befuddled by the presumption in this offer. Tommi persisted. 'Didi, if you can articulate this downturn, this slide into…what are we going call it?' He mulled, darkly intense for a concentrated second, then grinned as he found his phrase; 'this fall into the warm amorality of a slow dance with a first cousin…I like that—Didi, if you can describe that for my readers, you'll be performing a real service. I mean it. Try, Didi. Tell me your anger. Your desolation. Give me something to hang my story on.'

Belfort's eyes bulged. His trembling fingers wrapped into a fist. 'I'll beat you. I promise.'

Then Didi Belfort walked away.

But he made the mistake of glancing back. Tommi was ready.

Didi Belfort was swamped in another pool of white-green light…

And Tommi was gone by the time it faded.

As Belfort's addled eyes recovered, he stood gazing at Tommi's empty chair. He told Anne-Marie, 'He's lucky this isn't two hundred years ago. I could kill him and no one would say a word. Cut him to bits, feed him to the goldfish in the courtyard. One little problem solved.'

Anne-Marie did not respond to that. She left money on the table and split from Diabolik. She had her own problem to solve, something in her heart that needed answering right now. Plus she had a million things to ask him. Mainly about Pearl. Stepping into the street…

There: He was loping away, almost gone into the darkness. 'Hey! Wait!'

He stopped and turned. 'Are you following me?'

'I like the work you do.'

'Prove it.' A dare. Everything about him was a dare.

Breathless, she took him by the arm. 'You have to come with me.'

He did not resist. They walked together. 'Here…' sliding open the side panel.

'You live in this thing?'

'*Oui*,' uttered cool and low: Where else would I live? She gave him water. It came with a soft lick on his salty cheek, letting her curls fall over his bloody eyes. She hoped he was happy as she undid his belt and proceeded to wrap a lithe poodlish tongue around a lovely Bonneau bone.

## – 8 –

## Pumped-up cops

Chief Instructing Judge Richand denied Commissaire Néon's request for a mandate regarding the suspicious deaths of three leading citizens on the same day. Procureur Michel Souviron hated legal messes that touched the community's elite — because Michel was one of them, and a very political animal. Because the thing was far less than clear, the proc had shrugged, deferring to the best judgement of his chief magistrate. Gérard's reading of Claude's report seized on the essential fact that Dr. Petrucci had failed to establish anything more than cardiac arrest. As coincidental and oddly similar in certain outward aspects as they may have been, in each instance a heart attack was just a heart attack. Since there were no extenuating circumstances or marks, no contusions, lacerations or the like, nor any forbidden or lethal substances found inside the victims' systems, and since the three sites had been dusted and picked over by IJ and pronounced clean, all a prudent judge could do with Claude's new file was crumple it up and toss it in the waste bin.

The commissaire pushed the coincidence. 'Same girlfriend. This high profile social thing? Come on, Gérard — at least give me a preliminary.' Before he could reply, Claude blurted, 'What does Michel say?'

But it was the judge's call. And Gérard Richand was a fan of facts and rational ideas — not so big on hunches. He felt no need to debate it. 'It's all just back-page fiction, Commissaire. Nothing to hold it together. Sorry.' No murders nor tangible suspicion thereof had been established. Therefore, in official parlance, 'No case to answer.'

Gérard Richand's decision did not surprise Inspector Nouvelle. Heart attacks. No evidence. There was only Pearl Serein. She was trying to assuage Claude's abiding spite for Gérard Richand when Monique burst in with a copy of that evening's paper, open at the Letters page.

### Mistaken Identity

*Sir, I would like to put right an erroneous claim made by your society writer. In her column yesterday she referred to me as a former institutrice maternelle. In fact, I hold an Education nationale certificate, still valid, qualifying me to teach the primary levels. Gaining such accreditation entails a basic post-secondary degree and at least one year of specialized training. By contrast, in this region maternelles proceed directly from secondary school into a two-year training program, and in many areas, completion of secondary credits is not compulsory at all. In short, the difference between the two vocations is one of pedagogical degree, and, I should add, an increasing salary differential as seniority is accrued. Pearl Serein.*

Followed directly by: *We apologize.* The Editor.

Aliette was impressed. 'The lady's tougher than I thought.'

But it did not alter 'No case to answer.' Claude raged a bit, then sulked. Monique put her *Le Vrai Tommi* file away. Aliette knew Claude couldn't let it drop completely. But she could.

There was work. There was love! You could say she was pursuing her own deep hunch.

A week later, the morning after the Mari Morgan's verdict had finally come down, Inspector Nouvelle awoke to the sound of a banging balcony door. Overnight, April in Alsace had reverted to its usual self—rainy and inconsistent, with a blustery wind from the north. Then the phone rang.

'*Oui? Non!...merde!*' She dressed, fed Piaf, went out and hailed a cab.

Cars and trucks were massed in front of the old Legal Arts building in Rue Maginot. Word had spread like wildfire. Reps from all the local press and media were scrummed in the foyer, yelling questions at a stone-faced uniform guarding the lift. Those who recognized the inspector began yelling questions at her. Aliette pushed past, ignoring their noise, protruding mics, flashes, the red light over the eye of a video camera. As she stepped into the waiting lift, a woman stepped forward. The thickly painted eyes of television reporter Tina Trintingant, known as Cakeface at Rue des Bons Enfants, locked onto hers. A camera peered over Cake's shoulder.

Aliette smiled, touched the button, the lift door slid closed. When it opened again, another uniform escorted her to the end of the hall: *Georges Pugh, Avocat.*

Maître Pugh had been on a losing streak lately. This was satisfying. Georges' losing streak meant a winning streak for cops such as herself. Yesterday, there'd been a memo from the courthouse the minute the Mari Morgan's verdict was pronounced. And a moment of quiet, professional satisfaction. Bye-bye, Flossie Orain. Aliette had known Flossie was guilty half a year ago. She had testified in February, then moved on. The verdict was affirmation: Sometimes the world worked right. But she had nothing personal against Georges Pugh.

Now Georges was dead. Famous boyfriend number four.

Pugh's secretary was sitting in her usual place, shocked but tearless, waiting to be instructed. Going through to Georges' office, the inspector found Claude Néon, Raphaele Petrucci, three more uniforms, one snapping Polaroids, and two SAMU paramedics. The city's most colorful lawyer was seated at his desk, a pallid statue. It was a study in pressure: his shirt and tie like soiled tea towels, his besieged hair exploding in disjointed clumps, his glass of scotch still clasped in his left hand. His vacant eyes stared through the open window into eternity.

'Same thing?' she asked.

Raphaele nodded. 'Heart attack.'

'Last night,' Claude said.

'We're saying eleven…maybe ten hours ago,' Raphaele added.

At a cursory glance, Georges Pugh's death betrayed no signs of struggle, no blood.

As the inspector nosed around the office, Claude indicated that Raphaele and the SAMU team could proceed with transferring the body to the morgue. Raphaele hesitated. He knew Claude was blatantly ignoring the *non* from Gérard Richand. Claude snapped, 'Get moving! I've already talked to Souviron. He says do it — he'll smooth it out with Strasbourg.' Followed by a not so subtle huff,

'Richand can stick it in his fat bum.' A proc's OK trumps a magistrate's no. His own ass covered, Raphaele directed the removal of the body. With Georges removed, the empty spot on the blotter protecting the surface of the antique desk loomed large—the spot where his hand had been firmly placed at the time of death.

It was a basic desktop writing pad, more decorative than functional: a square of green blotter paper under a sheet of plastic, the two surfaces held flush by embossed morocco shoulders. Slotted between plastic and paper were keepsakes: photos, ticket stubs, cards, a blue ribbon. Something was missing from the place where Georges Pugh's hand had been—this easily deduced because the blotting paper retained its original rich green where the missing object had shielded it from sunlight.

'A photo.' Aliette carefully slid another photo from the other corner of the blotter (Pugh at the helm of a motor-yacht) and fit it perfectly to the blank spot. 'A photo of her?'

Pugh's secretary was summoned. She barely glanced at the spot. 'That woman.' A flicker of distaste sparked in her face. 'Topless, with Georges on his boat at Lac Como.'

Basic question. 'So, who wants a picture of Pearl?'

'Someone who loves her,' Claude replied. 'Someone who wants her for himself.'

In describing the frustration of watching a gifted man in the process of tragic, 'almost wilful' self-destruction after splitting from 'that woman,' the secretary sounded a lot like the filmmaker's assistant, but ten years older. Matronly. Had she kept a motherly flame alight for Georges?

The security guard who worked the night shift confirmed Pugh had stayed late and had been alone in the building, according to the log book. He said one reporter tried to follow him in when the Maître had returned earlier in the evening—at exactly 6:17pm. How did you know it was a reporter? Because he was badgering Maître Pugh for an interview. What did the Maître say to this? He threatened to sue the man's paper, adding: 'Maître Pugh used to love all those people, they were always in and out for interviews and pictures. But since he's been losing…' A rueful shake of his head to acknowledge a tragic turn of fortune. What did he look like, this reporter? A basic description was clearly one of Tommi Bonneau. But he did not come in? No. You never left your post? Yes, I made my rounds, like always, to see who's in, but the door was locked tight, all alarm systems in place, you can check the computer. Thank you — the security guard was dismissed.

Aliette leaned out the open window. Below it, a good ten feet, was a ledge only a brave cat could negotiate. This was the only link to the offices on either side of Pugh's. There were no windows in the wall of the next building, at least forty feet across the gap. There was a dank alley six storeys below. The only ladder long enough would have to have come on a fire truck. Maybe IJ would find a print from a climber's shoe? Maybe.

Claude Néon said, 'We damn well better find an MO or we're in for a rough ride.'

They left the uniforms to seal the office.

Back at the Commissariat, the phone on Monique's desk kept ringing and the energy kept rising as Claude laid it out for his assembled team. They now had four dead men. If murder, that meant serial. But, 'barring a breakthrough downstairs, all we have is coincidence and the tiniest B&E. Nothing was broken and we're not sure how they entered...' There was one possible tangible link to Georges Pugh's seized-up heart: The photo that was not there. 'We're looking for a basic drugstore printed photo of Pearl Serein sitting on the bow of a boat.'

'Topless,' added Aliette. It was weird, but it *was* about this Pearl Serein.

Claude confirmed. 'Topless is an incentive. I'm sure Gérard Richand will be more amenable if we let him see the lady's tits.' All the more so if the city got to see them too. Which it would — Commisaire Néon was learning how to work these things. But they had to find the picture. 'Keep it quiet. This picture is just missing property from the scene.' He began portioning out assignments. 'Patrice and Jean-Marie will focus on last night. Pugh's secretary, the security people, his clients — the more obvious ones first. If it means closing down a lab or two, then so be it...'

'Don't start a war,' warned Aliette. It was her unwritten privilege to warn, critique and otherwise keep an eye on Claude's leadership decisions, especially as they pertained to her patch. Fighting the people who controlled the drug trade only worked with negotiation and trade-offs.

'No,' Claude agreed, 'no wars, very cool.' He pressed on. 'Guy, Jeannot, you'll make a wider circle. First three victims: any enemies including family. Anyone pissed enough to kill for love and nuts enough to do three more to make it into a game. If you need background, it's all in my computer: money, taxes, drugs, tics and politics, whatever you need. Under *pearlsboys*. Monique will send you the file.' Junior Inspector Bernadette Milhau would reread everything in Monique's assorted clippings. Claude would approach the woman in question…

Aliette left them to it — she had her own very busy day ahead, thank you very much.

The inspector was intrigued but worried. Four lovers down. Heart attacks? There was obviously something occurring here. But she was sensing something wrong in Claude's reaction. Claude couldn't help but see it big and was making it bigger by the minute. The guys were lapping it up, bursting to get out there. Pumped-up cops are easy targets. Yes, for bullets, but far more so for those who want to tear a strip. An instinct made her want to back away. It was his obsession, not hers, and it was growing. Aliette hoped Procureur Souviron was truly onside with Claude.

## - 9 -
## CLAUDE CALLS ON PEARL

Stepping into the open-concept mansion in the sky, Claude Néon was nervous, immediately out of his element. He had never been in a lift that opened directly into a home, let alone a home like this one. He looked out at the Vosges, misty in the distance—this was the highest point between here and there. He'd been announced by the uniformed concierge back at ground level and Pearl Serein was waiting for him, composed, wary. Everyone's wary when the police come calling.

Claude apologized for intruding.

Pearl shrugged, 'It's all right. Not busy...Just reading.'

Claude asked, 'What are you reading?'

Like any obedient citizen, she handed over her book.

'*Three-Cornered Room*?' Some Japanese novel, in translation. He didn't know it.

She mumbled something about it being a classic. Her father had recommended it. 'Years ago. I still pick it up from time to time. Whenever I feel removed from myself like this.' Pearl said it was the story of a woman with one part missing.

Claude asked what part that might be.

She replied, 'Her compassion.'

Claude blanched. He was in no way prepared to pursue a literary discussion, much less an existential one. He did know that sociopath killers display a fundamental lack of compassion toward their fellow human beings. He asked, 'Who's your father?'

'No one special. He's dead...He had a bookstore.'

As gently as he knew how, Claude broke the news of Georges Pugh. She knew, of course—it was all over the radio. Pearl stayed quiet, inside herself: what can a person do? Claude eased toward the inevitable questions. After their less than smooth first meeting, this time Commissaire Néon took extra care to assure Pearl Serein that she was under no obligation to reply.

She emerged from her quiet to assure *him*, 'But Monsieur le Commissaire, I want to reply.'

Claude smiled, deferential. 'Of course. Your reputation.'

'No!' Eyes flashing, not in the mood for deference. 'That is not about my reputation. What you're referring to is a fairy tale. A silly fantasy. We have to be clear.' Pearl Serein turned away and stared at the distance. Her own private distance. She added, 'Or I won't reply.'

'Fine. Perfect.' Claude asked, 'Where were you yesterday afternoon and evening from two till six or so?' From the time Georges Pugh left the courthouse under the weight of another high-profile loss till the time he'd signed back in at his building.

'I shopped…I have a new dress and a sales woman to corroborate that…I played tennis at my club. Then I came home. I walked… through the park.'

'You weren't at the courthouse by any chance?' To see Georges fail.

'No. Why would I be?'

'Just that you and Monsieur Pugh had a history. I mean, you were there for—'

'As you probably know, I had a personal involvement with someone directly involved in that case. I find court boring. Only morbid people with nothing to do go to see such sordid things.'

'Did you have any contact with Georges Pugh yesterday?'

'No, not directly. I haven't talked to Georges since autumn.' She shrugged. 'But he was at the club yesterday afternoon when I was there. Does that count?'

'You saw him there?'

'No, I saw his car in the lot. Bright gold. Hard to miss. By design, I should add.'

Pearl closed her eyes and breathed. Claude understood. Georges Pugh was the worst kind of flashy, attention-seeking, egotistical lawyer. But he had to ask, 'Why didn't you see him?'

'I didn't *want* to see him. He could never let go. It always gets so stupid and—'

'Then why did you go to thé club?'

Pearl Serein lifted her Japanese novel out of Claude's hand, her brown eyes heavy with exasperation. 'I had a lesson booked. I will not stop my life because of some man.'

'No.' It was lucky she said that. Claude caught himself going straight back to the mess he'd made during her visit to his office. He eased up. He looked around. 'This is beautiful.'

'Yes.' Peremptory. Saying it added nothing useful to the matter at hand. She told him, 'I had my lesson, I had a shower and dried my hair and went home. Georges' car was there when I was on my way out. He could've been in the bar or eating or God knows where. I know he was supposed to have a lesson. But I did not see the man. I did my best *not* to see him.'

'How do you know he was going to have a lesson?'

'Remy mentioned it...Remy Lorentz, the tennis pro at the club.'

Ah. 'There, you're helping me already.' Another cop smile. 'According to our timeframe, this Remy could be the last person to have spent any meaningful time with Georges.'

'Remy?' Pearl's eyes went wide. 'They were going to work on his serve.' (*Le service.*)

'We'll have a word with Remy.' Claude took out his pad and jotted down the name. Pearl's mouth moved, tentative, as if she might think a word with Remy would not be useful. But she stayed silent. He asked, 'What about the others?'

She flared again. 'What *others*?' She understood the question. She resented the implication.

Claude stayed calm and explained. If she honestly wanted to help, she had to accept the strong possibility that she'd spent intimate time with a killer. The list of her ex-lovers, who had to be considered both suspects and potential victims, was now down to three: Didier Belfort, Bruno Martel and Raymond Tuche. Claude ran his hand along the back of a creamy leather *fauteuil*. 'Monsieur Belfort. He gave you this place?' That got a silent yes. 'Is he still involved in any way? I mean, is he the kind of man who might believe he still had a claim?'

Pearl marched across the room to her writing desk, sat and began sifting through the drawer. Claude began a casual tour of the room, admiring, touching…she was a big reader, four shelves chock full of books. He ended up by her shoulder as she continued to search through her desk. He couldn't help but notice the open invitation lying there.

*Spring Follies! Saturday, May 1*
*Champagne and dancing to celebrate the season*
*Members and friends*
*RSVP Gaston for group tables*

'Going dancing?'

'Is there a law against it, Commissaire?'

Claude just smiled. They both knew it was none of his business. He backed away.

Pearl continued rifling through the overflowing drawer, frowning, muttering, 'I might. I've been cooped up here far too long…Ah! Here…' Bringing Claude a business card. 'This is my notary. He will show you everything you need to see. The place is free and clear and completely mine.' That settled, Pearl seemed to retreat inside again. 'I can't really explain it. Didi insisted.' Then, softer, retreating still further—searching for further clarity? 'Didier Belfort is a very talented, very spoiled, very passive-aggressive overgrown child. He also owns or has access to ten other homes around here and over the river. I had no home. It was a lovely gesture but not the hugest sacrifice. You know?' Claude mulled this. Pearl added, 'If you really need to know, Didi also paid my entry fee at the club. We met through tennis.'

'I see,' said Claude.

Did he? Pearl appeared to doubt it. 'Didi's too wrapped up in himself to kill anyone.'

Following this thread, Claude asked, 'And Duteil—he gave you a lot of money?'

Staring with disbelief into a cop's intrusive eyes, Pearl murmured, 'Yes.'

'How much?'

Now her placid face twisted slightly. 'Do you really need to know?'

'Not really, not just now… But enough for someone to kill for, do you think?'

'I don't know.' Pearl pondered it. 'Depends on how much importance you give to money.'

So money was a sore point. Pearl's dour mask was firmly back in place.

Claude tugged it again. 'Were you in it for the money?'

'No!'

'No?'

'Monsieur Commissaire, I'm a schoolteacher. I was raised over a bookstore. It is not in my blood to be in anything for the money.'

'Then why did he give you all that money? Were you making plans?'

'We weren't together long enough for plans.' But Claude needed to know more — for her sake, for his sense of her. So Pearl said, 'I asked Jerôme the same thing. He told me, This is all I have to give you, this is what I do. That seemed a bit sad, but it was obvious he needed to do it. So he could feel secure in the way he felt about me. Do you know what I mean, monsieur?'

Claude did not answer that. He asked, 'Then you left him for Pugh?'

'No. I just left him. There was no connection.'

'But everyone says —'

'I don't *care* what everyone says,' she hissed. 'My heart does not have a sign on it. *Merde!*'

Pearl whirled away. Claude waited till the mountains calmed her.

She approached again. 'Georges can be very persuasive.'

'Mm. And now he's dead too.'

'Poor Georges,' Pearl murmured.

'*Poor* Georges? Some of the slime I could tell you about that he's gotten off...'

Pearl nodded grimly. 'I know all about them...impossible to live with a man like that.'

'Impossible?'

'The grubby thing behind the brilliant words. It's there forever.'

'Who would kill Georges Pugh?'

Pearl held steady. 'Lots of people. Look at the life he lived.'

Claude returned to his list. 'So then came Raymond Tuche.'

The sculptor. After the lawyer.

'So?' Bristling. She really hated all this stuff about her boyfriends.

'These men are dying, madame.'

Pearl Serein deflated with a weary sigh. She wrapped her arms tight across her breast, stress leaking from her face. 'Raymond has his problems, but after Georges he was like fresh air.'

'Seen Ray lately?'

'I haven't seen anyone lately. I mean men. I play tennis with the women. I come home. I read.' Flashing her book about a woman with a part of her soul gone missing.

Claude wielded his pen. 'Which women do you play with?'

'The women on the ladder.'

'Ladder?'

'The tennis ladder!'

Pearl had a temper. Claude stepped back from it. 'Please. You said you wanted to help.'

She relaxed. 'Sorry...Raymond has been at a sanatorium since December. Le Cure Curé. He checked himself in. If Raymond forgets his medication he's very capable of de-compensating. Drastically. His emotions are volatile but he's not dangerous.'

'On a voluntary basis?' Tuche could walk out of his sanatorium whenever he felt like it.

Pearl countered, 'Commissaire, if Raymond ever hurt anyone, it's likely to be himself.'

'OK.' Claude felt the truth of her statement. He said, 'Which leaves Bruno Martel.'

Pearl asked, 'How could *he* kill anyone? He's not here. He's been out at his farm since...' She trailed off. Pale. Full of quiet sighs. It went without saying: Since he'd been dumped by Pearl.

'He was your last...uh, your last involvement. Why did you leave him?'

She shuddered, flustered. 'Because I didn't like him.'

'He wasn't happy about it.'

'No.'

'Jealous?'

'They're *all* jealous, monsieur Commissaire. But Bruno Martel will never admit to something as low as jealousy...*Quel bordel!*' This last whispered into silence. What a god-awful mess.

Claude gave her space to breathe. Finally asked, 'You can confirm last night's whereabouts?'

'I was here.'

'Can you prove it?'

'I have no idea. Do I need to?'

He didn't know; she might. Claude gave *himself* some space to breathe. After a good long gaze at the mountains, he asked, 'Would you be willing to help in a more active way with this?'

'If I can.'

'Good. Merci.' Claude pushed the button to call the lift.

Pearl Serein came near, Japanese novel clutched tightly in her hand. 'Monsieur Commissaire, my men are...' She paused. What? The lift arrived. Claude pulled back the door. 'My men are my mistakes, but they are not murderers. I would know. I would have a feeling. Any woman would.'

Not every woman, Claude Néon thought. Some women are as blind as bats. But he held his peace. Stepping into the lift, he left Pearl Serein standing with the world spreading out behind her.

He spoke with the puffy concierge, who confirmed Madame Serein's comings and goings and final return the previous day. 'But there is a back stairs, I assume?'

'*Oui*...but...' A large shrug. Why would anyone with a private lift bother climbing?

When Commissaire Claude Néon walked out of Pearl Serein's building he was fairly sure Pearl did not kill men. He felt it. A cop's certainty. A man's instinct. He stood out front, gazing up. He thought she might be looking down. She said she would be willing to help. Help Claude Néon solve this. He checked the time. The proc was not for another hour yet.

Monsieur le Commissaire strode back into the foyer, and back into the lift.

The concierge inserted his key in the top button, 'Voila.' And stepped out with a servile bow.

Are you meant to tip? Claude wondered as he rode back up with a special request for Pearl.

## – 10 –
## Bruno weeps

Inspector Nouvelle was on her way upstairs with a briefcase full of paperwork. She'd been up late preparing for a lunch meeting with Swiss FedPol Agent Franck Woerli, her Swiss counterpart in the recent border operation. He would in turn be eating with their Italian link next week. The political element required a constant and careful coordinating of facts. '*Salut.*' She met Claude Néon on the second landing. He was bright-eyed with intent. 'So? Best friends now?'

'She's going to cooperate.'

And a bonus! Procureur Souviron, under siege after Pugh, had convinced Strasbourg to send (and pay for) a heart specialist from the university to work with Raphaele Petrucci. In a backdoor sort of way, the hysterical press surrounding Pearl's dead loves was working in Claude's favor.

Aliette smiled. 'Good, Claude.' His hunch was turning into an obsession — but one he could run with.

'Yeah, good.... And you?

'Have to get ready for lunch with the Swiss police.'

The two cops continued in their separate directions.

Pearl was punctual, waiting at the door of her building when Commissaire Néon arrived. They headed for the river. They would start at the beginning, with Didier Belfort. Claude explained his thinking. 'Confront them. If you're there with me, something will give.' It always did. If Pearl could handle it — if she honestly wanted to help the police do their job, they might clear this thing up directly.

Pearl nodded, quietly truculent. She'd do her bit. 'But I still don't believe I slept with a killer.'

They arrived at a refurbished warehouse complex, another of the architect's noted projects. Didi Belfort's studio was adjacent, a done-up loft, his latest fabulous residence. They were greeted by a diminutive woman with wildly cascading red hair set against a million freckles and milky blue eyes who was clearly quite gone on some drug — it was plain to a cop, if not to a former schoolteacher; though Pearl seemed to nod knowingly as the woman fumbled and spilled trying to simultaneously tie the sash on her housecoat and sip the drink in her wobbly hand.

She was Charlotte, Didi's cousin. Her French was thick with Black Forest German. 'I have been taking care of Didi,' she told Claude. Her distracted gaze came to rest on Pearl. 'This woman has made much harm, no? Cunt.' With that, Charlotte began to shut the door.

Claude blocked it. 'I want to see him.'

'Didi is at his tennis.' Then she belched. The hand holding the sash came up to cover her mouth. Her housecoat fell open. She fumbled to regain a proper balance of decorum.

Seeing there was no point in further chat with Charlotte, Claude released the door.

He walked a weeping Pearl down to the riverside promenade. The flow was silvery on a grayish spring morning. Pearl's tears glistened as he softly assured her that she did not deserve that kind of abuse. She leaned on his arm. He respected her courage and sense of civil duty in agreeing to accompany him. During this mid-morning interlude Claude Néon again felt the fragile thing at the core of Pearl Serein. The thing beneath the pride and temper. The heart that was in need.

But she was OK and wanted to continue. Insisted, 'Yes! I said I would... Let's go.'

So they headed north to the club in search of Didi Belfort.

They found Bruno Martel instead.

The club was at the foot of a cul-de-sac. An unused château on an overgrown property had been purchased and extensively remade into the city's chicest club. Parking and ten tennis courts had been laid down around the grounds, three handball courts designed into the carriage house (by Didier Belfort). A pool was added to the patio area, changing rooms and showers installed in the basement. Card, billiard and private dining rooms now filled the elegant nooks on the second floor to complement the dining, bar and ball rooms on the main. A barber, hairdresser, manicurist and masseur each had mini-shops as adjuncts to a shiny fitness facility on the third floor. There was a security box at the gate, with a sign: Members Only.

In fact, the Quarter Racquets Club was three blocks from Commissaire Néon's new home in the north end, but he had yet to explore this little lane. Making the down payment on the house had been a reckless gamble. A boy from the streets of Paris, he was still tentative as to his status amongst the provincial bourgeois. But tennis couldn't be *that* hard, surely.

Pearl said, 'Why, there's Bruno.'

'Martel?' A giant with a Jesus beard and hair, all in white, was shuffling along, a woman, also all in white, was at his side. Like they were out for a walk in their pyjamas. Claude pulled over. Rolling down his window, he watched the man approach. 'What's he doing here?'

'*B'en*, going to the club, obviously.'

'I thought he was in the mountains.'

'So did I.' Adding, 'Looks like Agnès got her wish.' Pearl's catty side rang clear.

She meant the woman holding Bruno's hand.

Claude asked, 'Are they allowed to wear that kind of stuff to the club?'

'For lunch it's not a problem. Bruno wears only white. He says it's more enlightened.'

Claude had done a search on Bruno Martel: Sold insurance, then financial planning, had morphed into motivational speaking, usually from a financial strategy angle, then hit it big when the therapy movement boomed. A large man, his mass contained an expansive energy that became his calling card when Bruno had discovered a gift for hugging. He began to bill himself as a healer. He'd opened a center in town and transformed a farm in the Vosges into a spiritual retreat, strictly secular—lots of cows and shit to balance out the quasi-religious group hugs and meditations. If you were feeling especially forsaken, Bruno offered *Une Semaine Face à Face*, a one-on-one week with himself, secluded in a converted muck room attached to his barn. The experience, described as 'duo-innering,' was monitored by Bruno's personally trained staff. In the many articles and TV news spots produced on the spiritual farm, the healer always promised that an intense week of duo-innering *Face à Face* was guaranteed to ultimately expose 'the heart inside the heart.'

Time alone with Bruno cost a fortune. You signed on with a promise of nondisclosure.

Claude Néon always found it hard to believe people bought into such touchy-feely bullshit. But in getting the facts from Pearl Serein, he'd been careful to avoid implying as much. Though vexed with her ex-lovers' apparent inability to be graceful in losing the prize that was herself, Pearl refused to undermine the professional credibility of these men. Now here was Bruno Martel, walking down the street. Shambling was a better word. A bear of a man—a bear that had swallowed a barrel of beer. 'You spent a week in a room alone with him without coming out?'

'Two. He insisted. An extra week. He didn't make me pay. Bruno's not about money.'

'What happened?'

'I can't tell you. I signed a contract… He has incredible presence,' she murmured. 'He has helped a lot of people.'

Claude repeated his bottom line: 'People are dying, madame.'

Pearl acquiesced. 'We talked. We had sex. Meditated.'

Meditated. Claude had never meditated. For two weeks? 'Were you afraid of him?'

'Monsieur Commissaire, I'm not attracted to men I'm afraid of. That's not logical.'

'When you left, he didn't attempt force?'

'Of course not!' She was mad that Claude still did not get this central thing about her men.

'All right.' Claude got out of the car, indicating that Pearl should too.

She obeyed, nervous, and stayed very close as they stood on the curb.

The woman Pearl had identified as Agnès was pale skinned, with straight black hair cut short in the common workaday style. In her enlightened whites Agnès was ascetic, dancerly. When her eyes fell on Pearl, she stopped dead in her tracks, stern face registering scorn, maybe fear.

Like a ship that needs a lot more room to put the brakes on, Bruno Martel kept going. 'Pearl?' Agnès reached to pull him back. The huge man did not notice her restraining move. '…Pearl?' Peering as if through fog. 'Is it really you?' Massive arms spread, the prelude to a world-sized hug.

'Yes, Bruno. It's me.' She did not offer a kiss. Stayed well away from his hug.

Bruno seemed at a loss until Agnès stepped into the void. 'Agnès!' (You have to say it the French way: *An-yes*, pushing softly on the *yes*.) 'Agnès is now my special assistant,' said Bruno.

From deep inside Bruno's large embrace, Agnès demanded, 'What do you want from us?'

Claude answered. 'We'd like a word with Monsieur Martel.' He flashed his ID.

Martel stood mute, eyes locked on Pearl. Up close, Bruno Martel showed bulging pock-marked cheeks, a pin-like nose descending from between button eyes a tad too close together, thinning hair swirling down over his ears and collar from a central bald spot, the whole mess held together by the patchy, biblical beard. For the life of him, Claude could not figure out Pearl's attraction to the man.

Two weeks! Pearl having sex with Bruno Martel? Claude was truly baffled.

Freeing herself from Bruno's arms, Agnès started in on Claude. 'Leave us alone!' Whatever the problem, Bruno knew nothing about it. He had been in seclusion since February. He was in a very delicate transitional state. Could the commissaire not see that? Agnès was aghast at his presumption.

Claude said, '*Bon*. It can be here or in *garde à vue*.' A huge bluff without a clear mandate.

Bruno said, 'I will answer your questions.'

Claude said, 'Good. Now –'

But Bruno was addressing Pearl, not Claude. 'I sense anger, Pearl. Anger at your life.'

'I'm not angry, Bruno. It's finished. It's gone from my mind.'

Bruno Martel didn't hear this. He said, 'All things can be transformed by an ever-deepening spiritual perception and activism. Early on in my innerings I discovered gratitude, I learned the importance of feeling grateful for the pain in my life, especially as regards the heart...' Bruno's large hands began to move. 'The more forgiving and grateful you feel for all that pain, the more you will appreciate that pain only reflects your inner state of mind. I've been alone meditating on these things for several months. I have been examining my heart. And your heart, Pearl — I know all about your heart.' Again he reached. Pearl Serein did not respond.

Agnès purred, 'Bruno, please...' She moved back inside his arms. She stroked his cheek.

The only forewarning was his ears, sticking through his greasy hair and turning a bright translucent red. He began to emit a gurgling sound. The gurgle congealed into a frightening train of wretched dry coughs. Agnès held Bruno tight — like hanging onto a shaking tree trunk. Then Bruno loosed a preternatural howl that rang in the street with such incredible force that Claude Néon instinctively felt for his gun. The man in the security box at the club gate stepped out. Pushing his special assistant away, Bruno Martel clutched his breast and bent double, face in hands, huge body convulsing. Then rising again, an outsized man, sobbing chest-wracking outsized sobs, torrential tears flooding down through his scraggly beard. And he whimpered: a high-pitched, squeaky sound. 'Pearl?'

Claude let go of his gun. Always a disorienting sight, a big man breaking down like that. He hesitated, then dared to rest his hand on the shuddering shoulder. 'Come on, man, pull out of it.'

Pearl touched Claude's arm, whispered, 'Bruno believes in crying.'

But Claude found himself resenting it. This dreadful spilling, heedless of another man's presence. It had something to do with manhood. It made Claude Néon feel too much like an invisible cop. Claude waited for Pearl to respond. She knew him — she had spent two weeks *face à face* with Bruno. He finally demanded, 'Can't you do something?'

No. Pearl was shaking her head, resolute. Not my problem. Let Agnès do something.

Agnès wanted to take care of it. 'Bruno…Bruno?' She was wary as she tried to calm him.

Claude had seen similar caution in the faces of the bomb-squad guys.

Bruno's stupendous crying had brought the neighbors to their windows. Cars heading into the club were slowing. Claude held up his Police ID, waving them by. Everything's under control.

But it wasn't. Beside him, Pearl Serein uttered a chagrined, 'Oh, *merde*.'

Because Tommi Bonneau had arrived.

'Hey, Pearl!' Already moving in, flashing pictures. 'What a brilliant coincidence!'

Blinking away diffusing ripples of green-white light settling in his eyes, Claude stepped protectively in front of Pearl Serein. 'If you even think of running that.'

'It's a free country, Commissaire… Beautiful! Totally perfect!' Never even looking up from behind his lens, flashing off shot after shot, Tommi Bonneau was undeterred.

Claude stuck his ID card square in front of Tommi's lens and raised his voice. 'You leave!'

'Bugger that…' Dodging, clicking away, 'I'm an accredited reporter, I'm in the street, I'm covering the news, it has nothing to do with you. Bruno's one of my best customers. Eh, Bruno?' Reacting to the same green-white flashing, the healer had fallen silent. Thank God. But his tears still flowed, a monumental river of broken-hearted pain. As Tommi circled, taking pictures, Bruno's button eyes seemed locked to Tommi's lights. From behind his viewfinder, Tommi commanded, 'Talk to me, Bruno. Come on, I need a quote… Pearl, if you could move a little closer to Bruno.'

Pearl's defence was to look bored. 'Stop it, Tommi.'

'Could be a wonderful moment, Pearl. Where's your sense of history?'

Pearl Serein opened her mouth to reply—

'Bruno!' Agnès shrieked, frantic, tugging at his oversized arm.

With a heavy shake, Bruno sent her staggering. A bystander amongst a crowd of bemused club members caught her before she fell. Stumbling like Frankenstein, Bruno Martel began to run. The crowd watched the distraught healer lumber up the street. Tommi Bonneau took off after Bruno, flashing shot after shot after shot. They disappeared around the corner.

Claude Néon would have liked nothing better than to chase them down—and smack them both. But he was needed. Agnès was screaming, 'Did you really need to do this? Are you happy?' She leapt at Pearl, pummeling. Pearl tried to protect herself, yet remained oddly mute. Claude watched for several dumbfounded seconds before summoning the wherewithal to pull Agnès away and deliver her, flailing, into the arms of the club security guard. He hugged a weeping Pearl.

Agnès wailed, 'She ruined him! She ruined everything!'

A city police car pulled up. Two uniforms rushed to take charge.

When Agnès calmed down, they got her papers, took the information over to Claude.

Agnès Guntz lived a few streets away. Tommi Bonneau was waiting when they arrived—affecting a hang-dog Lucky Luke pose, Tommi pointed. 'He went that way.'

Agnès bared her teeth. 'Stay off my property, you pig.'

Tommi smiled. 'I am off your property, madame.'

'Just ignore him,' Pearl advised.

Claude made it clear. 'Fuck off or you're in trouble.'

Tommi took another picture as Claude and Pearl followed Agnès Guntz inside.

— —

PJ Inspector Aliette Nouvelle was sitting at a table in the Rembrandt Café with Swiss FedPol Agent Franck Woerli, enjoying coffee after gobbling down Willem van Hoogstraten's special Pig's Feet Sausage served on a bed of sauerkraut and a bock of Jupiler beer. The meeting had been productive. With some simple tweaking of names and dates, the French and Swiss would be in sync on the latest multinational police action. Her portable buzzed. 'Sorry, Franki. Excuse.'

Monique. City had called. The commissaire was caught in the middle of an incident with Pearl Serein. 'At the gate to that club in the north end…Quarter Racquets?'

'Merci.' Aliette made her apologies and grabbed a cab. After some confusion at the club gate, she was directed to the residence of Agnès Guntz with basic information as to the situation.

The north end is prosperous. On a peaceful spring day there were hints of new flowers peeking over garden walls. Well-heeled mothers pushed well-planned children strapped in well-designed *poussettes*. Joggers passed, intent on health, unconstrained by work. The elegant corner-lot house of Agnès Guntz — a divorcee who had done well by it — was typical: pinkish terra cotta masonry, three tall stories plus a half-floor lined with dormers. A gargoyle in the lintel was a sign of roots. A high stone fence shielded the Guntz residence from Tommi Bonneau, waiting out front in the suspended ambience of a leafy afternoon. 'What are you doing here?'

'Working.'

'Haven't you done enough for one day, Tommi?'

'I serve the story, Inspector.'

'I'd think twice about publishing those pictures.'

'He's a bit of a *nul*, your commissaire.'

'He'll fight you if you want it, monsieur. Count on it.'

He ignored this. Returned to his habitual fiddling with his camera.

Crossing the street, Aliette was distracted by screeching tires, the wailing *pan-pon, pan-pon* of uniforms arriving. A voice cut through. '*Attention!*' She narrowly missed being run down by a jogger rounding the corner, earphones on, eyes focused on the house of Agnès Guntz. *Imbécile!* he cursed, veering to avoid her. A beautiful jogger but less than neighborly; his almond eyes in a ruggedly tanned face registered a flash of pure disgust for the careless woman.

'Pardon!' Startled. But the inspector easily noted a man very interested in this house.

He kept running, eyes locked on a bedroom window, oblivious to the arriving police cruiser.

And now a radio news team roared to a dramatic halt. More *pan-pons* in the distance. The rush was on. Calling to the uniforms, 'Keep them well away,' Aliette pushed through the gate, hurried to the door, let herself in with the briefest knock.

Pearl Serein was in the salon, huddled on a sumptuous divan, head in her hands, weeping. Agnès Guntz was in her kitchen in a state of rigid shock. A trail of strewn and shattered objects led the inspector down the basement stairs. Where she found Claude, puzzling over victim number five:

Bruno Martel, squeezed into a sooty corner behind the ancient heating-oil tank, slumped on his large backside, soaked with piss, stinking largely—and quite dead. And yet his eyes were wide, seeming to stare up at whoever happened to find him. Like some child caught?

'What in the world?'

Claude hadn't a clue.

## – 11 –

## Adding murky innuendo to the mix

*Failed police action adds murk to healer's death.* By Serge Phaneuf, *Le Cri* Crime Desk.

Disturbingly unresolved rumors surround the sudden death by apparent heart failure of well-known new-age guru/healer Bruno Martel yesterday. Martel, 40, was found dead at the residence of Agnès Guntz, Martel's current companion and Executive Director of the Martel Meditation Center and its subsidiary Spiritual Farm.

Légiste Raphaele Petrucci confirmed the cause of death as, 'heart attack,' before he accompanied Martel's body to the police morgue where, it is assumed, it will be autopsied in context with four recent and similar deaths. Jerôme Duteil, Jean-Guy Gagnon, Pierre Angulaire and Georges Pugh have all died within two weeks, all of heart attack, all (with the debatable exception of Duteil) well before their natural time. While no criminal action has as yet been tied to this coincidental series of fatalities, PJ Commissaire Claude Néon was observed attempting to speak to Monsieur Martel minutes before his death. When Martel bolted the scene and took refuge at the Guntz residence, it was Néon who, upon entering the house, discovered the body in the fruit cellar, where Martel apparently sought to hide. From what, is the mystery, as is a more detailed description of the heart attack that felled him.

Monsieur Martel was known to be on several medications in aid of his considerable weight and attendant blood pressure issues.

Commissaire Néon offered no comment as to the coincidental aspect of Martel's passing, nor regarding the presence of socialite Pearl Serein with him yesterday at the aborted 'interview.' Néon would only say that in light of his own presence, investigation of the 'semi-suspicious' circumstances would be handed over to Commissaire Duque and the city police.

> *It is commonly known that Madame Serein was romantically linked with Monsieur Martel, as she also was with Messieurs Duteil, Gagnon, Angulaire and Pugh. It is assumed that Commissaire Néon's attempt to confront Monsieur Martel yesterday afternoon is connected. Madame Serein was not available for comment. All calls to PJ offices last evening were referred to City Police. Spokesperson Martine Wangen said there was no more information at this time. Referring to the fact that Monsieur Martel had just emerged from three months of 'deep solitude' at his retreat near Rhinau, a distraught Agnès Guntz expressed outrage at what she termed 'an unconscionable breach of privacy during a highly sensitive time,' and laid the blame for the death of 'a beautiful, enlightened man' unequivocally at the feet of 'blundering police.' 'I will be talking to our legal advisors,' said Madame Guntz. She would not comment as to the presence of Madame Serein.*
>
> *It will be for City investigators to determine the parameters of a police action apparently gone askew, and whether the Divisional HQ of Police Judiciaire ought to become involved.*

Inspector Nouvelle stood by as her Commissaire sorted through the ramifications.

A 'police action' in Serge's murky headline, failed or otherwise, presumed a case. The rest was left to conjecture. Bad optics, to be sure, but not as bad as it might have been. The matter of possible professional misconduct had not yet leaked beyond the confines of the Court. If the Instructing Judge wanted to issue a statement censuring the *Police Judiciaire*, it wouldn't help any, but Gérard Richand wouldn't. Not with Procureur Souviron finessing it with Strasbourg. All things considered—and last night was a communications nightmare—Claude could not complain. In fact, he was damn lucky and he knew it. But if Divisionnaire Norbert Fauré became involved, that could change and seriously. Claude had to say the right things today.

Tommi Bonneau had heeded the proviso regarding pictures of cops. The photo accompanying that morning's *Le Vrai Tommi* gave away nothing of yesterday's shoddy spectacle. Rather, Tommi's offering depicted Pearl and Bruno in a snowy mountain scene from an obviously happier time. But all other major celebrity gossip issues had been left to slide. Tommi Bonneau's entire space was devoted to the **Local Scene**.

*In light of the tragic death of Bruno Martel: Your scribe was at the scene yesterday, scant minutes before he left us. While it is for the police to decide whether this was another in a series of murders (indeed, it is for the authorities to tell us what exactly is going on!) we, you and I, gentle reader, should consider only the cold fact of death in the face of heroic love and take heed.*

*Bruno's was a world of dreams and confession. It had lately been sealed off from the larger world by the mystery of one heart's failed desire. The healer was scheduled to emerge from his well-known seclusion and—we hoped—share the secrets of a broken heart. I was standing there, I heard Bruno say, 'Your heart was there with me, Pearl…I know all about your heart.' These were Bruno's last words to Pearl. Tantalizing! Profound? Before she could respond, the police came between them. Regrettably, all I can report is that Bruno Martel was trying in his way to share with Pearl. We have all watched and waited. Now we'll never know what this pilgrim knew. Had Bruno discovered something in his muck room? It seemed so. I heard him speak of gratitude. I thought of Pearl Serein. But the dream and the reality are two very different forces. All lovers know this.*

*Yesterday the forces of Law and Order brought Pearl and Bruno together again—too suddenly, too carelessly, too drastically. Tragically. 'Bruno was too fragile for such a moment. This was not right that they should intrude the way they did,' lamented Agnès Guntz, the healer's special assistant, in reference to Pearl's unannounced arrival in the company of her policeman, PJ Commissaire Claude Néon.*

*What happened yesterday? Is it murder or something more sublime?*

*Let the authorities find the physical evidence to make their case. For Pearl, and for those of us who live in her image, it is a matter of the tender things that have no name except Love's Enquiry. The tragic bottom line: Bruno Martel is gone and Tommi is bound by principle to go on record with the thought that Pearl-plus-a-cop brought sad destruction.*

Watching Monique's eyes tear up as she read it aloud over coffee was embarrassing. The more pressing concern was public perception tying Claude to Pearl Serein. Forget about suggestive murk from the Crime Desk. Tommi Bonneau's was the far more dangerous insinuation.

'The man's so full of shit he's choking,' said Claude. 'A world-class jerk-off.'

But he had to get going, to Strasbourg, to explain himself to the divisionnaire.

Aliette accompanied him down the stairs to the second-floor landing. 'Just tell the truth. Don't talk too much. *Bon route, bon courage.*' (Have a good drive. Hang tough.) She would manage the shop. Then she went along the hall to Commissiare Duque's office, to confer with the City team.

What was Bruno Martel doing in the basement? Claude had surmised, and Aliette agreed, that Bruno had run down, frantically looking to hide from someone. Or something? Hallucinations left over from an overdose of seclusion in his muck room? Despite the mess of thrown and broken objects — which pre-supposed a chase if not a struggle, there were no clear signs of anyone else at the place of Bruno's dying. Blood pressure issues? Maybe this time they'd find a drug to blame it on. They'd have to wait for Raphaele Petrucci's best advice on that.

Jean-Marc Pouliot of *Identité Judiciaire* was at the table. 'Dusty down there. Néon was the only other presence, at least as far as shoe prints go. Néon knew enough to keep well away. We can prove that, if need be. As for Martel,' Jean-Marc was flummoxed. 'It's like he saw a ghost and died.' And he was vexed. 'Why can't any of them die with their eyes shut?'

'If you don't like ghosts, talk to Raphaele about his voodoo theory,' the inspector suggested.

Captain Mathieu Deubelbeiss was Duque's second in command. He looked up from the provided files. 'Ghosts or voodoo, fear of a sort seems to be a recurring problem here.'

'Raphaele will tell you it occurs pretty regularly,' she responded. 'But fear can be slotted into a sub-category of stress — which is probably a more useful context. At least that's what we've been hearing. Losing Pearl Serein was a very big deal for all these men. Martel was highly distressed when he ran from the club gate,' she noted. 'She set him off. Pearl Serein. Seeing her again was obviously upsetting, if not terrifying. And Bonneau was harassing him.'

Commissaire Duque said, 'My sister used to mind that Tommi Bonneau. I mean years ago. She'd do babysitting when she was needing pocket money... Scrawniest little runt. Strange what people turn into. Can you imagine spending your days producing that claptrap?'

Deubelbeiss said, 'Bonneau says he followed Martel to Guntz's front gate, then waited.'

'That's where we found him,' Aliette confirmed.

'There's nothing of Bonneau on the lawn or around the doors,' said Jean-Marc Pouliot. 'Others, not him. Something may have happened in the yard.' Sliding a pile of photos to the middle of the table. Images of shoe prints on the grass. 'Trainers. They line up with Martel's.'

Aliette said that according to Pearl Serein, Bruno Martel only wore spiritual white — which apparently included high-top basketball trainers.

Pouliot continued, 'Martel's hands are all over the patio door. That could be from any time recently, I mean since he got back from the mountains, but...' The prints on the grass. 'I'd bet there was someone else there. *Too many* prints. Unless he was doing a dance.'

A passing jogger was also wearing trainers. A rude jogger, staring up at a bedroom window.

For that matter, so was Tommi Bonneau. *Was* he? The inspector struggled to adjust her inner camera. But all she could conjure were the man's devastated eyes, those long fingers fiddling with lenses and exposures. 'And the fence? Any of the same marks there?'

'Nothing immediately apparent,' said Jean-Marc.

Commissaire Duque was apologetic. 'We could look more, but we're still pretty much betwixt and between on directives here, I'm afraid.' He meant a budget.

They were in all in holding pattern till they knew for certain they had a crime.

'But, you know,' said Jean-Marc, with the weary candor of a technician long used to never having enough time or resources, 'there are trainer marks all over the stairs and bedroom, not all of them Martel's. Or hers.' Because Agnès Guntz also wore spiritual white. 'Who else goes in that house? Does she have children? Other people connected to this spiritual farm business?'

The officers at the table all took notes.

'In fact,' Jean-Marc went on, venting, 'I'm getting fed up with rubber soles. The film guy's building, Pugh's office, the first two places. It's mainly the SAMU and your people coming and going—no one's faulting them, don't misunderstand me. I mean these are still just heart attacks. But I really wish people would be a little more professional about these things.'

Commissaire Duque, bemused, assured Jean-Marc Pouliot, 'We'll issue a directive to wear the moon suits and matching boots in the event of another heart attack.'

'*And* to be very careful around all windows, no matter what level,' added Aliette. 'The window directly above the patio door was wide open.'

'Her bedroom,' noted Captain Deubelbeiss. 'So?...nice spring day.'

'Three of our sites are in rooms five and six floors up. A third floor would be easy.'

Pouliot shrugged. 'No signs of a ladder. Garden fence would leave you less than halfway up.' Those chateau-like homes often had upper rooms thirty, even forty feet above the ground.

Inspector Nouvelle requested that the uniforms canvass the north end for a jogger. 'All in white.' She described a handsome though less than pleasant man who seemed preoccupied with Agnès Guntz's bedroom window when he'd gone running by. 'And he didn't stop to watch the show. Which is odd.'

Commissaire Duque said, polite but pointed, 'I gather you won't be dropping this completely.'

'We will be at your disposal, Commissaire.'

Duque understood. The *Police Judiciaire* was not meant to be working on this file and that was how the City team would approach any problematic eventuality. He stood, signaling the end of the meeting.

'For what it's worth...' Jean-Marc Pouliot had one last thing. Rudimentary dusting revealed that Bruno Martel and Agnès Guntz were both reading the new bestseller on evolutionary psychology. They'd also found a copy at Georges Pugh's home. With Jean-Guy Gagnon's copy, that made three out of five victims who'd apparently been reading to discover more about their own little place in life's larger scheme. 'I mean, in case it fits with ghosts at windows.'

Merci, Jean-Marc.

## – 12 –

## A CHAT WITH RAY

Claude called from Strasbourg. He had survived his visit with the divisionnaire. Whatever else—meaning Claude's less than brilliant tactic of bringing Pearl along—it seemed the big boss agreed it must be murder. They needed to get a handle on the why and how. If she was interested, Claude suggested low-key interviews with the last two remaining lovers. 'Could you take care of that? The docklands. Both Belfort and Tuche are down that way.'

Tiring of paperwork, interested despite herself, Aliette said, 'Fine.'

Claude reminded her that they were walking on legal egg shells—a quiet, low-key chat was the order of the day. 'But Fauré is with us,' Claude assured her. 'He said good things about you.'

'One of my very favorite people,' Aliette replied.

It was a nice walk on a spring day, past City Hall, the courthouse, down through the business sector and on to the docks. There were barges lined along the wharf, loading, unloading. Aliette marched in the sunlight, enjoying the physicality of stevedores, the tang of decaying fish and industrial waters, the pinky haze of potash dust on the wind, the blunt largeness of everything.

The grungy working sector ended, the highly priced 'reclaimed' area began. Aliette entered the airy sandblasted space of a refurbished warehouse, knocked on a door at the end of a sky-lit hall. The petite exotic redhead who answered said Didi had gone to his club for his tennis lesson. As forewarned, this was Charlotte. When the inspector asked for her take on the situation, Charlotte's opinion of Pearl Serein was coldly obscene. She said further that 'my Didi' was preparing to sue *Le Cri du Matin* and demanded to know what the inspector could do to expedite the process of putting Tommi Bonneau in jail. The inspector advised the best strategy was polite cooperation, and she left her card. 'Please have Didi call us.'

How could Pearl spend time with a man who would spend time with someone like *that*?

She continued along the landscaped promenade to Le Clinic de Répos et Cure Curé, which was located in another remodeled warehouse. Put it under the rubric of 'spa,' or 'sanatorium,' the kind of facility designed to handle out-patient overflow. Operated privately for profit, but one could claim a partial rebate if one's problem fit a proper category.

Raymond Tuche, the locally celebrated but famously unstable sculptor, had a room on the fourth floor overlooking the river. Aliette was accompanied up by a pleasant nurse. Tuche was sitting on his bed, clad only in pyjama bottoms. In greeting his visitor, Ray did not smile. Or cry. Ray was flat, medicated to a gray point the pleasant nurse described as both voluntary and comfortable. 'We always aim for comfort, then build from there. Well, perhaps *re*build is more apt. Eh, Ray?' Ray folded his arms across his skinny, hairless chest. 'Ray's always popping in for a rest and we admire him for that. He knows his soul. But he's an artist, I guess he has to. Eh, Ray?' She gave him a big smile. No response. Though widely acknowledged to be only marginally sane, Raymond Tuche purportedly possessed 'a totally anthro-mythological sense of proportion.' Or so some art critic had said. Probably in *Le Soir*.

The nurse smiled more discreetly for Aliette. 'Saves us a lot of trouble. The system, I mean.'

And Aliette was discreet in asking if this latest rest was the result of damage wrought by Pearl.

'Pearl was not a good idea for a delicate guy like Ray,' the nurse opined. She explained that Ray suffered from borderline personality disorder, which was not illegal and did stop some people from daring to love, but could be dangerous. 'But,' she noted, 'Ray's problems go far deeper and further back than a broken heart.' Upon presentation of the proper mandate, Ray's file would show this in no uncertain terms. Aliette did not tell her they already had Ray's file.

The woman smiled and left them.

She reopened the door almost immediately. 'If you have one of those wireless phone things in your bag and he asks to use it, don't let him.' Same smile. Same exit.

Ray perked up. 'I need to tell her something.' He meant Pearl Serein.

Aliette knew Ray Tuche had a tendency to call in the middle of the night and stay on the line till dawn. She told him, 'The lady said no, monsieur. You have to learn to live with it.'

The artist's response to her advice was to cry. Just like that — tears flowing. But quietly.

How Pearl caused tears! Aliette was motherly, but stern. 'Come on. Get a hold of yourself.'

Ray whined, 'You don't know what I gave that woman!'

No, she didn't. When it comes to love, who knows what anyone gives to another? And who understands the impossibility of receiving someone's most precious gift? A bright afternoon sun highlighted the pervasive dust surrounding Raymond Tuche, indeed, attaching to him. The cool tile floor and melamine desktop were spattered with dried droplets of modeling clay. As the nurse had explained, Ray could not stop creating. Shapes in a row along the windowsill attested to his urge, each a variation on the famous drumstick-shaped monument dominating the sculpture room at the Institute which Ray claimed was a metaphor for the erogenous parts of Pearl Serein. When Aliette pointed out that he and Pearl had not gotten together as a couple until three years after he had created this landmark piece, Ray said, '*B'en*, that only enhances our shared destiny.' Defiant, he told her, 'You don't know what it's like to be a sculptor.'

'True. Although I do like that piece you did for the foyer at the bank.' Jerôme Duteil's bank.

'Everyone does,' said Ray. 'That old Nazi should've paid me twice what he did. What I mean is, you start with a piece of rock. OK? A real piece of rock — from the *world*, not from a fucking mix from a packet from the hardware store. I'm talking about elemental material, *tu sais?*'

Aliette tried to be encouraging. She knew Ray's inhibitor drugs were a stop-gap. Recovery, if it happened at all, would come with maturity, and the real therapy occurred through talking. Dialectical behavior therapy aimed to get BPD patients to identify their upset emotions, then pause—that is, sit back and think about them, rather than acting on them, consumed by impulse. The inspector only wanted to aid this process. She asked, 'Monsieur Duteil's a Nazi?'

'Sure.'

'Why would Pearl love a man like him?'

'She didn't. She loves me.'

'I understand.' One of Aliette's strengths was an ability to soothe. Raymond Tuche felt this and looked up—into her eyes. Don't fall in love with me, thought the inspector, just talk to me. She knew people like Ray tended to be quickly and heavily attracted, then equally disappointed (read: devastated) when it (inevitably) all comes crashing down. Love.

'And then you work on it,' concluded Ray. His eyes narrowed. He breathed.

He meant the piece of rock, his basic start point, before Nazi bankers, before Pearl Serein…

Aliette asked, 'And did you always love her?…before, back at the Lycée?'

'No…' Drawing this declaration out, as if it were a thing he'd never realized. 'That was too long ago. That was before I had the power to create what I've created.'

'But you knew her?'

Ray shrugged. 'Never had a class with her. I remember walking past her every day in the halls. But I lived in the north end. She lived…I don't know where she lived.'

'Above her father's bookshop,' prompted the inspector.

'Raymond Tuche looked out his window. Or at the miniatures along the sill? Ray's focus was askew. 'You could say Pearl did not exist and never would've if not for the power of my hands.'

'No.'

'And my heart.'

'It must have been a shock to see her go off with J-G Gagnon.'

The flat eyes of Raymond Tuche showed no hint of registering this name. Nor any of the other names. As Aliette gently made her way through the list of rivals, Ray stayed silent (as was his right) and (more to the point) apparently unknowing. All the while his celebrated hands moved around an invisible shape…Well, Ray Tuche shaped his most important thoughts with his hands. She patted one of them. 'I know it's painful, Ray—but do you have an opinion on the fact that five of these others have died?'

Ray asked, 'How could there be others? Don't you understand? I created her!'

There was anger there. Claude had shared Pearl's impressions regarding Raymond Tuche: her advice that on his bad days he was capable of anything. But being capable of anything is global, murder is specific; the 'how' of murder usually dovetails with the core of a man. And they still had no definitive idea as to how these supposed murders were happening.

She asked, 'But what about Tommi Bonneau?'

'Photography is *so* easy!' Ray fell back on his bed and stared at the ceiling. 'So fucking easy.'

Poor Pearl, thought Aliette. Then again, a girl is free to choose. No?

'You've been very helpful, Ray…We appreciate it.' Standing to go, she looked around. 'Not a bad set-up here. You've been popping in and out a lot lately?'

'Not so much. Been staying. Resting up. New project…' Ray pointed to his head. 'Have to be in shape to start, you know? No one knows what it's like to be a sculptor.'

'Not a tennis player, you?'

The club was another tweak. They knew he was a member. Or his mother was.

'Me, no…I just use that place for haircuts.' And Ray clearly hadn't had one in a while.

Claude was back in his office when she returned to the commissariat.

She doubted Raymond Tuche was a killer, but noted a volatility likely impossible to predict.

'And Belfort?'

'Missed Didi Belfort again. Another tennis lesson.'

'Damn. I stopped in there on my way back… We'll catch up with him. Maybe we'll see him on the dance floor.' He passed her with a folded card. 'Think I'll go. I think you'd better come too.'

*Spring Follies! Saturday, May 1*
*Champagne and dancing to celebrate the season*
*Members and friends*
*RSVP Gaston for group tables*

'It's just work,' said Claude, adding, 'It could be fun.'

'Dancing?... But why?'

'I have a feeling.' A feeling that something could happen. 'I mean, so much of Pearl's life revolves around that place... All *their* lives.' Claude felt he should check it out.

'Is she going to be there?'

'She's determined not to let these guys get in the way of her life. Even if she doesn't show, I'm sure the members will have some things to tell us. We could have a drink with Didi Belfort.'

'Yes. And Charlotte...lovely woman.' The inspector mulled it. The card was expensive vanilla bond. On the face, an engraved logo: *CRQ*, the Q drawn with a finely inked web and abnormally long stem, a stylized racquet's grip at its base. Not too original, but it didn't have to be. The letterhead proclaimed *Le club des raquetteurs du quartier*. 'Who is Gaston?'

'He's the manager. Nice guy... I mean, once you get past the silly snooty act.'

For the second time that day, Aliette Nouvelle said fine, no problem. It was just work. There were worse assignments. Yes, it could be fun.

But Saturday was tomorrow. She had nothing to wear!

She left in a rush, took the long way home, made a chaotic pass through the boutiques.

And the man Aliette Nouvelle might love laughed about it as they snuggled with their drinks. She happily drank the last of the wine and explored the possibilities.

Perhaps she should have stayed more low-key — there in his bed, he was growing dubious.

So she began to play it down. Saturday night? Work the club dance. Strictly procedural. Maybe nail a killer. 'And for her protection — though we don't even know if she'll be there.'

'Maybe I'm not totally comfortable with this after all.'

'It's a good strategy. I can go where she goes. Certain areas of the club, I mean.'

'Where your commissaire cannot?' He smoothed her hair.

'Or any other man. The powder room is often the key to the mystery. Surely you know this.'

'Ah. But are you under cover?'

'Not at all. We'll talk tennis—me and Pearl, I mean.'

'Maybe you should let your commissaire handle this one alone.'

She laughed and drew the remaining bit of blanket from his body, gently climbed on top.

Then she lay her head on his belly and reassured him. 'It's only work.' Which was the truth.

But.

She'd spotted a dress that could be perfect, she had a hair appointment for ten next morning.

She was looking forward to it. Something different. Although they were making beautiful progress in this new relationship, he hadn't yet taken her anywhere quite like a dance at the club.

## — 13 —
### Dancin' the night away

Dressing was precise and procedural, decisions at every phase. Piaf watched knowingly as the inspector tried the raspberry *soustien-gorge* again, but finally discarded it in favor of the steel blue camisole made exclusively for her pleasure by a murdered seamstress named Ondine Duguay. Wonderful how that steely tint transformed into a silvery dream-like shade with the slightest shift of her body. The *AN* monogram embroidered in black in the region of her right hip added subtle presence, something like a professional secret… Then her gown: a sleeveless wide-strapped sheath of brushed viscose, burgundy with a light-sensitive two-inch panel running down the right side from armpit to hem, six fingers above her knee. Depending on her movement and the ambient light, it flashed plum, mango, scarlet. Very nice… Hair. Eyes. Lips. Single gold bangle. Lapis studs. Moroccan pumps. Teal calfskin purse from a boutique in Basel. Perfection! The inspector was feeling quite complete when the commissaire arrived in a cab.

The evening was mild, aperitifs were served on the terrace. Aliette could not spot a familiar face as she and her date stood by the pool sipping pastis, self-consciously making sure their conversation was as animated as everyone else's.

And Pearl Serein. Would she show?

Claude had lots to talk about. Surely it was clear by now that a certain judge would do well to heed a policeman's proven instincts. 'Richand's got no respect for experience. No nose for the heart of the matter. It starts with us, not him.'

'Shh! Claude…' It was very likely someone near them would know Gérard Richand.

'I don't care. He's a stuffed-up ass.'

Despite the Martel debacle, Claude was brash. After yesterday's chat in Strasbourg he knew his rapport with Divisionnaire Norbert Fauré cut far deeper than mere rules.

Hardly. Fauré's position was unknowable, purely political, depending on the moment. Claude was dreaming, caught up in the moment. But there was no point arguing, not tonight. She sipped her drink, surveying the garden, the pool. 'It's nice here.' Her parents belonged to a place just like it — in Nantes. She'd spent a lot of adolescent hours at the club. She rarely mentioned it, and never at work. After eight years and counting, the life in Nantes seemed like another world.

'Not bad,' said Claude. A little too offhand. 'Did I mention that I joined?'

'You *joined*?'

'Well, on probation — at least that's what Gaston called it.'

'On probation. Not a bad place for the likes of you.'

He smiled at her lame joke. She grinned at Claude's new status. They sipped their drinks.

Her eyes moved past him. 'There's the guy who almost ran me over.' And even more beautiful in a light gray suit than in his jogging outfit. He looked like that sloe-eyed singer from Quebec. What was his name?

Claude followed her eyes. 'Who is he?'

'No idea. I told Deubelbeiss to look for him.'

'*Bon*. We'll have a word.'

But it could wait. Because the man called Gaston came out the dining room door and rang a bell. Supper was served. The guests moved into the ballroom-dining area where linen-clad tables awaited, aglow with floral scented candlelight reflecting and refracting through bottles of the best of the rich ruby and amber-gold local vintages. Probationary member Claude Néon and his guest had been assigned a table with Mylène and Alain, a pair of accountants, and Annick and Nicolas (*Nic et Nic*), an older couple, he a retired investment banker. Aliette had seen madame somewhere before. 'I know we've crossed paths…' The lady agreed. But where?

Gaston was acting as maître d'. To start, he was pleased to offer consommé or tomato juice and a plate of foie gras slivers on rye crusts. Following on, guests had a choice of lamb medallion, poached lake trout, chevaline tournedos or shark filet, each served with small portions of green beans, baby carrots, beets and flageolets. Then salad, the cheese tray, lime sorbet and biscuits…slices of pear and a digestif to finish. Aliette went with the horsemeat, bloody and tender, verging on sweet. Claude would have the shark.

A festive luminescence bathed the diners' faces and danced along the edges of crystal tureens overflowing with the loose softness of pansies and petunias, washed the smooth edges of heavy bone china ringed in gold leaf and embossed with the venerable club crest, rested delicately on the tines of similarly branded silver forks as the well-manicured hands holding them paused to make a point. Gaston moved from table to table, making sure everything was fine. The two cops began to enjoy themselves. Aliette did not mind that no one reacted when she replied 'inspector' and all attention flowed to the commissaire. Not that anyone made direct mention of Pearl Serein — these people knew what it is to be polite. To his credit, Claude stuck to the truth, admitting 'it's mostly administrative… No, not that much of cops and robbers at all.'

When Annick teased Claude about his controversial testimony at the Mari Morgan trial, Aliette blurted, 'So *that's* where! You follow these things?'

'Follow them? Dear girl, I had a seat reserved in the third row. I never missed a day.'

Accountants Mylène and Alain had spent their Saturday afternoon at the cinema, being thrilled by the new American thriller that was causing such a furor. Another French film had been remade by Hollywood. 'The guy flies a miniature jet through the New York metro,' explained Alain, 'from Harlem to Wall Street… Superb!'

'I wept,' confessed Mylène. 'All that adrenaline! Too much for me.'

'There was never any jet in the original,' complained Annick. 'It's ridiculous how they steal from us and tart them up.'

'It's just a movie,' chided Nicolas.

Annick shot back, 'But it's *our* story…it's French!' She was a patriot.

Neither Aliette or Claude had seen it yet. Claude said it was on his list.

'It's not the stories,' mused Nicolas, 'it's the business.'

'Made 100 million its first weekend,' reported Alain.

'U.S. dollars,' added Mylène. A world record at the time.

'While our own industry can barely survive,' rejoined Nicolas. 'When I was working I could fill a prospectus for a film in two months, some in two days. Like buying a diamond for a beautiful woman: a pleasure to take the risk. A duty! My old firm won't even read them any more.'

'I think those Americans must have deep problems with self-image,' declared Annick. 'Manhood, *quoi*?'

Mylène agreed, 'It's true, none of them are very attractive. But perhaps that's not the point.'

Annick smiled at the younger woman. 'What else could it possibly be?'

Alain puffed his chest. He liked American movies and would spend his francs as he chose fit.

Claude nodded yes to that.

Nicolas refilled their glasses. It was not a night to argue.

They gabbed on, and as the wine flowed a cop could easily forget why she had come.

But not completely. Aliette's gaze drifted around the room, picking out a judge from the assize court. Some lawyers she knew... No sign of Pearl Serein. No appearance by Didier Belfort and his horrid Charlotte... Ah. There was Rose Saxe of *Society Notes*, sporting gold buttons and epaulettes and too much lipstick again as she leaned dangerously close to the ear of the beautiful jogger.

The inspector asked Nicolas, 'Who is that...with Rose Saxe?'

'That's Remy. Remy Lorentz. Our tennis pro.'

By the tone, the narrowing of Nic's eyes, the inspector gathered he was not a fan. On the other side of Rose Saxe sat a man with silver hair in formal white evening dress. Monsieur Saxe? He concentrated on his red wine while Rose remained in deep strategy with Remy — he didn't seem to see or care that Rose's hand was very busy all up and down the younger man's arm as she made her heated points. Or that Remy's hand was enjoying Rose's knee. Well, it was spring.

Around ten, as the bar staff circulated with cigars, and guests wandered away to the ladies' and men's, Gaston announced the entertainment. The evil looking singer said *bonsoir* on behalf of *The Lonely Blue & Sad Times Band*, then counted them straight into a highly energized and absolutely danceable version of Berthe Sylva's classic...

*Frou frou, frou frou: par son jupon la femme...*
*Frou frou, frou frou: de l'homme trouble l'âme!...*

Great song!...about underwear. By the time it took the guests to adjust their eyes to the malevolent faces, outfits and hair of the ones who'd come to sing for them, their feet were also moving. Before the second refrain, the entire club was up and dancing. Yes, it was only work, but the two cops were in the thick of it, Aliette Nouvelle moving her body against the luscious silk inside her dress, grinning at Claude Néon — who was proving himself pleasingly adept at moving in time. Responding to the quicksilver pops of a soloing guitar, he spun her around, brought her over and through, and people near them formed a clapping circle. They tried a slow dance. Claude led strongly through the deepest valleys of the saxophone's swoon. Aliette was having fun, soon sweating under her silk. She smiled for a wandering busboy and he hurried to find them beers.

Then two more... Twirling and gliding, Inspector Nouvelle boogied on.

It was during the second set, around midnight, when her well-bounced bladder told her it was time for a break, that she left Claude Néon standing by the blaring speakers, mesmerized, happy like she'd never seen him before.

After freshening up, the inspector found a door and stepped out for some air.

Cooler now, a surface of dew on the *chaises-longues* by the pool, the garden soft in darkness, alyssum, begonias, impatiens, petunias impeccably arranged...a gardener's trowel left lying on the step of a stairway leading down to a basement. From down those stairs the inspector's trained ears caught the sound of a quick breath of laughter. Another cautious step, she looked — a natural response, anyone would. Remy the tennis pro...and someone...Rose Saxe peeked out from behind his shoulder! Spring Follies? These two were pushing the theme of the evening to its forbidden limit. Aliette blushed, continued strolling. Don't worry, I won't tell; I'm not even a member.

But *Society Notes* fell some in her esteem. Rose Saxe must be at least twice that Remy's age.

She went back in. Lining up at the busy bar in search of more beers for herself and her partner, the PJ cop allowed the assize court judge to engage her in clubby chit-chat. He was a director. They were discussing the issue of entrance fees and yearly dues, more particularly sliding rates for couples and families, when a busboy came rushing though frantically calling, '*Au secours!*' (Help!) A brawl had erupted on the dance floor.

Aliette left the judge in mid-explanation and ran for the ballroom.

Remy Lorentz was pounding away at Alain the accountant. Claude Néon groped at the edges of it, ineffective in his efforts at pulling them apart. Mylène, Alain's accountant wife, continued dancing maniacally and very drunk through pools of light, oblivious to her husband's little war. Rose Saxe's stout husband, pink with booze and rage, was flailing, trying to land a fist on the snake Lorentz. The man was old but the ugly thing in his eyes was ageless.

The band played on, diabolical, inspired!
*C'est la nuit, c'est la nuit*
*C'est gratuit, c'est gratuit*
*C'est l'esprit, c'est l'esprit de pleine nuit!*
—*oh oui, oui oui oui oui…!*

Tom-tom solo. Shrieks and whistles from all sides. The crowd was stoked, loving it!

Aliette finally registered Pearl Serein behind the knot of brawling men. She was sparsely elegant in a bone-white crew-necked tunic cut to mid-thigh, hair loose, skin brown. She appeared frozen in panic under the band's frenetic lighting, awash in waves of pounding music. The inspector noted the helpless eyes of an unknowing fool who has done something very wrong, no idea what. Then Claude Néon stepped past the faltering Alain and punched Remy Lorentz hard in the face. Remy fell back into the melee, blood bursting from his nose. Claude had no time to savor it. Immediately he was fending off a ragged man groping desperately for the lady at the center of the storm. Raymond Tuche. Where the hell?…with dust in his hair and dressed in all the wrong clothes. Claude tried to maneuver the deranged artist—but got bashed out of the way by Remy's return lunge. Claude swung back at Remy. Another round of tit-for-tat pounding began. Leaving Ray alone in front of Pearl. Aliette saw him go down on his knees, imploring Pearl through the delirious noise… while Pearl just stood there looking at him, helpless, a piteous sight if it weren't so absurd. All the while, the band's roving strobe light raced in time with the machine-gun drumming. For a searing instant the sculptor's eyes were smashed by the strobing light, revealing wild fear, uncomprehending terror. Aliette watched as Ray Tuche reeled, unseeing, phantasmagorical, a soul stripped bare… But the strobe moved on, defining more moments of violence in stark tableau, each man like a statue for a series of split seconds, the most apparent thing the savage at the core of each man's eyes. Elemental. Not attractive.

Dark-age crude was another thought that came to an inspector's mind.

Claude, in the midst of it, showed no better or worse than any of the rest.

The band smiled a group smile, oh yes, very diabolical, and pumped the music even higher.

Gaston came running, leading a squad of waiters.

'Claude!' Aliette Nouvelle went moving through and around chaotic members.

Someone splashed something all over her left side. '*Merde!*' She smelled brandy…

Then the strobe light hit her eyes full on: one, two, three, four, five pulsing rings that left her blinking, unable to see anything but greenish shadows for fully half a minute, as if submerged.

When her vision cleared, Pearl Serein was gone.

And Raymond Tuche?… Where?

The fighting continued, unreal inside the ungodly din, the ravaging strobe, the entire scene transposed to negatives and excruciating noise. The inspector managed to communicate Pearl's sudden absence to Claude—then she ran from the hellish room.

Her first instinct sent her down a half-flight and into the ladies' locker room — still a place where a girl can expect at least a few moments free of an overweening man. But there was no Pearl Serein to be found here.

Aliette was standing in front of the locker room mirror contemplating the blotch across her midriff for a blank moment when the pounding music suddenly stopped mid-note. Someone must have pulled a plug. She heard the inevitable *pan-pon!...pan-pon!* of uniforms arriving. Good. Her second instinct was to pull her dress over her head, grab a club towel from the pile and soak it in cold water. Damn, damn, damn!... She worked away in her underwear.

*Quel bordel* — a brand new 900-franc dress!

After using the club hair dryer to the best of her limited ability on her damaged dress, Aliette Nouvelle emerged from the ladies' room, feeling a mess, to find an unnaturally calm Gaston placating the City squad while lingering members sipped yet more drinks, not at all worried — *au contraire*, excited! *What a great party.* She heard Gaston saying something about people having reputations, everything was fine, no one would be pressing any charges. Her tablemates Nic and Nic were too old to worry about their reputations. They said the police had arrested Alain and Mylène. She gathered many more guests had cleared out via the garden and over the wall as the cops had poured in. Remy Lorentz had run like a goat, straight over the garden wall!... It seemed Rose Saxe and her hubby had also disappeared.

But where was Claude? Gaston had no idea. He was sorely disappointed in the commissaire's behaviour, none too subtly implying that Monsieur Néon had sparked the whole disaster. Gaston doubted Claude would have his membership nomination approved.

Aliette could only assume Claude had gone after Raymond Tuche, who had gone after Pearl Serein. Very out of control. Growing concerned, she called the Cure Curé from Gaston's office. They hadn't seen Raymond since his departure earlier that evening. No, they had not tried to stop him, he was free to come and go as he pleased. Yes, he'd mentioned something about dancing.

She conferred with the uniform in charge, asked that he conduct a search of the club grounds and direct all mobile units to keep an eye out for a seriously discombobulated Ray.

And Pearl Serein? And Claude Néon? Where? She took a turn through the upper levels of the club. Hoping to find Claude and Pearl and Ray cooling out over a game of billiards? No such luck, Inspector. She waited another half-hour on a bar stool, but none of the uniforms on hand could find any trace. The members were drifting off. Soon it was just staff, desultory, used to these things, or so it appeared, cleaning up after another fun night at the club.

Claude? *Claude!* Fighting a horrible premonition, Inspector Nouvelle retrieved her shawl from the vestry and proceeded home alone. Sure enough, there was a message waiting on her phone. He was with *her*...up there. Aliette peered through the night at a single dim light at the top of the building across the park. He had left the number. He answered forthwith.

'Claude?...are you all right? What happened?'

'Dancing. We were dancing. Then Tuche appeared, totally demented, giving Pearl a hard time. Then Lorentz—he's dancing with the accountant's wife and he gets into it with Tuche...it kind of boiled over.'

'But Lorentz was with—'

'We're fine now,' added Claude.

We? Dancing? 'You'd better come down from there. You should hear what that Gaston was telling the City sergeant.'

'I can handle Gaston. Pearl needs me. Just go to bed.' Pause. Claude added, 'Please.'

Please? It sounded like an order. In a bit of a trance, she put the phone down and obeyed.

## – 14 –
## For Claude?

She picked it up again early Sunday morning, listened to the City dispatcher's grim news.

She dutifully relayed the news to the number at the fabulous penthouse across the park. His murmured explanations as to best police procedure didn't fly. Not this morning. Aliette Nouvelle was deeply disappointed in her commissaire. 'What in God's name were you thinking?'

'Our role is to protect the public, no? Yes. I told you something would happen. Well it did and she was alone. She was at risk — given the situation and the facts such as we have them.'

Maybe Claude was right. Raymond Tuche had been found dead earlier that morning.

'Oh, *merde*. Where?'

'The club. In the sauna. Yes, another heart attack. Or whatever.' And Didier Belfort, the last of Pearl's remaining exes, had been unaccounted for since yesterday afternoon. But neither of these facts would soothe the feeling of betrayal. 'So now what, Claude — off to mass with the missus?'

'Ha, ha. I am going to stay right here with her till we find Belfort.'

'Ah. Sunday by the pool then? That's nice.'

'Inspector, it's not the time for this. You think it's easy walking her through this? I want you to go to the scene and confirm information with Petrucci.'

'Will we have the pleasure of your company? I mean *both* of you? Perhaps I could talk to her.'

'No and no. I told you, she's a wreck. You will organize a search for Belfort, into Germany if necessary, and you will keep me informed. And you will —'

'Claude, I'm working for Duque.'

'Duque knows we're ahead of him on this. And you will find and talk to Lorentz and—'

'How could you punch such a beautiful man, Claude?'

'Because he's a fucking out-of-control maniac. And if he resists in any way you will call for assistance and bring him to *garde à vue* and tell him next time I see him I will—'

'It is hard to have faith in your methods, monsieur.'

'Will you please try to get a handle on your reactions? It's work. All right, Inspector? Clear?'

'Yes, sir!' Wham! She rang off. Clear as fucking mud.

What a prick. What a centerless man. And in front of all those people!

Miserable, the inspector fed her cat, dressed and headed out to work.

'My lord,' Aliette breathed. 'Raphaele, he clamped down!' Raymond Tuche was folded into a corner of the sauna. His tongue had been caught at the final moment trying to squirm its way between clamped teeth. In death, the artist aped those horrific images of electroshock therapy.

'Heart attacks hurt.' It was becoming the pathologist's refrain. It was far too early on a Sunday morning, Raphaele Petrucci did not look much better than she felt. 'What happened here?'

'Here? No idea. Upstairs, the dance turned into a brawl. He got caught in the middle of it. Maybe even caused it, it's still not clear.' Aliette studied Ray's eyes: wide and bloody, the same terrified aspect she'd glimpsed the night before as he crawled through the battle on the dance floor, desperate, crawling to his Pearl. 'I've never seen a man more terrified. It was macabre. The band kept playing while they went at it, incredible noise, they had this strobe light going. For a few seconds there, it was like I could see right into poor Ray's mind. Completely boggled.'

Petrucci glanced at his notes, 'His heart was hurting him already. He was depressed.'

'Ray was broken-hearted.'

'Clinically, not poetically.' The pathologist pulled a rubber glove over his hand, opened an envelope, removed a vial of pills.

'These were in his pocket.' An anti-depressant called Méridien, a Prozac clone, praised for its effectiveness in dispersing the veils of depression, also known to produce negative side effects such as heart trouble and impotence.

'Both Pearl and the nurse at the cure mentioned that Ray wasn't helping the cause if he forgot to take it — which was often.'

'And a strobe light was the very last thing he needed,' Petrucci noted.

'Really?'

'If his nerves were already fragile, the effects could spark real damage. It's horrible, but at least there's sense to it this time. At least I've got one little thing to tell our professor from Strasbourg.'

'Lucky you.'

'What is wrong with you this morning?'

'Nothing.' Aliette turned away from Raymond Tuche, Raphaele Petrucci, the entire mess.

'And Néon? Where is he, anyway? I thought — '

'Néon's been taken hostage, Doctor.'

'What are you talking about, Inspector?'

She shook her head and walked away, through the taped-off men's locker room, out into a sunny Sunday morning. There was a small crowd of club members waiting outside, some already in their tennis whites, unclear as to what was going on and where they were allowed to go. Captain Mathieu Deubelbeiss of the City Police was sorting through assignments. The inspector politely suggested that one Remy Lorentz, tennis pro, be detained — the club office would have his coordinates, and to make sure all units were still on the lookout for Didier Belfort. She would also put a team on the noble's trail.

Deubelbeiss had no objections. The media had got wind of the tragedy and were gathering at the club gate, held in abeyance by two uniforms. Nothing like a bit of Sunday news. Mics, note pads, cameras, the TV truck. Cakeface was looking sleepy underneath her TV gunk. 'Ask Captain Deubelbeiss,' Aliette pre-empted Cake before Cake could even ask, and kept walking, through the club gate and up to the corner, where she caught another cab.

Returning to the commissariat, she climbed the quiet stairs to the third. Monique was not available. At her mama's in a village lost in the Vosges. Just Bernadette Milhau on Duty desk, a bit sulky, getting tired of being junior. Aliette made calls, woke people, ruined breakfasts, altered plans. Sorry, our commissaire is in a bind—not that there's anything we do can save his useless soul. By noon the team had been rallied and sent out to find Didi Belfort. Instructions: Mathieu Deubelbeiss is in charge—clear any action first through him. Call Claude at Pearl's as often as you need for hints or suggestions from the lady—clubs, restos, friends, hideaways, country inns. If going to the Belfort family's wine properties north of the city be sure, be sure, be sure! to read your map. If crossing the line into the next prefecture, call Commissaire Lefèbvre. (Claude's counterpart in the next district, always prickly about turf.) She made a call to Freiburg, requesting counterparts there to pay a visit to the castle in the Black Forest and redoubts of several other of Belfort's maternal-side cousins around the region. For Claude. Why? Good question...

Aliette Nouvelle pondered this as she grabbed yet another cab. '33 Rue Pontbriand.'

## — 15 —
## Tommi's place

There are charming pockets lined with creative renovations now, but for the most part the east end is unattractive, the dull result of cheap, hasty rebuilding after wartime destruction. The house at 33 Pontbriand was another plain, two-story cottage, a two-tone Deux Chevaux parked in front the classiest thing in sight. Tommi Bonneau answered her knock clad only in a bathrobe, a pinky sleep-starved glaze coloring his eyes. 'Well, speak of the devil. I hear some cops are quite the dancers.'

She barely blinked. No big surprise that Tommi had spies planted at the club. 'And I suppose you've heard Ray Tuche is dead.'

'Just got the call. Means another rewrite.'

'What exactly are you trying to prove here, Tommi?'

'I don't prove anything, Inspector. I report.'

'Sure. But why?'

'Because it's part of the story?' Tommi paused. Hugged himself as he mulled it. The morning air was cool. 'Something about a broken heart? The down side of a life like hers?'

'Pearl's?'

'She's my subject.'

'You followed Georges Pugh on Tuesday, looking for an interview. You might have been the last person to see him alive. Bruno Martel too, for that matter.'

'Didn't help me any,' he replied tersely. Tommi Bonneau looked straight at her, feral eyes hardening. 'Maybe if they'd known, they might've talked to me.'

Aliette felt his sangfroid like a quick punch. 'If they'd known they were going to die?'

Tommi shivered, massaged his arms. 'Is there anything in particular I can help you with?'

'May I come in?'

'Why?'

'These men are dying. Maybe you can help us.'

'I don't have to let you.' True: as someone who tiptoed along the fine edges of Article 9 on a daily basis, he would be familiar with similar laws designed to protect citizens from spontaneous visits from the police. 'And I have company.' Aliette acknowledged the sound of footsteps directly above, followed by a door closing, bath water flowing, a certain smile on Tommi's lips. But she held her ground. And he was clearly up and working. So he shrugged and stood aside.

Her eyes adjusted to the gloom. To her left, Tommi's dining room was a chaotic home gym, littered with weights and exercise machines. Glancing in, a nosy cop. 'Keeping fit?'

'Only way to survive the pace.'

So why such a sickly look to the man?

'You want Pearl Serein? Come…' leading her through the messy kitchen, flipping on a rear room light. There was Pearl, larger than life-sized on the wall, dominating a cluttered studio.

Much larger than the life of a quiet schoolteacher. Like a poster from your favorite film. Not a profile, and not face-on; a three-quarter shot: you could see her hair wisping up behind as she leaned on folded arms. She appeared to be listening with a calm, rapt attention, her lips just parted. No smile — the smile was in her eyes, crinkled softly in a sort of delight. Tommi had captured something, to be sure. But a yellowish, metallic tint corroded the magic of her presence, and she was curling at the corners, and there were messy claw-like rips across her enigmatic gaze.

'Your Pearl's looking a bit the worse for wear,' mused Aliette, ever sceptical of icons '— like she's been fending off too many desperate men?'

'She is a bit bashed up,' conceded Tommi. 'Backed into her a few times. Some of my set-ups? She's been keeping watch here ever since she started up with Didi Belfort.' Gazing at his heroine, he sniffed in rueful response to a cop's dry observation. 'Yes, too many desperate men, Inspector, and never the right one — sadly. We do want her to be happy in the end. I'll print up a new one, one of these days. Here, these are more in keeping with our Pearl...' proudly opening a drawer.

The inspector sifted through image after image of this most sought-after woman: alone, with her boyfriends...and here she was with Claude, who was confronting Bruno Martel. Aliette lingered over it, interested in Claude's expression: The hard-set jaw, narrowed eyes, crouched posture, tensing shoulders, ready to fight. She asked, 'What's the big obsession, Tommi?'

'Not mine. Theirs. Pearl has something to appeal to every heart.'

But there was something distinctly proprietary in his ghastly eyes as he closed the studio light.

She followed him back through the kitchen to his study. The shades were still down, one dim lamp burned on a desk overflowing with a computer, printer, phone, fax, books, papers, a couple of cameras. Aliette glanced at the glowing screen. He leaned across and switched it off. 'Sorry—my editor's my only critic till it's on the street.'

'The commissaire did not enjoy your last piece.'

'What? Bruno? My readers have been wondering about poor Bruno's fate for months.'

'I mean the insinuations about him.'

Tommi shrugged. 'Then he'll hate what's coming... Think she'll like him?'

'He's the commissaire. How could she not?' Trying to laugh. Choking on it.

'Fantastic storyline. But a pretty stupid cop.'

Who could argue? But she was perplexed. 'I always thought your stuff was just for a laugh.'

'Some people might think that. My readers and I call it news of the soul. Ask my editor. *Le Vrai Tommi* is second after the horoscope in readership.' Responding to Aliette's clearly signaled scorn, Tommi sighed. 'Look, ethnic cleansing makes you angry and you can't sleep: Scum in uniforms. Politics makes you poor and bitter: A bunch of self-serving thieves. Your football team loses and it all seems completely absurd, and what can anyone do? There's a lot going on out there but it's too far away, too horrible, too impossible to make a difference, so why bother caring? Most people aren't involved in much of anything except themselves and most can barely manage that. But on the back page there's this princess by the pool, boobs all brown and lovely, some rich man sucking on her toes. You may see it as silly and cheap, but my readers see an image of love. Heroic love, as a matter of fact, because for better or for worse, it's far bigger than they are and it's like a kind of glue. Holds this ugly world together, lets people dare to relate one last little bit to this sorry global village.' Tommi smiled. 'The Pearl Sereins of the world are about the only way the little guy can care about anything bigger than himself any more, and feel like it means something.'

'But it's such soft-brained mush.'

A shake of his ponderous head: wrong. 'No, it's life. Falls under "human interest," Inspector. Humans are interested in each other. The vagaries of the heart are the meat of culture. We care about it and we discuss it as extensively as we're able. If you have a problem connecting with it, well,' Tommi patted his own heart, his bloodshot eyes expressed a sort of sympathy; 'you're a cop. Maybe you just can't. At least not when you're working.'

She nodded, dumbstruck. Maybe I just can't.

He averred, 'No, it's not big-time like a Stephanie or a Fergie or a Di. But Pearl's our star. That woman is the most fascinating thing in this dark little corner of the universe. It's Tommi's job to gather all the news that fits. Both the high and the low of it. And they are so greedy. Her men. You think I'm mean? Georges Pugh took all the glory. He got to touch her and he reveled in it. He loved it! They all do. But they won't share a thing when she does a number on their hearts.'

'Not greedy, monsieur. Private. Obviously it's private.'

'No, no, no, Inspector. Greedy. You get what they had, you have to share.'

Tommi Bonneau was on a roll. Inspector Nouvelle quietly egged him on. 'Have to?'

'You say it's cheap, I say it's timeless. Large. Prototypical — it's like a god's shadow on a wall: scary, inspiring, but it's our own shadow too and we know it. They do what we want to do but would never dare. They make love and die in front of all of us. Only divine love bestows the keys of knowledge, Inspector. There's some more

Rimbaud for you. These guys are as close as we get and Tommi's gentle readers crave it.'

'I don't want to make love in front of anyone except my lover.'

'And who was your lover again?' Tommi was daring her.

Aliette ignored it. She began to peruse the books piled on his desk. What was a gossip writer reading? Page-marked volumes were piled high. *Les liaisons dangereuses*, *La morte amoureuse*, *Manon Lescaut*, *Carmen*, *Hérodias*, *Nana*, *Lulu*… All lush classics, some had been called works of genius. *Salammbô*: Flaubert's study of a sacred virgin in ancient Carthage who drives a man to destructive craziness because she will not return his love. A teacup was resting on Balzac: *La peau de chagrin*, a study of one Foedora, formidable in her beauty, inflexible in her sense of what she wants. A copy of *Les fleurs du mal* was lying open — that dark and marvelous garden, on every page Baudelaire's vision of feminine beauty as a thing unholy, deadly, fascinating, perverse and essential. This poet was the man who coined the term *la femme fatale*. The inspector picked it up, read, 'O fangeuese grandeur! Sublime ignominie!' She asked, 'Is this for inspiration or something?'

'Research,' replied Tommi. 'Everything is research.'

'And which one,' wondered Aliette, 'is Pearl?'

'They're all Pearl.'

'Bit of a difference between yourself and Baudelaire. Eh, Tommi?'

'Sure. Baudelaire's dead. And these days people want direct quotes. And a picture, of course.'

'On the back page of the newspaper.'

'Back page is as good a place as any. No one reads poetry any more. Now it's me.'

No answer to that, only another question: 'Could she really be so dark? A primary teacher?'

Tommi's smile was wan, depleted, the smile of a man who'd been up late enjoying himself. 'Darkness is in the eye of the beholder, Inspector. I bet you'd know that better than most. But so is the light that attracts us, no?'

Mm, tell me about it. On the bulging shelves she saw lots more interesting things to read. More poetry: Dante, Petrarch, some

Americans, Irish and English, Persian love poets. More novels. The Republic's major thinkers were also represented, Diderot, Descartes, Voltaire, Montesquieu, Pascal…and don't forget de Sade. And Plato got to be there with them, as did a lot of eastern religious stuff. And art. Food and health… 'You read all this?'

'I dip in and out. It's all useful. Wouldn't keep it if it weren't.'

And birds. Photography, Audubon's prints, much biology… 'Ah, right. My spies tell me you started with the bird column.'

'Birds are interesting,' said Tommi.

'As interesting as Pearl Serein?'

As if in response, there was a peeping sound in the shadows at the far end of the room.

Aliette approached the bird in the cage by the shuttered window. A finch. *Chardonneret*: the meager light obscured the rich crimson of its cap and mask, but she recognized the distinctive white sidebars extending from the fringe of the pate, ringing the back of the eye and wrapping below the chin. The species was common in garden feeders and kitchen cages, their colors and song a pleasing diversion. Her grandmère had kept one. She watched it shuffle along its perch.

Tommi Bonneau joined her. 'Some days, yes. Even more so.' Opening the gate, Tommi extended a finger. 'Eh, Bert? Are you interesting?' The bird hopped on and was lifted out and up close to an inspector's eyes. 'The homing instinct is only the most obvious thing. The way they mate. The way they build. The way they sing to each other. We hear a three-note song, they hear a complete pattern. Very sensitive, even neurotic — or something like it. There's a syndrome called Displacement Activity. It's as if their nervous system shorts out and one instinct cuts into the middle of another. They've been observed suddenly interrupting sex and attacking their mates. Apparently it revolves around problems of motivation and communication, and origin and evolution.'

'Sounds like a lot of people.'

Tommi sniffed a laugh. 'Some days I think I learn more from birds than I do from people.'

She tried to touch Bert the bird, but he skittishly avoided her. Tommi guided him back inside his caged home.

But birds and poetry were distracting. This was a business call. 'Can you tell me where Didier Belfort might be when he's not at home?'

'Didi? In a cloud...the man has about five different habits.' Casually lifting one of his cameras, Tommi Bonneau lined up Aliette Nouvelle. Another dare.

She ignored it. In the street, she could threaten him with consequences. Here, this was the necessary trade-off, Tommi's price for her unmandated visit. 'I know that. But where does he hide?'

'His studio.' Click.

'No.'

'His mama's castle.' Click.

'On my list.'

'Wasn't dancing last night? Didi's quite the dancer if he's got the right mix of pills in him.'

'No.'

'Can't see him killing anyone, though,' Musing. Click. Almost imperceptible.

'Not asking for your opinion on that, Tommi. Only where he cools his heels.'

'The clubs downtown. Try Diabolik? I saw him there the other night. Please smile, Inspector.'

Aliette would not smile for Tommi Bonneau. 'Which night?'

'Oh, a week ago at least.' Click. 'And there are all the family places. Over the river too.'

Tommi took another picture. She blinked.

'...his mother's castle in the Black Forest, the wine property at Bergheim.' Click.

'That's enough, Tommi.' Quid pro quo.

'Never enough, Inspector. Always something there.' He stopped, but he wanted more.

Too curious. She sensed this Tommi Bonneau could shoot on and on. Till he saw what?

A voice called from upstairs. 'Tommi! Where's your hair dryer?'

'I'll be there in a minute!'

Aliette knew that voice. She was sure she knew it. But it was none of her business.

Before leaving the house on Rue Pontbriand with a list of places in Germany and Switzerland, she thanked him for his help. And now she warned him, 'I am off the record, Tommi.'

Tommi told her, 'The crime page can talk about cops. *Le Vrai Tommi* sticks to love. I'm happy to see you. Spies are spies, *n'est-ce pas?*' He flashed a smirky smile before he closed the door.

The old Westfalia van was indeed parked in the street. Not hiding. Why should it be? And why should Aliette be sad to see it there? Not her business. Anne-Marie was free to sleep with whatever man might please her. As was Pearl Serein. As was Aliette Nouvelle.

But people made such stupid choices, time and time again.

And that can make a person sad.

## – 16 –
## Sunday's bitter end

When she returned to her desk, there were more calls, finally one from Claude. She informed him, 'Mathieu's people are talking to Remy Lorentz…No, no sign of Belfort anywhere.' In her opinion, Belfort's absence posed a heightened risk to an already seriously compromised commissaire.

'Why? There's only one way into this place.'

Refraining from anything smug or angry, objective — *a good cop* — she tried to help him see it from the other side of the equation, how other investigators were bound to start to see it: Because Raymond Tuche was dead. Because he and Claude had been seen in a violent situation within hours of his death and they — Pearl and Ray — were known to have been in love.

'She never loved him.'

She suggested statements like that were nothing if not incriminating. And because Claude was now with Pearl Serein.

'Protecting her.'

Regardless, certain people were wanting to speak to Claude and Pearl, officially — that is, in *garde à vue*. 'Michel Souviron is expecting you…both of you — before he gives you to Gérard. It's an opportunity that may not come again, monsieur.' Because the Sunday news reports were quickly spinning Pearl Serein and Commissaire Claude Néon into a very hot item (which was totally predictable, you ass!) and that wouldn't help his case at all.

With a word, Claude expressed his contempt for the Sunday news reports.

He conceded that the proc's support was valuable and forever iffy. But, 'Tomorrow,' Claude said, holding tight to the logic of the boyfriends, the not-unreasonable thought that he might himself now be a target. The pattern indicated the killer would be trying to get at him, and soon.

And Pearl? He felt they were both better positioned ensconced at the highest point in the city.

'Claude, Claude, Claude. What if you're the killer?'

'Me?' Big pause. '...But that's absurd.'

'But it's a way of seeing it. Coming in right now would be the smarter thing. Let Michel protect you — from Belfort *and* the rumors.' Claude and Pearl the assumed couple: this was highly volatile where it touched the public's view of it. 'So you spend the night in jail? It's no shame.'

No. 'Tomorrow.' They were safer where they were, legally and existentially, if not physically. 'No way I'll let anyone put us in a cell for the night. Press sees that, it might as well be over.'

'The divisionnaire has indicated that you should surrender. Are you going to force the issue?'

'Such bullshit. Look, Fauré likes *you*. Tell him I'm asking for the night to land the noble.'

'And what if he says no?' Divisional Commissaire Norbert Fauré was not one to be disobeyed.

A large sigh at the other end. Aliette suddenly wondered if Pearl was there. Rubbing his stressed-out neck? Claude burst in on this soft image. 'Let Fauré come up and arrest us. The vultures are all here. Let him walk through *that*, cuff us and lead us away. Hm?'

Bitterness aside, the inspector had to admit that Claude had learned to think strategically. No, the divisionnaire was not to be disobeyed, but the appearance of chaos within police ranks in his fiefdom was something else again. The media vultures would just as soon eat Norbert Fauré as Claude and Pearl — Fauré had lots of tasty political fat clinging to his large presence for them to chew on. Still, the inspector counseled, 'Better to come in of your own accord. Show the community you've nothing to hide. Push the Belfort angle. Let Fauré deal with the media on those terms.' If Didier Belfort *was* out hunting the men who courted Pearl, he would have to break through police lines to get at Claude. If innocent, Belfort turned himself in and submitted to questions. 'Or he stays low, runs. Whichever way, it becomes Fauré's problem. No?'

'That could take weeks,' rebutted Claude, but tentatively. Realizing he'd put himself in a tricky corner? 'What if we never see him again? We all know Richand's the worst for keeping people.'

Aliette couldn't argue. There is no concept of bail in France. One is either released from interrogation with a promise to remain available, or kept while further investigations are carried out. Provisional freedom is at the discretion of the instructing judge. More than anything else, the *détention provisoire* rule has given the justice system its ominous reputation of favoring the notion of guilty until proven innocent. Gérard Richand could and would keep them if he had any doubts at all. In that sense, walking into a jail cell for the night had nothing to do with a declaration of good faith. It would only make the judge's decision that much easier. And while Procureur Michel Souviron could be an ally, he would never publicly challenge his own chief magistrate.

'*Bon*,' Aliette murmured. 'It's your case, monsieur.'

Claude said, 'Find the noble.'

'Working on it.'

'*Everybody stays in contact with everybody else.*'

'*Oui, oui.*' She rang off, promising to keep him in the loop.

And she would. Because it's our duty... But Aliette Nouvelle was no longer feeling urgent. If Claude Néon was so sure he belonged up there and not down here, let him stay up there. Claude's bluff would certainly be called tomorrow morning. There was also the thought of Claude being sent to some outpost in the Massif Centrale, disgraced, never to be heard from again. Who would logically take over the PJ team here at Rue des Bons Enfants?

She watered her plant and gathered her stuff. She heard the phone ringing in Monique's office as she started down the stairs. She kept going, ignoring Junior Inspector Bernadette Milhau's request that she take line one. That's it for me today. Sweat, Claude. You deserve it.

Coming out of the winding streets of the old quarter, crossing the *rond-point*...

Claude's 'situation' had turned into a siege. The crowd in front of Pearl's building was growing, buzzing, spilling into the park, a circus of media and curious folk conjoined in their desire for something to happen. People clutching newspapers stood around surmising. Gossip. Grungy human curiosity. Who can claim to be above it? The inspector wandered through, anonymous, studying their expectant faces. What did they think they'd see? A happy couple waving down at them like royalty? Or maybe a pair of desperadoes trapped by their passion and cornered by the law, embracing there on the edge, then throwing themselves into the evening sky? Both those things, probably, and a thousand variations. The grist of the story was universal. Its details lay in all these separate hearts...shifting, fantastic, thrilling! All anyone had to do was pick up a copy. *Le Vrai Tommi* was a door to larger dreams. And they were hungering for that.

The balance between knowing and wallowing was seriously off. It vexed her.

Aliette lingered in the crowd, checking faces for clues to the empty thing behind each life that had allowed this spectacle to happen. Shhh! cautioned her better voice, Stop being so righteous, Inspector. People want to know about it. It's normal.

So she walked away from normal, climbed to her third-floor hideout, lay down for half an hour, then took a good long shower. Opened a bottle of beer.

She had a perfect view from her balcony. She sipped beer and ate warmed-up leftover *tarte flambée*, observing the throng with Piaf. Celebrity gossip, the scent of crime, people milling, the truck from the regional TV News shining under the evening sun. Perhaps enjoying it? It *was* something exciting for a lonely person on a Sunday evening.

Inspector Aliette Nouvelle was lonely again after a passionate winter, the happy spring of a normal life in which she had dared to think of making plans. Inside, the phone was ringing. She let it — in a mood to inflict some pain on a secret lover.

Love *is* indeed a mystery, but ah what a fool to be so deluded.

Of course it was Claude. Didn't you figure? You must have (gentle reader).

Who else could it have been? *But why?*

It's that stupid light of attraction Tommi Bonneau was talking about, the one that counters the dark. Beyond that, Aliette couldn't say.

Because people are desperate to make love with someone they can understand? A kindred spirit. A pretty basic reason. For this cop it was another cop... You get offered a beautiful face — Raphaele Petrucci's for example, but there had been others — and you turn it down. Well, you have to start to understand: you are on the kindred-spirit path, *ma belle*.

Because beauty lies inside the eyes (her mother said), and you finally believe you recognize it?

Because you have to believe your mother?

Because it was logical? One cop soul reaching for another, making love like police procedure.

*What?* Beauty lies? Or was it Mother? Aliette Nouvelle sipped beer and watched the fun across the park. She could not stop her eyes traveling, sliding up, up, up to the dim light at the highest point, till, slightly drunk, definitely bored, she left it, drew the curtain and sat there on her bed.

She thought it could be helpful to have something to read just now. A good book's an essential piece of survival gear for lonely Sundays. But like the rest of it, this was too sudden — whatever book she needed right now, it was not at hand. Aliette had let her reading lapse, had sacrificed it for nights in front of the television, maybe some music, or just talking. You know?... all those kinds of pre-bedtime sharing things. All for Claude Néon.

## - 17 -
### Good cop, bad cop?

Claude Néon spent Sunday feeling pulled by a tide of inevitability. It began with a sense of being above it all — the sight of the traffic circle as a toy-sized pinwheel, the flow of tiny cars, knowing the city was watching. His wake-up call from Inspector Nouvelle had not been encouraging. *What were you thinking?* Truth was, he hadn't been. He had reacted. Pearl was frightened, her steely dispassion had deserted her, she was overwhelmed with guilt. Claude had spent hours trying to calm her after the chaos at the club, given her camomile tea and aspirin, put her to bed... But at some point, he had to ask her the same question. What were you thinking by appearing like that at the height of the frenzy? Had she been *looking* for something to explode?

Well, it had. And now another one was dead. Tuche.

Claude was at the barrier, contemplating the sparse Sunday morning traffic and Aliette Nouvelle's balcony door, thinking the inspector was not being totally professional about the situation, when Pearl was suddenly there beside him, soft and sleepy-faced, offering coffee. He saw the outline of her body where the morning sun shone through the oversized T-shirt she wore as a pyjama. She moved, her body disappeared. Claude was confronted by an impishly grinning Jean-Guy Gagnon, emblazoned on the T-shirt above his signature greeting, '*Bonjour!...this is your wake-up call.*' Claude accepted the coffee but put it aside when he saw the cup carried a beatified image of Bruno Martel's bearish face, a memento from the spiritual farm. He declined the offer of Jerôme Duteil's gold-plated razor, left behind, long forgotten. Claude preferred to go unshaved.

He informed her of Tuche and she cried again. He let her. He would let her come to him.

She began to. Claude and Pearl talked in spurts and fragments, then separated, then found each other and talked some more. This was not difficult—inside, outside, so much space up here! The deck surrounded the apartment. The south-west side featured a landscaped terrace where Pearl kept her garden. He watched her gather fallen tulip petals. 'To the memory of Raymond,' she muttered, scattering orange and mauve bits of dead flower around a fiberglass female torso, modeled to scale and mounted in the earthy bed. Claude felt a pang, realizing the model had been *her*.

There was a backboard and half-court built against the windowless north wall, 'in honor of how we met,' Pearl said. How she'd met Didier Belfort. She smashed a ball till she was sweating, said it helped alleviate the stress. Claude promised himself he would learn to play tennis.

Inside, looking north-east and decorated with framed posters from Pierre Angulaire's films, was a mini-gym-cum-laundry-room where Pearl could warm up before her usual run in the park.

He would not allow her to go for a run in the park. For her own safety. Not with a murderer on the loose. When she complained, Claude reminded her that he was a man trained to keep her safe from harm. Sullen, she acquiesced and went for a swim in her pool. Got a glass of juice and read her book—her Japanese novel. Claude climbed the three-meter ladder to the board suspended over the pool. It had to be one of the highest points in the city. He felt he could touch the mountains.

'You can have it,' she told him. 'I haven't been up it once. Scared to death.'

She read. Claude stood alone in the sky. You couldn't hear the city. Only the wind.

A crowd began to gather far below. Her phone rang constantly. Nerve-wracking, but he warned her not to touch it: only media jackals. He knew Strasbourg was also wanting a word, but, sorry, unless the PJ team's two-ring-stop-and-try-again code was in play, Claude refused to answer. When they made contact, he and Pearl conferred, and he passed the information on, guiding his team in the hunt for the missing Belfort. He would be proactive. He would shape this thing.

But beyond his portable phone and his gun—neither of which he'd carried to the club—he was missing the file he'd been compiling. He needed these basic tools. Monique was not around. Because Inspector Nouvelle was being such a bitch about it, he instructed Junior Inspector Bernadette Milhau to go into his office, open his computer, find the *pearlsboys* file, print a copy of the Belfort pages and deliver it, along with his government-issue revolver, in his desk drawer, to the concierge downstairs. 'And the book that's there... Yeah, put that in.'

Pearl was a big reader? Well, Claude Néon would be too.

In due course the package arrived, delivered direct from lift to living room by the discreet man in the valet coat and hat. (Pearl said no, one did not tip salaried staff.) *Bon.* Claude felt better equipped to drive the search and deal with any eventuality. Didier Belfort would certainly have access to the building if he wanted. If he dared.

Pearl scoffed bitterly, 'Claude, you're pushing this into fantasy land.'

'Pearl...' Why did she refuse to imagine it? 'Anything is possible when it comes to a man who feels his pride has been abused, his heart broken.' Claude took her hand and held it in both of his. 'I can understand a person not wanting to face the fact of having been intimate with a killer. I see it everyday.' Pearl tensed at this. 'I know the heart doesn't need it and will do all it can to make the mind deny. But a policeman has to see through to the thing in the mind that can't resist the cry of the heart. You can sometimes see it straight off, plain as day. Sometimes love is love,' explained Claude. 'Other times it can be a hell of a thing—I mean the destructive thing at the heart of it. You can't fathom it. It stays unsolved. That's the worst: something horrible, brutal, unsolved. You might solve the crime, but you'll never solve the person.'

Pearl let her hand relax. 'What do you mean, love is love?'

'Only that people react in a predictable way and one can usually predict those people.'

'Yes?'

'Sure. If spontaneity has a link to the soul, then you have to believe the crime of passion is one of the more purely imaginative of acts, an instinctual thing, and the law allows it to be defended as such. By framing it as irrational to start with, the police and the courts can go at it in the kind of clinical way they need to, you see?'

'I think I might. Law is rational. Love is not.'

'Of course the psychologists are getting adept at making pictures for us. So many of these types are so bland. Evil is just a bored little man.'

'Looking to fall in love?' Pearl's eyes were wide as she beheld him. She seemed to recognize something. She gently withdrew her hand.

'Yes... Well, not exactly. Not the way you'd think.' Claude ran with it, talking too much, he knew, but couldn't stop himself. It had to do with his credibility. 'Now the obverse of spontaneity is calculation. Blinds drawn. Evil takes charge. Serious planning, absolute care in concealing... People say they can sense danger coming. They can't. What they hear is their own fear.'

'What do you do?'

'Fight fire with fire. Face it with a colder logic, a darker cast of mind.'

'Are you saying a cop is someone who's bad but can control it?'

'More like someone who's been trained to understand where others stop understanding.'

It was then she whispered, 'Merci, Claude.'

Claude finally felt Pearl knew why he, of all of them, was there.

Later, he left his command center, got a beer from Pearl's fridge. Took his book. The sun was warm, they spent the latter part of the afternoon by her pool, he in shirtsleeves and barefoot with his pants rolled up, she in her bikini, though not topless as in the missing shot taken on Pugh's boat.

Claude mentioned this, calm, professional but pointed, striving for more intimate ground.

Pearl said she had no copy of that picture and could barely remember that day. All that remained of her time with Georges was her brass paperweight—the bust of a famous jurist.

Yes. Claude had been contemplating it while making his calls from her desk. Pushing it further, he said, 'You have all these trophies, but no gallery.'

Her mouth drew tight. 'My gallery is private... I put it away.'

'I think I need to see it, Pearl. Your private gallery.'

She studied the page in front of her, a page in *The Three-Cornered World*. 'Because you think you might find that picture of me and Georges.'

'We've been looking for it. If you have it, we need it.'

'I'd hate to have your job,' said Pearl. Before he could reply (what *could* he reply to that?), she stood, wrapped a towel around her hips in sarong fashion and headed inside.

He followed but waited respectfully at the door to her room as she took a shoebox from her armoire, opened it and began to sift through. Slowly. Then quicker, her face clouding. By then he was standing at her shoulder. There were several envelopes filled with photographs, many of them old snaps from another time, adults and children, none of whose faces meant anything to Claude. Growing frantic, Pearl spread them on her dresser…let them fall haphazard on the floor.

There was no picture of Georges and Pearl on the boat at Lac Como. There were no pictures of any of them, Pearl's sorry line of famous men. There were no pictures of Pearl.

'Someone has taken every one!' Weeping again—from fear, and a deeper sense of violation.

Claude logically thought Didi Belfort. He led her into the salon, a calming hand on her shaking shoulder. Sat her down. Went to make some herbal tea. And tried to help her help him do his job.

'Tell me more about Didi. Does he give you trouble?'

'Just a headache…' It appeared she had one now. 'He's so melodramatic about everything.'

'But would he kill?'

'He never laid a hand on me.'

'Not you. The others… Think, Pearl! Think about the kind of man he is.'

She closed her worried eyes over her steaming tea and thought, but could not add to what they already knew. But her puzzling opened the door to Claude to ask,

'Why were you there last night?'

'I was lonely.' Barely a whisper. He waited. 'I had to go… I couldn't just sit here.' Stronger now. He waited. 'Sit with all this…

this death. I needed to go and have a taste of life. Show them! You understand, Claude?' He nodded, mirroring her complications. And waited. He sensed Pearl was rising to a place he hadn't seen since Thursday. Her spirit. The fight in her. He liked that she seemed to understand him now — his role, his presence; but he'd liked her better on Thursday. It was complicated for him too. '...I went to show them I'm not the cause of their pathetic little hearts and... Oh *mon dieu*.' Huge sigh. She was sinking back again, into it, her guilt, the weight of it.

'I understand, Pearl.'

She nodded. Shrugged.

The evening rolled in, the place was still. No more calls...no answer at Inspector Nouvelle's. Claude had to hope the team was out there searching, closing in on the noble. Pearl was deep inside herself and Claude backed off with the questions. He sensed the theft of her pictures had numbed her — somehow more than the death of the ones depicted. Or so it seemed to Claude. She sat staring at something just beyond the tip of her nose. Grim. Befuddled. A slow, constant shaking of her head. She seemed without earthly weight as she cut bread, prepared a salad, arranged cheese on a plate, opened and tasted a bottle of wine — nothing of the woman inside, just a pair of hands at work.

Wordlessly, she laid two places on the coffee table. He accepted wine, sat on the lush divan and turned on the evening news. She joined him. Silent, like a long-time couple on a routine Sunday, they watched Cakeface tell the story. The front door of Pearl's building was the reporter's basic setting. The uniformed concierge was posed there for effect. Claude bet he'd been bribed by Cake.

She eyeballed the camera: *This morning's news of the death of sculptor Raymond Tuche has burst the simmering pot that is the Pearl Serein affair wide open. Six suspicious deaths and counting. The authorities are scrambling. The city waits for an explanation...many citizens have come to the Parc de la République on a glorious spring Sunday to catch a glimpse of the woman at the center of the storm. Pearl Serein, reclusive and evasive at the best of times, is barricaded in her luxurious penthouse atop the exclusive Place du Parc, here behind me. We have had no luck communicating with Madame Serein today. She is* said to be in the personal custody of PJ Commissaire Claude Néon. The police, no doubt, have lines open to Commissaire Néon, but the situation remains unclear and somewhat ominous.*

Cut to a body bag being wheeled out of the club, pigeons flying.

Cake VO: *Raymond Tuche was last seen alive in the middle of a wild brawl at the posh Quarter Racquets Club last night. He was found dead this morning in the sauna in the men's locker room. All initial reports describe a heart-attack victim. The body has been taken to the police morgue and we await further findings. It is the sixth such death of a prominent local man within two weeks, all of whom have been linked romantically with Madame Serein.*

Cut to view of body bag being carried out of G. Pugh's building.

Cut to same being carted from the house of Agnès Guntz.

Cake VO: *No criminal cause has been officially declared but pressure is mounting on justice system authorities…*

Claude saw Pearl weeping again as she watched. Again he held her hand. He let go of Pearl's hand as they cut to Commissaire Néon — his official corporate shot. 'What the bloody hell?'

Cake VO: *The dark element flows from the fact that Commissaire Néon was seen dancing passionately with, then aggressively escorting Madame Serein from the elegant party that erupted in a wild brawl at the well-heeled club, apparently within an hour of the estimated time of Tuche's death. Our information is that Tuche's protests to Madame Serein sparked the brawl. City police are conducting the investigation. Monsieur Néon has been incommunicado all day. A spokesperson said the commissaire is ensuring the physical safety of Madame Serein till architect Didier Belfort has been questioned.*

Cut to head shot of Belfort.

Cake VO: *Perhaps the largest irony here is the fact that it was Monsieur Belfort who first wooed Madame Serein and brought her to the public's attention, and, upon the termination of their liaison, made a gift of the 11th floor redoubt where the shadowy cop and beleaguered lady currently hide…*

Cut back to Cake, now in the park. She speaks to the camera while moving through the crowd: *Meanwhile, it is not exactly an atmosphere of fear which binds all these good people here this evening. No, let's say it's —*

Pearl jabbed the remote, Cake and the crowd disappeared. 'Bitch!' hissed Pearl and ran from the divan to her writing desk.

Claude, stunned, bemused…helpless, watched her snatch pen and paper from the drawer and begin to scratch a note. He roused himself and approached with caution. 'What are you doing?'

'I am writing to her station. She is being absurd and irresponsible.'

'Pearl…'

'And wrong, Claude—just plain wrong! And I am going to let them know.'

Claude presented a face of exaggerated calm. 'Wrong about what?'

Pearl's face bent with incredulity. 'Were we dancing passionately?' He didn't like the way she said it. 'And it wasn't Raymond who started it, it was Remy. She's wrong about everything. It's a travesty!'

'It's normal. Cake's always more interested in effect than details. It's the nature of the beast.'

'Cake?'

'Nothing.' Claude watched her scribble her complaint. He was smiling, but sadly. He felt pity for Pearl and was experiencing a kind of dawning awe at the vastness of his own mistake.

'She should not be allowed to say things like that.' Pearl signed her name. Proffering the pen, she told him, 'And you're going to sign this with me.'

Claude shook his head. 'Forget it. It doesn't matter. All that matters is that she's saying it.'

'But it's bullshit!' (*Conneries!*)

'I wouldn't advise it. You're here too. You're my accomplice and my lover.'

She whined, 'But it's not right! This is *not* a real situation!'

He begged to differ. 'You're damn right it's a real situation.'

Pearl pounded the letter with an outraged fist. 'We'll give them this! You take it to them. You make them take it. They'll have to read it on their broadcast—if they have any integrity at all!'

'Pearl…' Claude hesitated. Was she strong, or cold? Obstinate, or simply stupid? Again, she left him wondering. He felt an urge to say *bonsoir, madame*, keep your doors and windows locked, and get himself the hell back down to street level, take his lumps, leave this goddamn thing. Finally, he laughed, 'Of course they'll read it! You could send them your poetry and they'd read it. The papers would run it on their front page.'

Pearl's fierceness went all twisty. 'I don't *have* any poetry.'

'Then your thoughts on the new global marketplace. They'd love to know. They need a handle for their story, Pearl. They can't operate in a vacuum. It's a losing battle, believe me.'

'Claude! ...I want to tell them their reporter got it wrong. Horribly wrong. It's what any self-respecting person would do. Has to do. Surely they want to know.'

'Not really. Not when their star hound's got the sweet scent of rich underwear up her nose.'

'Don't be disgusting.'

'I won't be disgusting if you won't be dumb. OK, Pearl? Deal?'

'Deal?' Pearl rose from her desk, threw her letter in his face and walked away. '*Merde!*'

'Right.' Claude picked up his suit coat and put it on. It was ripped and rumpled from the *quote* wild brawl at the elegant party at the well-heeled club *unquote*. He told her, 'Sorry, as a public official it would be wrong for me to countersign. You want me to leave?'

Pearl gazed out at the city that would think she was complicit with a rogue cop and nibbled on her pen. 'No,' she muttered, 'I don't want that.'

'Then don't say a word...' discreetly removing his coat; 'it'll only make it worse. Now, right or wrong, we're going to have work around them and that's not easy. Our first strategy is silence.'

'*Our* strategy?' was her pointed reply. But her outburst seemed to have settled.

'I'm sorry.' He shrugged. 'You seemed so alone in this.'

Pearl nodded... She accepted that.

She cleared their supper off to the kitchen and poured herself another glass of wine.

Claude took a breath and dialed Inspector Nouvelle's apartment again. No answer.

He could not bring himself to go out on Pearl's deck and look down.

They shared the last of the wine, watching the gloaming spread across the mountains. They talked about tomorrow. She asked, 'What will we do?'

'We'll talk to them. Tell them the truth.'

'They'll put us in separate rooms. I've seen the way they do it.'

'They're not bad people. They respect the truth. They recognize it. Just don't waver...' He reached for her hand. She let him hold it. 'There's nothing to fear if you've nothing to hide.'

'That's the thing,' she murmured. 'I've no idea what I'm hiding, but I fear I must be hiding something. Why else would this be happening? The way everyone's watching? I can't sleep at all.'

'So tell me about it.' He felt her move closer. 'Try, Pearl... You can tell *me*.'

Pearl told him her dream, a recurring dream, absurd and disturbing, of Tommi Bonneau out in the moonlight doing flips on her diving board like some demonic *saltimbanque*, perfectly agile, beautifully balanced, '...and he lands so softly, like Peter Pan! There is always applause from the city below, and Tommi bows...' while she lay trapped and mute in her bed.

Claude shrugged. 'You could talk to J-P Blismes. A psychologist—he sometimes works with us.'

'I can't stop their stories, but it's not who I am,' Pearl said.

'I know.'

'I'm not a bad person.'

'*Some*one's a bad person.'

Pearl shuddered (and he felt it). 'But *is* it me? Could it be?'

'Don't think that way. It doesn't help. Please, Pearl...'

'I'm scared, Claude.'

'It's normal.'

Fear (and a little wine) defined a place within the nexus. He took her in his arms. Pearl let Claude hold onto her but that was all. 'Don't. Don't make it worse... Till she left him with his sense of duty and badly aching testicles. For the second night he lay down on the pull-out hidden inside that same divan. He tried to stay alert to sounds, but was distracted by lover's nuts and strategy.

All available units were hunting the noble. Divisionnaire Fauré had backed off till morning. Claude hoped Michel Souviron was standing pat. He'd need Souviron tomorrow — he had no faith at all in Gérard Richand. He'd given up on Aliette Nouvelle. Of course they had to talk. He supposed he was a bastard. But it would settle. She would see it. Two cops is not a good idea and they'd never hide it forever. Nosy Monique was on the verge of guessing, and once she did, the entire world would know. It had been a nice moment, a comfort during winter, but Nouvelle-Néon was a non-starter.

She had to see it. She had to know this… Claude Néon lay there mulling.

Did he sleep? Did he hear a threatening sound? Claude was jolted.

'Are you a good cop, Claude?' Pearl asked this as she slid warmly in beside a startled and somewhat embarrassed commissaire. The erection she gently patted had been standing in the middle of his sleep like a streetlight; now here she was, leaning against it.

'Try to be,' he mumbled, moving away from her, slightly…yet opening his arms.

'I believe you,' she whispered, moving into his arms, now putting him between her legs.

Not inside herself — just there. Pearl smiled at him, dimly, the same uncertain tone in her face as in her voice, then she buried her face in the crook of his neck as if to sleep.

There was an indeterminate time of tentative fingers, unclear legs, closed-mouth kisses, dry-lip nuzzling, vague heat, the muffled sounds of vaguer want and need. Then he was inside her.

The strangest thing is always the look at that instant. This held true for Pearl.

They made love like two people who did not really want to wake up, neither one on top nor bottom, movements desultory. That was all. Baudelaire would have been disappointed.

Claude was less than fulfilled…

He awoke to Monique's call and another erection which he quickly piled with blankets. No luck finding Didi Belfort. He was expected to present himself (with Pearl) to the divisionnaire, without fuss, down at the entrance to her building at eight sharp. Police solidarity was key now. Perception was going to be everything, and it would start with the walk to the car...

Yes, yes, fine. Claude confirmed details.

Pearl, soft-faced like any other woman in the morning, was lying there, watching him talk.

They prepared separately, and in silence. He used Jerôme Duteil's forgotten razor to clean his worried face. He used an offered toothbrush, didn't ask whose it was. Her apartment was resplendent in the clean light of early morning—he took one last look as they stepped into the lift.

She asked him again. 'Are you a good cop, Claude?'

Watching the floor numbers light up, flash off as they descended. 'Yes.'

Pearl stared deep into herself and said, 'I hope so.'

As if she felt something was again lacking in yet another man?

He took it to mean her fear was growing. He had to.

They emerged together hand in hand, the way defeated politicians will with their wives, or like film stars who've been through tragedy, or convicted CEOs. The wife, the lover, the friend, it helps soften the grim image. They met Norbert Fauré waiting in the lobby and proceeded to the door.

## - 18 -
### Didi discovered

Monday morning traffic jerked spasmodically around the *rond-point* as some motorists slowed for a look. Impatient others blasted on shrill horns. The crowd was growing by the minute, noisy, expectant, most grasping copies of *Le Cri du Matin*. Inspector Aliette Nouvelle certainly had hers. Tommi Bonneau had warned her Claude would hate this morning's column. **Local Scene:** *Regarding Saturday's tragedy. A delicate balance was disturbed, a fragile energy shattered. We have lost Raymond Tuche. We have lost his beautiful vision. While our Pearl continues on, now in the company of her policeman. Protective custody? These are dry official words. I for one am having trouble accepting them. What is happening?*

Yes, Claude probably would.

A contingent of uniformed officers had formed a line and stood linked arm in arm, creating a barrier to allow free passage from the door to the waiting car. Members of the media jostled for vantage along its inner edge. Cakeface was in the thick of it, easily seen in a royal blue knit suit, microphone ready. Cake's cameraman was stationed on the roof of the TV truck. Aliette watched him diligently keying on the reporter as she pushed and shoved with the others, waiting for Pearl to emerge. She saw Tommi Bonneau up near the building entrance, stooped and disheveled, eye glued to his viewfinder, free hand holding his light aloft. Waiting for his moment.

The couple could be seen conferring with the divisionnaire as he prepared to escort them from the lobby. There was a prolonged moment of preternatural silence when they appeared, Claude looking grave, but not as grave as Norbert Fauré, who was older, craggy, and looked to be bearing the weight of this scandal like an aggrieved papa. Pearl was jittery. Her alarm deepened visibly as the silence broke, the crowd started up again with its raucous noise, the media pack surged forward, calling questions, flashing lights. Aliette could see Claude's hand wrapped tightly over Pearl's while Fauré led the way. Two or three reporters, Cakeface being one, squeezed through the human barrier and confronted the entourage with mics. The uniforms began to manhandle these strays out of the path. Cakeface resented it — the poor *flic* who grabbed her came away with an ugly gash over his right eye. The crowd went 'oooh!' when they saw the blood. Cakeface straightened her hair and starting waving her mic in the air, making sure her man atop the mobile unit had her in his frame.

That cold green-white light from Tommi's flash and many others bathed the scene.

Fauré raised an arm and motioned: one finger — come.

Five plainclothes men came bursting out of the two cars parked at the end of the line.

Fauré's team knew exactly what to do. They efficiently bashed their way to the stranded trio, formed a wedge and began to move. They were not as big as elephants but they did know how to proceed *en groupe*, and any person, including a telegenic reporter, who stood in their way was summarily ploughed aside. The crowd fell back. The only sound was the percussive 'hup, hup, hup, hup!' from the escort, a sound deliberately designed to override all questions. Aliette was impressed. A perfect example of men making excellent combined use of both the larger physical upper body and the concomitant instinct nature had provided in a totally unnatural manner. Moving to the side of Junior Inspector Bernadette Milhau, she was about to point out the absolute left-right, left-right *robo* footwork which made the exercise a thing of such precise beauty —

— when a scream stopped the juggernaut dead in its tracks.

Then another. A woman, terrified, obviously. But *where*?

Cop and media antennae simultaneously searched the suddenly still morning.

One more scream… 'There!' — by the corner of the building, in the lane leading round to the parking at the back, and shaking her arms about her face in that universal way people will when expressing deep and sudden fear, as if trying to wave the sight away from her eyes, the very idea out of her mind. She was older, hair wrapped up, an apron tied around her belly, just setting out on a day dedicated to cleaning someone's luxury apartment. Clearly not a local woman. Turkish, more than likely. Probably with no idea what was happening on the Local Scene.

Uniforms ran toward her. The crowd flowed after.

Aliette and Bernadette dawdled along behind. This was not their operation.

There was a pile of garbage by the entrance to the garage, waiting to be removed: crates, cardboard boxes, discarded furniture. The uniforms approached, sidearms at the ready. One by one they stopped, looking around, shrugging. So? A kindly Cakeface guided the traumatized cleaning lady forward, a gentle arm around her quaking back, demonstrating police and media *could* work together, even with immigrants. The woman jabbered and shook, pointing at the pile. *In* the pile! The cops closed in, tentative, trying to follow her scattered directions. One of Fauré's men saw it first. '*Mon dieu!*'...then everyone, as he went to it: A long, wrapped coil of newspaper, propped up as if it contained a bound-up carpet to be discarded, a hand protruding as if signaling, 'Here I am.' Another cop rushed to help. They pulled away the paper. Another wave of green-white light as Tommi and the rest of the pack clicked away with fervent focus...

A dead man, standing as if frozen, in his tennis whites.

Smoothly, like water, word filtered back. Didi Belfort! The crowd edged forward. They were held back. The body was covered. They could only watch from a safe remove while the authorities examined and conferred. *Pin-pon, pan-pon!* The SAMU team arrived. More police vehicles. More media. But after thirty minutes, many of the onlookers lost interest and drifted away.

Inspector Nouvelle, still not needed, but standing by and waiting, watched people dispersing. She wondered, Were they feeling satisfied? cheated? witnesses to history? or merely late for work? She wished she had survey cards to hand out. Someone would cherish the information. Probably make lots of money with it. Musing, yawning, she noticed Pearl Serein split away from the out-going group of citizens. Their eyes met for an instant. Pearl looked so much like all the rest of them.

The inspector belatedly yelled, 'Hey!' as Pearl ran, quick and deft, across the *rond-point* and into the old quarter.

The first one after her was Remy Lorentz, tennis pro (not yet in his whites). A good runner—this she already knew, but was Remy not meant to be in *garde à vue*? That's what happens when you stop taking calls and have some beers... Next came Claude, running flat out, billowy, less than elegant. Then Junior Inspector Millhau, who had a much more telegenic way of running... Cake's cameraman, well-positioned on top of his truck, spun on his tripod, one eye glued to his viewer, fingers wrapped around his lens, total concentration as he followed the action... Then Fauré's men, followed by a ragged parade of hustling uniforms, then the frantic camera wielders.

Tommi Bonneau was lagging at the rear, jogging fitfully, looking back, then looking back again, as if not quite certain whether he needed more shots of a dead Didier Belfort.

Or a shot of a fleeing Pearl.

Aliette caught his eye. He waved, *Salut*...kept following along, to see what he could see

But they were unable to find Pearl Serein—not hard to disappear in the old quarter.

Two of Fauré's large men returned with a hostile Remy Lorentz in tow, actively resisting, loudly insisting he was 'her friend, damn it! just her friend!' as he was bundled into a car.

Captain Mathieu Deubelbeiss dispatched a team to seal Pearl's apartment.

Surrounded by media he refused to acknowledge, PJ Commissaire Claude Néon stood ready to face the divisionnaire, ready to take it like a man.

Surprisingly, Claude was allowed to leave, albeit with an order to be at the *procureur*'s office at exactly two PM, 'with a very comprehensive report, monsieur. A great deal will be riding on it.' Menacing, but without theatrics. Aliette had to admire Fauré for playing it out so coolly in the face of the cameras and mics. She remained quiet. *Don't-worry-Claude*s and *it'll-be-fine*s were of no use at this point. Claude drove off in the back of his official car. She walked. When she arrived at the commissariat, his office door was shut. Monique had cleared her desk, ready to receive his pages for editing, typos, underlining, straight margins—all the things that make the difference.

The inspector spent the better part of her morning with the City team, down on the second floor. Charlotte Griss-Freiss, Didier Belfort's diminutive cousin (half-sister? this was still not clear) was brought in for an interview with Captain Deubelbeiss. The police had visited and called several times Saturday and Sunday, to little effect. Confronted with the reality of her Didi's death, the woman's cantankerous manner softened. There were still many holes, but Charlotte did her best. Belfort had a tennis lesson every day. He usually came home livid or depressed. A week or so ago they'd gone out for an evening of dancing at Diabolik. Bonneau had been there with his horrid camera, there'd been an altercation, a tantrum. 'He stewed about it for days.' Friday, like every day, Belfort had got up, dressed for his tennis lesson, '...he plods about in the morning, I sleep, ignore it as best I can. A beating. He kept muttering about a beating as he tied his shoes. I'm sure it's what I heard. Could've been that disgusting gossip, or it could've been tennis—honestly not worth listening to, poor Didi.' Then he'd left and she did not see him again. 'No, he takes his car.'

They made a call to the club. Gaston said he would canvass his staff. Ten minutes later he called back. Yes, Belfort had been in the locker room Friday morning, staff and several members could vouch for that. He always arrived in his car and left the same way, everyone Gaston had asked was sure... Saturday the place was busy as usual, and Saturday night the club lot was full, what with the party—lots of people coming and going, members and guests alike, lots of silvery high-end German coupes very much like the noble's, no one could say they had seen him on the premises any time Saturday. Before he went back to his chat with Charlotte, Inspector Nouvelle asked Deubelbeiss, 'Could you ask her to be more specific about this run-in with Bonneau? At the club downtown?'

Aliette sat behind the one-way, listening in. Tommi Bonneau had admitted seeing Didi Belfort at Diabolik. He was not exactly lying. But taking pictures, threatening to sell them in Paris? Tommi hadn't mentioned that. What game was Tommi playing with his so-called story? Obviously he pushed the limits of Article 9. But professionally. She was beginning to feel it must be somehow deeper. She returned to her desk and called *Le Cri*. Was transferred. 'One little question, Tommi.'

'I'm listening.'

'Are you honest?'

Some people would slam the phone down. Tommi Bonneau was different. He liked being dared. 'As honest as I need to be, Inspector. Like you?'

'Merci, monsieur. We'll be in touch.' Could she respond to a dare?

With the large possibility looming that they — the local police, both PJ *and* City — would be formally relieved of the matter within the next few hours, an army of uniforms began to comb the streets for Pearl Serein. Jean-Marc Pouliot from *Identité Judiciaire* was sent to go over Raymond Tuche's room at the Cure. His colleague Charles Léger was pulled away from his examination of a burned-out crack dealer's van discovered by the potash terminals and dispatched to Pearl Serein's building. 'See if you can build some kind of trail.' Front, back, from the ground to the 11$^{th}$ and back again. Inspectors Patrice Lebeau and Ricky Roig headed down to the holding cell to talk to Remy Lorentz. Again. Captain Mathieu Deubelbeiss was apologetic on behalf of his own guys. Yes, they'd spoken with Remy yesterday. Good long chat. But the club was not pressing charges against anyone for Saturday night's debacle, and beyond that...well, they'd released him.

'Poor guy has to work for those types every day,' Officer Beyer noted, gesturing through the one-way, where Charlotte waited the next go-round, vacant as a doll.

'Couldn't be easy,' Officer Herrscher added, backing up his partner.

Aliette informed them that Charlotte was not a tennis player. But she agreed, No, it couldn't.

Then Inspector Nouvelle requested permission to have a look through Pearl Serein's place before the larger investigation went into full force. Mathieu Deubelbeiss saw the logic in that.

Deubelbeiss asked her, 'Could you make sure he comes down here? We need him to explain his movements leading up to Saturday night. Won't take ten minutes. I know it's distasteful, but…well, he should.'

He meant Claude. She agreed.

Claude did too. He humbly went down to chat with Deubelbeiss before heading off to his appointment at the courthouse.

## - 19 -
### Stifling folds of love

Aliette returned to Pearl's building. The strutting concierge in the silly Napoleon suit inserted his service key in the lift panel, into a unmarked keyhole above the 10$^{th}$ floor button. 'Voila, madame Inspector. Please remove the key as you leave the lift or the rest of us will be stranded.' She thanked him and turned the key. The lift rose, and with it a tremor of anticipation in her gut. Voyeuristic anticipation. She was finally going to see where Pearl Serein hid with her special life.

The lift opened directly into the living room. Well!

She went from room to room, not as a cop — just to see. Stepped outside, admired the garden and pool, the diving tower, the backboard at the far end where Pearl could work on her backhand. Not too shabby, not too shabby at all. She stood by the rail, enveloped in the midday breeze.

There was Piaf, miles below, a white speck.

The inspector commenced the basic exercise of picking through the woman's life. She peeked into Pearl's fridge (light yogurt, half a quiche, milk, limp carrots, an unwrapped hunk of muenster, apple juice, five cans of Fischer beer), balanced her cutlery...not as expensive as it looked, checked her wine rack. She perused the notes scribbled on Pearl's kitchen calendar (hair, tennis, tennis, mother? tennis). She gazed dumbly at wine stains on Pearl's chic de Boers divan, the Navajo carpet in need of a fringing, the German sound system with the English speakers, the juice glasses from a Turkish bazaar... There was a book on the floor by the divan. Aliette picked it up. *MATING*...in smaller print, *An Analysis of Devotion and Betrayal, Marriage and Divorce: How evolution shaped human love.* Aliette had scanned a review in *Marie-Claire*. They were calling it evolutionary psychology, a hybrid of sorts, wherein the Naked Ape and Charles Darwin sit down with Sigmund Freud. Overleaf, two quotes to entice the reader. From Nisa, a woman in a !Kung San hunter-gatherer village: *When you have lovers, one brings you something and another brings you something else...Your husband also gets things and gives them to you. Do not all women live this way?* And from an American billionaire: *A lasting relationship with a woman is only possible if you are a business failure.'* The premise was fundamental: *'Human beings are genetically designed to fall in love, but not, alas, to stay there. This groundbreaking, often shocking, study ties together...*

A credit card marking the reader's place fell out. She picked it up. A gas card, in the name of Commissaire Claude Néon, expiring at the end of June. Well, everyone had been reading *MATING*. Why not our commissaire? Though Pearl appeared to favor fiction. From *Madame Bovary* to *Le Petit Prince* to the American *Fear of Flying*, her books, lined neatly, covered a good range of the human predicament which love and evolution had so far created. And some pedagogical stuff: Bettelheim, Montessori, Piaget, Steiner. Plus *Le guide Hachette des vins* for 1992. *Le guide familial de l'homéopathie*. A biography of Jeanne d'Arc...But no *Fleurs du mal* in Pearl's library.

Hardly anyone reads poetry any more.

In the bedroom Aliette found pictures scattered on the floor around an ancient shoebox—old snaps of parents, dogs, Pearl in younger...*much* younger days. Souvenirs: happy, sad, sweet and personal and real, leading back through the times of a woman's life. *So* normal. On the bedside table, amid clock and pills, pencil, pad and phone, a comb, a stray earring, a brooch, some buttons and a spool of thread, quite at home in this mess of innocuous flotsam so authentically one's own, was another book, translated from the Japanese— *The Three-Cornered World* by Natsume Soseki, an acknowledged master from the turn of the (prior) century. There was a woman depicted in silhouette on the cover, walking modestly away, alone under her blue parasol in the shadow of a mountain. It is the story of an artist who wants to paint a woman who fascinates him but cannot because there is something missing from her complex character.

Inspector Aliette Nouvelle knew *The Three-Cornered World*. It was a book from those first years in a city she had never visited or imagined as a girl, a time of getting her bearings and, despite no lack of male attention, being lonely. One endless Saturday, she had wandered into a used bookstore, where the proprietor, sensing something, had recommended it. Aliette returned to the shoebox on the floor, reconsidered the old Polaroid of Pearl's papa. She *remembered* him! And this same book had spent time beside her own bed. She had read it closely and taken it to heart.

Pearl Serein's copy opened to the part about the Maid of Nagara, a folk tale within the story. When two men fall in love with her, the well-born Maid cannot decide which one she wants. Her anguish leads her to the riverside, where she throws herself into the swirling gorge. Aliette knew the despair of the Maid of Nagara grew out of the hopelessness of choosing. Choosing love.

And having love choose *you* so wrongly.

There was romance galore out there to fill the lonely hours, endless variations on zipless fucks and femmes fatales and a never-ending line-up of modern thinkers to explain each passing fantasy, but for a woman waiting in an emotional holding cell, the *Three-Cornered World* was reality. Can you read a person from what they're reading? It was just a book, but the inspector suddenly felt a true step closer to the elusive Pearl Serein. Aliette guessed Pearl had followed these same pages up along the misty path of solitude—her heart was by a river, her sin was wishing to be away from it all, a character wanting nothing to do with the story *they* had put her in…While down below men like Claude and seven others, and Tommi Bonneau and a city full of gentle readers, were all searching for a clue. Pearl had been hiding in this story. A story that wasn't even French.

…the inspector was suspended, ruminating when she heard a sound from the front.

The lift door sliding open? A woman's voice exclaiming, 'Isn't this fabulous!'

Aliette crept up the hall to find Rose Saxe fingering the milky leather covering the divan, much in awe of Pearl's domain. A man in a gray work shirt with grease stains on his forehead was standing by in the entrance area, one leg inside the lift door, waiting, nervously twisting a rag in his oily hands. When he noticed Aliette, his face flushed.

He cleared his throat several times. Rose Saxe turned. The haughty demeanor, the beginnings of a gesture — but what to say? With the help of this oily man, Madame Saxe had got past the police barrier. She was breaking the law.

'Rose Saxe! What a surprise!' Aliette, effusive hostess, flashed her police ID card. The woman nodded slowly, circumspect... Guilty. 'And to what do we owe this unexpected pleasure?'

'Just a story,' muttered Rose. 'I had no intention of...ah...' She breathed, stared, nonplussed.

Aliette helped the visitor through an awkward moment. 'What do you think? Spectacular, no?'

'Yes...' suspicious, knowing she'd been caught, 'though it could use a cleaning, I dare say.'

Aliette was businesslike as she sat on the de Boers and crossed her legs. Patted the cushion adjacent. 'Sit, please.' Rose obeyed. The inspector looked over her shoulder. 'Who's your friend?'

'Arthur. He works in the engine room. I have the key to a friend's place on the seventh.'

'Well, that's handy... You can go back to your engines, Arthur,' she ordered politely, playing the role (but flashed her card again just to be sure). The oily man was glad to leave. He stepped back inside the lift, the door slid shut, they were alone. 'Now, Rose,' said Aliette, biting her lower lip, still not sure of the right words. Then, with a slight gasp; 'I'm sorry!...can I get you anything?'

Rose glanced at her watch, put her grossly red lips in a kissing position, considering. Barely noon, a bit early, but resistance would be impolitic. 'Campari with a twist would be just perfect.'

'Not a beer?' asked Aliette, rising.

'Well of course — if that's what you're having...'

'I love beer!' she gushed, heading for Pearl's fridge.

Madame Saxe was closer to sixty than fifty. Her treated ash-blonde hair was tied back in the tight formal manner of bourgeois women throughout the Republic, bound in an elegant black ribbon. Aliette guessed the lady's chin had been tucked a time or two. Sporting gold buttons again. Rose's wattle-ridged neck kept turning, craning, her eyes bright with ill-concealed curiosity. She longed to snoop from stem to stern. Aliette offered a glass. Rose dutifully took a sip.

The inspector pointed to the lipstick smudge on the rim. 'Is that Russian Red, by the way?'

Madonna's color! A little bit of fun with Rose. (And Madonna was also getting old.)

'It is...' Taking a tissue from her purse. 'Did I see you at the club the other night?'

'Perhaps you might have.' The inspector was diplomatic. 'I saw you.'

'But do I know you?' she inquired, leaning forward, peering. 'Who's your husband?'

'I don't have one.'

'Well, it's more fun without one, isn't it?' Rose dabbed the tissue to her lip.

'I wouldn't know,' confided Aliette. 'I've never had one.'

'They have different feeding patterns than we do.' Rose took another messy sip of her beer, sighing, relaxing, 'I do envy the younger generation.' Arranging herself yet again, she declared, 'Inspector, you know we're only too eager to strike up the best of relations with the police on this.'

'We?'

'My editor and myself. *Le Soir*. I honestly hope we can work together.'

'Glad to hear it,' Aliette spoke true. 'But that will be up to you, won't it?'

Rose Saxe heard subtext. Wary, she raised her glass as a sign of agreement.

The inspector returned the gesture. Looking out at the beautiful distance, she said, 'So tell me, why exactly are you doing this? There's no party here, madame.'

'Purely a business decision on the part of my editor. I know the lay of the land, you could say.'

'And you have the key to a friend's place on the seventh,' Aliette noted. 'But, tell me, did you ask for this, Rose?...May I call you Rose?'

'Of course you may. And I'll call you...?'

'Aliette.'

'Aliette. I didn't ask—I suggested, he saw the logic. These are my people.'

'Your people?'

'I've known all these poor men — except Jean-Guy Gagnon, we never saw much of him — some of them quite well.'

'Monsieur Duteil.'

'Went to school with his wife...but Ray Tuche, Pierre, Georges, Bruno, Didi Belfort, they were all bright young lights and very sociable, and that's my world.' Gazing around the spacious room. 'We used to see Didi all the time. We were so looking forward to an evening in this wonderful home, then he took up with her and disappeared. Can you imagine not sharing a place like this?' Rose was rueful. 'And now we've lost poor Didi too.'

Aliette agreed it would be a fine party house. 'But why,' she wondered, 'would Pearl invite people to a party if they write snide remarks about her and get things wrong?'

'That letter?' Rose smiled. 'Did you ever see anything so absurd? So tiny?'

'She stood up for herself. I think she has more character than you give her credit for.'

Rose sniffed. 'A question of being graceful. Obviously it's beyond her. We were talking about Jerôme Duteil, not her little teaching *bac*. There's something wrong with that woman. Apart from having a ruinous effect on some very good men, she's too secretive. Anti-social. If you're going to snub your nose, you should have friends around to protect you. That's what my husband says, and he's a lawyer. He should know. .'

Aliette responded to the cue. 'Don't think I've run into him. Do you have the same last name?'

'Not professionally,' said Rose, but declined to mention her husband's name. 'Pearl Serein has no friends,' she continued, 'at least none we know of. Just not interesting. Very low.' She must have noticed her host wince at this. 'Yes,' she conceded after a dainty gulp of beer, 'you're quite right: a horrible thing to say. But it's what she is. Father one of those tedious woolly men with a bookstore. A *used* bookstore. Dies...American mother gone back home. Not much of a base at all, *quoi*? No, really quite gauche and probably troubled, I've always said.' Rose reprised her smile. 'Of course a person can *make* herself interesting. What life's all about, isn't it, Inspector?'

Aliette asked, 'What about Remy Lorentz?'

'What about him?'

'Remy is quite adamant he's a friend of Pearl. Highly protective, in fact. Willing to fight.'

The eyes of *Society Notes* grew narrow. 'What are you saying?'

'Only that you could be sitting right on top of a very hot lead. For your story?'

Rose blushed slightly. 'Fight? Perhaps…He's a very hot-blooded boy. But never kill.'

'Nobody has said anyone's been killed,' replied Aliette, 'The medical-examiner says heart attacks. Seven in a row. Strange but true. A mystery, most certainly. But as such, no criminal case, not in the least.'

Rose stood, clearly slighted. 'But that would mean I do not have to discuss this any further with the likes of you.'

'I'm afraid you do, madame. Not only did you break and enter in coming here…'

'I did no such thing!' Rose went striding to the lift and pressed the call button.

Aliette followed. 'You also violated a police barrier. Both highly serious crimes.'

'I know how you people work. Don't think I don't. Michel Souviron is my good friend.'

'It is a very small town, indeed,' Aliette said. 'I almost feel like you're my cousin. Has Michel ever explained our Cousins Program? It helps us cops fit in.'

Cousins brought Rose up short. 'You know, Aliette, we could help each other, we really could. Pearl Serein is going to have to explain herself. She owes us an explanation and I have the connections to ensure she provides it, one way or another. I'm sure it will dovetail with those same legal gaps you are trying to fill. My story will open some eyes.'

'And I'm looking forward to your story.' Aliette patted Rose's arm. A dear old cousin who had never quite learned to do her lipstick. 'But if we are going to work together, it means we have to be allies and not enemies after your story hits the street. Yes? It means I'm looking forward to reading your story *first*, madame. You get a scoop,

I want it too. *D'accord*? Safety is paramount. We wouldn't want to hurt anyone who's not really involved. One lawyer is quite enough. Right, Rose?'

'I take your point.'

'And I'll trust you to keep our meeting off the record.' There was silence till the lift arrived and the door slid open. Coldly professional, Rose Saxe extended her hand. Aliette shook it. 'Rose, I am so glad you caught me. It was lovely to see you. We must do it again.'

'*Au revoir*, Inspector.' She bowed. The door closed

A little bit of fun, *oui*. But really quite a horrid Rose. *Quoi*?

Then it was back to the places a detective is meant to go: Pearl's drawers, back of closets, behind the mirror. There were no weapons, needles or vials, and not a single picture evoking time spent with the most eligible men in town. Nothing about high romance. Or murder. Nothing like that at all. Just banal souvenirs and a cherished book. The inspector sat on Pearl's bed, left unmade and chaotic like the waters in a swirling gorge, and read it again. Before throwing herself into the gorge, the desolate Maid of Nagara leaves a poem:

*From leaves of autumn flushed with love,*
*A pearl of dew shakes free*
*And falls to shatter on the earth beneath.*
*So too must I, to flee Love's stifling folds*
*Drop from the world.*

## – 20 –

## INQUISITION

You call it the Courthouse. We call it the Palace of Justice. The term is apt. History doesn't disappear, it only changes, and the notion of the palace keeps us humble. Downstairs, the courts are in session. The rotunda is the hub, a public place through which busy people revolve, conferring, advising, getting stories straight, awaiting their moment in court, or pondering a losing argument, savoring a win. Despite the activity, all voices seem hushed in pervading deference to the institution. The Law. Upstairs this sense quickens. A secretary's heels clack, disembodied...till she enters with copies for everyone. Then she sits and prepares to record the proceedings. She looks good, but it's the last thing you want to think about. These offices and antechambers are called *le Parquet*. It is here that the *procureur* and his staff and the instructing magistrates (in a separate suite) examine the pros and cons of bringing another person's life before the court. The window in this room where you are being interviewed may be open wide on a pleasant spring afternoon, but the sounds of the city don't quite touch your ears. And it is humbling, to say the least, how the rest of your senses will join with your ears in creating a memory of how free and casual (*unexamined?*) it all was just out there. It has only been two hours since you walked in that door, yet *out there* feels like a memory. A wide gulf between the Romantic and the Law. And yet—

Though Claude Néon tried to be logical and factual, a murky personal element kept seeping through. 'The first time I saw her? In the paper. My secretary showed me. She was playing tennis.'

Tennis? The three voices coming at him throughout the ordeal — divisionnaire, *procureur*, chief magistrate — were, in effect, one implacable Voice of Authority.

'At the club...the Quarter Racquets Club?'

Was she with one of them? In this picture? One of her now-deceased men?

'She was alone. Practicing alone. That was the thing. Her separateness. It was almost fierce.'

That made you attracted?

'Not at that point. I mean, not as you imply. We had three dead boyfriends—this strange coincidence with her at the center. I read about her...I looked at the available pictures. I had a hunch, and, well...' Shrugging: you know how it is?

They only stared at him. Then asked: You actually met her when?

'After the banker's funeral. She came walking into the commissariat, out of the blue, to arrange for the other's transport. Gagnon. The one from the radio.' Claude told of the letter from the morning man's mother.

That was the first time you talked. Your impression?

'I thought...I thought she was difficult.'

Hiding something?

'Possibly...No, correct that. She wasn't hiding anything... except herself, perhaps.'

The divisionnaire said, '*B'en*, what else is there to hide? Especially with murder. Eh?' A bit cranky—old cops may enjoy philosophy, but usually only their own.

Claude elaborated. 'I mean she wanted nothing to do with us. The police, the law...She was only responding to a request from the mother. Being a good citizen. She wrote her name on the form and that was that.'

'But you were, if not suspicious, what?...intrigued?'

Claude bit a nail and nodded, yes.

'Speak for the record,' prompted Procureur Michel Souviron.

'I was intrigued. But like you said, there was no tangible link.'

No modus operandi. No *how*.

Earlier, in expressing his regret for the mess which they (*all of them*) had allowed to develop, Divisionnaire Norbert Fauré had introduced an analogy: 'Like building with three sides of the foundation filled, leaving the other one floating, for pity's sake!'

Chief Magistrate Gérard Richand felt wrongly included in his damning metaphor. 'This is still an issue,' remarked Gérard, clearly looking for support from the divisionnaire.

Claude, humbled and at their mercy, mumbled, 'Yes, officially speaking, still no MO.'

Fauré's professional disgust had already been vented. He just shrugged, effectively overruling Gérard. There was something here requiring their attention, even if it meant one crucial building block—*how*—would have to be left out of the equation for the time being.

They moved on, the three of them relentless, picking it apart:

When did you first decide to tie her directly to it?

'That afternoon, after she left us. I was with one of my inspectors, talking about the case. I realized the only way in was through Pearl.'

'What case?' asked Michel Souviron, polite, but pointed, lawyerly. The language here must be precise. Officially, because of the still-undetermined status of the matter, the meeting was the public prosecutor's responsibility. A divisional police chief had seniority, hands-on experience. If an enquiry became necessary, it would belong to the instructing judge. But in this particular legal instance, Maître Souviron le Procureur had the determining power. He did not have to remind anyone. Just the same, Michel was reminding Claude.

'The *possible* case…' Thanks for that, Michel.

'Which inspector?' Gérard Richand again.

'Inspector Nouvelle.'

'Was she assigned to it?' Another trapdoor, to demonstrate a less-than-capable Néon.

Claude alertly told him, 'No one was assigned to it. It didn't exist. We were just talking.'

'I like her,' commented Norbert Fauré.

To this, Claude nodded gravely, mirroring the older man.

Then back to sequence: In any event, you proceeded?

'The press was starting to gnaw at it. I did some background. I thought it prudent.' Claude pointed to his file, and to Monique's, and related his collation of facts surrounding the lives of Pearl Serein's men: their friends, enemies, business affairs, families…

Claude had brought this material to his interview in Strasbourg but Fauré had barely given it a glance. Leafing through it now, he officially wondered, 'Had a budget for all this searching, then?'

'No…' embarrassed, 'I…I had to take a first step. I had to start somewhere.'

'But you had no case,' reminded Souviron, always unpredictable in his support and point of view, siding here, then siding there. One never knew the source of Michel's position.

A slippery Souviron was vexing. 'I had a mystery!' snapped Claude, challenging him.

It was met head on. 'An emotional mystery, perhaps. Certainly not a legal one. It would appear you were working more for yourself than the State. Why?'

Claude stared straight ahead, thinking, We contemplate, discuss, make educated guesses and informed decisions. How exactly does our kind of 'work' take form? But he resisted the urge to give a speech. He answered calmly, 'Three dead bodies. Then Georges Pugh loses another case and dies that night in the same strange way — which made four. Unexplained.'

'Heart attacks,' corrected Gérard Richand.

Norbert Fauré ignored Richand. He asked, 'Did you suspect her?'

'No…I couldn't. As you know, I spent the day with her the day Martel…'

Fauré rolled his eyes. 'And Martel made five.' They'd been through that up at Strasbourg.

Claude bowed his head to acknowledge a mistake, but had to tell him, 'She's just a schoolteacher. Everything she owns had already been handed to her, gratis — by them. She had nothing to gain. She cannot and will not believe anyone would kill on her account.'

'Maybe they didn't.' The divisionnaire sat back, tapping his belly, an old cop musing.

'Maybe they didn't,' agreed Claude.

'When exactly did you and Pearl Serein become — involved? May we use that word?'

Claude didn't need the innuendo. It offended him. Why did Fauré…why did all three of his inquisitors look so dry and skeptical?

Surely there was more to these men's collective experience in sorting through the non-technical human beginnings of a crime. Any crime you could think of. There had to be! Technically, his error was obvious and Claude Néon knew the remedy: Any connection of a personal sort—family, business, *emotional*—with the subject of an investigation and you withdraw. Disqualify yourself. Hand over the file to a neutral and preferably distant colleague, someone at the far end of the hall to whom you've never had much to say. That person will do the best job for everyone concerned. (There wasn't any such person on the PJ brigade at Rue des Bons Enfants.) If you still can't leave it—the thought of the money, the sight of her body, that nagging need to remain involved—then you ought to retire, if only for the interim (this is allowed), until the case is officially resolved and your relationship has nothing more to do with the laws of the Republic. But they were far beyond that point now. To his boss's query, he insisted once more, 'There was no connection between Pearl Serein and myself when I started on this thing.'

To which the boss rejoined, 'That is not what I asked.'

'No. Sorry...' scratching the table with a fingernail. 'I suppose it was the night of the club.'

Dancing. This was hard to fathom. Perhaps Michel understood, but he wouldn't show it at this table. Gérard's eyes clouded. Fauré's old face pinched tight. Again the basic question: What could you possibly have been thinking? Claude absorbed it. The woman recording the meeting glanced at him, professionally vacant, fingers at the ready. Claude had to keep going and make it clear he had acted as a cop, in good faith, with a view to protecting Pearl, and, by extension, the community he had sworn to serve. He had to show them he never swerved in his dedication to duty in upholding what he and *they* stood for. Truth. Justice... He patiently explained the connections tying it to the club: a filmmaker (before he ran out of money), a banker and lawyer, the noble—'who'd been frequently observed in the locker room arguing with Pugh,' *and* the sculptor, who used the place on his mother's membership card and the bizarre Bruno Martel, both of whom were clearly still obsessed with Pearl Serien '...*and* that tennis pro we picked up this morning.' Given the situation—

Not the morning man? they wondered.

'We know the morning man had applied to join.'…Given the fact it was where Pearl Serein spent most of her time, it had seemed logical and proactive for himself and Inspector Nouvelle to attend the party at the club. Not as cops, as guests.

A question from the divisionnaire, to get something straight.

'No, Inspector Nouvelle and I are not involved. We work together. We decided her presence would help deflect from mine.' Thus Claude lied…for both of them. Staff liaisons are not against the rules — too normal, too frequent — there would be few cops left if such activity were officially banned. But they were frowned upon.

Gérard Richand said, 'I thought you said she wasn't assigned to the investigation.'

'Because there wasn't one,' added Souviron.

Claude smiled. 'She wasn't assigned. She was invited. To a party. You see?'

Norbert Fauré bit into his mid-afternoon Mars Bar. Through sticky teeth, he said, 'And so?'

Claude spoke of the band. The Lonely Blue & Sad Times: 'Have you heard them?' he asked, going round the table. No? 'They do this amazing version of "Frou-Frou."' And he told of the entrance of Pearl Serein onto the dance floor, alone and suddenly in the middle of it all, at the very height of the party, highly vulnerable, and how he had instinctively moved to shield her. 'A dance was the best way to stay near.' Insisting it was lucky he did because Raymond Tuche appeared and caused a scene and Remy Lorentz provoked a fight, and the mounting music and the frantic light had sent a bad situation completely out of control.

They listened to his every word. They asked, But did she ask for protection?

'Not in so many words. But she's probably the most vulnerable woman in the city. In terms of visibility, I mean.'

But she didn't say, 'Commissaire, I'm desperate here, I need your protection, your personal protection?'

'No.'

What did she say?

'She said we could dance.'

She asked you to dance?

'No.' Claude blushed. 'I asked her. In fact I talked her into it.'

Why?

'Something came over me.'

A need to protect? They were watching him. They asked, Where was the inspector?

'The inspector had gone to freshen up. By the time she returned, the place had exploded. We were separated.'

'I'd like to hear about it from her,' said Fauré, sipping coffee.

Souviron nodded. So did Richand — who made a note. They returned to the sequence:

So you danced, ended up in the middle of a brawl and then went home with her.

'Naturally, she was upset. I should say distraught. I had to get her out of there. I escorted her home.'

Straight home? A direct allusion to the death of Tuche, which occurred within that frame.

Claude winced. He hated that they would even think it. 'Yes. Straight home.'

Confirm it?

'Ask her.'

She's missing… And did you have relations with her?

'No!' Why did this matter? 'I slept on her divan. I was protecting her.'

You keep insisting on this…

They knew this game and they would not let up till they got what they wanted. But Claude Néon knew it too and he held steady. All he could do was continue on, recounting the hours between then and now. 'Yesterday we passed the day, I interrogated her on and off, I directed my people in the search for the noble, we ate together…I went to bed alone. This morning we came down to meet you.' Not the entire story, but the part that seemed most relevant to Claude.

Norbert Fauré drained his coffee. 'But you were holding hands when you came out of the lift. Why is this? I know I'm old, but — '

'She was afraid! Terrified.'

And you were protecting her?

Claude held steady—except for his ears. They were glowing, and he knew it.

And of course they caught it. They asked, Monsieur Néon, how could you believe you could conduct a love affair and an investigation at the same time?

'I was not conducting a love affair. I was protecting her. The situation called for protection. Neither of us ever said the word love. Or sex, for that matter. In my mind, I was protecting her. I was doing my job.'

They asked: In your mind?

'Where else?'

Norbert Fauré beheld Claude Néon. He wondered, 'Where else indeed?'

Claude relaxed. They'd got him, he knew. He'd got lots of others in the same manner.

Gérard Richand said, 'Did you or did you not become physically intimate with Pearl Serein?'

'Yes… Last night. Just once.' Twice would've been much better.

There was silence. Claude Néon believed he sensed a general sympathy in the room. He imagined they were seeing him like commissaires and magistrates and *procureurs* might see an old prisoner: someone who was bad, but a man nonetheless, and one whom they had grown to know over the years of his churning through the system. He imagined it was how they might look upon this type of man after he had lost his final appeal to the State for mercy. No, it was life, it had to be life, but there was still this bond between them all… Sighing long and wistful like said lifer, Claude stood and went over to the window. He stared down at the street.

They said, Please elaborate. It could take us closer to the heart of this odd matter.

Claude realized he was number eight on a list of seven men. He felt like he was already dead as he returned to the table and told them all about it. His last words as a commissaire? The bets were not in his favor. 'Well, she's an odd woman, not that I'm an expert. No expert at all. I'm a fool.'

They nodded. They might agree. They asked, Why are you a fool?

'I wish I knew.' He meant, I wish I could tell you. Tell you about Aliette Nouvelle. Now *there's* a woman who wanted me, but I had to get this big idea. 'Yes,' mused Claude. 'Why?' The court recorder waited. He said, 'I spent a day with her asking questions. I fought to protect her at the club. I did what I could to make her see the dark potential in this thing. I comforted her when she was feeling desperate. The more I found out, the more I felt like I could give her what those seven other guys could not. She is attractive, no?' He received nods from Souviron and Richand: yes, attractive. 'It all kind of rolled together. Desire. Some lucky moves. And something inevitable, something about my life…It made me feel like I was the one. The man for Pearl. I—'

Fauré cut in, 'Damn good reason to kill someone. At least in my experience. More coffee?'

Michel Souviron, being host, rose and backed toward the door to relay the order. Neither he nor Gérard Richand could take his eyes off Claude.

Who protested, 'No! To *protect* her!' Glaring at his superior, beyond caring. 'Who do you think I am?'

'Trying to find out, aren't we,' grumbled the divisionnaire.

Claude breathed deep and continued. 'I'd questioned her. I heard her talk about the others. She seemed to like them. She refused to say a word against them. But she didn't love them. There was always something missing.'

Like what?

'She couldn't tell me. Or wouldn't…'

Was she mad at them?

'More like disappointed. Worn out by their jealousy, their possessiveness…their need?' Claude shrugged. 'And I'd seen her react to Bruno Martel. Pathetic. A big man breaking down like that? Made me squirm. Goes against the grain to see it, you know? Pearl didn't bat an eye.'

Fauré grunted, 'She sounds cold-blooded.'

Claude thought about it for a moment. 'I was asking questions about her relationships, trying to get her to help me bring out a reason for any of these guys to be done in. Pretty basic: find the reason, find the culprit, even without an established MO. Some of those questions were raw. She was totally removed. She was trying to help, but she refused to believe it. Nothing in her would react to the fact of murder. Death, yes; murder, no. Nor to the pain that might compel a man to act in such a desperate manner. Martel was in agony, crying his eyes out. Pearl just stood there. She said, Oh well, that's Bruno. Yes, it made me wonder. But I'm still thinking, if it's not them, *it must be me*. I couldn't make that thought go away. Then last evening, after all that's happened, it was finally sinking in. Murder. We're up there together and we drink some wine and we're watching the thing on television. She cried and that was my cue. I tried my move. My big move. That was when I wanted to make love to her. What I mean is, it felt like the time had really come,' said Claude, looking round the table, meeting the collective eyes of the Law. 'But no, sorry, monsieur, she didn't love me, wasn't interested in sleeping with me. I was stunned, but I backed off. I don't push it, no…no way, I don't need that kind of trouble. You know?'

'She sounds just plain cold,' muttered Souviron.

Claude indicated, No. 'It was *my* problem. Not hers. I'd misread her. This kind of thing sends you in the wrong direction. I mean all the gossip. I was looking at her and thinking I was exactly what she needed, but Pearl Serein does not see herself the way I was seeing her…or the way those seven others did. Not in the least. She just does not believe this big story about herself. Can't. Won't. I don't know. But there's a gap.'

Gérard Richand was perplexed and maybe insulted in the way a righteous judge can sometimes be. 'But you slept with her, after all?' His tone was verging on accusation.

Fuck Gérard. Claude was anxious to give them the right view on last night. 'She wasn't helping me. I was ready to back off, look at it from a different angle. Protection could still be provided, sure, but it was a mistake, a waste of time—I mean my presence there. But she cries again, so I stay over…same routine, back to the divan. It's a great place to sleep. Beautiful to see the morning from up there. She came to me later, in the middle of the night.'

With information?

'A question.'

What question?

'Are you a good cop?'
And you made love to her to show you were.
Claude ventured a smile. 'Voilà.'
And you held her hand this morning.
'It was the least I could do.'
'Romantic,' commented Norbert Fauré, the old cop, laconic.
'Not really, believe me,' responded Claude.
Then they find Belfort in the garbage and she runs.
'Yes.'
They asked: But why?...why do you think she ran...right at the point when she had actually come to trust you?
Claude replied directly. 'Because of you. She's afraid of you. Of us...of this.' The Law.
Why?
'Because she's innocent.'
What does an innocent person have to fear from us?
Claude told them, 'If everyone else gets her wrong, why would she believe that we would get her right?' Then he rested. Vague, unprofessional, but there it was. That was his story.
'And seven hearts attacks,' said Fauré, pondering the pathologist's reports. 'But still no case.'
'No,' Claude admitted for the third time, 'not strictly speaking.'
There was the matter of Didier Belfort. The City team had already found the noble's car — in Pearl Serein's parking spot down on the second level of the building parking area. First estimation from Raphaele Petrucci had put the time of death at sometime Friday afternoon or evening.
They had Captain Deubelbeiss' notes, but still they asked, Where were you Friday?
'Friday morning I was meeting with the divisionnaire...' Claude tapped his file of notes.
Fauré nodded.
'Mid-afternoon, after I got back, I was at the club for an hour or so arranging things with Gaston...'
Gaston?
'The manager. I've applied to join. Then I went back to the office.'

Fauré's eyes were hooded, bleary. 'You've applied to join this club?"

'Yes.' Claude nodded warily.

Fauré leaned forward. 'And Friday evening?'

'I was at home.' In bed, lingering over a glass of wine with Aliette Nouvelle.

'Proof?'

'No.'

'I hear you got a new place befitting your new station?' Fauré said.

Claude indicated, Yes. But it was not the time to tell the boss of his new house in the north end.

Chief Magistrate Gérard Richand swiveled in his chair, tapped his notes, edgy, eager. 'I've got so much circumstantial here.' He would love to stick it to Claude.

Procureur Michel Souviron shook his head at Gérard. 'But you still have no MO.'

They asked, Was there anything else Pearl Serein told you that might be useful?

'She told me her dream.'

They were not interested in her dream.

They excused him from the room while they conferred.

## – 21 –
## The price to pay

A preliminary investigation would be conducted by the local *Police Judiciaire*, the focus and limit of which would be a search for Pearl Serein. Inspector Nouvelle would lead and submit all findings to the divisional office at Strasbourg. City Police Commissaire Duque would conduct an investigation into the circumstances surrounding the deaths of Bruno Martel, Raymond Tuche and Didier Belfort and submit all findings to the divisional office at Strasbourg. Remy Lorentz would be detained and interviewed in depth; both teams could have access. A specialist from the medical faculty at Strasbourg would be made (officially) available to work with Dr. Petrucci in determining the means causing death, costs to be underwritten by Strasbourg. All materials gathered would be considered by the divisionnaire and presented back to the office of Judge Richand for subsequent referral to Procureur Souviron. Lack of *prima facie* evidence connecting Commissaire Claude Néon or Pearl Serein to any of the victims had been duly noted, although autopsy reports on the last two victims were still pending. (Circumstantial evidence was another matter.) That Commissaire Néon had taken obvious steps, and in good faith, to present the suspect for questioning was also taken into consideration. While the investigation proceeded, Commissaire Néon would be suspended from duty with half-pay, his status to be reviewed by Division as more facts came to light and/or when the investigation was resolved. It went without saying that Commissaire Néon would take no part, active or otherwise, in any subsequent events pertaining to the matter, apart from what might be required of him in the way of testimony in a court of law. They accorded him the benefit of the doubt concerning his claim to have no idea where Pearl Serein might be.

The fact they had left the 'murder' aspect with Duque meant it was still a big huge nothing. Everything depended on Aliette Nouvelle finding Pearl. Still, it seemed fair to Claude, looking out the window as night fell over his untended garden. Fair because it was within the rules and he deserved the benefit of the doubt. He had leveled with them. Better to sit here than in jail...

The previous autumn, when prices were down and his confidence up after eight scandal-free months as PJ commissaire, Claude Néon had dared to make a downpayment on a residence in the posh quarter north of the Parc de la République. He had told himself it was in keeping with his new status. He had since told his mother he hoped someone would live there with him some day soon. Aliette Nouvelle had stayed over a few times, including a couple of smoothly domestic weekends, but preferred the bed in her apartment. She said it was less visible. She had wanted to keep their love affair quiet — had been almost fanatical in insisting on his silence. He'd thought she was being overly cautious, maybe paranoid. Now he was glad.

Now he was lonely. Claude opened a beer, cut himself a hunk of muenster and took his meal to the salon where he reclined in front of the *télé*, a free but somewhat restricted citizen, and watched the evening news. The lead story featured pictures of the morning's big event: look at Pearl run! Look at the commissaire run!...God, do I really look like that when I run? And now here was Norbert Fauré walking. Now a uniformed cop overseeing medics loading a bagged Didier Belfort into a hearse. And the disgruntled tennis pro, still trying to take a swipe at anyone within his range as he was packed into the back of a police car. Then Cakeface, dressed to the nines in blue: *Initial reports by the examining physician point to some kind of seizure. There are no marks, no signs of violence, exactly the same circumstances surrounding the six other unlucky lovers. In the meantime, Pearl Serein has gone missing, while the last of her known boyfriends, tennis pro Remy Lorentz and Commissaire Claude Néon, have been remanded for questioning. At this point, no clear motive or clue has emerged to cast light. Although love would appear to be at the center of it all, this bizarre string of deaths seems to be out of everyone's control. The most a citizen can ask is, Where will it end?* Cake signed off, unaware that a certain blonde cop had got herself into the frame and stood there, staring, bemused, over the reporter's shoulder and out at the watching world.

It prompted Claude to call Aliette. Her phone rang and rang... Where are you?

Twenty-four hours ago Claude could look down and see her apartment.

Not any more. He had returned to ground level.

There was shame. There was anger. A void in the vicinity of his heart was primary to both.

How to deal with it? Claude was not what you would call a reader. It was another reason Aliette had said she felt slightly out of her territory in his house: no books. ('Read, Claude. Don't become an old man who sits in front of the television. Nothing more pathetic.') Apart from the newspaper and a couple of best-sellers on management strategy, all he had to read were gardening columns. Having been raised in a 4th floor apartment in deepest, darkest Paris, Claude knew precious little about gardening. With the arrival of spring, Monique had been assigned the task of going through *Le Cri du Matin* gardening column in search of tips that might help her boss keep pace with community standards, because Claude's new home came with a garden he would be obliged to tend, the neighborhood being what it was. *Mon beau jardin*, twinned with the bird column on the back page of the second section, was overleaf from *Le Vrai Tommi*.

Claude was wishing he'd remembered to take that book as they left Pearl's place this morning. Evolutionary psychology: fascinating stuff about instincts. It had told him his own instincts were on the mark...that he was making the right moves, because when it came to natural selection and propagation of the species, female genes perceived a house in the north end as the most secure of nests to be feathered. But now? He had overshot the north end, hadn't he? Apparently. *Oui*. Bedazzled by the highest nest in the city, Claude had flown too high and something had gone wrong. What had possessed him? After all, he was just a cop. Perhaps the answer lay farther along in that same book... But there was no way he could risk going back and removing it from her place. Even if he pulled it off, he had already removed it once from another place (Gagnon's), and they would surely notice. He was not sure it wouldn't be a mistake to go and buy his own copy. They'd be watching him closely and drawing lots of conclusions, reading motivation into his every move.

No way he'd give that bastard Gérard Richand the slightest further crumb of circumstantial.

He considered the reading materials which remained at hand. But he was not of a mind for gardening columns. Or birds. He couldn't bear the thought of that cretin Bonneau. And now that he was temporarily out of the office, management gurus were not much comfort.

What about some music, then? Slapping it in. Turning it up to fill the space.

But the hard, fighter thing that usually connected him to his favorite band was just not there.

All Claude Néon really had for diversion was the television.

He sat, counting the hours till the late news report was aired, when he might see it all again.

# Part 2

The experience of romantic love is beyond all conditions, claiming devotion beyond all bounds... Romance feels fateful, feels like kismet, karma, destiny.

— James Hillman, *The Soul's Code*

## – 22 –

## A VERY SPECIFIC MANDATE

Tuesday morning, *Local Scene* cited the previous evening's television coverage:

*Did you see her face on your screen last night? I am speaking of Pearl in flight, her fear telegraphed, canceling her beauty. And did you see the artless buffoons trying to catch her? What a travesty! It has been close to three years since our Pearl and Didier Belfort shared the limelight. His was a sad fall, so unbecoming — the stories one could tell! …then dying the way he did, in such an ignominious manner, literally in the shadow of the palace he bestowed upon our Pearl. And now seven men are dead.*

*For those of us who study the ways of the heart, there is something truly dark at play here.*

*What is going on? We must have results — and the truth!*

'Bizarre,' was Dr. Gilles Conan's only comment as he laid the paper aside and accepted a cup of Raphaele Petrucci's famous cappuccino.

'She's the reason you're here, Doctor,' said Raphaele.

Conan smiled. 'I'd like to meet her.'

The renowned cardiac specialist from the university-affiliated wing of Hôpital Jeanne D'Arc had wandered into Raphaele's morgue yesterday without airs or introduction. It had been a chaotic morning dealing with the discovery of Didier Belfort. Raphaele had been up and down the stairs four times as jurisdictional priorities were clarified — whom you reported to made a difference in how you reported. The body had just been delivered, he was standing there, exhausted, gazing down at his newest customer, sharing the blank solitude of the dead the way he sometimes did, when the morgue door had squeaked and swished. '*Oui?*' Raphaele did not even look up, assuming yet more functionary communication from upstairs.

'Doctor Petrucci?'

Conan stood there, bag in hand, like someone's long-lost bachelor uncle. Into his sixties and a little ruddy in the cheeks, snowy hair thinning, but a twinkle in his gray eyes, and admirably trim and spiffy in green suede shoes, gray flannel, Harris tweed. Raphaele Pretrucci recognized him of course and adjusted instantly, welcoming the great man with cappuccino and biscotti. Apologizing in advance as he presented his notes, he pulled five hearts from a refrigerated drawer. 'Radio, cinema, law, God knows…' referring to the heart of Bruno Martel, 'and fine art,' tapping the tray marked Tuche. All he had were notes on the banker's heart. For this, he apologized again.

Conan made a joke about the lawyer's heart being a darker shade.

He complimented the coffee. The biscotti. (God bless you, mama!)

Then he donned smock and gloves and together they removed the heart of Didi Belfort.

Raphaele soon relaxed. 'I should have got them all,' he confessed, but he'd let the banker's get away. Dr. Conan averred that the banker was a senior citizen and in that sense an anomaly as regards pathology. Raphaele confessed again. 'I know I jumped the gun with victims two and three. But losing number one like that, I felt a sense of scientific duty and…' He shrugged: why not? A heart's not much use to the dead, much less the dead's family, whereas the police maintain a genuine interest that covers both the near and far sides of life. (In his role as *légiste,* Dr. Raphaele Petrucci definitely considered himself to be a policeman.) Then a third confession, this one existential: 'People think we're ghouls,' he murmured. He needed commiseration, if not approbation, '…and there were only two to start and it was just coincidence.' And Raphaele hastened to add that Strasbourg *had* granted permission to take the lawyer's, and, well, with these final three, he'd just assumed and gone on harvesting.

Conan smiled. 'It's hard in this old culture. My friends in America order them by the dozen.'

It did the younger man's heart a world of good. Shades of the mentor he never had.

They'd spent an enjoyable first afternoon analyzing and collating data.

This morning Conan was set to meet the investigators and provide his initial thoughts. It was coming up ten when Inspector Nouvelle and Commissaire Duque escorted Instructing Judge Gérard Richand into the morgue. Dr. Conan, polite yet perfunctory in greeting the two males, beamed as he shook the blonde inspector's hand. 'My friend Norbert has told me all about you.'

She asked straight off, 'And what do you think of our mystery?'

'It is enticing, Inspector.'

The judge followed directly. 'Any ideas where we might be headed?'

Direct and rather blunt. Gérard Richand had made it clear he did not like having his judgements manipulated from above. He believed they were wasting time and money. He resented Néon's gaffe on an almost personal level. In his way, Gérard had practically promised to be no help at all.

Aliette had warned Raphaele.

He'd promised their visitor would be carefully prepped as to the prevailing power structure.

So Gilles Conan was politely circumspect in telling Gérard, 'We've barely begun.' He mentioned the equipment he'd ordered sent from his lab up north.

'But have you ever seen anything like it?'

'Do you mean like heart attacks?'

'I mean like murder. I mean like physical evidence for same, Doctor.'

'Of course.' Personal biases aside, it *is* the instructing judge's duty and prerogative to ask the toughest questions. Conan knew that. Fetching his notes, he was thoroughly businesslike in perusing his preliminary findings...making the skeptical Richand stand back and wait.

Dr. Conan offered a professorial smile. 'Would a hormone satisfy you?'

Gérard Richand tilted his head. 'Which hormone?' His wife was obsessed with them.

'Noradrenaline.' Gesturing at the six hearts in their respective trays. 'These hearts are awash in the stuff, relatively speaking. I would guess the banker's was as well.'

'Noradrenaline,' repeated Judge Richand, suddenly bemused, staring at the organs.

'You can call it adrenaline.'

'From anger?' asked Aliette.

'Or fear,' said Raphaele.

'Or elation…even love,' continued the doctor. 'These emotions all register in the same place in the brain. 'That,' he stated, for the pleasure of Gérard Richand, 'is a physical fact.'

'But…' Richand sensed the next obvious question. You could see him groping to form it.

Honest scientist that he was, Conan helped him. 'But extrapolating beyond the boundary of the body is something else again. The external catalysts for each may be a world apart. And they may not be physical.'

Inspector Aliette Nouvelle was not as tied to the strictly rational as was Chief Magistrate Gérard Richand. The metaphysical, the *totally* irrational—these are often central to a criminal action, if not a police solution. She asked, 'Can a person really die of a broken heart?'

Doctor Conan was a scientist of the highest level. Perhaps for that very reason he did not automatically disdain metaphysical discussions relating to the heart. Not even when standing beside six pieces of raw meat aligned in trays. 'Same as dying of fright, more or less,' he replied. 'There are people down the hall at the faculty considering that very question. A spouse dies, the other follows shortly after for no apparent reason. They say he or she died of a broken heart. They're actually talking about unresolved stress throwing the heart into an irregular and fatal beat. They're trying to see how the emotion—in the brain—can change the electrical activity in the heart. It centers around the insular cortex, the same place which handles fear and anger. The insular cortex is like a junction point, you see?…where the autonomic nervous system, which controls automatic things like breathing and heartbeat, links up with the limbic nervous system, which is apparently the domain of fear, pleasure, stress, sexual arousal and the like. We know stress floods the heart with stimulating chemicals but we're still not sure of the sequence of events in the brain required to start the flood. Some think this place in the brain could be the key to sudden cardiac deaths.'

'Like these?'

'Just like these. Emotional catalysts: quite a fascinating juncture between pure physiology and, well, our poetic side.' Conan smiled. 'Seems we can't get away from it, even in pure science.'

Soon they were discussing love and death, probing links and overlapping perceptions — nexus points, as it were. Aliette Nouvelle was thinking she had an ally. One sensed Gilles Conan knew well enough how the heart is a main avenue connecting man the brute machine with the creature capable of sonnets. How love, the high and the low of it, is felt most physically in the heart — overpoweringly so at those most human moments, those times when we can't help ourselves from blurting, I never felt so alive! And how death is always a possible result.

'But murder,' argued Gérard Richand. 'You still haven't drawn the connection here. Not in the legal sense. Please tell me why in the world should we even think it's possible?'

In truth, an esteemed heart specialist didn't honestly know. 'Because there are always limits and there are always possibilities, and the heart will pull in both directions?' At this point, it was all Gilles Conan could offer.

Commissaire Duque spoke to support him. 'And because accessories must share the result of the action.' Meaning accessories to crime. Meaning the action causing death. Which is a legal fact.

'Anger, love, fear: your accessory is metaphysical.' Was how Gérard Richand saw it.

Conan asked, 'How can you investigate what you don't recognize as a possibility?'

Richand riposted, 'Exactly.'

Too quick; immediately frowning as the deeper implication filtered through his logic.

Aliette thought, Gérard, if scientists and cops can bring imagination, shouldn't judges too?

Duque, enjoying himself, said, 'It goes to intent, Gérard.' Which is a workable premise.

Sipping cappuccino, they continued to bat these notions up and down a row of stainless steel trays containing hearts. They passed around the collection of police photographs. A photograph of death is useful because so starkly compelling. But it also always seems like the ultimate oxymoron, requiring a thousand if not a million words you know will never come. 'Blood pressure could easily factor,' commented Conan as they contemplated the whale-like corpse of Bruno Martel. And likely many other things they were bound to find—in all of them. 'The sculptor's anti-depression meds were made to slow his electricity down. Being over-excited and lost in a barrage of strobe lights would be like walking barefoot through a lightning storm with antennae strapped to your head.' Because of these factors, Dr. Conan remained dryly objective. Yes, he was interested in the problem as it related to broken-hearted lovers. 'We're always on the lookout for any sorts of new directions...' But he would give reality its due. There had to be physical circumstances. Life *is* physical. Death too.

The most compelling exhibit on display was the fact of fatal coincidence.

But Gérard Richand did not come away convinced of a criminal act. He would wait for the expert from Strasbourg to offer him something more substantial than adrenaline, or till the police could provide him with evidence more rational than the idea of a life without Pearl Serein. He wanted something proving criminal intent before he would allow them to proceed as such.

Until such evidence was produced, Commissaire Duque's team really had no job at all.

And Aliette's mandate would remain severely limited: Find the woman. *Bon courage*.

## – 23 –

## A QUESTION OF CO-ENABLING

Inspector Nouvelle knew she needed to find out more from Tommi Bonneau. His 'story' demanded fuller explanation. The gossip's relationship to Pearl Serein's lovers was mean-spirited, bordering on antagonistic, but his relationship to Pearl was downright strange. The inspector's mandate did not provide for an *interpeller* order on Tommi. Nor did Commissaire Duque's. Meaning they could not compel him to talk. And even if Gérard Richand could be coaxed into summoning him, Tommi's editor would very likely fight it tooth and nail.

A prudent cop with scant wiggle room did not go rushing back to the house in Rue Pontbriand. No, Aliette took Monique's file of collected clippings and headed down to the courthouse, where she sat with Substitute Procureur Maître Cécile Botrel. They had worked closely together on the case against Flossie Orain. They trusted each other. 'Have you been following this thing?'

'Hard not to, at least this past week. Before that, no…not really my crowd.'

'But what do you think about it?'

'She's so bland looking.'

Which was interesting, if not useful. Cécile Botrel was gay.

Opening the file, the inspector found a clipping from a November day the previous autumn and passed it to Cécile: **Local Scene:** *High-flying defense attorney Georges Pugh seemed to be wearing two left shoes yesterday, wandering in aimless circles as he made a mockery of both the principle of a reasonable defense and his own golden reputation at the extortion trial of Bertrand Loftus…*another one of George's lovely clients, now gone away for at least six years thanks to the above-mentioned aimless argument. *That's three losses in a row for*

*Georges since the loss of Pearl. Following so sadly on the stumbling heels of Didi Belfort, Pierre Angulaire, and Jerôme Duteil, it appears bad luck is stalking those whom Pearl finds wanting!*

The sub-proc crinkled her nose, amused. She had lost a big case or two to Maître Pugh. 'Georges deserved a lot of things, but probably not that...Insult to injury. Pretty tasteless.'

'But he's on to something. Pugh was in a tailspin...' Tastelessness aside, Bonneau was right: Georges Pugh had started screwing up last autumn. The man had appeared lost, separated from his talents, failing utterly in front of everyone, his entire identity unraveling. It had been happening since his break-up with Pearl Serein. 'Same applies to Duteil, Gagnon, Angulaire... All of them. In a slide. Depressed, off-guard, vulnerable. Because of Pearl Serein.'

'And so? It's just back-page bullshit.'

'He calls it news of the soul. His readers hang on every word.'

'And depressives are known to suffer heart attacks. But that's not why you're here, Inspector.'

'No. It's her...it's these.' Pages of images. Tommi's commentary. 'I'd like your opinion.'

'My opinion is it's a low-level fantasy.'

'But what about Article 9?' The privacy law. Some French celebs live off it, suing anyone who uses their image without their negotiated permission. 'Why hasn't she sued him for his fantasy?' Aliette pulled the shot of Pearl on the city steps after the Duteil funeral, passed it across the table, quoting the cutline, 'Could it have ended differently?...It's like he blamed her for the death of Jerôme Duteil.' Spreading more pages in front of Cécile Botrel. 'Take a closer look. It's like *she's* the one who's responsible for these men's disastrous fall from grace.'

'And their dying?'

'You tell me. The fact is, they are dead. Now he's aiming at Claude.'

Maître Botrel sipped her coffee. 'What a stupid man he's turning out to be.'

Aliette bit her tongue and held her peace. Cécile began to read.

Pearl Serein had first appeared in *Le Vrai Tommi* two and half years prior, after an item on Brigitte Bardot's decision to sue her village veterinarian for allegedly aiding and abetting her schnauzer's heartbreaking addiction to champagne: *On the local sports scene, my spies at the Quarter Racquets Club inform me that interesting architect and international man-about-town Didier Belfort has a mighty serve. At six foot six and with a family fortune to back him up, who could doubt it? But news from the Tennis Section is that schoolteacher Pearl Serein's return is rock solid. Quite the match, I hear.*

Three weeks later, *Members of Primary One at Ecole Marthe-Richard took a day-trip across the bridge yesterday and into the Black Forest, where they made a tour of four-hundred-year-old Villa Freiss. Leading the way through the dark passages was none other than Freiss scion Didier Belfort. Making sure no one got lost and never heard from again was Pearl Serein, mistress to both the wide-eyed kinder and blue-eyed Monsieur B. The stuff of storybooks, n'est-ce pas?*

There followed notes on sightings at society parties and trendy bars throughout that autumn. Pearl the schoolteacher was invariably described as looking good, radiant, et cetera. But then, *Didier Belfort stomped out of Club Diabolik last night. The occasion was meant to be a celebration of Pierre Angulaire's new doc on the architect's contributions to the cityscape. Sources say the display might have had something to do with the ability of D's girl Pearl and Pierre A. to boogie through two straight sets!*

The next instalment found Pierre Angulaire's name in place of Didi Belfort's: *I'm told by those who know that director Pierre Angulaire has been screen-testing Pearl Serein. Neither the acclaimed filmmaker nor the much admired schoolteacher will say what's cooking. However, Pearl's leading man was heard telling a mutual friend 'it's only a test—but I believe she's got that magic.' Magic! We love magic!* Pearl and Pierre were beautiful. They lasted till mid-summer.

Then, *Pierre Angulaire tried to sell a dream but ended up losing the farm to the bank. In this case the farm is Pearl Serein, and the bank is banker Jérôme Duteil. Apparently it happened over lunch. A business lunch. This city's north end is still reeling.* A week later Tommi duly reported that Pierre had been spotted wandering in a disoriented way through Parc de la République in the rain, *lost without his rudder in a summer storm*, the clear result of having split with Pearl Serein.

Cécile Botrel blinked. 'Ouch!...He really does know how to kick a man when he's down.'

Aliette said, 'But it's part of the story.'

Then Tommi asked, *Who is this Pearl Serein? A lot of people are wondering, most particularly a well-known film director and the wife of a certain banker. We can hear a chorus out there, whispering it up and down the line. Where is she headed? What exactly is her risk rating?*

Cécile Botrel flipped though more pages. 'Does she never get to say anything?'

'Not a word,' confirmed the inspector, adding, 'This is what's so strange.'

Pearl Serein simply continued on, appearing to enjoy it—for a while.

Then: *Double loss breaks the banker...* when Georges Pugh successfully defends morning man J-G Gagnon against Jerôme Duteil's defamation suit (under Article 9), Georges becomes Pearl's new tennis date. Some excellent doubles action. Then: *One would think a man of Maître Georges Pugh's skills might be capable of making a better case when it comes to love...* as Pearl leaves Georges for Raymond Tuche. Georges goes into his tragic slide.

Then: *Raymond Tuche was spotted crying alone at a table yesterday afternoon, a table shared for eight magical weeks with our Pearl...* 'Poor Ray was reduced to blobs of clay.'

Cécile Botrel sipped coffee. '*Our* Pearl?'

'She's their star. The brightest in this corner of the universe. According to Tommi.'

'It is very weird. And still she says nothing?'

'Not for the record.' Aliette frowned, pointing to Tommi's shot of Pearl out shopping, tight-lipped, empty-eyed...and yes, very bland.

Then Jean-Guy Gagnon climbs into the saddle, starts calling his Pearl on-air. Tommi enjoys their lovey-dovey morning chats; though he taunts Pearl, exhorts her to *have a heart!* when she declines J-G's on-air proposal.

'But who in their right mind would accept like that?'

'No one. That's the thing. Claude said she refuses to buy into it.'

Then: *A morning man's rude wake-up call...* Pearl tells Jean-Guy, on-air, that she's in need of some time alone, that she's heading up to the Bruno Martel's spiritual farm for some serious introspection...Jean-Guy weeps on-air! And Tommi records the moment for his gentle readers. Then the pictures of Bruno and Pearl on a snowy mountainside. Excited notes about the couple's spiritual journey. But Pearl leaves Bruno on Valentine's Day. *Large tears!* writes Tommi.

And Pearl disappears from the *Local Scene*. 'Till two weeks ago.'

Sub-Proc Cécile Botrel was perplexed. 'What is duo-innering?'

'God knows...So what about Article 9? Could she go there?'

Botrel jolted slightly. Shaking herself loose from Tommi's gentle fantasy? 'She could if she had a mind to. Several times...almost every time.'

'So why doesn't she?'

'No idea.' Musing, 'It would be interesting to know. Although: most of those muckers have money set aside specifically for Article 9 suits, and they don't mind spending it because the profits outweigh the costs. A princess shagging in the swimming pool is worth a lot of money.'

'But they don't share it with the princess.'

'No. But I gather she has done quite well from this...story?' The inspector nodded to confirm — very well. The sub-proc mulled it for another moment. 'There's also the gap between calumny and malicious gossip. Maybe she fears having to explain where that lies.'

'Maybe. But she is not a gold-digger. Claude is certain.'

'For what that's worth.'

The inspector would not argue Claude's credibility.

Maître Cécile Botrel said, 'Look, if this Bonneau was a drunk, she'd be a co-enabler. But this is Article 9. A judge would tell him to stop, if she asked that it be so.' With a shrug, she began to put the clippings back in a neat pile. 'But Gérard Richand could have told you that.'

'Gérard doesn't want to hear about it. He finds it too demeaning. Like Claude affected him personally. Very angry. He won't allow this to be a part of it.' Collecting the file. Rising to leave.

'Gérard sounds a bit like her,' said Cécile Botrel. Like Pearl?... 'Merci, madame le Maître.'

---

There was lonely inspiration in a Japanese novel. But there was something else at play. It was the structure of the thing. The situation could not have existed without rumor, built into the medium of the so-called 'story.' Envy, curiosity, ambition, pride: a soapy drama of doomed celebrity. It took two to make it happen. The one who strung it all together. The woman at the center. Where *was* Pearl Serein? And why? The inspector met daily with her team.

'We've got an APB out all over the region. Trains to Paris, trains beyond.'

Had Pearl sufficient time to get herself beyond?

'I think she's closer...With a friend. Or...' Who?

'Unless she jumped a plane to America.'

'Run to her mama? Where was it?'

'Connecticut.'

Several members of the team took a try at pronouncing it. No one knew if they had it right.

'People do,' conceded Inspector Nouvelle. People run back to their mothers all the time. She herself was often tempted. *You know we're always here, dear*...But there was no sign of it at the airport, an easy half-hour away, neither in the security video log nor in airline receipts. The inspector wondered if Pearl's mother—in...Connecticut?—even knew of her daughter's situation.

Signs in Pearl's kitchen suggested they talked. 'Have we contacted her?'

Not yet. Everyone sat there—looking to her.

'I will.' It *was* her responsibility.

She went to her phone, spent half an hour getting the connection. It was still morning in America. A stilted chat—all in French, Pearl's mama spoke good French—yielded up the claim that there were no relatives of note nearby. As for friends?

'I wouldn't know, Madame Inspector. Not anymore.'

'Did you hear about this?'

'Well, yes… I hadn't heard tell of *him* for years. They used to be such good friends.'

'Pearl and Tommi?'

'I mean when they were very young… Now I gather he hunts her like one of his birds.'

Aliette assured her there was no need to come. Not yet. Promised to keep her informed.

And wondered what to do with *that*: Used to be such good friends.

## – 24 –
## AdrénalineAlors!

Captain Mathieu Deubelbeiss produced a file and dropped it on the table. '*Traceurs.*'

'No!' Forensics specialist Jean-Marc Pouliot was momentarily boggled. 'Are they *here* now? Where they pretend they're cavemen swinging through the forest? Ally-Oop?'

'Seems they are,' said Deubelbeiss.

*Traceurs. Free runners.* Also known as *parkourists*. The term *parkour* ties the idea of *le parcours*—a route, a journey—to *le cour*—a city courtyard. Climbing walls, leaping narrow chasms from roof to roof, the idea is to emulate the challenge faced by early man in getting from point A to point B before the concept of the road occurred. A *traceur* plots (traces) a course.

And it did indeed appear that this extreme sport which originated in the concrete jungles of the Paris suburbs had arrived in our provincial city. Mathieu Deubelbeiss explained that the city police had been receiving sporadic complaints from citizens hearing footsteps through their ceilings in the dead of night, 'but no one thought to think of these *traceurs* till Sophie here,' tapping the file, 'kind of fell into our lap.' A teenaged girl who'd ended up in hospital after misjudging a jump while following her boyfriend across the city skyline. 'Saturday night. They only come out at night.' The girl was an aberration. 'They're mainly male, in gangs, mainly from the HLM's.' Low-rent apartment blocks in ugly housing projects. All the activity surrounding Pearl Serein had left the matter un-investigated. 'Too new. Didn't make the connection till just now. Not at all.'

'They're not exactly cavemen,' Aliette ventured. 'There's a lot of very calculated style.'

'So we gathered,' Deubelbeiss agreed. 'And not your gangs of car-thief druggies, either. Ultra-fit. You'd have to be, the risks they take. It's like a religion for them, the way Everest is for climbers. They live for it. Sophie says it's the biggest adrenaline rush of all.'

Inspector Nouvelle wondered, 'But do they go around scaring people to death?'

Deubelbeiss signaled negative. 'I got the sense they couldn't be bothered. It seems it's only about themselves. A challenge. A way of proving themselves, an identity thing.' He passed her a piece of official paper. 'Sophie will tell you all about it. Very passionate.'

'Interesting,' mused Jean-Marc, '...from evolutionary psychology to *le parkour*, so many people tapping into prehistoric imperatives for fun and inspiration.'

Yes, and even in a dullish mid-sized city. Something was definitely in the air.

The pale girl in traction in room 454 at Hôtel Dieu already had a visitor—probably a boyfriend. Neither was too happy when the nurse ushered in the police. 'Mademoiselle Sophie Glarr?' The inspector met grim, taunting silence. It took a flash of her ID card for the girl to answer, '*Oui*,' and the boy to back away from the bed. 'Please. I'd like to talk to you for a minute.'

'What about?' demanded the boy. Automatic. Automatically surly.

'I'd like to talk to Sophie, monsieur, five minutes...'

Boy and girl traded glances. White girl, probably local—the pale Germanic face, a Maghreb-tinted boy. Lots of varied young people were finding each other these days, mainly in the HLM's, anything could happen when you were hanging around waiting for something to do. If they stuck it out and made a life, their babies would be beautiful. Sophie Glarr shrugged—with her eyes. Her face was the only part of her she could move. The boy backed reluctantly out of the room.

Aliette asked, 'What happened?'

'I fell.'

'But why were you even up there?'

'Why shouldn't I be?'

'Not your property.'

Sophie Glarr shook her head, just slightly, it was all she could manage, but the message was clear: another stupid cop. 'I go where he goes.' Her look said, That's the story, lady. Don't bother me about 'property' because I just don't care.

'But you slipped.'

No response.

'Is it fun?'

Fun? Sophie eyes met Aliette's. She murmured, 'It's about something you'll never understand.'

The door opened, the boy was standing there. 'Yamakazi,' he said. Same frank eyes as Sophie's. Aliette waited for an explanation. 'In Zaire it means a strong spirit in a strong man.'

'Or woman,' reminded Sophie, challenging him.

'You have to prove it to yourself,' said the boy.

'You're not from Zaire,' said Aliette.

'It was the name of the first crew — in Paris.'

'Crew?'

'We travel with our friends.'

'What's your crew called?' This was posed to Sophie. Sophie's eyes looked past Aliette.

She turned. The boy was unbuttoning his shirt. She read *AdrénalineAlors!* hand-painted in glowing orange across the black T-shirt covering his wiry but obviously muscled chest.

## - 25 -
## SOME PREHISTORY

She walked into *Le Cri du Matin* on a whim, and found Tommi Bonneau in a corner of the sprawling newsroom, in a cubbyhole next to Births and Deaths. He was on the phone. He nodded a *bonjour* as he scribbled notes. She backed away. Five minutes later, ringing off, he gestured her in. 'My source in Cannes. Big time of the year for me. I'd head down if it weren't the Pearl crisis.' Tommi looked horrible, like he hadn't slept in a week. He shifted into business mode. 'How can I help you, Inspector?'

'I need some background.'

He shrugged. He did not have to ask on whom.

She sat down, pulled out her notebook, found a clean page. 'I gather you're old friends.'

'*B'en*, we grew up together. Primary, high school, the whole bit.' This was no big secret.

'I'm not from here, monsieur.'

'Neither is that fool you work for.'

Breathing deep, rolling with it, she suggested, 'Let's stick to Pearl, shall we? And you.'

'Are you friends with everyone you grew up with?'

Again. 'Not me, Tommi. *You*. Pearl…Please.'

He smiled. That teasing thing. He asked, 'You going to tell me your source here?'

The inspector told him flatly, 'No.'

His smile disappeared. He seemed mystified. By stupid police? Tommi sat back in his chair. 'We *all* grew up together, Inspector. Except Jerôme Duteil, obviously. But even old Jerôme was a local boy. Different neighborhoods, mind you — only weird Ray Tuche and snobby Didi were born and bred north-enders. If memory serves, Didi even had a class or two with Pearl after he was booted from some posh Swiss school. I told you: This is very local. Our very own fairy tale. Everyone knows everyone in this place. But friends?' A shake of his head. He waited.

'And what about her?'

'We haven't said three words in... Lord, twenty years.'

'So you must hate her.'

'Hate her? What are you talking about? Why would I hate her?'

'For ignoring you. For never saying a word. For making your life so difficult.'

'On the contrary, Pearl's silence makes her *better* for my story.' His smirky smile flashed. 'And she doesn't totally ignore me. Look at the pictures. My camera knows she's looking. Always. Mm?' He rolled his bloodshot eyes, perplexed that she would even suggest such a thing. 'But it's not personal, Inspector. It's a *story*. I'm a journalist. I'm here to dig out the story. The real story. The story *behind* the story. You know?' Tommi sniffed, gruff, dark. 'I mean, if I did happen to be interested, in the sense of, you know, *interested*...yeah, sure, I'd probably be pounding the wall, cursing Pearl. But I'm not...' He sat up, leaned across his desk. 'Ask her.'

'I will. When I find her.'

Tommi folded his long arms and considered Aliette. 'Where do you think she is?'

'It's why I'm here, Tommi... Maybe there's a trail somewhere in the background.'

'What do you need to know?'

'Why aren't you interested?'

'She's not my type... Never was.'

'What type is that?'

'I don't know. She was into sports. I was quiet. I had a camera...' A shrug, remembering. 'I was a quiet boy with a camera getting interesting shots of birds, Inspector. It got me my first job, but not too many dates.'

'A quiet boy with a camera?' Aliette risked a smile. 'You realize you're describing the perfect serial killer?'

The smile earned a spontaneous laugh. 'I'm flattered...I think. No, we were pals when we were kids, but by the time we got to the point of liking in a boyfriend-girlfriend way, we'd gone our separate ways. She was really into her tennis, and…I don't know. Jocks, I guess.'

'Like Remy Lorentz?'

'He was an asshole then and he's an asshole now. For me it was birds and *mon appareil*…' patting his trusty camera, there on the desk at his right hand; 'all I cared about. Yes, we've always known each other but our paths never crossed again till all this.'

'The story.'

'*C'est ça.*'

'I wonder why she never sues…I mean—if it's no longer personal.'

'Because as soon as she sues, she admits she's a star. A hero! Our Pearl rolls through 'em like the mountain rain. Beautiful!…I'm no shrink, but I think she hates the idea of all that responsibility. Lots of dissonance there for sure. One of these days we're going to find out where she goes to work it out. In the meantime, we can imagine her turbulent passion, Pearl's fingernails clawing into the next man's back. Eh, Inspector?' Aliette recoiled. He smirked. 'One wonders how to please her. And who? That's the key to a happy ending. No?'

She recovered. 'Everybody wants one.'

'Néon scared her…Obviously. Why did she feel the need to run?'

Aliette signaled no, she wouldn't go there. Background, Tommi…back, back. She asked, 'But how did Pearl suddenly arrive on the scene? Is there a beginning prior to the beginning of Pearl Serein and Didi Belfort that I should know about?'

'Not really.'

'What does that mean?' Not really wouldn't do—not with seven suspicious deaths. 'Was she in a convent? Was she living in América?'

'With her American mother? I believe I know who you've been talking to, Inspector…Either of those would be excellent starting points. The boring fact is she was with Remy Lorentz and—'

'With?'

'They were going out. She was teaching kindergarten—no way she could be a member of that place on what she was making—he was earning his keep batting balls to members. She would come to play with him there. Somehow Didi Belfort got her number, called, she said yes. And it started.'

'What do you mean, somehow?'

'That has never been clarified. If you people bring her in for questioning, do me a favor and ask her how she got hooked up with Didi. My readers would love to know.'

'We wouldn't tell you, Tommi.'

'Well, maybe in court. This would definitely come to light in court.'

'Maybe…' Maybe in court. 'His cousin says he was on his way to give you a beating on Friday morning.'

'Didi?' Tommi laughed, delighted. Then surmised, 'He may have been a bit perturbed after our encounter at Diabolik.'

'Which you neglected to mention.'

Tommi met her eyes. 'I believe I mentioned seeing him there. I may not have mentioned his state of mind. So much of what I do depends on the exclusive, Inspector. Please don't take it personally. And I'll do same for you. OK?'

'OK.'

'Didi's got a good eye for space. The rest of him's out to lunch. Drug addict…Didi couldn't beat an earthworm. Anyway, I never saw him. I was not quite home on Friday morning.'

'Could you prove that?'

'Sure.'

'Nice girl?'

'So far, so good.'

She asked, 'Why not ask Remy Lorentz how Didi got her number?'

'I did. He just spat at me. Total cretin, I'm not kidding. My readers would never consider Remy Lorentz to be one of Pearl's boys. Socially, he's just not in the same stratosphere. It's prehistory—you kiss below a certain level, it doesn't register.' With an imperious wave of his large hand, Tommi dismissed Remy Lorentz.

'And the others. Were you friends? Before?'

'It was a big school. You knew people, kind of…but we were all too different. Ray Tuche was an arrogant mental case and Didi was living in another century. You learned how to work around those kinds. Bruno Martel was…just boring, basically. Bruno surprised a lot of people later on with his success. Me for sure. Georges and Jean-Guy were OK, I suppose. But different crowds. Pierre and I were in the camera club together, but, you know…' A shrug. 'We could talk about photography but not much else. We drifted apart. We all drifted apart, the way everyone drifts off and into their own life. It's normal… No, it was just Remy. And Pearl. Same street. But too much history. I doubt I'd have ever run into any of them again if they hadn't moved me over from birds.'

'Then it was war.'

'No, Inspector. Then it was *love*. I heard about Didi and Pearl. I saw a story that fit perfectly with where they'd put me. I went for it. Added some local value to my product. Voila.'

She put her notes away, eased back into her coat. 'Any idea where she might be?'

'None. That damn cop…'

She warned him silently. His eyes were bleak. Extending a hand, she thanked him for his time.

# Transcript of interview with Remy

Chief Instructing Judge Gérard Richand opened the inter-office courier envelope and removed the transcript of a recorded interview conducted by Inspector A. Nouvelle with Remy Lorentz.

AN: Remember me?

RL: No.

AN: I saw you at the club the other night.

RL: Good for you... What the fuck am I doing in here?

AN: Surely this has been made clear. You have to explain your relationship to Pearl Serein, and—

RL (sound of subject hitting bars with fist): I've told five different people! We are just friends!

AN: —and anyone else who might be connected to her situation.

RL: This is bullshit!

AN: Please. You mustn't speak like this... Especially to the judge. He will assume you have something to hide and keep you here till he finds out what.

RL (silence for extended moment): She was terrified. She needed someone. Anyone could see it.

AN: I tend to agree... But Judge Richand wasn't there. You have to stay calm and lay it all out for him.

RL: Thanks for nothing.

AN: You know, monsieur, in point of fact, she did have someone.

RL: Who?

AN: Us. The police.

RL: That Néon? He's a jerk-off.

AN: Perhaps it's all just bad timing. Your movements on Tuesday evening two weeks ago?

RL: We went through all this on Sunday...On Tuesday I finished my teaching day with Maître Pugh. I practiced alone for a bit. I went for a run, I came back to the club, I had my shower and left.

AN: Where did you go?

RL: To see a friend.

AN: Pearl Serein? (Silence...) You did say she was your friend.

RL: No.

AN: Which friend, then?

RL: A friend who has nothing to do with this insanity. My movements can all be accounted for.

AN: A friend who has a key to her friend's place in Pearl Serein's building? That friend?

RL I have a friend. That's all.

AN: Monsieur Lorentz, frankly, this thing with Madame Saxe, I don't understand the attrac—

RL: It is none of your business!

AN: It could be. It really could. (Silence...) You are right, for the moment. But we do need to understand the confluence of your, ah, friendship with Madame Serein with Madame Serein's relationships with Messieurs Pugh, Belfort, Tuche, Duteil and Angulaire.

RL: What about the other two! Why don't you pin those on me as well, you useless—

AN: No one is pinning anything on anyone. But neither Monsieur Gagnon nor Martel was known to play tennis. Although I will get to Monsieur Martel in due course...Now, to return to Tuesday evening. You were the last person to spend any meaningful time with Maître Pugh. I hope you understand this and that it is vital that you account for—

RL: We worked on his goddamn backhand! One hour. Two hundred and fifty francs. That's it.

AN: Madame Serein said you were going to work on his serve.

RL: She does not know anything about my life or my business.

AN: You said she was your friend. (Silence...) Why would she mislead us? (Silence...) Any thoughts?

RL: Mislead you?

AN: You say backhand, she says serve. Why? (Silence...)

RL: Are you serious?

AN: Obviously I am, monsieur. Any thoughts on this contradictory information?

RL: I have no idea.

AN: Why were Maître Pugh and Monsieur Belfort fighting in the locker room?

RL: That has nothing to do with me.

AN: Was it about Madame Serein?

RL: Usually, yes.

AN: What did you work on with Monsieur Belfort on Friday morning?

RL: Nothing much. He was too hungover, as usual. Probably drugged out of his weird mind, as well. I tapped a few balls his way. Put in my hour... Total waste of money, but that's his problem.

AN: Why did you start a fight with Raymond Tuche on Saturday evening?

RL: Because he's a drooling ass and he was making a horrible scene.

AN: But what did it have to do with you? (Silence...) From what I understand, you did not accompany Madame Serein to the party...in fact, you were actively preoccupied with at least two other women there. No? Why? (Silence...)

RL: I hate Raymond Tuche. Ever since...(Silence).

AN: Since?

RL: Since forever! He has always been a complete and utter—

AN: What do you mean, forever?

RL: Since the Lycée. (Silence) We grew up together.

AN: I see.

RL: Do you? Good. Now let me out of this fucking cell!

AN: And you grew up with these other men.

RL: Yeah. Except Duteil, obviously.

AN: Is that why you're so angry, Remy?

RL: I am not angry.

AN: Because you grew up with them and you were better than them at all the games, but now you have to work for them? Is that it?

RL: She belongs with me! Not them. OK? It is very simple. And wrong. (Smashing sound.)

AN: Then why isn't she with you?

    RL: *Oh, fuck this. Fuck this. Fuck this!* (Sound of head banging steel.)

    AN: *We need to understand the nature of your friendship with Madame Serein, and your relationship to these men.*

    RL: *I teach them how to play tennis! I work for them!*

    AN: *And do you work for Madame Serein?*

    RL: *No…*

    AN: *You give her free lessons.*

    RL: *We hit some balls together sometimes.*

    AN: *So you are friends.*

    RL: *I've only told you this about a thousand times.*

    AN: *But you are looking beyond that.*

    RL: (extended silence.)

    AN: *Monsieur Lorentz, you do sound like a friend in a certain kind of way. But I have to tell you it does not look good. Your attitude. Your basic outlook here.*

    RL: *Are attitudes against the law now?*

    AN: *No, but you are incriminating yourself, at least circumstantially, especially as regards Raymond Tuche. You were also dangerously near the scene of Bruno Martel's death. You seemed very interested in the residence of Madame Guntz. Why was this?*

    RL: *None of your business.*

    AN: *You really ought to disclose everything you can that can mitigate your circumstances here.*

    RL: *Oh Jesus…Because we had a thing, all right? After her marriage, before she fell in love with that fat phoney. It's natural to look to see if she's around when I do my run…I've explained all this!*

    AN: *Is it natural to climb her fence and go into her garden?*

    RL: *She used to leave her back door open…*

    AN: *And Monday morning. Our information leads us to believe this entire matter starts with Monsieur Belfort, Madame Serein and yourself.*

    RL: *I was her lover!* (Another sound of steel banging, rattling.) *But we broke up…She hated me—for selling her.* (Sound of another very bitter laugh.)

    AN: *Selling her?*

RL: *For God's sake! Pearl and I were playing, Didi Belfort comes moping along looking for someone to hit with, I told him I'd rent him my partner... It was one of those crazy things that just happen sometimes...a whim, a dumb joke, it just popped out. She didn't think it was funny... maybe it wasn't. She went to play with him. It caused a fight and we were both holding out, not speaking, you know the way you sometimes do? Belfort suddenly calls her up from out of the blue and asks her for another game. She said yes—just to get me. And that was it. She was gone.*

AN: *How much did you sell her for?*

RL: *Does it matter?*

AN: *It could.*

RL: *I sold her to Belfort for a thousand francs.*

AN: *That's four times your regular rate.*

RL: *More like five back then.*

AN: *Are you sure Pearl Serein is your friend? Now, I mean. (Silence)...Monsieur Lorentz?*

RL: *(Silence)...It was such a shame. I mean a shame that she would be with him. What a waste.*

AN: *Monsieur Lorentz? Your relationship at this time?*

RL: *She's wasting her life. Look. Proof's in the pudding. None of them last. Pearl's lost in that world. (Silence...) It breaks my heart.*

AN: *She does seem to have that effect. (Silence) Did you know where she might be?*

RL: *No.*

AN: *Would Tommi Bonneau hide her?*

RL: *Bonneau? A total geek. She wouldn't go near the likes of him with a barge pole. (Silence.) It's me. Pearl belongs with me. It's just a matter of time.*

AN: *Please explain that. What would cause her to—*

But the judge stopped reading here...

## – 27 –
## Constructing a deeper view of Tommi

'I went to see Sophie Glarr. I got a demonstration from her friend.'
'And so?'

*AdrénalineAlors!* Her own adrenaline had been pumping hard just watching him perform. It *was* like a performance, the fluid scaling of the walls, the bursts of pure speed, the elegant leaps across precarious space. The touch-down. The backflips and handsprings were just for show, but they had looked like magic set against the rich blues and pinks of dusk. She had gazed up at his sweat-shiny face gazing down. No smile—it was a steely look of proven pride. Then he'd loped off into the night… 'Says they can go anywhere. Says it depends how brave you are.'

Captain Mathieu Deubelbeiss knew Inspector Nouvelle well enough to read her pauses. 'But?'

'Those kids could care less about Pearl Serein. That kid could easily get to our victims' windows. But they are the exact opposite of the kind of people who have to have a Pearl Serein.'

'Even so. Everyone's inspired by somebody.' The captain bent to his notes. 'His name?'

'No idea. I didn't ask, he didn't tell.' She shrugged. 'That was our deal for the demo. I just wanted to see what it is they do. And how they think.'

Deubelbeiss put his pen aside, pushed a memo across his desk. 'Richand's releasing Lorentz.'

Aliette nodded, not surprised. 'Poor Remy. Doesn't get much respect.'

'We'll watch him. Richand should have a chat with *him*.'

He meant Tommi Bonneau, passing the inspector that morning's *Cri*.

### Local Scene

*Dear Pearl, Wherever you are, the Law can't touch you (and never stood a chance).*

Aliette agreed. 'But he won't. Gérard refuses to lower himself to allowing this as a factor.'

'Factor or not, that gossipy ass is pushing his luck. Fucking disrespectful.'

'He doesn't mean you, Mathieu. He means Claude.'

'I know. I mean Article 9. Néon screwed up, but he doesn't deserve that.'

'He might.'

Deubelbeiss disagreed. 'Néon is us, Inspector. Have you talked to him?'

'No. But I've talked to Tommi Bonneau.'

'Why is he doing it?'

'He needs a foil — for his story. For his readers? It's about love. Not police.'

'It *says* police and it reflects on all of us.'

'Pretend you're a duck, Mathieu. Let it roll off you. Any kind of reaction will only make it worse.'

Aliette left Mathieu Deubelbeiss and knocked at the office of Commissaire Duque. 'You say your sister used to mind Tommi Bonneau.'

'Yes. They were up on the fifth. Father was something at Peugeot — a desk, not the line. His mother, I don't know. Good enough people as far as I ever knew. Both gone now, I believe. Yes, Margie was up there often of a weekend at one point, earning a few francs.'

'Would she...would you...mind if I gave her call?'

'Not at all.' He wrote a number, an address, presented it. 'I'll tell her you're coming.'

William Tell is a regional hero, shared on both sides of the border. Our Swiss neighbors have given his name to ProTell, the national anti-gun-control lobby, first-cousin, philosophically speaking, to the American NRA. Here in our burg we have honored the fabled archer with a life-sized painted plaster statue reminiscent of no one so much as that other American mainstay, Ronald McDonald. He stands forever dour, if not freezing, in short pants, crossbow in the at-ease position, at a corner along (where else?) Rue Guillaume Tell. And young Walter Tell is depicted sitting on a stump by his father's knee, the famous apple waiting on his head. The inspector stepped down from the tram, paused a moment in appreciation of this elemental father/son moment, then walked a block and rang at the door leading to the apartments above the pharmacy.

Madame Marguerite Dandurand was a less chiseled version of her brother. Same dolefully cavernous gray eyes and solid nose, the mouth that seemed forever tightly pursed, same fine gray hair… mainly, she shared the commissaire's height, that rangy, knock-kneed presence. Her place was a large three-bedroom flat on the third, somber on the street side at this hour, and made more so by the bulky hardwood furnishings, so pervasive in pre-IKEA generation homes across the Republic. She shared it with her retired husband (a desk job with *La Poste*) who was '…off on his annual spring bicycle tour with his pals. The boys still need to let loose — who am I to tell him no?' Aliette smiled, attentive. Three silver-framed photos, two girls, one boy, showed three sets of Duque eyes in slightly fuller paternal-side faces. Madame murmured, 'One in Paris, one in Strasbourg. Three grandchildren… And one no longer with us.'

One of the daughters.

'I'm sorry.'

'Life brings many challenges.'

The kitchen got the morning sun. And, for easy reference, a view of Pearl's diving tower. 'It is bizarre,' said Madame Dandurand as she sat and poured their tea, 'but then again, not so much. I mean, when I read this…this nonsense? — is that what it is? — I hear an echo of that little boy. I always enjoyed his bird column. But this strange thing, it reminds me of how he was.'

The inspector nodded. 'I don't know if it's nonsense either.' Then ventured, 'It couldn't be, not if so many people follow it so religiously.' Then asked, 'What was he like?'

Marguerite Dandurand, clarified, recalling as she dipped a Bastogne biscuit in her tea. 'I don't mean the nasty thing. Tommi was a polite enough child. And gentle, I suppose. Only child — hard to know. But it's something else. I know this from my own. It's...It's what they hope for.'

'Who?'

'Children. He expresses that. Do you have children?'

'No.'

She stared past her kitchen, into the morning. Straight at Pearl's. 'Tommi was always staring out the window. I'd read to him. He loved his story. He would hear it — every word, but it always looked like he wasn't. I remember that. It took me a few tries before I could get used to reading to a boy who did not seem to be listening. But then I'd get to a tragic part, a part where things weren't right — D'Artagnan is left for dead, Rumplestiltskin mocking the miller's daughter's hopeless guessing — every story has to have a moment like that, and *then* he'd suddenly turn and demand, Why? Why did that have to happen? Very intense. I remember, so many times, trying to explain those parts had to be there, for the ending to be worthwhile.'

'Did he believe you?'

She shrugged. 'He'd insist that I finish. I would offer to leave it — we could do something else. He always had to know the end. But he was rarely smiling when I put him to bed.'

'Children are literal.'

'Of course. It can be worrisome.'

'Now he reads a lot of poetry. I went to see him.'

'Say hello to him for me if you see him again.'

Aliette looked beyond, toward the disembodied diving tower. 'Did you know her?'

'Pearl? No, not really. I never sat for them. They were a few doors along. I saw her in the street with her American mother...an American mother was something interesting. Never really noticed Pearl. I was bigger. Looking after Tommi was a job — I mean, he was a handful in his little way, but then his parents came home, I got paid, I went back downstairs and carried on with my life till the next time. And you know, gradually, it just ends.'

Aliette smiled. She'd done a bit of babysitting too. She began to finish her tea.

Marguerite Dandurand was still mulling the fact of Tommi Bonneau. 'I was happy for him when he got the bird column. And before that, sometimes you'd see his pictures. Then his name was there in the paper three times a week and I'd read it. Even started noticing some of the birds.' Her gaze stayed in the distance. Her voice dropped a tone. 'Then my daughter. Our eldest…She died. A love affair that broke her heart. She decided life was not worth it. And she left us. That was hard—the hardest thing ever. Such a happy-go-lucky child, the last person in the world you'd ever think could get so trapped in such darkness.' She turned back to her guest. 'Sorry. It was fifteen years ago. We've dealt with it, learned to live with it because you have to. But this Pearl story…this nonsense that isn't nonsense, I find it often throws me back to that sad time. My daughter was the opposite of a Tommi Bonneau. She would be the one giggling when everyone else was dabbing their eyes. Including me. I noticed it. Of course. You notice everything. But she seemed to go along all right. School. Boyfriends. Work…She was in the Gendarmes, down near Doubs, following her uncle's path. Then this one relationship fell apart and it was too much for her to bear. You just never know, do you?'

All Aliette could do was shake her head.

Marguerite Dandurand picked up another biscuit. 'Tommi Bonneau still seems to be worried about that horrible line. Why and where the dark side starts. I don't want to read him, but I do. I suppose I have to. I want to know—I need to, although I don't really believe I ever will.'

The inspector took this, plus some suggestions—the *lycée* was an easy walk, perhaps some of his or her old profs could shed some light?—and continued on. Along Rue Marianne, the doors Marguerite Dandurand had talked about were waiting. Doors with numbers. Then stairways. But Tommi's parents had died. There were no more Duques—hadn't been for years. Four doors along, Pearl's father's store was now notions—buttons and ribbons bedecking the window in the place of books. Sad, somehow, when a bookstore disappears. Crossing the street, the Papeterie Lorentz was still there, at least in name. She glanced in. A tired-looking man glanced back. Remy's papa, no question. Used to be as beautiful as his son. And as angry? She smiled and walked away. Did not want to talk to him. Suddenly confronted with the chance, she wondered what good it could possibly do. Remy had told her everything she needed to know yesterday afternoon. Remy was peripheral. Not part of the story.

Was Remy peripheral back *then*? As she headed off toward the school, Aliette tried to imagine kids in this street at different times of their lives until their lives grew too different for this street, and for each other. Madame Dandurand's words provided a frame: Tommi, intent and literal, vexed when things went wrong in stories; Pearl, vague beside an exotic American mother. But friends with Tommi? Remy's nasty bitterness provided another view. Aliette trusted Pearl's mother's sentimental vision of two kids more than Remy's juvenile anger. 'They used to be such good friends.' Why would she lie? ... But then, kids do turn into adolescents, and some of them are good at tennis, and others definitely are geeks.

The noisy energy of the school pushed away her useless thinking. Lycée F-A-Bartoldi, for Frederik-Auguste, another regional star, famous for giving the Americans their iconic statue in the harbor at New York. Inspector Nouvelle knew the place. Six weeks prior, she'd sat in an unmarked car monitoring the operation as Junior Inspector Bernadette Milhau had gone about busting two senior and very bright girl students known back at the office as the Hashish Twins. That had been a good day—the principal welcomed her warmly. Today's business was entirely different. The woman was unsure if she should smile or scowl as she consulted with a secretary.

Yes, one teacher from the time of Tommi Bonneau was still around.

Monsieur Jean Gregoire. A thin, tobacco-pallid, graying *philo* teacher, he had supervised the student newspaper during his first years on staff. 'Don't do any of that volunteer work anymore. Now I just rehash my notes, I'm afraid,' he told her, brash and cranky, 'I'll admit it to you, I admit it to anyone. Only way to protest the cutbacks... Two more years, I'm gone.'

Aliette said they experienced the same frustrations with the Ministry of the Interior.

As for Tomas Bonneau, 'Never said much in class, absolutely nothing memorable. About as logical as any run-of-the-mill teenager, I guess, but certainly never the *philosophe* in embryo one dreams of finding. But he was our go-to man when we needed a good photo for the paper. I got a feel for him there… Always brought in excellent stuff. Mainly birds, that was his passion. The boy did not mind climbing a tree to get his shot. I mean to the very top. You'd worry. But he'd get whatever you needed. In fact, I admired him. He understood how the light would work, used it perfectly. Total dolt with a camera, me — I'd no problem writing a letter recommending him when he went out looking for a job. Happy to. No need to go further in school. He'd found his talent.' Jean Gregoire reached for the newspaper on the corner of his desk. It was open at the back page. 'Can't say I hold him in much esteem now. Silliness. He probably should have stayed with birds.'

'You follow it?'

'I feel I had a hand in these people's lives. Deaths too. I mean, philosophically speaking, you understand.' A flat smile behind his disclaimer. An old prof's professional hazard.

'But she's not dead. Is she?' Pearl. A rhetorical question.

'She might as well be. Of course I'm speaking on a conceptual level here. If she's not dead, she's dying.' Meeting the inspector's quizzical gaze: 'No more boyfriends. Yes? No boyfriends, no Pearl.' Tapping the paper, 'Bonneau knows this. In any case, I can't remember *her* at all. Which doesn't mean much. It's a big place, I am just a lowly philosophy prof. You see?'

It was somehow harder to respond to a philosophy prof who hated his life than to a woman whose child had destroyed herself because of love. But Monsieur Jean Gregoire graciously gave her the next name to try. Merci. And on she went, following a serpentine trail through the past in a city where she would always be a stranger, attempting to impute cause and effect into the vague nexus linking Pearl Serein and Tommi Bonneau and seven iffy heart attacks.

But despite a city full of gentle readers, so many of whom had crossed paths with Pearl or someone that she'd loved…or hated — oh, yes, lots of people still carried grudges in this town — there was no tangible trace of *her*. There was only *le vrai Tommi* Bonneau, heedless, building the next arc in his *grande histoire*. Whether for business purposes or something more central to the soul of himself didn't matter, the man could not leave it alone.

### Local Scene

*How pathetic! That one woman can elude the Police so completely speaks volumes of the abilities of the man at its supposed head...Quelle crise d'esprit! Where is leadership? Where is Pearl?*

A spiritual crisis? Everyone on both teams at Rue des Bons Enfants knew it was Claude now — dead central to Tommi's sense of drama. In disgrace? An embarrassment to the force? They could not let that distract them. With Commissaire Duque's blessing, Inspector Nouvelle crafted a memo to her judge requesting an Article 9 charge on behalf of Claude Néon, not the citizen but the member (still on the payroll) of the *Police Judiciaire*. Captain Mathieu Deubelbeiss agreed their MO had to include the fact of Claude Néon's well-being. Monique was instructed to CC the divisional office in Strasbourg.

And there was also the personal element, an abiding worry that was Aliette's alone.

*A faithless bastard?* She couldn't let that matter either. How was *his* heart these days?

## − 28 −
## Claude in exile

Exile from the job was cruel and unusual. Claude Néon had been unsure where to begin to fill the time. The garden was waiting for him, but he went to the club instead. No sense hiding. They were watching him — he knew that and expected it, but tennis was tennis, with or without Pearl Serein. He'd gone to plead his case with Gaston, who listened, detached, cop-like, in fact, and said he'd have to run it past the membership committee. Claude went back to his yard and started to dig. Two days later, around the cocktail hour, he was sitting in his kitchen like a zombie after a futile afternoon with his planting when the telephone rang. Gaston said, 'OK, we'll give it another go.' Claude's probationary membership was renewed.

'Merci.'

'Act like a member, not a cop.'

'Understood.' So he'd washed his face and gone to the club — a short walk — and had his cocktail there. Scotch on the rocks. Single malt. He'd signed a chit. That made him feel bona fide, if not welcome. Because no one said a word to Claude Néon. After such an easy-going chatty supper a week ago with the inspector beside him, it was a rude surprise realizing he hadn't the foggiest notion how to re-engage. Act like a member? He'd made a promise to Gaston. He sat there smiling till he finished his drink, mumbled '*bonsoir*,' and strolled out. What now? A haircut?

What about a sauna? Claude Néon felt moist heat from the showers as he descended to the basement area. He paused to consider the B&W glossy tacked on a notice board by the locker room door: Remy Lorentz grinning at him. The notice urged everyone to sign up for a session with Remy and get in shape for the new season. An hour honing your strokes with Remy cost 250 francs. Claude had not dared ask Gaston if and how Remy's status had been affected by Saturday night.

He had no idea how Remy had fared in *Provisoire*. Horrible to be out of the loop.

There was an older member, naked on a bench, carefully sprinkling talc over a hoary belly, sagging scrotum, and between his bony toes. He eyed Claude the way people everywhere will eye a cop suddenly in their midst. Acting like a member, Claude picked up a towel from the pile. The older member said, 'You were damn lucky.' (*Vous avez pas mal de chance.*) Claude wanted to say, No, I was a dumb ass. (*Un vrai con, moi.*) But he did not. He smiled, yes, I was lucky. 'Seven to six,' the older member added. 'You should know you've got a friend in Gaston.'

The older member returned to his fastidious sprinkling. Another naked member stepped out of the shower. Claude stood there on the verge of panic. Seven to six? Seven to six? 'Ah! The vote.'

The older member looked up, suspicious, covered his crotch with his towel.

'Democracy's a beautiful thing,' Claude averred, tossing his unused towel back on the pile, thinking, I am a lucky guy but maybe we'll leave the sauna for another time.

The naked member drying himself said, 'In the hamper…' looking toward the corner.

'Ah, the hamper.' There were many things one didn't know. Claude obediently retrieved his towel and put it there. See? I can do exactly like you're meant to. And left.

Claude ended up skulking by the tennis courts, busy with fours and pairs on a warm Thursday evening. He watched carefully, noting different skill levels, trying to gauge where he might fit in, a careful eye on shoes, racquets, shirts and shorts. Saturday he would head downtown and shop. Or maybe drive to Basel. The Swiss had better tennis players, maybe they had better gear. Suddenly he found himself looking through the fence at Remy Lorentz, alone on court 10 with a bucket of balls.

Apparently Gérard Richand had not found a reason to let Remy rot in jail. Remy was damn lucky too. Claude wondered if he knew it. Probably not. The handsome pro was methodically—

angrily, it appeared—smashing bullet serves across the net. He did not respond to Claude's presence at the fence—he continued smashing serves, each one accompanied by an ugly grunt of exertion.

Claude Néon wondered if one must do the grunting bit. He took a quick mental count and decided that about half the members he had observed did, and of the half that did, the majority were female. Hmm... But if the pro did it... When his bucket was empty, Remy picked it up and went to the other side of the net and began to gather up the balls. He seemed deliberately disinclined to acknowledge Claude. Fine. Claude would not say a word. He would watch. When all the balls were back in the bucket, Remy went to the service line on the other side and began to hit again—at which point Claude began to walk away. Without a word, Remy's bluff was called. Before Claude took ten steps, he heard the pro's snide warning, 'Forget it, man. You're just another little conquest.'

Ouch! It hit Claude Néon dead on. But he stayed low-key—the only way to win, especially at a place like this. 'Is that all she's into? What about tennis? She promised she would teach me.'

Ignoring tennis, Remy added, 'Forget about it. When she shows up again, it'll be with the next one. She'll walk right past you... Count on it.'

Claude considered that. 'And will I be dead?'

Remy Lorentz shook his head like he'd seen far too many men like Claude. (Especially at a place like this.) He followed with another heavy-duty groan as he slammed another serve.

As Remy got himself back to the start position, ready to hit the next serve, Claude could not resist wondering, 'So did she teach you to groan like that? Or vice-versa?' Claude tried groaning from the sidelines as Remy tossed his ball. It caused Remy to swing wild and miss completely.

Claude said, 'At least, that's how I remember it.' And winked.

Would Remy have come off the court and fought with Claude? He was under a very stern order from Judge Richand to keep the public peace. (Would it apply at a private club?) And would our suspended commissaire have reprised his Saturday night performance and most likely lose all hope of ever being a full-fledged member in good standing? Claude did not like the tennis pro and was feeling quite prepared to rub his lovely face against the steel-meshed fence. More than prepared: Standing there daring Remy Lorentz to try his luck, Claude Néon sensed something inevitable at play, something bigger than himself. Exiled or not, he had to keep moving forward.

Claude realized he was glad he'd bumped into the awful Remy.

Claude Néon would pursue his bid for membership in good standing, but Remy Lorentz reminded him that he was cop, first, last and always. It was a moment of clarity in a week filled with distracted non-direction. Claude savored it, adrenaline surging. Cop energy. His life blood.

It was suddenly diluted by the next intruding presence. Claude turned to face a miserable looking Agnès Guntz, former special assistant to the late Bruno Martel, all in white again — for tennis, not meditation — suited up for a lesson with Remy. Her cool regard sent a clear message: Claude was hateful. She moved quickly through the gate and onto the court.

Claude remained silent. He lingered till Agnès and Remy gave up waiting for him to leave and began to hit. Agnès Guntz began to grunt with each effort to return the ball.

Walking home, Claude contemplated an uncomfortable dissonance between grunting and the club. Not what you'd expect… But who'd expect a rough-hewn cop to ever be a member? Life was filled with dissonance. Claude was unaware of a hooded jogger passing on the far side of the street.

Though he wouldn't be the least surprised if he had noticed. Of course they were watching him.

Our commissaire is sometimes dangerously compulsive, but not entirely stupid.

## – 29 –
## EXPERT OPINION?

Friday. After speculating as to whether or not a certain American starlet was wearing underwear when she'd crossed her legs repeatedly during a interview with the German press at Cannes, there was this at the bottom of *Le Vrai Tommi*: **Local Scene**: *To Pearl... Come home! Everyone needs you (including some people we don't really like).* It came with a shot of Claude Néon watching Remy Lorentz hit serves. *Tying up some loose ends? Or looking for another fight? A sidelined cop watches a partnerless pro.* Clear and nasty. And how did Tommi hide himself so completely? The shot presupposed a rooftop or a tree.

After attending to an in-box full of tedious boss-like administrative duties, Aliette Nouvelle went down to see the doctors. The morgue door squeaked once as she swept through and once as it swung closed behind her. The inspector was welcomed effusively by Gilles Conan. 'Bonjour!... Up to our ears in it!' Gesturing at the work area, proudly proprietary. Corpses, hearts, paperwork, and all manner of instruments and machines.

And so? You've had a week. The basic question: 'Why did they all die of heart attacks?'

Enjoying his mid-morning cappuccino, the famous doctor was delighted to explain what they'd established. In all seven hearts the key mechanical factors at play could be deduced post-mortem. After *again* walking her through the likely susceptibilities found in each, Conan pronounced, 'given lifestyle, drug regimens or the lack of preventive measures, these organs all show dangerously vulnerable states of wear and/or extraordinary stress on the vascular system.'

She liked him, but there was something too casual. Too academic? 'I need to prove murder.'

Gilles Conan smiled, commiserating. He knew her need. 'However, as for a common point of attack leading to death, this remains obscured.' Why? Because the crucial electrical factor could not be known. 'An EKG might show it, but a body has to be alive.' Conan shrugged. 'In this modern era, you could say death is the absence of electricity.'

'Electricity?' Benumbed by a litany of oxidants and statins, too much booze, nicotine, sleeping pills, anti-depressants, Bruno Martel's weight-loss drugs, Didi Belfort's love of Debutal…Aliette Nouvelle gazed at the lifeless organs on display in a line atop the counter.

'Well, yes.' Leaving the hearts, crossing the floor to where five well-worked corpses rested on gurneys, tapping each on the top of its head with his pen as he paced and expounded, 'The brain receives a message then sends another one down the spinal cord in response to what it's just been told, telling adrenaline to form in the nerves, which are the delivery system. Nerves…electricity. That is what's common to these hearts which have been *attacked*, as we call it. It's hard to get more specific after death, when there's no more electrically induced rhythm to analyze. The traces of the attack in each are much the same. These six,' mused Conan, returning to the hearts in their gleaming trays, 'and, I would guess, the other man as well, died… um…quickly, yes, but like I say, with their various constitutions, conditions and drugs contributing, it's fairly certain they each died in their own kind of way, likely at a different rate of passage. That's the electrical factor.' He considered that last idea for a moment. 'Yes, each man dies differently.'

'Even if killed the same way,' added Raphaele Petrucci. He knew what she wanted to hear.

Aliette frowned. 'How differently?'

Dr. Conan slowly shook his head, Sorry, no idea. 'Just different. Varying health and pharmacology. Nerves and systems operating at different speeds. As for a catalyst, the pain of love is just as likely as sudden fear or sustained panic or abiding anger. We can't know. Still, all of them probably bore a macabre kind of witness to their own deaths, if that's a help…' Conan was beaming, too obviously enchanted by the intensity of the cop with the silver-blue eyes. He wanted her to push him. He wanted to tell her everything he knew, and more.

'Why?'

'A flood of adrenaline affects one's sense of time. Things that happen in a moment can seem drawn out.'

Fascinating. But she was feeling something similar: as if suspended, contemplating veiny lumps of meat, while the over-eager eyes of Gilles Conan studied her. (Of course she knew it.) From deep inside this suspended place she stared at Conan: Not good enough. 'We need to show that they were killed, probably by the same person, therefore likely in the same way. I need something in common and tangible that leads from the heart to the life it drove.'

It came across with cold insistence, fusing the antiseptic air inside the morgue.

The doctor took an instinctive step back from the inspector's confrontational tone.

Big difference between expounding and making excuses. He looked like he'd been slapped.

Raphaele Petrucci's heart caught for a beat. He had seen it before, and *felt* it—the sharp tear to the soul that came with being found wanting by Inspector Aliette Nouvelle. He dreaded the thought of an alienated Dr. Conan saying *I don't need this* and heading straight back to his faculty in Strasbourg. Raphaele stepped forward. 'What about some freshly baked biscotti?'

He was ignored. Gilles Conan was not used to being found wanting. 'This woman you're looking for,' he mumbled, ironic, tripped up by her challenge; 'this Pearl. Tangible. Common?'

A twist of the inspector's mouth conveyed her unamused response.

Blushing, Conan hurried past it, 'And, given their social status and professional profiles, this thing psychologists have dubbed a Type-A personality—all inherently aggressive, action oriented, focused on achievement at all cost, said to thrive on confrontation, testing limits, and therefore prone to the stress naturally associated with any and all of these things. I'd say they share *that*.'

'Physical!' blurted Aliette, feeling stressed but not about to die. 'I need something physical!'

'Stress is physical,' countered Conan, steely, now eyeing her with his own questions: who is this cop? 'The stress of love, stress of work, loneliness, sadness, grief, fear, failure. Type A and failure can be a deadly mix... Any negative emotion can affect the flow of blood to a dangerous degree, Inspector. Surely you've experienced these things. You've felt them — *physically*. No?'

'Of course. But I cannot put stress in a plastic exhibit bag and present it to the judge. There has to be some tangible quality common to these heart attacks that I can use to demonstrate a modus operandi and prove murder.' Aliette did not put much stock in Type A's...or B's or C's.

'I told you the day I arrived here: Adrenaline.' Gesturing to the storage drawers, Conan added, 'Each of our five bodies has totally depleted adrenal glands. We could cut them out and put them in your plastic bag.' Quietly snide now. As if addressing an uppity intern.

Aliette turned away from the doctor's sarcasm. Closed her eyes. Breathed. She did not need Conan as much as Raphaele appeared to. But she did need allies. You always need allies, on the street, and in every professional nook and cranny the justice system holds. Needing to salvage *some*thing here, she did what her mother had taught her. She smiled. She apologized. Neither was difficult. 'I'm sorry. I'm on the verge of something with this, but I'm blocked.'

Folding his arms, sighing largely, letting his own Type-A adrenaline surge abate, Conan seemed to accept this. He was sorry too. 'We are working for you, Inspector.'

'I know you are. I'm only trying to cover all the bases. I need to. I've got a judge obsessed by rules and the man watching over me is a realist, and —'

*'My friend Norbert?'*

She nodded. Divisional Commissaire Norbert Fauré. 'A total, down-to-earth realist, and —'

'— and I know for a fact a lot of good work has depended on him being exactly that.'

'Which means I have very little room to move, Doctor.'

Conan's bright smile returned, spreading back into the kindly avuncular territory that seemed its natural place. 'But you — are you *not* a realist, then, Inspector?'

'Yes, yes…of course I am…' moving to the five corpses, pallid, rubbery. 'But if every man's heart attack can be different, then reality is relative. Or at least that's what you'd have to think.'

'I couldn't agree more.'

Behind them, Raphaele Petrucci breathed a quiet sigh of relief.

Aliette extended a hand toward the five dead lovers. 'Why won't one of them give us a hint?'

'It is frustrating,' said Conan, approaching, 'believe me, I know the feeling of needing a solution.' He wanted this cop's respect. 'A death mask only shows death. But that's the thing… I mean to say, we're starting to believe there is so much more in the act of dying. We're starting to suspect it may not be the agony poets have traditionally ascribed it, nor the flat, abrupt transition to the other side of zero we see on our machines. I mean, in *some* cases. Obviously a bullet in the head…' A shrug. But, 'Have you ever seen a bird caught in the jaws of a cat?' She nodded. (Piaf's dark side.) '…no struggle, as though it knows, in a bird sort of way, and has given itself over. And many people, at the end of a long battle with cancer—just before the end, they seem to collect themselves and become calm. It's beautiful. Affects anyone who's with them—it's so important that one leaves gracefully, if at all possible… Do you know anything about endorphins?'

'I know they make me feel…um, special?…when I go for my run.'

'Good word, Inspector. And just as that feeling overrides any physical discomfort you may have when you run, we now think the dying body knows the end is imminent and that for the last time those peptide hormones—endorphins, as they've come to be called—are released and attach to the cells responsible for the pain. And mitigate it. And so the body composes itself for death. It's remarkable. Only fair too,' he averred, 'after all the pain some go through to reach that final point. And it may even be more than that. An awareness. A sense of moving through…a final bath in beauty? These men may have gone that way. A heart attack might provide the mind with that same kind of window in its final moments. One of these days someone will let us know.'

'Their final thoughts for Pearl?' mused Aliette, leaving the bodies, turning back to the trays,

There was a silent moment as they stared down at six hearts which had suffered.

Then, vague and flustered, the inspector thanked the doctor and left.

Gilles Conan accepted more coffee and a biscuit. He shared a quiet secret with Raphaele. 'Who knows what a man or a bird is feeling when they die? Ideas like that are really just people like me trying to think in the opposite direction of all the hard knowledge.' Sipping his coffee, crunching biscotti. 'Half of what I told her is no more than an educated guess.'

'She really does have to find hard evidence, or this is just for practice.'

'Of course she does and I think she will.'

'Then why tell her things like that?'

'It can't do any harm when you're stuck at zero, can it?'

'I don't know… I don't understand how she works.'

Gilles Conan said, 'I enjoy watching her think, your Inspector Nouvelle.'

Monique knew a frustrated inspector when she saw one. She was solicitous, offering Friday afternoon tea and a cookie with two more memos. Chief Magistrate Gérard Richand's response to her request for an Article 9 regarding Tomas Bonneau and/or *Le Cri du Matin* was No.

'Merci, Gérard.'

And Strasbourg had called. They had received her package containing the same request, plus copies of the columns that prompted it. Divisionnaire Fauré would drive down to meet with Inspector Nouvelle on Monday morning.

'Oh, Lord…Nothing beyond that?'

There was mention of lunch together. Did the inspector know of an enjoyable spot?

Boggled, Aliette took the notes, declined the tea, collected her things and went home.

## — 30 —
## Tracking instincts

*Local Scene: Our police have failed us twofold. Once: through uncooperative communications and non-results. And twice: in a policeman's patent inability to keep Pearl from running. By inability I do not mean the force of his office, but the power of his love. His arms could not hold her, his net cannot drag her back in. This man's failure looks bad on all of us...To all my gentle readers: Keep your eyes (and hearts!) peeled for Pearl. If you have a clue, we'd love to hear it. Love is the operative word. And you could win a romantic weekend in Paris for two, courtesy Le Cri!*

Unbelievable. Aliette gulped her coffee, burning her throat, dreading Claude's reaction.

Maybe he was being wise and avoiding the back page. Or strong? One could only hope.

When her breakfast had settled, she put on her cheap disguise and went out. One does not cease being a cop on Saturday — especially when there is nothing else to do. Stupid life! And surveillance is mundane and deadly repetitive, a true test of a cop's commitment. But Aliette was not the hooded jogger tracking Claude Néon on Thursday night. She had, wisely, left that job to Captain Deubelbeiss, who'd assigned it to an officer whom Claude wouldn't know from Adam.

She had jogged past the house in the north end the evening of his suspension. Too painful.

Too confusing, how the endorphins could make her forget anger, leave judgement suspended, passing...and re-passing the house in the north end, gazing surreptitiously, *protectively*, the endorphins working chaotic magic on her mood, visualizing Claude Néon's long body meshing with hers — how she missed it! — while freeing a more inner voice telling her to let it go, knock on his door, kiss and make up. Take him straight up to their bed. Yes, *their* bed. Exclusive territory of Claude and Aliette. The body remembers longer than you want it to. It was getting bad, this need. But Aliette Nouvelle resisted. Today she jogged toward the east side, in a silly hoodie, further concealed by wrap-around shades, pink beach-chick beach cap and Walkman headphones.

The house in Rue Pontbriand was quiet, curtains drawn. The old VW van was parked across the street. Aliette thought of Anne-Marie. Somehow her friend had hooked up with Tommi Bonneau, found the next exciting thing for her aimless life and latched on. Resisting the urge to strongly advise the wayward waif was almost as hard as not running straight back to Claude. Almost. *Was* Anne-Marie a friend? Not really. She was Georgette's friend, who was Aliette's friend, sort of—an odd nexus of companionship forming around a shared link to Jacques Normand. But the Normand affair was fading into history and the ties that bound the three women were fragile, verging on disappearing, harder each day to see the point. At least for Aliette. Life moved on from one case to the next. This thing called friendship tumbled like shards in a kaleidoscopic box.

But as a woman? Aliette was concerned for Anne-Marie.

What would it be like being with a man so completely (so publicly!) devoted to someone else?

Aliette did a few slow circles of the block. At a certain point she saw Anne-Marie leave the house, climb into the van and drive off. Alone.

She mulled the possibilities—and was about to knock on Tommi's door (in total disregard for the magistrate's order) when the man appeared, stepping out on a Saturday, camera bag slung over his rangy shoulder. The inspector followed Tommi Bonneau. He headed into the old quarter, a popular Saturday destination. There was no need to run. She had only to stay at a discreet distance as Tommi wandered up one street and down the next—tight old streets, charming in their old-world colors, flower boxes, half-timbered vaulted roofs, and filled with Saturday people enjoying their warm authenticity. But Aliette Nouvelle was working and it looked like Tommi Bonneau was too, stopping people, camera at the ready, asking them something, getting them to smile, snapping a shot, then moving on, acting on their information, going in and out of a hundred doors. Thus she followed him to the Rembrandt Café. Where she had to pause to parse more possible ramifications.

Aliette knew Willem van Hoogstraten was another hard-core devotee of Pearl Serein. The day she'd lunched with Swiss FedPol Agent Woerli, Willem had offered a dessert called Chocolate Pearl, proudly described on the menu as 'inspired by the lady of my dreams.' Just chocolate pudding laced with Kir — very tasty, but what did that make Willem to a man like Tommi Bonneau? And there was the fact that Willem and Anne-Marie were very regular friends. Confronting Tommi in front of Willem might force Anne-Marie into a dangerous position. At the very least, Anne-Marie would be lost forever as a possible source. Or at least till the end of her love affair.

The inspector stood there in the street, trapped in a game of hurry up and wait.

The Pearl effect? It was ridiculous that Pearl Serein had created this conundrum.

But Tommi Bonneau came back out in short order and ambled off.

She followed. No more pictures. No more ducking in and out of doors. Tommi retreated back to his home. Deduction: Whatever he'd been looking for, he found it at the Rembrandt.

She would talk to Willem. Alone. Not today.

She called it quits, exhausted, not physically, but spiritually, instincts on the blink.

Aliette Nouvelle didn't really care where Pearl was. With luck, she might stay gone.

# Part 3

It is enough that you are able to take this view of life, and see this decadent, sullied and vulgar world purified and beautiful in the camera of your innermost soul.

— Sōseki, *The Three-Cornered World*

## – 31 –
## Pearl's Kiss

Question: How do you get from a media-engorged police escort to this lost place?

Answer: You run. As everyone is sucked toward the ghastly fact of a dead Didi Belfort wrapped in newsprint, you run, blindly, panicked, no idea where, till suddenly you're in the Rembrandt Café, at a corner table in the shadows, cowering, face in your hands, weeping, struggling to control it. Thank God it's the kind of place where people keep to themselves.

And then there's Willem, concerned, gentle, 'Is there anything I can do?'

'Please,' she whispered, 'I'm very confused. All I want is privacy.'

'Come.' Guiding her into his kitchen, where he left her alone with a bowl of chocolate pudding, still warm. It calmed her. Of course it did. Everyone loved Pearl's Kiss.

When he returned to prepare the next order, Pearl asked, 'Why are you doing this?'

'You have many admirers who believe your life is special.'

Plain fact? Or yet more expression of a mass delusion? Just then she had no choice but to take it at face value. She huddled in Willem's pantry, wretched and wary, till the mid-morning lull.

When he spirited Pearl upstairs, he said, 'You'll be more comfortable here.'

She insisted she should leave. He insisted, 'It's the least I can do.'

And he didn't really believe she'd still be there when he climbed up again at the end of the day.

But she was. So Willem opened wine and cooked for Pearl. Asked her questions. Let her talk.

That night she told him several times, 'This is not who I am.'

Which raised the question, Then who are you?

'I don't know what to tell you.' She asked, 'Does one repay a kindness by indulging a lie?'

Which left Willem confused. But Tommi said—

Pearl touched his lip, to shush him.

She asked Willem, 'Do you believe your childhood was the best part of your life?'

He didn't know. He didn't really think about it much…could barely remember it.

Pearl told him, 'Tommi Bonneau and I were friends.'

Just friends? Willem's wine worked on Willem too—of course it did—and some of Willem's questions were not quite right.

Pearl had flared. 'We were children! We were best friends and then we weren't. OK?'

OK.

'Suddenly our lives were changing. It was finished, our magic world. There are so many people in a life. Some go in different directions, you lose sight of them. You know how it can be, surely?'

Willem did.

'We haven't said two words to each other since… I don't know when. Years.'

Then why did Tommi write these things about her?

'I don't know. I don't encourage him. I try to ignore him. But I can't hate him. I can't sue him—that would only make it worse. And I don't *want* to. It's not about a court order or money. I'm not Brigitte Bardot…' Trailing off, feeling guilty. Trapped. 'It isn't fair. I am not complicit in this!'

Willem believed her. But he asked her about love. How could he not? The local goddess of love is sitting at your table, insisting she's beholden to your kindness. And that she loves your wonderful dessert. 'Merci.' Willem poured more wine and asked.

'I do try,' Pearl promised. 'You *have* to try… I don't play games. It's as pure as I can make it. And I believe in it. I do. I mean, *c'est l'amour!* Do you think I'd take a seventy-one-year-old banker to my bed just for money?' Before Willem could answer, Pearl assured him, 'There was a real charm there and I was attracted.' Willem believed her. She told him, 'They may not work out, but I am attracted to the good thing, not the bad.' He sat silently as Pearl stared at her image in Willem's kitchen window, and at the diving tower in the distance, melding with her reflection, enveloping her face. 'All this death. Do you think anyone will ever come near me again?'

Willem told her, 'You don't *feel* dangerous…What about that cop?'

'Claude? He's another man lost in a fantasy.' Then on the strength of almost an entire bottle, Pearl recited, 'From leaves of autumn flushed with love,/ A pearl of dew shakes free/ And falls to shatter on the earth beneath./ So too must I, to flee Love's stifling folds/ Drop from the world.'

Willem had toasted this effort. Bravo!…what was that?

From a favorite book. A favorite passage. Passion…hopeless passion, the stifling folds of love, how impossible it can be. Which Willem naturally had loved to hear. *This* was Pearl Serein.

Of course Willem never touched her. He just listened. Then put her to bed.

And then?

Then she was gone. Walked out the kitchen door after breakfast. *C'est tout.*

## – 32 –

## Saturday at the Rembrandt

The weekend edition of *Le Soir* hits the street by noon. Regular readers were intrigued to see Rose Saxe's byline on the front page. Many more not-so-regular readers had scooped up copies.

Headline: **Murky Link To Pearl's Past**. Subhead: **Cri Columnist Should Come Clean**.

*Is le vrai Tommi really telling all there is to tell? The question merits asking.*

*A writer who neglects to disclose a key element of his main character's past may well be hiding something crucial in the present. Is this fair in asking a reader to understand said character? Why didn't Tommi Bonneau tell us he and Pearl Serein were childhood friends? Surely this matters, and all the more so now that 'our' Pearl has disappeared.*

*Last Monday morning socialite Pearl Serein fled a police escort taking her for questioning concerning the suspicious deaths of seven former lovers. Madame Serein's flight and disappearance capped a bizarre ten days of heretofore unexplained heart attacks. Police have so far remained tight-lipped concerning the cause and circumstances surrounding the deaths of Didier Belfort, Pierre Angulaire, Jerôme Duteil, Georges Pugh, Raymond Tuche, Jean-Guy Gagnon and Bruno Martel. The official line remains: No case to answer pending the results of ongoing autopsies. As of this writing, Madame Serein is still at large, the object of an intensive regional search.*

*For the past few years a featured part of Le Cri du Matin columnist Tomas Bonneau's column, known as 'Le Vrai Tommi,' has focused on the former teacher's love life. The ongoing saga has made Madame Serein a much-admired, if unwilling, star. Madame Serein has consistently distanced herself from the press. This reluctance only seems to add to her attraction. Indeed, even as the city waits, Monsieur Bonneau continues to bang the drum, imploring his heroine to 'come home!'*

 *A hiatus has prompted others to step back and wonder, Where did this come from? How did this all start? Since Pearl Serein first emerged on the local scene on the arm of Didier Belfort, no one has asked for, and — more strangely — no one has offered any substantive background behind this love fantasy. And yet there is a city full of readers who know that Pearl and Tommi go a long way back. Apart from the late Jerôme Duteil, all the players in our local drama do. This reporter's notebook is filled with links and contacts stretching back to a schoolteacher's earliest years in Rue Marianne. Why was this never mentioned? Are we really so thrilled that we're afraid to ask and maybe break the spell? Something is out of kilter here.*

 *If Pearl Serein were indeed a fantasy figure — that is to say, a person in the business of being famous, leveraging her role in the Local Scene, whether through coordinated photo opportunities or, indeed, loudly publicized lawsuits under Article 9 — there would be no need for background. We would all understand the game. We would enjoy it, or ignore it. But Pearl Serein is not that. She is a schoolteacher who happened to meet a man. And then another. Seven boyfriends notwithstanding, Madame Serein has never said a word, positive or negative, to move this narrative along.*

 *Pearl Serein is no fantasy. But neither is she engaged.*

 *What then? A victim? Co-conspirator? What gives? Who is she? We are all partly to blame for never pausing to ask these basic questions; indeed, for being too emotionally wrapped up in our Pearl's amazingly romantic ride.*

 *But the major part of the responsibility surely rests with the man who 'created her' — out of nothing, as it were. Monsieur Bonneau has never claimed or implied any personal connection to the woman whose fortunes he has taken it upon himself to record. But it exists, and deeply so.*

 *And now our Pearl has disappeared.*

 *Where is Pearl? This is a crucial question.*

 *We might well also ask, What is Tommi trying to prove?*

 *Should we be worried? Should we feel like fools?*

 *Where is this story coming from? Where does it go from here?*

 **Ed's note:** *This is the first of a series by Rose Saxe, a reporter with her finger squarely on the pulse of this town. In the coming days, Le Soir readers can look forward to these exclusives:*

*Monday: Rose Saxe talks to teachers and friends*
*Tuesday: A mother in Connecticut*
*Wednesday: Tracking the transition from the birds to the stars*
*Thursday: A chat with child psychologist J-P Blismes*
*Friday: When stars are fading: A round table featuring four of the city's most enquiring minds*

The regulars at the Rembrandt Café studied these words as they sipped their coffee, their beer, a Saturday afternoon pastis. They contemplated an accompanying grainy black and white photo of two smiling kids: a much younger Pearl and her friend Tommi. Engrossed, no one seemed aware of the presence of one of the two personalities at the heart of Rose Saxe's provocative reasoning.

Tommi Bonneau was moving slowly through the Rembrandt... pausing, looking up, as if to note the gentle dispersal of light through the vaulted windows. Some patrons briefly met his curious stare, then went on with their reading. They did not relate the nine-year-old on the front page of *Le Soir* to the 'probing eyes' icon on the back page of *Le Cri du Matin*. When Tommi wandered through to the kitchen, the door swung back and forth its usual four times behind him.

Willem van Hoogstraten was preparing fresh coffee. 'Can I help you?' Although he'd never seen this man's face, he recognized him immediately. A suddenly rushing heart showed in his eyes and revealed the fact that Willem had been waiting for this visit.

Taking the measure of Willem, Tommi smiled. 'Nice spot. Never had the pleasure.'

'We're a bit of a local secret.'

'I love secrets... Haven't seen that Pearl, have you? Some people say she stopped in here.'

Willem shook his head—too quickly, a deep raspberry color rising too spontaneously in his milky northern cheeks.

'May I have this?' Picking up one of Willem's hand-lettered menus.

'Of course.'

'Pearl's Kiss?'

'A sort of tribute.'

'I think I'll come back and take a picture.'

Fighting panic, struggling to control his shaking, Willem gestured: be my guest.

Tommi bowed and left the kitchen.

'Oh, *merde*!' Anne-Marie was flabbergasted. She was at a table in a shadowy corner with Georgette Duguay. She'd been brooding, hadn't really noticed the tall man who'd come in. 'Don't let him see me!' Sinking into her chair, pulling the *Le Soir Style* section up in front of her face.

Georgette turned and gawked. 'What a horrible-looking man. Who is he?'

'Never mind... Please!'

'Well, I don't blame you for hiding.'

'And please shut up! You don't even know him.'

'But I can *see* him.'

'Looks aren't everything, Georgette. *Mon dieu*!... Just be cool!'

The artist's model coolly raised her glass in a mock toast to a street girl's altruism. But it was empty. 'I could do with another one of these...What say?' Craning her elegant, much-studied neck, searching the room for Willem.

Preparing his coffee, considering Tommi's disturbing gaze, Willem van Hoogstraten realized he was afraid. Not for himself—for Pearl. Willem would never assume to be a part of it. He was just a simple man who had tried to do his bit. He had no idea how to confront the eyes of Tommi Bonneau, much less his camera. He'd spent a difficult week realizing he had no real notion at all as to the heart of Pearl Serein. And now this. Willem lifted his tray and pushed through the door. He could barely focus. He forgot where he was, went to the wrong table... twice! Regulars were watching Willem—blushing, flustered.

He finally placed the order with its rightful owner, then hurried to his two friends.

Willem couldn't carry the weight of his secret all alone.

Anne-Marie said, 'She was *here*?'

Georgette said, 'That was *him*?' Then turned to Anne-Marie.

Ignoring Georgette's accusing stare, she said, 'Could we have another round?'

Willem fetched pastis, more water, and poured one for himself—badly needed.

He took a break and tried to explain.

When he finished, Georgette said only, 'I would like to read this book about this maid.'

There was a respectful pause. Anne-Marie and Willem both knew Georgette had had a mother, long ago, who'd flown away off a trestle bridge, another victim of unkind love.

Anne-Marie tapped the front page of *Le Soir*. 'So this is true?'

'Seems so. At least from what she told me.'

She asked, 'But why would Pearl tell you things like that?'

'I guess she needed to. Poor thing, she was very stressed.'

## - 33 -
### Just a guy with a camera

Georgette said, 'Your Tommi made Willem tremble.'
Anne-Marie responded, 'He's not *my* Tommi.'
'But you wouldn't mind.'
'One day at a time, Georgette.'
The older woman patted the younger woman's hand. Sipped her drink.
And forced the issue. How did this happen—you and Tommi Bonneau?
Anne-Marie tried to explain. About the night at Diabolik. And after…
…well, no, not every delicious detail. She just said, 'Voila, that's how.' A shrug, a street-savvy smile. 'He's fun. It's been a bit of wild ride, if you know what I mean.'
Georgette asked Anne-Marie, 'Then why is Willem scared?'
'Oh, you heard him—he's worried about Pearl. You know how Willem is.'
As was usually the case, when closing time arrived with early evening, Anne-Marie and Georgette Duguay were the only two guests remaining in the Rembrandt. And normally—on any other Saturday—Willem would have brought a bottle and helped them finish it off. Not this Saturday. They watched him arranging tables for tomorrow. He wanted them to leave…
No, still not a word as Willem fastidiously arranged the table next to theirs.
Anne-Marie was losing patience. 'What are you so worried about?'
He paused. 'Everything. I feel I've got this entire thing so completely wrong.'

Georgette, never known to be subtle, said, 'You'd better invite us up, Willem.'

'No. Can't. It's been a trying day. I need a quiet night.' He continued placing spoons just so.

So they paid their bill and put their coats on, wondering as he saw them out.

Willem van Hoogstraten bowed, blushing, gaze averted, bolted the door behind them.

Before she left the van, Georgette admonished, 'You tell Tommi that Willem is our friend.'

'She's his job,' Anne-Marie retorted, dismissive. 'He's just a guy with a camera.'

'Tell him!'

Sure. *Salut*. And they parted at the corner.

───

Bitch. Anne-Marie resented Georgette's damning judgement.

She drove on, back into her little world…

You think he's ugly, Georgette? You should see him when he's up there on the roof. When Tommi throws back his head, lets the night wind fly through his hair. When he calls out, as if to the entire city, '*When the wind is high, I feel madness!*' And with an evil wink that makes her instantly wet, he whispers, 'So said Diderot.'

Then he runs.

Anne-Marie has never met or even heard of this Diderot. But of course she follows. In Tommi's words, *Un bel petit parkours*. Running out across the rooftops, down through the back streets and along deserted midnight docks, all acceleration, covering ground at a rate that leaves the ground weightless, a sensation of slicing the night air, wide open, of being outside space.

She can't follow everywhere. But watching Tommi vault from balcony to sill to railing as he scales the sheerest sides of buildings, leaves her dripping. And amazed.

Occasionally they'll sight others and this is another revelation. A community of people, all runners, fearless and beautiful, like herself and Tommi Bonneau. He told her, 'We're like the first people, Anne-Marie. Us, them, we travel against a backdrop of night in any direction our hearts send us. There's no else like us. We're brand new!'

Anne-Marie wished she'd told Georgette how, when you meet a guy like Tommi, it makes you question all the times before. But she knew Georgette would tell her thinking this way is her life's big problem. Did she need to hear that? She knew it. It happens with each one: This is the big one, this is the only one that's real. Yes, this girl's life's big problem. But how can she help it?

Running with Tommi in the dead of night…surely this is love. It has to be.

But saying that — Georgette would only turn the knife a little deeper.

Then why did she hide when he came in today?

Because there was something wrong and she needed to think.

Because Tommi was fun. But he was angry. Too angry.

And because Tommi only talked of *love* when he was doing Pearl.

Tommi's studio was like a shrine. Anne-Marie could understand that. Pearl's fabulous! She knows she would not be there with him if it weren't for Pearl. She even told him, 'If you love her so much, why not ask her out?' No hard feelings on her part. 'I mean, I understand.'

Tommi told her, 'It's not like that. It's like she's my Béatrice.'

Béatrice? Hearing that, Anne-Marie felt doubly jealous and must've looked at him wrong.

'Pearl is my job, OK? My work. Got it? If you don't believe it, go away. I don't need that shit.'

'No,' agreeing. Fine. Cool.

…But *why*? Why the need? What was there? She gnawed at it in her way.

Like most men, he had a need to explain his heart's obsession. Or try.

'Hints,' said Tommi, 'hints and secrets. We take pictures because of the secrets they contain — secrets we can't fathom any other way. Look at Dante, seeing the glory of God reflected in Béatrice's eyes, *I believe that so piercing was the ray/ which I endured that would have been lost/ if from it I had turned my eyes away* …Look at Petrarch, seeing perfection once in Laura—and living by it his whole life! It's there. It's our duty to keep searching. We look for hints of perfection.'

Right. And it was Tommi's job to know all these famous people. Anne-Marie knew a Béatrice but not a Laura. Béatrice the film star, the one in *Betty Blue*. Famously fucked up, but dangerously *belle*, someone a girl like her could relate to. Anne-Marie had seen the film six times. She'd even made a pilgrimage to the beach town in the south where they filmed it. 'You know *her*?'

Tommi would sigh when she said things like that and run his fingers through her curls. He talked about a guy called Henry, an American in Paris. 'Henry Miller…He said, *The task of genius, and humanity is nothing if not genius, is to keep the miracle alive, to live always in the miracle, to make the miracle more and more miraculous, to swear allegiance to nothing, but live only miraculously, think only miraculously, die miraculously…*'

'He said that?' Could he speak French, this Henry? Wasn't Pearl's mama American?

'He's dead…and he didn't *say* it, he wrote it in a book.'

'Ah.' Like that Diderot, she'd finally figured out. Anne-Marie was not a big reader of books.

'He's a man you would've liked. Very into sex.'

'Sex is healthy.' Sex is fun!

'Sex is energy. Sex is the vines on the wall.'

What? Tommi would say things like that. And it left Anne-Marie feeling lonely, even when she was right there beside him, pushing against him, wanting more, always more…

'Cartier-Bresson says, *In whatever one does, there must be a relationship between the eye and the heart*. When the master says it, you believe it. We go through the eye to the heart.'

Who? Anne-Marie had no idea. Sounded like another nob.

Tommi told her, 'I believe it. I've seen it, this perfect thing.' Tommi said he had seen it there in Pearl. 'My job is to immortalize this woman—to poeticize her. It truly is. My Béatrice.'

'I see,' said Anne-Marie.

Hardly. Well, not really. Not at all.

But she *felt* it. Anne-Marie's heart sensed that a woman like herself hardly registered on Tommi's heart's scale of virtue, that movie and rock stars and the *Local Scene* were as close as she'd ever come to Tommi's heart's ideal. *Of course* she felt that. It wasn't the first time Anne-Marie had resigned herself to the fact she would have to settle for being the one in a man's bed but not in his heart. And when Tommi reached for her, she rolled back into his arms. Ready, willing and able. Mm! Whoever he knew, whatever he believed, there was no denying the fact that *she* was here, right now, with him. And she *wanted* to be here. Because men like him were her addiction. Her instinct told her not to push too far. She listened, but so much was beyond her.

So she watched and, mainly, *felt* him…

Tommi Bonneau believed these things he told her. It was clear to her. He believed it more than anything — including love. The kind you can actually touch. And when she was with him on the rooftops, running with him, she saw him from a close-up vantage no one else did — not even Pearl Serein, and she knew she should take what she could get when it came her way and enjoy it till it came to a head. Which it would. Because it always did.

She needed to believe she could take Tommi's pain and make it better.

But she was sharing Willem's uncertainty. Why should Willem be afraid of Tommi?

Anne-Marie held her born-to-be-faithful heart in abeyance, forced her mind to ignore these looming worries as she guided the van back to the house at 33 Rue Pontbriand.

## – 34 –
## Sunday's worse than Saturday

Anyone with boyfriend problems knows Sunday's worse than Saturday.

'*Salut?*' Aliette approached the battered old Westfalia van. Anne-Marie was sitting at the wheel. She had seen the inspector and pulled over. The inspector had not seen her — she had been walking aimlessly, far from anywhere that mattered, honestly trying to give it (and herself) a break. Now here was Anne-Marie, pulled over, wanting a word, and the inspector was surprised. Anne-Marie never sought her out, she mainly tolerated the cop who was Georgette's standoffish friend. For history's sake, mainly. Sympatico, as required — that was Anne-Marie's basic position.

Anne-Marie seemed almost lethargic, tired eyes exuding a well-fucked Sunday absence. Lucky her. Before Anne-Marie could speak, the inspector said, 'Just tell me one thing — is she with him?'

'No. *I'm* with him.'

'I meant hiding. Working on this thing together. You know what I mean.'

'We haven't seen her.'

We. How touching. Fine. *Alors...* 'What can I do for you?'

'Look after Willem.' Which meant, Take him off the street.

'Willem? Willem's a private citizen. Until Willem breaks the law, it's Willem who looks after me, and I pay him for the attention.'

Anne-Marie just stared.

'Has Willem got a problem?'

'Willem broke the law.'

'Really. What did he do?' Aliette knew Anne-Marie knew more about the law and its ins and outs than most people you might meet — hard-won knowledge gained from a street-faring life.

'Go ask him. Just make sure he's not at risk.'

'At risk?'

She grinned thinly. Shrugged.

Aliette envied her amazingly wild jet-black curls. 'OK. We'll have a talk with Willem.'

'Thank you.'

She asked, 'What about you? Are you at risk?'

Anne-Marie instinctively retreated. 'Risk is a matter of taste.'

No cop could argue with that. She tried to get serious. 'But these guys are dying. And he's —.'

'No!' Anne-Marie was with him. She would defend him. 'He has his camera. His story. His big ideas about manhood... And he's a pain in the ass like all the rest of them...' Her eyes went soft, looking for the cop to understand. 'But how does that kill anyone?'

'Then what is Willem's problem?'

'Willem's scared.'

'Of what?'

'His shadow?' Shaking her head — this is a gift. Don't push me.

'I can't help if you won't tell.'

'I'm not asking for your help. It's Willem.'

Aliette nodded. OK, I'll accept your gift. Then, 'So...' trying a smile — a two-girls-out-on-a-Sunday kind of tone. 'You're looking good. It's going well?'

The veteran street girl just rolled her eyes: Don't bullshit me.

OK, fine. But Aliette *was* truly interested. 'How long?'

'A few weeks.'

'Too early to say much, then?'

'A little.'

'What's so great about him?'

'There are certain things we like to do together.'

'But Pearl? I mean —'

'She's just his Béatrice,' sniffed Anne-Marie, defiance hardening those huge dark eyes.

Béatrice. Right. 'OK. Thanks... You keep an eye out at your end for me?'

Sure. The van pulled away.

The inspector's aimless Sunday walk now had a destination. At the Rembrandt she ordered beer and frites. When it arrived, Willem took a breath and asked, 'Are you going to arrest me?'

'Let's talk about it first. I might be willing to negotiate.'

'You?' Willem blushed. 'I didn't think you'd be—'

'Stop it, Willem. Take a break. Tell me.'

It wasn't terribly busy. He saw to a dessert order, presented a bill with a coffee refill, came back and sat. After he told her how he'd sheltered Pearl and his instant fear on the occasion of Tommi's visit, she had to tell him, 'You should have told us.'

He repeated, 'Are you going to arrest me?'

'I will if you keep asking. Why did he make you nervous?'

'I don't know. It was like he was looking right through me.'

'Are you hiding Pearl Serein?'

'No.'

'But?'

'She asked me to keep it a secret. There is such a thing as honor, you know.'

Aliette sat back, sipped beer, munched another frite. 'I know, Willem... I know.'

'But...'

'But?'

'She's not who I thought she was.'

Aliette felt a kind of bitter pity, the two emotions mixing like a burning soup. She asked, 'And what was that?'

Willem wasn't sure. 'She told me her life's ambition is to start a kindergarten just for boys.'

'Isn't that sweet.'

'I suppose.'

She asked, 'How could she possibly be what you thought she was?'

He asked, 'Are you going to arrest me?'

## − 35 −
## Remy aggrieved

Aliette Nouvelle was not the only one out walking aimlessly on a Sunday. Remy Lorentz had no lessons booked that day. He'd woken up and realized he was bored with hanging around the club, waiting for the next bored woman. He'd been vaguely hoping a bit of tennis with Agnès Guntz would help her get past the shock of Bruno Martel. Maybe they could take up where they'd left off. Good idea, but much too quick. That same old problem — Remy was impetuous. It never served him well. His mother had told him. *Pearl* had told him. Agnès had retreated. She needed time. She needed space. She actually seemed to like that fat phony. Remy could not call Rose Saxe — not on a Sunday afternoon. And he wasn't sure he wanted to. Her story in yesterday's paper had bothered him, had sent him back to places he didn't want to go. He was walking, trying to understand this nagging irritation. That cop with the blonde hair had planted the seed. Replanted it — because he'd put it out of his mind. Necessary. Because he was never going to make it to Roland Garros, but you had to earn a living and teaching tennis at the Quarter Racquets Club was about as soft a touch as he would find. But it was always there: Remy had always been better than the rest of them. Tennis made Remy a star when he was twelve. He'd been featured in the school paper every year for winning something — Bonneau had taken his picture. They read about him. Hung around him, like the girls did. They tried to be his friend.

Yes, and now Remy worked for them.

That cop had gone straight to it. Forced him to face it. Again.

Now Rose Saxe was throwing it into the streets for everyone to pick through.

The thing that rubbed closest to the bitter heart of it was that he wasn't even mentioned. That was wrong. If there was going to be a history of Pearl, Remy Lorentz had to be part of it.

Remy's mama—five years gone now—had told him love made life bearable. Especially a life spent in service to people who took you for granted. Mama, who'd passed all those years behind the counter in the tiny stationery shop with Remy's moody pa, would know. No matter how high Remy had got in local, then regional tennis circles, she always told him, 'Find someone on your own level. Don't be a dreamer. It never works.'

Remy believed her. Remy had been with Pearl, and Pearl had been on his level. Their paths were parallel, if sometime distant at certain points along the way. Two small shops across the street from each other, the life in a small apartment directly above. Pearl's American mom was good at tennis and Pearl had inherited it. From retail to tennis, they shared much, they understood each other, he and Pearl. Then teaching. Because, no, Roland Garros, Wimbledon, Forest Hills…the larger tennis world beyond was not in the cards for Remy Lorentz. It took a while but he came to terms with that. It took some time for Remy to find Pearl…to find her *again* after the heady days of being an up-and-coming tennis phenom, which, let's face it, were days filled with champagne, interviews, blow jobs on demand. Oh, man! Hard to let go of a life like that. But finally, after a year of anger, too many blind bursts in dead-end directions…then depression… he had allowed himself to make a call and see what Pearl was up to.

Teaching. The little ones. It was her mission in life.

Pearl helped Remy find his stroke again, so to speak. She helped him understand that he could teach tennis and still enjoy life making the most of the 'lovely talent' nature had bestowed. Lovely talent. Those were Pearl's very words. He kept them like a mantra. She pointed him toward the club. Encouraged him. Straightened his tie and sent him off. He got the job. She helped him deal with the death of his mother. They knew each other. They were doing well, even if Pearl was never anywhere remotely near to being one of those excellently willing tennis groupies always waiting by the exit ramp, always up for whatever. Well, there's no perfect life.

But before she'd died, Remy's mama had said they were good together. He and Pearl.

Then one dumb mistake — one silly moment of impetuous assholerie: 'You can have her for a thousand francs, man.' — and Remy lost Pearl to Didi.

Didi Belfort was so not-Pearl. Watching Pearl and Didi on the court, Remy knew that Didi knew it too. No way you can be with a woman who won't ever let you win a point. Pearl played hard. Didi played like a panicky giraffe. It wouldn't last. Impossible. It was her little gesture — to show him how things would have to be. Remy could see it every time he saw them.

And, OK, Remy got it. No more asshole. You say *au revoir* to poor Didi — we will move forward, with respect. I promise.

Then Tommi Bonneau put Pearl and Didi in his column on the back page of *Le Cri du Matin* and everything changed. Putting a picture of Pearl and Didi out dancing in the same space as a shot of a tanned and water-beaded Johnny Halliday with an arm around his newest amour on some beach ensured everyone would see it — and see it in that light. Especially Didi, if not Pearl.

You never knew what Pearl was thinking. Remy always thought he did.

Didi. Pierre Angulaire. The banker... Remy got to watch them, sitting there naked on the men's locker-room bench reading about the fun they'd had with Pearl the night before. That was when Remy began taking up those silent offers the ladies made while he was demonstrating the basics of the backhand. Had he ever actually liked any of them? More to the point: Had they liked him? Not much. Not past those few minutes of hot fun...

Remy's sullen meditation brought him to the house in Rue Pontbriand. He knew he shouldn't be standing in front of this door. Two cops, that judge — they'd all told him in no uncertain terms. Back off. Stay cool. Don't paint yourself into a frame.

He should walk on. But didn't. Remy knocked. Hard. Kept at it, till the door was opened.

Bonneau was still in his pyjamas. 'You? What the hell do you want?'

Bonneau was taller. Always had been. But he didn't take care of himself. That had bothered Remy since they were five years old, neighbors but never friends in Rue Marianne. He said, 'You look like hell, man.' And punched Tommi in his sagging mouth and knocked him flat.

He walked in. 'Getting in shape, are we?' Taking a gander into the weight-strewn dining room while Tommi regrouped, struggling to his knees. 'About time,' muttered Remy, and turned and kicked him. Tommi fell over, curled up, holding his gut. Remy told him, 'You're the cause of all this. You fucked up my whole life with your bullshit. Hers too… What have you done with her?' He looked in the dim study. Saw nothing but a bird and a million books. Demanded, 'Are you hiding her here, you weird ass? If you are…Pearl!'

Remy kept going, into the kitchen, through to the back. 'Ah.' There was a life-sized picture of Pearl on the wall—ripped, fading, a Pearl from some years back. And more faces in a pile of 8x10's, smoky, washed out. Who were *they*? Remy was puzzling over a ghost-white face when Tommi came in. Geeky Tommi—who picked up the tennis racquet lying by the door. Remy sniffed, 'Forget it, man. She'll never play with you… Who's this supposed to be? Looks like Bruno…the eyes, and that's gotta be Didi. Is this like art or something?' Sorting through the pile, very unconcerned about Bonneau.

Tommi said, 'You know I hate tennis. This is Didi's. He was going to kill me with it.'

Top-of-the-line composite. Light. Flexible. But hard enough to dent Remy's well-shaped skull. Tommi smashed Remy on the back of the head. Several times. What a mess.

But Tommi was angry too.

## - 36 -
## Pushy Rose

Sunday evening.

Sipping a beer, Piaf circling her ankles, the inspector punched in Tommi's number from the comfort of her bed. She got his answering machine brusquely instructing callers to 'go through my editor.' She left an airy message: '*Salut*, Tommi, Aliette Nouvelle here…I'd be interested in seeing prints of those shots we did the other day…was thinking it might be something nice for my mother's birthday. Oh, and I'd love to hear your take on that Rose Saxe thing. I'm around this evening. Give me a call.' She left her number. Did not honestly expect him to call her back.

One minute later, the phone rang. '*Oui*.'

'Inspector?' A whisper. Someone who had embraced her clandestine role.

'Hello, Rose.'

'Was it all right?'

'Perfect. Looking forward to tomorrow's revelations.'

'Look, there's really not much more I can do with this thing the way it stands.' Sounding as if the matter were another party that was getting a little flat.

'But they promised a series.'

'All done—on my editor's desk. I want to take it further. I was thinking I could try something from a police point of view. You know? Spend a day in the car with a detective. That sort of thing. Can you to set it up for me?'

'I don't think it would help your cause, Rose. All it is at this stage is surveillance. Terribly dull. Making the rounds…we watch, we wait.'

'Watch what?'

'The streets. Known haunts. The bus station. Trains. Planes. Some people...'

'Which people? My people?'

'I can't divulge that.'

'People want more from this story.'

'I agree. But a surveillance diary would never satisfy your readers, not with Tommi turning up the heat the way he is.' She tried to encourage her. 'You're on the right track, Rose. Really. I'm impressed. Maybe we could talk further at the end of the week. I mean—'

'Hold a moment...' Aliette heard Rose tell someone, 'Court ten...be right there.' Rose returned, 'Sorry.'

'Not a problem. Nice evening for tennis.'

'Maybe one of your detectives knows her,' suggested Rose. 'Maybe he loves Pearl Serein like all the rest of them. It could be the thoughts of an inspector hunting an old friend. Mm? I'm a good writer, Inspector. Just give me the thread of another angle and I can develop it.'

'The only cop who knows her has been taken off the case.' She thought about it. 'You could try the pathologists. Now there's a world of broken hearts. Your readers would love the two men working on it. They both have buckets of style. I could set *that* up.'

'Are you palming me off, Inspector?'

It was this disquieting persistence. 'Not in the least. I'm giving you a thread.'

'Aliette...' said Rose, her tone now softer, motherly, angling, 'we're in this together, my dear.'

'Rose, I appreciate your enthusiasm, but people cannot be distracted. Or compromised. Their thoughts on Pearl, from whatever angle, have nothing to do with their work. We're not ex-friends or fans, we are instruments of the law. If we went in that direction and it came to light, defense advocates would find the tiniest things and—'

'Let me shadow *you*. I'll do a profile of a commissaire-in-waiting.'

Such a pushy woman. 'You're kind. But again, highly inappropriate. Our current commissaire is on leave and I fully expect to see him back on the job before too long.' Aliette the diplomat.

Rose was blunt. 'Can we not move past this polite veneer? We are talking serial murder here.'

'We don't know that yet, madame. And you must not even think of suggesting such a thing.'

'I can take this so much deeper, Inspector.'

'I have to let you go, Rose. I'll be in touch.'

Ringing off, wondering if the lady understood her role. The cousin game was often delicate.

Within a minute, the phone rang again.

'*Putain!* you're not my friend.' And he hung up. Such an angry Tommi.

Sipping beer, running a toe along Piaf's back, wondering, Could Anne-Marie handle that?

## — 37 —
## Lunch with Monsieur le Divisionnaire

Inspector Nouvelle ate her cereal slowly and deliberately. Then she combed her hair, applied make-up, donned a serious gray suit. Took the gun from the back of her sweater drawer and put in her briefcase. Couldn't remember when she had last carried it. Hadn't needed it. So many other much more subtle ways of getting the job done. But Norbert Fauré was a hard-nosed traditionalist and a gun was *obligatoire*. A brisk walk to work cleared her mind.

Stepping into Monique's office for coffee and the usual Monday morning meeting to make sure everyone was headed in the right directions, she was met by a picture of Claude in rumpled clothes, spade in one hand, a flat of geraniums in the other, befuddled, utterly at a loss in the face of the intruding lens.

**Local Scene**

*Why are we not surprised to learn Commissaire Claude Néon has been relegated to gardening duty while the search for Pearl Serein continues? A leave of absence? How genteel. One fears for the flowers in his care. After all, look at the mess he made with the rose that is our Pearl.*

A grim PJ team lingered over coffee, suffering with their exiled leader, letting righteous anger simmer. The inspector's first bit of business was to draft another memo to Gérard Richand. Please! Silly words are one thing, pictures of cops looking like fools are dangerous. Not exactly in those words, but Gérard would hear her. She was with Monique, making sure the thing went off ASAP with a photocopy of Article 9 and a *perfect* photocopy of the offending page attached when Monsieur le Divisionnaire arrived. Early. At least half an hour.

'I have a very full schedule.' He accepted a coffee and a plate of biscuits and took it through to Claude's office. He shut the door. Message: I am not part of this debacle. The inspector finished with Monique, returned to her desk for her notes, checked her face and hair in the ladies' room mirror. Then went in. Fauré was standing at Claude's window, nibbling a biscuit, 'Well?'

The man's presumptive presence irked her. 'We've been talking to and watching members of each victim's family, as well as her own connections, past and present. But no sign of her.'

Finishing his biscuit, he started a cigarette. 'Been looking across the river?'

'Sir, anything beyond our jurisdictional lines would be for you to arrange.'

He shrugged his indifference to territorial protocol. 'You have contacts—it's your beat.'

'Don't forget, she's a schoolmistress...the little ones.'

'Néon's exact description. So?'

'I can't see her going anywhere near my contacts for love or money.'

The divisionnaire sat in Claude's chair and made a note with Claude's pen. Aliette, always momentarily fixated watching people make their various notes, observed a still-vital, highly pragmatic police professional under the rumpled world-weary veneer.

He looked up, caught her staring. 'Other ideas? Observations?'

'We're monitoring the media.'

'Absurd,' he muttered.

'Perhaps. The regional paper has assigned one of their columnists to do a series on it. Her first piece came out on the weekend...it's generating reactions.' Rose Saxe's effort was discounted with a roll of Fauré's smoky eyes. Aliette pressed on. 'This is a small place. People feel connected to a situation. Sometimes they say more than they mean to.' He sipped his coffee, drew on his cigarette, turned his gaze toward the mountains. She added, 'I'd like to take a closer look at Bonneau, but my judge won't let me.' No recrimination; a simple statement of strategic possibility.

The tiniest sniff expressed succinctly Norbert Fauré's measure of Gérard Richard. 'No?'

'Insists we have to find her first. He really detests the love and rumor element.'

'Well, he's doing his job.' Like the lowest-grade traffic cop was implied. Then, offhand, too casual, he asked, 'And how is Monsieur Néon?'

Aliette suppressed a smile. She heard cop guile, loud and clear. 'Our contact has been minimal. Monique...our secretary? She's visited twice. Moral support. And gardening columns. He seems to be weathering the storm...Our friends downstairs will have much more on that front.'

'*Bon.*' Stubbing his smoke, he pondered it.

Commissaire Duque's City Police team had been ordered to watch PJ Commissaire Néon. Distasteful, but not unwarranted, the most logical of moves, so much so that Claude would surely know what was occurring. Inspector Nouvelle was being apprised of developments but was excused, along with her team, from participating in this aspect of the investigation, the better for morale when the thing was resolved. Norbert Fauré had excused himself as well, the better for his own credibility. But like any prudent cop caught up in such a thing, Aliette had been proceeding under the assumption Fauré would have his hand in deep regardless.

So it was dreary, this charade of questions to which the answers were already known.

She waited, blank and professional, for him to pronounce.

Whatever he had in mind, Fauré decided to wait. 'Let's hear what Conan has to say.' Finishing his coffee, he took two of Monique's cookies for his pocket.

The inspector escorted him down to the morgue. She was embarrassed—she could see Raphaele Petrucci was too—as Dr. Gilles Conan went through the same spiel she'd suffered through on Friday, heading toward the same non-conclusions.

The cagey divisionnaire seemed to know exactly what to do: He sighed with undisguised boredom through his hoary nose and fired up another smoke.

Flustered, Gilles Conan recited, 'Tobacco smoke cooks the blood and curdles it like milk.'

Norbert Fauré absorbed this with a blasé grunt. 'We all have to die of something, Gilles.'

'You won't enjoy it, my friend.'

'Are we supposed to enjoy dying?'

'I believe we are—and it *can* be beautiful. It is a part of life, no?'

'I enjoy these.' Fauré puffed deeply on his Gauloise.

Conan reddened. 'You are free to die as you choose, but really Norbert, your smoke does not help the forensic process...Mm?'

Gauloise dangling from his purplish lips, Divisionnaire Fauré threw up his hands in mock surrender and walked out of the morgue, presumably to finish his smoke in the street.

Aliette watched him go, uncertain as to how Conan's gratuitous display would settle.

'Don't you worry,' soothed the doctor, 'Norbert Fauré is a practical man. He understands good science cannot be rushed.'

'I hope so.' More for Raphaele's sake than hers—he was the one who stood to lose most from Conan's leisurely approach. She left them to it and joined Fauré on the commissariat steps. It was a nice May day. Would Monsieur le Divisionnaire enjoy a walk before eating?

'You walk?'

'I do, usually. It's not far.'

Lighting up yet another cigarette, he gestured: Lead on, Inspector.

Holding the door for Norbert Fauré, the inspector prepped him with some local cop lore. 'Jacques Normand used to eat here all the time.' Said with a bit of cop pride as she bid him enter.

Fauré paused, as if repositioning her in his mind. 'Ah, *oui*,' he said, and stepped inside.

The noonday sun was refracted through the Rembrandt's high portals, affording Willem's guests shady nooks for privacy amid oscillating patches of pure light like diamonds on the floor. Today's special was fried carp, a local delicacy drawn from the streams of the Sundagau district on the southern boundary of Alsace: cut into strips (with tail if you wanted), rolled in a semolina batter and fried in peanut oil, served with a lemon on the side, mayonnaise sauce and a green salad; preceded by leek soup, followed by a choice of the cheese plate or a dish of Willem's chocolate mousse. Monsieur le Divisionnaire chose a bottle of Tokay Pinot Gris in the Bruderbach style from a respected domain at Westhoffen, at the north-most end of the Wine Route...

Wine from the north, fish from the south; most eclectic. Willem approved.

Fauré sipped water and asked, 'This thing about love...Néon. What do you make of it?'

*What?* It caught her off-guard. She felt her ears heating — God, I'm so automatic. She sipped her own water, attempted a casual reflection. 'It can certainly get in the way of an investigation.'

'When we talked to him, he kept insisting he was there to protect her. That any relations which developed did so like some kind of inevitable trap.'

Aliette, breathing evenly, shrugged politely: so?

'Is he the passionate sort?' wondered Fauré, also as polite as protocol would have it.

'Sir, I wouldn't know.'

He smiled, flat and enigmatic. Whether or not he believed her was suddenly one of life's darkest mysteries. Aliette was beginning to squirm as Willem reappeared with the wine. Norbert Fauré tasted, accepted and signaled Willem to pour. The inspector stared dumbly at a glass of *pinot gris*.

'He mentioned you and he were at the party at this club of his...you were wearing —'

'With respect, sir, I know what I was wearing.'

'I don't doubt your respect. But tell me, why *were* you there?'

'He asked me...he needed a date.' Hadn't Claude explained all this?

'Doesn't know many women then?'

'I don't know who he knows. And he's not actually a member... just probationary. He felt it was related to the case and I was a logical partner to team with for that part of it.'

'Back-up?' Sipping wine. Lidded eyes looking down into it, instead of across at her.

'You could say. As you know, there was a brawl and victim number six occurred shortly after.'

A cursory nod. He asked, 'Nice place? Good time?'

She was confused, suddenly trying to protect herself. And Claude. 'Sir, I don't see—'

'And all contact since that night has been strictly business.' Not a question; an observation.

Voilà: her suspicions as to Division's supposed hands-off position were confirmed and more so. She could only nod, *oui*, and wait while Willem placed their soup and spoons.

'Never been a member of any club,' Fauré mused, 'unless you count the divisionnaire's quarterly get-togethers. Which I don't.' Rueful. 'It's strange to me how economies of scale in holes like this allow for things one can't rightly contemplate up north. Almost a disincentive. Eh?'

Aliette tasted her soup and smiled at Willem — excellent! — as he placed their salads and added a fish knife to each setting. She only shrugged at Norbert Fauré. What was she meant to say? Small is beautiful. Small holes included. Where was he pushing this?

'You're not a member of this place?'

'No.'

'Not the club type, you?'

'Not exactly.' In fact she had spent many childhood and adolescent hours at her parents' tennis club in Nantes. But Aliette Nouvelle was not inclined to share with this man.

Fauré finished off his soup in eight rapid spoonfuls. Taking a piece of bread, thoroughly swabbing his bowl, he told her, 'I would like to revisit this idea of you and Néon going dancing.'

'It was one night,' said Aliette. 'We're well past that episode.' She spooned her soup at a measured pace.

'Perhaps we could recreate that moment.'

Delicately breaking her bread, studying it. Then meeting his eyes. 'Why would we want to?'

'This club remains a locus — and what else have we got? Precious little. Adrenaline — according to Conan. And love... Love for this woman, Pearl Serein. But everyone associated with this accursed thing has been a member of that club. *Alors...*' Popping soup-soaked bread into his smoke-stained mouth, 'Néon is the latest object of this gossip writer's ridiculous darts. He has time on his hands and he's been spending a lot of it at this club. Learning tennis.' The divisionnaire seemed perplexed as he paused to sip his wine.

Aliette sensed he found the notion of Claude and tennis somehow wrong. Un-cop-like?

Fauré dabbed his lips, laid out his thinking. 'Néon is perceived as the latest suitor for the lady's affections — failed perhaps, if one believes Bonneau, but that's all to the better since the killer strikes at her failed lovers. And if the killer is a member of this club, which you'd have to think he — or she…this *is* a possibility, Inspector — might well be, and if Néon were to appear there in the right sort of situation, then something might occur. Like last time? If you were there with him, better prepared, mind you, you might succeed in intervening. You *are* known for your sense of timing.'

Her cheeks (not to say her ears) were burning and she knew it showed.

He leaned forward, the better to impart professional confidentiality. 'Inspector, I don't care about your personal relations with Commissaire Néon. What I do care about is having this thing resolved before the center collapses around what remains of our integrity in this godforsaken place. For which I am ultimately responsible. Not you.'

Willem was waiting with two specials. Fauré took knife and fork in hand. Inspector Nouvelle had lost her appetite. As Willem set her plate down, he bent close to her ear. 'Are you all right?'

'What?' She emerged from a breathless space, heart pounding. 'Oh…yes, yes, fine.'

'Do you want more water?'

'Please.' She resumed a careful examination of her crust of bread.

Fetching water, Willem van Hoogstraten watched her, concerned. The inspector was perspiring. Her face, usually so calm, somehow inspiring, was drained of the thing he loved to see. She looked like she'd been in bed for a week with the flu. Willem had never seen her looking this way.

When Willem returned to their table, the inspector's dining partner was savoring his fish. 'Good,' he pronounced through a full mouth. Reaching for his wine, his suit coat fell open, exposing the handle of a holstered gun. Guns in the Rembrandt! What was going on? Did it have to do with Pearl? Willem felt unwell himself. Bowing stiffly to the compliment, he moved to pour water for Aliette. His hand unsteady, he asked her quietly, 'Do you need an aspirin?' He was loath to leave her alone with this man.

'I'm fine, thank you, Willem.'

He continued to watch as he made his rounds: the man with the gun talked on, the inspector not meeting his eyes, barely touching her food—which Willem knew she loved.

When they left, she glanced at him, deepening his discomfort with a pale, apologetic smile.

Returning to clear and re-set the table… The man had left a twenty-franc *pourboire*.

Willem was not sure he wanted it.

## – 38 –
### Breakthrough?

The divisionnaire would set it up. He would speak with this Gaston person, the man at the club. All the inspector would have to do was show up on Néon's arm. 'Good lunch.' Patting *her* arm as he left her at the second-floor landing, heading off to meet with Commissaire Duque and Captain Deubelbeiss. Then it was down to the courthouse. Busy day indeed.

'Good lunch?' Monique passed her a reply memo from Gérard Richand responding to her request for an Article 9 against *Le Cri* and Tommi Bonneau. The judge said no. Again. He noted that despite certain rhetorical turns, Bonneau's innuendo was essentially personal as opposed to institutional. And it had nothing to do with heart attacks. He intimated that, given the context, a counter lawsuit could serve to derail the entire process. He advised her to focus on her mandate. Which was: Find Pearl Serein. *Good lunch?* Aliette Nouvelle felt sick. She sat at her desk, unable to concentrate on more paperwork forwarded by the Swiss police. A two-page memo from Children's Judge Tuillot regarding her pending disposition as to the Hashish Twins was a meaningless blur. The inspector's heart was racing.

It was anger — Norbert Fauré spying, far beyond the context of the situation!

It was frustration — she had worked hard and *faithfully* to guard the special thing that was herself and Claude Néon. She needed to believe Claude had too.

It was fear — fear of the judgement Fauré might pass.

It was not right. Not fair that her heart should be used so coldly...

It was a lonely moment, a professional hazard, confronting one's true place in an endless line of dispensable pawns. Aliette Nouvelle juggled people all the time, didn't she? She did. And a heart was often central to the balance. The inspector was feeling the coldness at the heart of the law.

Monique buzzed. *Identité Judiciaire* might have something for her. 'Merci.'

Five minutes later, a breakthrough. Forensics specialist Jean-Marc Pouliot waved her over to his bench. He turned on his projector. 'Resin-coated paper: scraped from beneath the noble's fingernails.' She gazed, trying to read the magnified image. What exactly had Belfort sunk his claws into?

"With traces of silver and gold."

'Explain. Please.'

'Photographic paper, to be more precise,' added Jean-Marc, clicking up another transparency.

'Photographic paper?' It looked like nothing so much as several microscopic turds.

'I've found silver halide and gold, along with traces of sodium thiosulfate. The silver halide suspended in gelatin is the surface of the paper, the gold would be residue from the toner solution used in the photographic process. The sodium thiosulfate would be from the fixer.'

Her first guess was automatic. 'Could it be newsprint? I mean, he arrived wrapped up in it.'

'Perpetrator's a fish dealer perhaps,' suggested Pouliot's partner Charles Léger, joining them.

'No, no,' muttered Jean-Marc, meticulously focusing another slide. 'Different process altogether. This is definitely from a photo. Not well rinsed, I'd say. Still traces of the fixer... Photo image breaks down, turns rather metallic-looking with exposure to light.'

'And yellowish?' Aliette Nouvelle heard the buzz of revelation in her brain.

Jean-Marc mulled it for a moment. 'Yes, bronzy, yellowish, sort of a used-up tone.'

Voila. 'Merci, messieurs.' *Bravo les IJ's*! That odd metallic look of the enlarged and somewhat tattered print of Pearl Serein in Bonneau's studio! Didier Belfort had been inside the house in Rue Pontbriand.

Carrying a photocopy taken from an enlarged slide — it really didn't look like anything — she went to the second floor. Duque and

Deubelbeiss were in the conference room, mulling their meeting with Fauré. 'We were just talking about you,' said Duque, gesturing her toward a chair.

She didn't doubt it. She felt both men watching her as she sat down.

It was coming up five when Monique buzzed. Gérard Richand was on the line.

'*Merci... Oui?*'

'Can we have a word?'

'Of course.' Opening her book. 'When?'

'Now, if you can manage it.'

Now? Most judges would be heading home at this hour. 'I'll be there in twenty minutes.'

Aliette Nouvelle and Gérard Richand knew each other well, the way ex-lovers sometimes do — no longer close, yet one still has a sense of the other that extends beyond the job. She could feel the judge's raw nerves through the telephone line. Feeling caught in the middle here, Gérard? The inspector had felt Norbert Fauré's gray, relentless pressure impinging on her own best instincts. As had Commissaire Duque. Job descriptions meant little when mandarins grew cranky. Had Fauré imparted his message to Gérard Richand as well? Was an old cop squeezing a purist judge? She hurried out.

The courthouse was quiet, all courts adjourned since four. Climbing the stairs, passing secretaries heading home, Gerard's among them. 'Door's open. He's waiting.'

'Come in, come in...' gesturing without looking up, gazing dully at his notes. She took a seat. Now a perfunctory smile to greet her. 'Just wanting to make sure we're on the same page.'

'This, I assume?' Dropping a copy *Le Cri* on the judge's pile of reading, open at the photo of Claude, lost and stupid in his spring garden. On the strength of their past intimacy, Aliette could be less than formal and not get slapped.

'Yes. God, yes,' Lamenting. 'My poor wife's become addicted. Souviron sits there studying it. My staff...the divisionnaire was growling about it throughout our chat. It's too absurd.'

'Maybe not absurd...Maybe time to move on Bonneau? He's turning Claude into a bullseye.'

Gérard seemed to laugh privately. 'That's what we need to discuss.'

'I don't think it's funny, Gérard. I think he's at risk.'

'Néon's a professional—he'll handle it.'

'Like the others?'

'He has no choice.'

'I think it's very close to boil-over time. It's dangerous.'

'He has to bear up. His career is on the line...' a quick, tense shake of his balding head. Poor Gérard, she thought—he really found it distasteful, truly believed Claude had got far less than he deserved by way of censure. 'He lets his silly adolescent passion create this ridiculous mess for all of us, and that includes you, and I for one will not—'

He was taken aback as she produced a reprint of her second memo requesting an Article 9 charge against *Le Cri du Matin* and Tomas Bonneau, and laid it on top of the rest of his materials. Second try in one day. Pushing. And Gérard Richand was not accustomed to being pushed by cops. 'But I sent my response to this. Did you not receive—' The judge stopped himself mid-stream.

She could read him, yes. And he could read *her*—gazing into him.

Pointedly wondering, 'What's the problem? Gérard?'

Yes, she had latitude. But he would not be pushed. He flared. 'The problem? *This* is garbage!' A voice that boomed, a large sweep of his arm demonstrating his contempt, sending *Le Cri du Matin* flying from his desk as if it were unclean. Her memo was swept away with it.

The inspector scooped up the mess of pages and quite brazenly put them back in front of him. Pushing past the limit? She was past caring. It suited her to see Gérard Richand less than certain. Being on the same page required it. 'Not garbage, monsieur. A *love* story. Talk to him. He'll tell you himself: Tommi does love. That's his purpose and it is a very high-minded one.'

'Well he treats it like garbage and Néon looks like a fool and I take it personally!' Glaring, he reminded her, 'And you should too!'

'But the man who runs me is going to leverage that garbage to get a result.'

Gérard's glare and flush abated. 'His people were supposed to respect the order. If not, what is the point?' Sighing, eyes clouding, fuming, 'I have standards, Inspector. *Some*one has to.'

The inspector smiled her sympathy. Message: I would *never* lump you into the same slimy bin as the principal actors in this sordid situation. But she insisted, 'Have another look, Gérard. Tommi Bonneau treats love as though it were what we all hoped it would be. Love is sublime. Love is ennobling. Love is the biggest challenge and the most profoundly simple secret in any man's heart—and his readers hang on his every word. It's the ones who fail at love that he treats like garbage. Pearl Serein is some kind of yardstick for Tommi Bonneau's idea of love *and* the men who want to make it. He harassed the men who failed with Pearl Serein—and they all died. Now he's after Claude. Fool or not, we have to protect him... I mean, this is our duty, no?'

'You are allowed to attack a man with words, Inspector—even ridiculous ones. To a point, this is fundamental to our system. And Monsieur Bonneau has not passed that point. At least not as far as this office is concerned. Souviron will stand with me on that. As for Néon the private citizen, that's his affair and he has chosen to stay silent.'

Aliette said 'He's still my colleague, Gérard. Yours too, when you get down to it.'

Richand's pinching shoulders, hardening eyes, said in no uncertain terms, 'No way. *Not* mine.'

And he told her, 'And those men still died of their own account.' Pearl's failed men. But perhaps Chief Instructing Judge Gérard Richand noticed *her* rising color. It was easily evident in a slender neck he'd once kissed with exceeding care. 'What do you care what happens to him?' Gérard knew the professional history of Néon and Nouvelle. Everyone did.

But he couldn't know their emotional present. Could he? She had no more faith in Norbert Fauré's integrity than Gérard did. An ugly, brutal, manipulative man.

She could not ask her judge what that old prick had been sharing as he'd made his strategy known. All she could do was plead, albeit calmly, 'Let me go into Bonneau's house — for an hour. I know I will find links, if not evidence, that can move this thing forward.'

Gérard Richard sniffed, hunkered down. 'What links?'

'Pictures. Pictures of Pearl... And maybe her. She could be there.'

Again, Gérard Richard laughed darkly. 'Would he be hiding her?'

Aliette refused to laugh along. 'He could well be.' She ached to tell him the larger story. But for her own sake, and for the trust of Commissaire Duque, she had to play a game with Judge Richard. 'How do we know until we look? That's my mandate. No?'

'If you have solid cause.'

'What if it's true?' Pulling Saturday's *Le Soir* from her briefcase, she slapped Rose Saxe's *exclusive* on his desk. 'Bonneau and Pearl Serein — some puppy love thing that's got all twisted? Wouldn't be the first serial killer to carry a flame like that.'

Gérard Richard barely gave it a glance. 'Just more muck we have to wade through. That won't open any doors. Don't read any more of it, if you want my advice.'

'I have to, Gérard. At this point there's nothing else.'

'Well I don't!' Surging... Then Gérard Richard deflated, weary of parrying with Inspector Nouvelle. 'We have to prove murder or we'll never be rid of this mess.' He shrugged away the notion of Pearl hiding at the center of the storm. 'Even if we found her sitting in front of his television giggling and completely complicit in this wretched thing, we still need to know the hows and whys of murder for Bonneau to be compelled to reply to the court.'

'Fine. Pearl or no Pearl, I could get you what you need to compel him.'

'What?'

'Pictures.'

Gerard stared glumly at his papers, as if stuck with a stubborn suspect who would not change her story despite all reason. 'Exactly how do pictures link to heart attacks, Inspector?'

'No idea. But it is not just Pearl Serein that's gone missing, monsieur. Apart from Tuche and Belfort — who did not die inside their homes, at each stop along the way, pictures of Pearl Serein have disappeared. Even Martel — he'd just moved into his new girlfriend's home; she told us she found a photo of Pearl Serein with his things. But it was gone when they went through the place.'

She had his attention again. And again he posed that logical question. 'How do you know this?'

'The commissaire was investigating.' Claude was a safe place to lay this transgression.

'Perhaps he has them.' A cynical sniff. 'Mm? Do we see our bold but foolish commissaire passing his days in retirement with pictures of Pearl Serein?'

'He's not the one who's obsessed.'

'No? Then why he is no longer on duty?'

Aliette would not go there. 'It's Bonneau, Gérard. Pearl Serein is his life's big cause.'

'Inspector, these words, these pictures, they are nothing but a distraction. Are you listening? Back page. By definition — a pastime. They do not cause heart attacks. How could they possibly be related?'

'Let me go in and find out!' Did she shout? Pretty close. She took a breath and quietly repeated her request. 'For my colleague's well-being, we *need* to go into Bonneau's house. One quick look before the divisionnaire puts Claude Néon out there like a sitting duck.'

Gérard Richand managed a smile, if rather snide. 'But you'll be with him. The divisionnaire has complete confidence.'

That stung — as it was meant to. She took a moment, nibbling at her thumbnail, then inquired, 'And how will this operation read on my new mandate?' Her mandate to root out Pearl.

Gérard's smile rested in place. But it grew softer. 'It won't. It will be an informal date. Like the last time — although quite against your current mandate. And the terms of his suspension.'

'And if something happens?'

'Which Fauré fully expects.'

The inspector was hearing Chief Judge Richand attempting to lead her, much as she'd been attempting to lead him. She knew him, professionally and personally, and now she was feeling his concern coming through despite his distaste. 'I don't think I like what you're telling me, Gérard.'

'Nor me. It's why I wanted to make sure we understood each other's position going in. OK?'

'OK. I appreciate it. But what can I do?'

'You could say you were busy when he calls. Or you could say it's against the rules and you don't want to compromise the investigation.'

'I can't do that.'

'For your colleague's well-being? Don't worry, no matter who he shows up with, they'll be watching him every step of the way.'

'I can't.' *Who else would he show up with?*

'You could. You should. Fauré's a hard man. But you *do* have a mandate.'

Yes, he was protecting her. She smiled. 'Thank you. I will keep it in mind.'

A vague shake of his ponderous head. He did not want thanking. 'I'm doing my job, Inspector. To the best of my ability. The record will show that. The rules will bear me out.'

'You can still call me Aliette, Gérard.'

'I am advising you, Inspector, not to ruin whatever measly substance this absurd thing might have. Or your career in the process. You people are on shaky enough ground as it is.'

'What about Claude?'

'I don't understand why you defend him.'

'I don't expect you would.'

'He betrayed our trust. Yours included. It won't bother me if he sinks in his own mess. I don't see why it should bother you.'

'I can deal with my own life, Gérard.' She sensed he was fishing for a confession. That his concern came with a quid pro quo. Well, to be a cop was to deal in trade-offs. But this was not about being a cop. Sorry, monsieur, my lips are sealed — Fauré's slimy intimations will have to do.

Richand nodded. OK. No confession. 'Still, my best advice is: Stay home.'

They sat there staring at each other.

'Pearl Serein…' Gérard twiddled his pen, musing bleakly. 'Do you think she's still alive?'

She shrugged. She didn't care. She asked again, 'Let me go into Bonneau's for half an hour.'

'No. Duque wants a word tomorrow. Something from IJ. Maybe things will change. Until then, we stick to the line we're taking till we find her or the doctors give us reasonable cause.'

'We'll get closer to our cause if we go inside Bonneau's house. I know we will.'

'We have an expert from Strasbourg working on it, Inspector.'

'If you could call it that.'

He nodded once, noting her contempt for the non-results of so-called experts. Then Chief Judge Richand took up his pen and shook his head, boggled by it all. 'You can watch Monsieur Bonneau. I dare say you already are. But you will not—and this is a formal instruction—go near him. If you are coerced into doing something you shouldn't, the court will deal with it, according to the rules of law. As for me, I'm still waiting for a rational, scientific statement explaining how a criminal act causing death was committed. And I am waiting for a missing woman to be found. *D'accord?... Inspector?*'

'Don't you see, Gérard? Do you really not see the link to pictures of Pearl Serein? And the link from there to Tommi Bonneau? He is the source of this thing... Gérard?'

'Don't *you* see that if we respond to that cretin in any way, our position in the eyes of our public is utterly undermined?' Easing back into his plush leather chair. 'Can't *you* see *that*?'

As she was leaving, the judge was jotting a note.

## - 39 -
## Flying blind

Two hours later, a softening spring sun was beginning to decline… Rose's column in that day's *Le Soir* was headed *Pearl and Tommi: That was then…*

The full-page piece, overleaf from the Editorial page, included an allusive photo of a street sign signaling Rue Marianne and a view from earlier days of Lycée F-A-Bartoldi. The narrative meandered, weaving together varying interpretations of local history. Gay culture advocate Léo Lacan insisted Tommi Bonneau was a nerdy camera fanatic who wanted nothing to do with girls, Pearl Serein included—whom Léo remembered as 'modest and withdrawn and not at all boy crazy.' But Bernadette Leclercq, who described herself as a 'full-time mother,' said, 'I always suspected they had something going.' But Louise Montvalon, now a real estate agent, implied that Bernadette Leclerq had always had a 'bitter streak.' Louise Montvalon said the 'golden age' of Pearl and Tommi was pre-teen, that the pair were 'definitely the talk of the town at ten,' adding, 'a time when love is pure, maybe purest.' This latter scenario was more or less backed by retired philo prof J. Gregoire, who had overseen the student-run weekly journal at Lycée F-A-Bartoldi. He remembered Tommi Bonneau taking excellent pictures of whatever was required, although his passion was clearly birds, not girls. But retired bio prof Paulin Soublin, who had organized the student photography club, recalled 'a wall full of student-body beauties adorning our darkroom, all provided by our club star, Tomas Bonneau.' Although Soublin could not recall a dewy Pearl amongst them. 'Mostly blonde…and much more, let's say vibrant,' noted Soublin, adding that he still cherished a pile of these classic shots, and that, 'I don't remember her at all.' Marguerite Dandurand, a neighbor who had minded a very young Tommi, would only say that, yes, she was aware they'd been friends. And that Tommi Bonneau had loved a good story. Several other former neighbors added wistful, if vague, recollections of the street.

Tomorrow's instalment, *A Mother in Connecticut*, promised further revelations.

Folding *Le Soir*, Inspector Aliette Nouvelle tucked it under her arm. She was leaning against Anne-Marie's old Westfalia van, observing the house in Rue Pontbriand. All views within were closed up tight. She had been mulling Gérard Richard's advice on the long walk from the courthouse to the east end — with a brief detour to give Piaf his supper. She had dispensed with her run this evening; she hadn't the energy after a debilitating day, courtesy Norbert Fauré. She was beginning to agree with Gérard that acquiescing to Fauré's crude idea was a no-win game. Nor had she bothered with a silly disguise this evening. There was no more point, not after today. She was back to basics — a cop in the street, in plain view, waiting, observing the source of her problem. She would not knock on Bonneau's door. But if Tommi Bonneau came out that door, she would ask for his reactions. It was all she could legally do. Reduced to pushing buttons.

Well, we do what we *can* do. And see what might transpire. She waited, heedless of breaking her supposed cover.

…*Pok*! A quick, hard, punching sound.

Certain firearms can make a sound like that when discharging and the trained inspector reacted by instantly hitting the ground.

But it was the sound of something punching a clean hole through glass. She raised her head. There was a bird, flying low and straight at her position. Whoa! She ducked again. Without veering in the slightest, the bird flew into the side of Anne-Marie's van, smacked against it with a feathery thud and dropped onto the pavement, an inch or two from the inspector's eyes.

Aliette pulled herself to her knees, wondering; What does a bird feel when it is dying?

Looking over her shoulder at the house — the glass that had been broken was the blinded window in Tommi Boneau's front room. She saw the vertical blind that had been opened a crack, fall shut.

Would Tommi come out? The inspector stared at the window, daring him, and waited…

It did not appear that he would. She turned her attention back to the bird... It was dead.

Poor bird. Bert? Tommi had called it Bert. Now what? She could pick the thing up, knock on his door and present him with this pathetic body. Accuse Tommi Bonneau of killing it.

Cruelty to animals: could that get her a mandate to search his house?

It occurred to her that this was not just a dead bird. This was another victim that had flown straight from the source — the house she wanted to enter but could not. She has seen it come out of that house. She had seen it in the act of dying. Or being killed. One of Tommi Bonneau's victims? Crashing through a window aside, Bert had had the entire sky and he had flown straight into a car. Flying *blind*. Why did that happen? She *knew* she knew the answer — or at least the beginnings of it.

But it would not come clear inside her mind. Too excited, feeling cop endorphins kicking in.

She thought, No, I'll take poor Bert to the morgue instead. Opening *Le Soir* to its full broadsheet expanse, Aliette rolled the small feathered body onto it. Then she gathered the edges carefully together into a sack-like package. Grasping the package gingerly like those good people carrying bags of doggy turd home from the park, she took off, now wishing for her jogging shoes, keeping half an eye out for any movement behind her. But there were no steps in her wake.

Responding to the dismissive thing he'd perceived in Norbert Fauré's smoked-out serpent eyes, Dr. Gilles Conan had decreed he would stay in town for an evening or two in lieu of the hour commute back to the capital. He and Raphaele Petrucci would pick up the pace, work late, maybe crack this thing. But before they started their evening investigations, it was Raphaele's pleasure to take him out for supper. Inspector Patrice Lebeau found the two doctors at La Piédmontaise, one of the pathologist's favorite local sources of Italian cuisine. He had ordered for both of them: *Bistecca à la Florentine* — aged ten days, marinated for three more in a mix of olive oil, lemon juice, garlic and sage. It was on its way. They were savoring the bouquet of a Barbera D'Alba '89, chosen by Conan, debating an interesting vegetal quality at the farthest reaches of the mouth, when Lebeau rushed in, breathless, insisting on behalf of Inspector Nouvelle that they return to the commissariat forthwith. They weren't happy with this command, and even less so to discover a dead goldfinch curled on the same gleaming metal pallet where the six victims' hearts had been displayed in a line that morning. Inspector Lebeau told Légiste Petrucci, 'She's upstairs making some calls.'

Raphaele sprinted up three flights…went in without knocking. 'What the hell are you thinking?'

Aliette was indeed on her phone. She held up one hand—wait!—as she told the party at the other end, 'Gérard, I assure you I would not disturb you like this if it were not of the utmost—No, we haven't found her… Gérard, you have to stop being so…' She caught herself before she said it (so Raphaele would never know) and took a breath before amending her request. 'For old time's sake, Gérard?' Raphaele's dark eyes narrowed. He'd heard rumors about the inspector's early days in this city. That tone, that one little phrase spoke volumes. '…yes, Gérard, I know every single consequence and repercussion, and I will personally accept the weight and force of each of them.' There was a long pause, after which she simply said, 'Merci,' and hung up.

To Raphaele, the inspector put the pointed query: 'Why is it men always have to make it crystal clear they're not going to help you if you make a mistake? I hate that.'

She brushed past him and headed for the stairs.

'Is it only men who do that?' asked Raphaele, following hard on her heels. Aliette did not answer. 'Well, I'm here to tell you the same thing, Inspector. The man downstairs is one of the top men in the region…the country! A dead bird? Is it a joke? He likes you, but you're really pushing it.'

'It is not a joke! Give me a bit a credit, please.'

'We were about to eat!'

'Is he angry?'

'Hasn't said a word…I know he was excited about eating.'

'He'll be excited by this.'

'I hope so.'

'I know…I know: for *my* sake, right? Not yours.' Banging through the doors to the morgue.

In lieu of steak, Dr. Conan was sipping coffee and munching the *panettone* sent along by Raphaele's mama to help her son solidify his alliance with the eminent man from the university. His professorial eyes indicated he was willing to hear her problem.

'I have two questions. One: Can you tell me if this bird was blind before it died?'

'Probably not,' said Conan, wiping crumbs from his fingers. He took a light and shone it. After several shakes of his famous head, 'I really can't tell you. Why do you need to know?'

'I have a suspect who is not supposed to be a suspect. He's off-limits. This bird was his pet. This evening I watched it fly straight through a window pane and into the side of a car. Once it smashed through the window, it had all the room in the world but no idea where it was going. Whatever happened to it occurred in a place where I cannot go to look.'

Conan smiled, protesting, 'But it's just a bird.'

She ignored it. 'Second question: Can you tell me if any of our lovers were blind at the time of their death by heart attack?'

'Maybe,' replied a suddenly cautious doctor.

Turning to Raphaele Petrucci, she demanded, 'Did you check their eyes?'

'Yes,' said Raphaele. Meaning: but only in a cursory manner, a basic matter of course.

'But not to that extent,' said Conan, interceding on behalf of his more vulnerable partner.

'Why not? It's possible victim number seven died inside that house. Or shortly after visiting.'

'Didn't occur,' Raphaele admitted. A pleading tone. *God, how fast it changes,* thought Aliette. And Raphaele Petrucci saw this. He glared back at those contemptuous silvery eyes. 'It was their hearts!' Adding, '…Eyes don't show much of anything after death.'

Dr. Conan was already pulling open the drawer containing the dead noble — *all* of him, not just his broken heart. The two scientists aimed lights and dropped chemicals into Didi Belfort's eyes, then pulled out Raymond Tuche and began to do the same.

Aliette paced, sighing out loud with nervous exasperation.

Raphaele looked up. 'You're not helping.'

'But the bird...I need the bird!' She came to rest beside the tiny corpse. Laid an uncertain fingertip on the lifeless feathered skull. 'This bird lived inside that house.'

Raphaele could only shrug, unclear as to procedural legalities.

'Physical evidence!' she hissed. 'From inside his place! If I don't have it, Richand couldn't give the smallest damn if everyone he's ever shot is now walking around with a white cane.'

Conan looked up, dubious after exploring the sculptor's eyes. 'Shot?'

'Photographed. Tommi Bonneau...' Gesturing at the bird. 'How else would that happen?'

Raphaele said, 'But Pearl Serein's not blind.'

'I'm not talking about Pearl Serein. It's her men. They're dead. I want to know if they were blind.'

'But why does it matter?'

'Raphaele, for God's sake...I don't know!' Suddenly struggling to regain the control essential to credibility. 'Think of Claude! He's been stalking Claude with his unholy camera. Please!'

Conan muttered, 'Need some help here.' He had Tuche's left eye clamped open and needed an extra pair of hands to position the head and steady a microscope under his light. Raphaele Petrucci was suspicious, assessing silently as he obediently gave his attention to the doctor.

Aliette watched them for an empty moment. Then she turned to Patrice Lebeau, dutifully waiting by the morgue door. She took him aside for a word — after which, he dashed away.

'I can see some sort of deterioration on the back of the retina,' reported Conan, 'but the man's been dead for more than week. We really don't have the right equipment here and I can't honestly say I'd know what to look for even if we did... I do know an excellent ophthalmologist at the faculty who would be delighted to —'

Aliette interjected, 'He's got this elaborate camera set-up.' It was too late to care if Raphaele, or anyone else, deduced her unsanctioned comings and goings.

'I beg your pardon?'

'Lights and cords all over the place.'

Conan shrugged. 'This is normal for photography.'

'The electricity you were talking about...in the brain...and the heart?'

'Yes?'

'I...I *don't know*! But it fits and you have to give me something to get me through that door!'

Dr. Gilles Conan backed away from the force of her. Offended? Not again...*please*.

She tried to atone. 'I'm sorry.' This professor was open to suggestions. Was he open to the vagaries of the environment in which she had to do her work? 'I'm not sure how to put this. I've pulled the judge away from his supper. He's coming down here. It has to be tonight or I'm done. I don't know how you scientists do it, but sometimes a cop *has* to make a move.'

'Scientists proceed as scientists,' grunted Conan, 'These could be burn marks...' Pondering it, opening the next drawer, uncovering the remains of another formerly highly eligible man. 'Why don't we see if these others have the same marks on the back of their eyes?'

They hauled out Bruno, Georges and Pierre, lined them up with Ray and Didi, and had a look.

Aliette waited, pacing in circles, rubbing her temples, trying to will a flash of brilliance.

## – 40 –
### The judge could see

Gérard Richand was no crusader. There was really nothing to crusade for—or against—in this dullish mid-sized city where they'd placed him and where he'd stayed. Where he was comfortable and doing well. No crusader; but he believed in what he did and believed he made an honest effort.

Gérard had come away from his meeting with Norbert Fauré feeling cynical. His meeting with Inspector Nouvelle had brought that feeling into high relief. He hated to bring it home. It had gnawed as he helped his two young boys with their homework, then eaten supper with his wife. He was just sitting down with some tea and a book when Inspector Nouvelle had called.

Gérard was reading poetry. He often found it an antidote to the masses of legalese he waded through every day. It helped stanch the bitter aftertaste of the words of unscrupulous divisionnaires.

Not Baudelaire. Too florid, too resolutely decadent. Gérard preferred an Apollonaire, so solid, honorable in his seeing, or a Paul Verlaine, champion of *les nécessités de la vie et la consequence des rêves* (the necessities of life and the consequence of dreams), and he sometimes even allowed himself to imagine he shared the same deep gaze as these large men. Or the ascetic eye of an Irish priest (also called Gerard)—his poem about watching a bird fly. Perfect. And he loved the abstractions of Stevens, an American, whose playful logic Gérard found so highly stimulating precisely because it almost, but never quite touched the cooler legal logic that was his own.

Poetry was relaxing. Refreshing. Now, rudely pulled away, here he was, back at work.

Inspector Nouvelle was presenting him with a dead bird, explaining, 'We believe this bird may provide a link to physical evidence inside the home of Tomas Bonneau.'

Dr. Gilles Conan backed her up. 'There is a definite possibility of burn-type scarring common to each victim's eyes. An overdose of extreme light is logical. The way things stand, we would be irresponsible not to investigate thoroughly.'

A bird?

(...*you were happy in spring/ With the half colors of quarter things,/ The slightly brighter sky, the melting clouds,/ The single bird, the obscure moon—/ The obscure moon lighting an obscure world...* Sometimes Monsieur le Juge had an urge to send a few cogent lines or even an entire poem along with his memos and decisions. But he never did.)

Folding his arms across his chest, Gérard remained silent, listening to Dr. Conan talk about electricity and light until Inspector Lebeau joined them. With a quiet word to Inspector Nouvelle, who in turn whispered something to Dr. Petrucci, the bodies and hearts of Pearl Serein's lovers were hastily wrapped and replaced in their respective drawers. The only dead body on display when Inspector Lebeau escorted in the seedy elfin man with ragged hair, streaked goatee and gray-tinged smoker's skin, was the bird's. Inspector Nouvelle introduced Paulin Soublin, a retired high school biology teacher. Gérard Richard took note of the name—Gérard's wife, a local woman, had been excited to find her old bio prof included in that day's instalment of *Le Soir's* new series devoted to the Pearl Serein scandal. His wife liked calling it a scandal. As opposed to a circus.

Monsieur Soublin bowed. Presented with the deceased bird, he stroked his horrid beard in a bizarrely vainglorious manner and pronounced, 'To photograph a bird or a woman, this is certainly a spiritual thing in that one must seek and wait at the same time. Yes? I told Bonneau this and he took it to heart. Some of the young women at the *lycée* were perfect...quite perfect.' Gérard Richard planted his feet against encroaching vertigo. A retired teacher, and spouting such stupid muck. Observing Inspector Nouvelle and the two doctors defer to this gentleman, he retreated deeper still into a bemused distance. Pleasantries complete, they got down to the matter at hand.

The inspector wanted to know: Had this bird been blinded before it smashed through a window and into a car and died? The retired teacher stroked his beard. A tic, surmised Gérard. The pride of celebrity so apparent in his face when introduced was now shaded into doubt, maybe fear. Well, it must have been odd for Monsieur Soublin — the police morgue, a judge, two inspectors, two doctors, and a question. But of all the dead things being considered that evening, only the bird remained.

Without the benefit of any context that might prejudice his scientific opinion, Soublin warily accepted a pair of tweezers, took his place at Conan's viewer and looked through it into the eyes of the bird. He adjusted the focus for a hellishly long minute, then began poking with the tweezers. He gently plucked one of the eyes, trailing a gunky mass of tissue as he pulled it free of the socket. Making an incision near the base, he positioned the eye and looked again, muttering, 'uh-hum, uh-hum…' in a way that must have driven thousands of adolescents straight up the classroom wall. 'Yes,' he finally said, 'this bird's optic system was certainly damaged. This misting on the cornea? A burn. Somewhat like freezer burn, you see?'

'And what may have caused it?' prompted Conan.

'Too much light, most likely,' stated Paulin Soublin — this without any hesitation. 'It happens all the time in urban areas. They're easily stunned, traumatized …occasionally blinded.'

Hearing that, Dr. Conan motioned Inspector Nouvelle aside. As they conferred, Pathologist Petrucci began to go through his cappuccino prep routine. Patrice Lebeau waited by the door. Left facing the retired teacher with the unkempt fingers, Gérard Richand could think of nothing to say. He had never liked biology much. He asked, 'What kind of bird is this?'

'Goldfinch.'

'Ah.' Gérard's wife had been thinking she wanted a goldfinch, to keep her company now that both the boys were off at school. But this was not something he would share with Paulin Soublin.

Soublin asked, 'Is this related to the murders of my former students?'

Gérard smiled, politely unforthcoming.

When Dr. Conan and the inspector returned to the table, Monsieur Soublin was surprised to be thanked and summarily escorted out by Inspector Lebeau. The bodies, hearts and eyeballs of the lovers were pulled out and unwrapped. Petrucci offered coffee and *panettone* all around.

The doctor went over it extensively, talking about how the retina was not only like a camera, but also a brain, an information-processing nervous system unto itself, and about photo receptors, the transduction of light into electrical signals…and about electricity and heartbeat, heart rhythm and stress, then electricity again, and its correlation, emotion. He again considered the stress on men who find themselves alone with their hearts, their *lives*, feeling crushed, angry, susceptible…

Listening, *watching*, Gérard Richand knew Aliette Nouvelle had worked her dubious magic on Dr. Conan. It was obvious the man was smitten, entranced and beaming as he dared them to consider, beaming shamelessly for *her*, inspired, giving them the possibilities, drawing on a lifetime's worth of study, making theory sound like poetry.

While she stood there, so serious, highly impatient, waiting.

Gérard knew because he had experienced the same thing, personally (eight sweet months, nine long years ago) and professionally (every time she came through his office door): this intriguing cop's maddening machinations. More than that: Gérard knew he was going to grant her permission to ask the *procureur* for a redirected mandate which would include access to the residence of Tomas Bonneau. But not automatically. Never automatically. Gérard Richand would first consider and assess, and demonstrate *his* place in the scheme of things.

Gérard knew Aliette thought him stubborn, stuffy, tied to rules and principles. Well, he probably was. You had to be — if not, who were you? He had his reasons, she had hers — different roles, different reasons. He thought, pace away, Inspector. The judge ignored the restless cop.

He sipped cappuccino, listened, asked questions, made notes.

And after a time Gérard Richand lost track of Conan's esoteric explanations. Yes, he could be interested in the effects of light, but he was far more interested in Conan's strutting, which was driven by Conan's blatant pride in his knowledge, the thing that made him who *he* was, and his strangely unabashed wanting more than anything to give his all for her. Inspector Aliette Nouvelle… As Conan drew links between a blast of light and the failure of a heart, Gérard began to draw his own. He was starting to see the problem as one of self-contained systems of logic within each man. Not logical like the law. More like the logic of a poem. This unsettling case was about men. Men's hearts. Hearts were all they had to go on. The *needs* of hearts. A common need? There was a pattern here that made sense to a judge who was also a man.

Gérard had heard two very different men assert their claim to Pearl Serein:

Claude Néon. Remy Lorentz.

Of all the things Lorentz had told him, most cogent were the answers to his very first questions:

'Why did you pursue her?'

'I was pissed off…had enough.'

'You were angry. At her?'

'No! At the Law. The System. Guys like you, the ones with the strings in their hands.'

'I see.'

'No, you don't see!' Remy Lorentz had been adamant. 'She belongs with *me*! She needs *me*!'

'She belongs with you? Why you and not them…the others?'

'My world!—not yours…Not the law. Not those rich pricks. That's *not* who she is!'

It was just there, at the locus of the workingman's invective and the caustic bile, the uniquely personal thing separating Remy Lorentz, humble tennis instructor, so irrevocably from the 'notable' men in the life of Pearl Serein. It wasn't social class or the specifics of intelligence. Here was a man's expression, from the heart, as it were, of where he stood in his perceived relation to *her*. It was this idea of love and a man's special province…

Then Néon: an impetuous cop stuck in a maudlin hero fantasy, believing he was the last man in the world, her inevitable and only choice: 'If it's not them, it must be me.' Believing it to the point of professional blindness. *It had to be me,* confessed the errant cop.

*My world!* insisted the loathsome jock.

Both had divulged a sense of inevitability where it came to the love of Pearl Serein.

Inevitability arising from a proprietary heart.

And as the scientist talked on, Gérard Richand considered Tomas Bonneau.

The gossip columnist was an even lower form than that cretin tennis pro, but: *Our Pearl…* the man continued to build this fantasy that Pearl Serein somehow belonged to him and his readers. *Love's inquiry. Those of us who live in her image.* Celebrity-driven trash, to be sure, but it was more than a fan club. It was as if Bonneau had set himself up as leader of an exclusive *populace of the heart* (the poet Stevens again, helping Gérard begin to see it clearly).

But here was a real question: Was Bonneau the disinterested creator of the fantasy of Pearl Serein, *a priori*, the hard X around which these discombobulated hearts revolved?

Or was he another player, like Néon and Lorentz? And the seven victims?

So mused the judge, yanked away from his reading for the sake of a dead bird.

It *was* just a bird. A goldfinch.

But the judge could see it might be a way of progressing, of moving one step closer to an answer. He almost smiled. Almost. Because Gérard avoided smiling when he was working. It was an absurd situation but a serious matter. He stood, taciturn, the way they expected him to, watching a learned scientist, in his element, doing his utmost bit to win a smile from Inspector Nouvelle.

It was the heart. It was a sense of ownership.

The judge could see it plainly.

## – 41 –
## Anne-Marie regrets

While the judge was in the morgue assessing, Anne-Marie was in her van, sipping wine, studying regret — the double-edged kind, partly bitter, partly sentimental, her mind going in circles, feeling a familiar emptiness, that mix of misunderstanding and mistakes. Tommi…Tommi, Tommi. Twenty days of crazy magic. Exquisite energy. That awful anger. She had known it would end like this — because it always did. But that didn't mean she didn't have to wonder why.

…At first Anne-Marie couldn't believe Tommi Bonneau wasn't completely cranked on speed. He was insulted when she'd dared to hint at it. His body was clean. He said his drug was light. 'Electricity, Anne-Marie.'

Electricity? She did not know much about it. It worked in guitars. Hair dryers. Kettles. Light bulbs — sure. But…His lights? So he showed her. It was horrible to see — his face ashen, his blasted red-rimmed eyes. But proof's in the pudding, no? Running: When Tommi powered away into the empty night, it was the best thing she'd ever seen. Tommi's body was sinewy and rock hard. The way he moved was creature-like in its intense exactness, large hands grasping ledges, railings — whatever there was to grasp Tommi found it and fastened on, long legs pushing, relentless. And he had a lumbering kind of energy when horizontal in his bed, an energy which built to a delirious hammering. She would dare him to go again. Tommi enjoyed being dared.

Anne-Marie was raw below and empty-headed. She hadn't eaten so much fish in her life.

'Brain food. You want the brain to be working as fast as possible. As fast as it was meant to.'

And his vitamins and supplements. Carrots by the bag-full for his eyes. Grapes, green tea and flax-seed oil, 'to keep the blood vessels open wide and clean.' He would sip a glass of wine, a heavily watered pastis, but she hadn't seen him do serious booze or gorge on sweets.

On the other hand, one evening they'd stopped at a certain door for something not quite legal. 'Growth hormone. Try some? Helps the heart pump more efficiently.'

Tommi could do 500 ab crunches, 100 pull-ups, 250 push-ups without stopping…100 one-arms if he wanted to punish himself for a lapse in concentration. Concentration was everything. 'The heart requires focus, Anne-Marie.'

Then he would sit for an hour and breathe. 'Breath is rhythm, rhythm is control of power.'

*Then* he would stand in front of his beloved lights and blast himself to the point of delirium.

It scared her—seeing him writhe in front of it, refusing to turn away.

But Tommi fought through it. Till he controlled it—sucking all that light into his heart.

He dared her to try it. She did. It hurt. It added nothing to her natural speed. It left her eyes burning, flooded with popping pools of over-brilliant flashing, her heart going wildly, her body needing to be used. Was that the power of electricity? The pulsing stopped but the light continued, an ever-deepening halo. 'I can't see, I get afraid.' Blinded, lost for that bottomless time as the green-white rings opened and opened, seemingly limitless inside her mind.

Tommi said, 'It's not because you can't see. It's because you can't think.'

'I don't understand.' Lying in his bed. Listening closer than she ever had to a man. It was not like the famous outlaw she had spent some years with. Poor Jacques, alone, overweight, maundering on about his lost heroics. You didn't really need to listen, all you had to do was be there. Tommi was not Jacques. Anne-Marie *listened* to Tommi Bonneau. She knew she would never remember all the complicated words—only the sound of them. And being mesmerized.

Tommi said, 'What is the opposite of fear?'

'Courage.'

'No. Exhilaration. Courage is flat. Exhilaration builds, like fear grows. But, yes, fear is where it starts.' Raising himself on an elbow, he pointed to his left eye: ravaged, the green faded and milky. 'The retina,' said Tommi, 'is the innermost layer at the back of your eye… it's where the optic nerve connects. It's got a quarter of a billion photo receptors and nerve cells. The iris, this circle of color around the pupil, protects the lens—it's a ring of muscle that opens to let in more light when you're in a dark room, or it shuts down to pinhole size in brightness to avoid overexposure. You squint in direct sunlight. Or when a light flashes in front of you, no?'

'*Oui.*'

'But an open iris can't always shut down fast enough when it's exposed to sudden bright light. That's why you see a pattern of light after the light flash. That pattern is an imprint left on the photo receptors. It's not outside—it's *inside*. You see it even if you close your eyes, right?'

'Right.'

'Light is physical. It's what you see. What's more important is what you feel. This fear. Why?'

Anne-Marie had never thought about it. 'Because it is sudden. I mean, it's a surprise.'

This pleased him. 'Good word. Surprise is fear, the reaction to something sudden, and being sudden, it's unknown, if only for a moment. When the eye sees something, the brain needs to focus on it. The brain has a need to understand…to *know* it. If the eye can't focus on the bright object, the brain can't process it—and you don't understand what the thing in front of you is. If you don't understand, you're afraid. And the brain's main message to your nervous system is fear. Instantaneously, it sends another message that produces that rush to the heart—adrenaline. And if you don't run, you at least hide; you turn and look away.'

She touched his serious face, admitted, 'I almost couldn't look.'

'No,' said Tommi, easing back down beside her. 'It's basic instinct to look away. That's why it all depends on your mind. On concentrating on beating the fear. On facing the light. Collecting it. And on alchemy—on transforming fear and disorientation into focus and exhilaration.'

Alchemy? She came close to his ear and whispered, 'But I wanted to be with you.'

Tommi didn't seem to hear. 'Life *is* electricity, Anne-Marie.'

'I believe you, Tommi.' Snuggling up. Inviting him to get plugged in. To her.

He shrugged her away. Still angry after Saturday. 'It didn't kill you, did it?'

'It's still horrible,' mumbled Anne-Marie, easing up, sensing there'd be no sex that night. 'Your eyes rolling in that manic way... like someone who's OD'd.' She'd seen it happen.

'*B'en*, that's what it is. An overdose of light. A hyper-quantity of light assaulting the cortex. '

'The what?'

'The part of the brain that sends the alert. Our nerve cells spark, one, then the next, and send electricity through our bodies and our brains. We act, we think, we act, we think, it never stops—all nanoseconds, micro-flashes up and down the system. Light is electricity and electricity is energy and the eyes are the best medium for bringing it into our body's system. My lights are like a supercharger. All you have to do is adapt your body and your eyes. Concentration,' he intoned, 'that's the key. Focus emotional confusion. Transform instinctual fear. Cultivate a physically centered belief in what the Taoists call the genuine idea and the body *believes,* regardless of instinct or mechanics. It's where you have to get to if the charge to the system is to be sustained and built to the point where the dragon is revealed and a man can acquit himself.'

Dragons? Dragons climbing walls. She rubbed his shoulder. Calm down, *cher*...calm...

'The strobe keeps strobing, the eyes stay open, light streaming through, the brain calls for more adrenaline—which kicks the nervous system to pump more blood. The adrenaline message becomes all-encompassing. It's a circuit, a wide-open circuit. The energy flows in, and you fly. But you have to be thinking right.'

'So I was thinking right?' For Anne-Marie, exhilaration and love were pretty much the same.

Tommi stared at the ceiling, brooding. 'The heart's just a motor. If you're not ready for it, the heart's mechanisms can lose control. And they'll fail.'

Which meant death.

For a moment, she was afraid of him. But no, she *wanted* to be here. She murmured, 'I heard women have stronger hearts than men.'

He mused, 'Mm, I heard that too.'

Electricity? This dragon thing? She knew it all came back to Pearl.

It was Tommi's deep contempt for the men who'd failed at loving Pearl. Didi Belfort. The spiteful anger he brought surging out in Tommi—hadn't she witnessed it first hand? 'Just another jerk-off... They don't concentrate on their lives. They lower the quality of my story. They've got money, the big rep, they think that's all they need to win a heart like Pearl's. What's worse, they even believe they deserve it. Sorry, you have be a true and perfect knight, my friend, nothing less will do.'

Tommi was in a war. She'd seen it before—this dark part of more than one doomed man.

Oh, *oui*, Tommi Bonneau was doomed. You didn't need carrots to see that.

---

A week ago Friday, as she was leaving after another out-of-this-world night with Tommi, she had passed poor Belfort cruising slowly along the street, searching for his door. She saw the broken shambles in Tommi's studio that evening, but she had no idea and didn't want to know. She'd waited while Tommi crashed the party at that club the next night, and returned, virbating like a dog that's made a kill. A week later she'd listened to Willem, stuttering with fear. And she knew something had happened yesterday—Tommi's studio was suddenly clean again, certain things were no longer there. Of course she didn't ask.

But she'd felt it last night. Tommi's anger. Boiling over.

It was wrong that Willem should be afraid of being caught in Tommi's war. If anyone was innocent, it was Willem. So a friend tipped off a cop. What else could she do? Now she was afraid that Tommi knew. Yet at the end of a day spent driving around aimlessly, she'd headed back to the house at 33 Rue Pontbriand. The hopeful thing was not quite gone, the itch was always there.

Would she ever learn?

She'd found him hunched in his study, surrounded by books, paper, computer things, camera stuff, tinkering. He had set up his lights. Bert was out of his cage, pecking his way through a scattering of seeds strewn across a small mirror placed on the edge of the desk. More letters from his editor were arriving on his fax machine—Tommi's readers were responding to the situation. There was also the hope of a romantic weekend in Paris for two.

She dared to be cheery. '*Salut*. What's happening?'

'Test.' He paused to scribble numbers in a notebook. Nary a glance for her.

Another test? It never ended. 'Poor Bert.'

Tommi didn't share her sympathy. 'Bert's a bird, Anne-Marie.'

'More like a guinea pig.'

'Somebody's gotta do it. Eh, Bert? Better to be useful than just another pretty face, no?'

'But he's so small, Tommi.'

'Yes, his heart's tiny compared to yours and mine, but his eyes are totally sensitive to light and he's easily startled. It's just a matter of scale.' Tommi made another adjustment and shrugged, 'I've been through a few Berts along the way....' another tweak, 'and I've learned a lot of things. The *real* link between Bert and you and me and this light here is the fact that vision's not just physical, it's also psychological. You understand that, Anne-Marie? What we see bears directly on how we taste, how things smell, even on our moods. I mean, if you want to be anthropomorphic about it, you could say birds are highly neurotic, and this is useful. Mm?'

She understood neurotic but not anthropomorphic. 'But why does Bert need to be tested?'

He ignored the question. Told her, 'I'm thinking a traveling halo has to be easier on the eyes than an alternating strobe. See? Four lights now—two over, two under, instead of three along the same plane. I'm going to build a halo around Bert and try pulsing at quicker intervals, around forty reps per second, but less intense. We'll just see here...'

She felt herself hating his coldness. 'So now you're going to kill him too.'

Making another meticulous adjustment, Tommi wondered, 'What's that supposed to mean?'

There was only the sound of Bert's claws scratching the mirror.

'Anne-Marie?...If you don't speak now, you can fuck off forever.'

'Those men,' she murmured. Suddenly so sick of his brilliant ideas.

'They failed their heart's test,' said Tommi, 'I didn't do anything except make them face the fact. It doesn't kill anyone. It doesn't kill *me*.' Another adjustment. 'It didn't kill *you*.'

Anne-Marie knew it had come to the moment where she had to decide who the object of her desire really was. A murderer? *Was* Tommi killing them? She honestly didn't know. She finally said, 'I could look away… If I wanted.'

'Yes, and that's the part I'll never understand,' said Tommi. 'There has to be something inside a person that wants to face it. Anyone *can* look away from it.'

'If you'll never understand it, why don't you stop?'

'Stop? Why don't *you* stop your nonsense? We'll just see how this makes Bert's heart go.'

No, she hated him. May as well speak plainly. 'Your work's useless, Tommi. Pearl doesn't like them. That's it. That's *all*. You can't make the heart do what it doesn't want to.'

'How do you know?'

How do *I* know? What a question. 'A friend told me.'

*Now* he looked up from his infernal calculations. 'What friend?'

And she couldn't stop herself. 'A friend who knows her. You know what else he said?'

'Tell me.'

'He said Pearl said, Poor Tommi's having trouble growing up.'

Tommi smiled as if he'd heard that one before. 'So many people in this town talking. Do you think it's true, Anne-Marie? Or just another bit of silly gossip? Mm?' His smile hardened. So: at least he believed her. She savored it for a spilt second.

Then Tommi made a move to grab her arm. 'Where is she?'

'Fuck off!' …jumping free. He lunged. She jumped again. He grabbed, she yanked herself free. In all the movement, one of them tripped his cable. Tommi's lights flashed. It stopped them both.

Bert was illuminated — for an instant each layer of his color was exquisitely etched, perfectly seen. Then he puffed his scarlet cheeks and spat the contents of his mouth — *pof!* His globe-shaped eyes wavered...but could not move, held absolutely by the framework of light that ran like neon, a luminescent barrier caging his tiny brain. Bert was just a bird and he could not look away. He stared into the light, his neck and spine twitching with each tiny pop of the flash.

Tommi watched for twenty seconds, then stopped it, muttering, 'Far too much.'

'Bert?' Anne-Marie expected the bird to simply keel over.

But he stood on the mirror. One dark orb of an eye twitched — as if he were somehow hearing the wind. Then he took off, flying in a frenzy, glancing off the walls and ceiling...the bookcase, all in strange bird silence, while Tommi rushed to the end of the room and ripped open the blind to give poor Bert some light... Natural light.

Bert reacted, shooting toward it like an arrow, and — *plak!* — right through the window pane.

When Anne-Marie came to the window she saw a woman bending over a shape on the sidewalk in front of her van. Then the woman was looking at the house. She recognized... 'Aliette?'

Tommi recognized her too. 'Ah, *merde!*' Then Anne-Marie felt herself yanked violently away from the window and the blind fell shut. They confronted each other. 'Another friend, Anne-Marie?' Tommi held her wrist. She saw his anger, and something like deep insult, the pain of betrayal. She felt his awful strength, a steel grip on her arm as he opened one slat on the blind a fraction and peeked out. They both saw the inspector leaving.

Anne-Marie tensed, preparing to be hit.

But he released her and went back to his desk. He sorted through the mess of papers. Finding the one he wanted, he muttered, 'It doesn't matter where Pearl is, it's too late.' Then Tommi began gathering his lights and power box together.

Too late for what? She took a step toward him. 'Tommi?'

He pushed her away — so hard she fell on her ass on the floor — and left the room.

A few empty minutes later, Tommi left the house.

Anne-Marie sat on his floor, vague amid the spilled-over clutter — his research, his inspiration, the models for his story. And now all these letters, surmising on the fate of Pearl Serein. So many people, so many hearts desperate to connect with the secrets of the heart *Le Vrai Tommi* had uncovered and shared. The one that brought the tears was barely two lines:

*Sir, If I could, I would send a violet to Pearl Serein, with a note asking humbly to be forgiven. But I fear it is too late.* Signed, Willem van Hoogstraten.

Anne-Marie let it fall to the floor. She forced herself to get up and get going.

Willem was her friend. Together they had believed Tommi's every word.

She drove to the Rembrandt. The door round back was wide open. So was the balcony door upstairs. Too late. She had an idea where they might be headed, but she knew she couldn't follow.

No one would believe the likes of her — no chance in hell that she'd get past the door.

So she had driven back to Tommi's, where she waited for Aliette. She knew the inspector would be back. Thinking, Come on, Aliette... Get here! Sipping wine. Bitter. Resigned.

## - 42 -
## Claude's mind

While Anne-Marie was sitting in her van feeling resigned, Claude Néon was hiding in his cellar, surrounded by flower pots, rotund planters, giant plastic bags of vermiculite and peat. 'Ah, *quel bordel!*' The gardening lady over-the-page from *Le Vrai Tommi* at the back of the second section was smiling blithely from the top of her column. This was a seriously demented woman. Claude had tried hard to follow her mixing instructions. 'As God is my witness, I have tried!' Insane gardening instructions were the very last thing he needed. 'Please God…' Trying to stay patient… 'ah, *merde!*' It was turning out all wrong again when Claude looked up to see shoes creeping by his cellar window. Polished shoes. Creeping by at nose level. Cop shoes. Those shameless pricks!

This impotent feeling.

This surveillance they'd put on—a team of unsubtle assholes from Division following him on his errands, into shops, his corner bistro, recording his every move. Now they were sneaking into his yard! It was too much. *Merde*…and double *merde*!

Stay cool, monsieur. Monique had told him gardening is good for the nerves.

Now, having had a good look inside his kitchen, they were creeping back. Claude heard two voices laughing in whispered tones. He lost it… '*Putain!*'

Claude Néon booted the bag of peat. The bag, still more than half full and compressed as tightly as the man attacking it, burst, spilling its contents throughout the room. Amazing mess!

But didn't it feel good, that one quick kick?—an alpha moment! *Oui.*

Then Claude Néon left the mess on his cellar floor and ventured out into the warm evening. He took the car—the quicker to get to the club. Six minutes later, driving into the lot, he immediately felt better. They could invade his property, yes. But Claude was beginning to value the fact that unless they had a sticker on their windscreen (and they did not), they could not follow him past the gate. Members only, you swine, you scum, you…

God bless Gaston for extending his probationary membership. Claude owed him, big time. He strolled to the locker room, opened his (probationary) locker, and changed. He had spent serious money for proper whites. A pair of English-made shoes cost 800 francs. And well worth it. Like the gate with the guard, the sticker on the car, these things were comforting in a way he'd never known.

He relaxed. He was getting used to being around naked men. He nodded knowingly as several members complained about Remy Lorentz. The pro had not shown up for work all day. Claude wanted to say, Well, what did you expect? But he held his tongue. Picking up a pail of balls, he strode out into the balmy evening and made his way to the practice court. He had not reserved. Luckily, it was free. He commenced slamming a ball against the backboard. First things first: learn this damn game, *then* find someone willing to play with him. Claude doubted he would engage the services of Remy Lorentz. Obviously none of the other members trusted him; why should he? Here in front of a wooden wall, it did not feel like he would need to. Maybe he was a natural tennis player… Smacking one…a little off balance (too much back foot, Claude), it flew over the board into the garden. He slowed his pace.

Then picked it up again—really leaning into it. Smashing a ball was a better way of coping than pressing wormy dirt into clay pots. Mm…wham! Soon he had a good sweat on. His stressed-out heart enjoyed it. Gardening? Sorry, not the type. Wham! Wham! Yes!

Claude became aware of two women watching him. Dressed for tennis. Both had three racquets tucked under their arms. He had begun to understand that a selection of racquets was the next thing to acquire after the expensive shoes. It registered that one woman was Rose Saxe. Ah, *merde* (again)—why couldn't they leave him alone?

But he smiled, the way one does, and tried to ignore them as he hit some more. Wham! Wham!

'From the shoulder!'

'...pardon?' Turning, putting the smile back in place.

'Less forearm,' advised Rose. 'Hit with the entire arm...from where your shoulder rolls...' grasping herself in this place, 'to the sweet spot.'

'Sweet spot?'

'Where the racquet meets the ball. The middle of the face.'

'Ah, the sweet spot.' Thanks for the information.

'And keep low. Bend those knees.'

'Got it...merci.' Claude prepared to hit.

'Do you want to hit with us?' Rose Saxe was smiling as he searched for an excuse. 'Come on,' she urged. 'We're just going to rally. You obviously need the practice as badly as we do.'

'This is fine,' said Claude.

Rose Saxe grasped the chain-link fence with painted fingers. 'I insist.' Adding, 'We should get to know each other.' And, with a sympathy he was meant to hear: 'I'm sure you could use a friend at a time like this.'

Claude Néon heard it loud and clear. The gleam in her eyes was grotesque. 'Well,' sighing, 'you're very kind.' He gathered up his stuff. 'Just let me use the, uh...the facilities.' That was what they said at this place.

'*Mais oui*...We're on court six—behind the pool.'

'Be right with you.' Claude jogged off toward the men's locker-room door.

Would Rose Saxe be his friend? There was no way he could imagine it and he had no wish to. Her unctuous offer signaled the end of his forbearance. Claude did not bother to change out of his whites. He knew the boys from Strasbourg working the *planque* would be camped by the gate where he'd gone in. He calmly snatched a floppy-brimmed tennis bonnet from an open locker, pulled it down to a suitably anonymous angle, went upstairs and made a furtive dodge through the club's more formal areas—indeed, he walked straight through the dining room and out the back door to the patio (where he'd sipped drinks with Aliette Nouvelle one fateful night), vaulted the hedge and hit the street running, heading for the source of the problem: that *connard* Tommi Bonneau.

Although he still carried his racquet, Claude was not thinking of pulverizing Bonneau with it. Not at all. He would confront the man and demand an apology. If it came to blows, he would fight, damn it! but with his fists — a private citizen having it out with a public prick. Consequences? Of course he considered it, he wasn't completely crazed — not yet. A break and enter? an assault? What of it? One way or the other, they were going to get him. And *they*...Gérard Richand, Michel Souviron, Norbert Fauré, even Aliette Nouvelle, would judge him. Oh yes. But it would be a judgement Claude Néon could understand, if not respect, because it would come from *his* world. Enough of this bullshit on the back pages. Claude Néon would act according to his impulse and, if need be, tell his story to the court of assize... The exiled cop ran on, adrenaline building.

There was no reply at the front door at 33 Rue Pontbriand, so he kicked it in.

Breaking rules, cutting loose, Claude was experiencing an incredible palpitation in his breast as he entered. 'Bonneau!' Calling into the darkness, 'It's Néon. Come out and face me!' ...No sound. He took five steps, gently pushed on a door. 'Bonneau!' A dim light glowed in a room off the hall outlining odd, large shapes. 'Bonneau?' Flipping on a light. The weights and training machines in the dining room gave Claude pause. Under the baggy coat, behind the druggy eyes, the gossip's wiry body must be mostly muscle. Should he get out? No. A B&E would be easily deduced and would mean the last of his credibility. Worse, a petty charge would be a waste of all he had suffered.

What do the English say? In for a penny, in for a pound. Bugger off, fear!

If there was to be a valid case of Néon versus Bonneau, he would have to bring it to a head.

But Claude was now feeling slightly different about the racquet in his hand.

Across the hall he found piles of books, an empty bird cage, a bullet-sized hole in the window, a menu from the Rembrandt on the messy desk...copied, perhaps fifty times, pages scattered on the floor.

Ornate, mannered handwriting, like from another century. Claude couldn't figure it, so he left it and made his careful way to the back. 'Bonneau?' Through the kitchen... Claude flipped another wall switch and stepped into a photography studio. He stood amid lights on stands, power boxes, wire and feeds, and photos strewn on tables. 'Bonneau!' Claude began to snoop, opening drawers, sifting through images. He studied Pearl Serein: eating, dancing, raising a glass, shaking an outstretched hand. Here was Pearl climbing the stairs after the banker's funeral. She was looking back as if wondering, *Why are you doing this to me?* That questioning look was a constant. In another drawer were many birds, extreme close-ups showing fixated eyes in tilted heads. It was unsettling, the seemingly sad look of a bird's incomprehension. In the bottom drawer there was a collection of drastically over-exposed faces, each as lost as the face on the Shroud of Turin.

Why? What was the point of these? Claude Néon knew next to nothing of photography.

Calling again, 'Bonneau!' But less so. The hot energy of vengeance was fading.

Going into the darkroom, turning on the red light, he stood within licking distance of a picture of Aliette Nouvelle. It was attached to a clothes peg, hanging from a string. She was serene, composed as if for a portrait. Claude Néon was stopped dead by the image of her face. Staring at it. Remembering that face, close up — far closer than the enigmatic face of Pearl Serein. This was a face he was truly coming to know. To love? That serious face. A cop face. And the rest of her. Beautiful. Fun. Thinking, God, what an ass I am. What a complete and utter fool... And so Claude Néon restarted — rebooted, as it were, much like a computer after it crashes. The portrait of the inspector caused Claude's heart to pick up and refind its original pace, bringing the energy in his body back into alignment with his anger. He hated the thought of Tommi Bonneau controlling her, placing her, urging her to smile and taking that picture.

Claude was thinking honor.

Wrong: It was possession. Pure envy. A surge of bitter jealousy.

But emotional semantics made no difference to Claude's heart. It worked. Angry adrenaline surged. He considered wrecking the studio. He could kick the place to pieces, like a bag of dirt or a door. It wouldn't be a problem. It would feel good... No. Claude decided to take a picture of himself instead. This would be the better way of talking to Bonneau.

There was a camera and a bracket holding four lights fixed to a tripod, placed in the middle of the room facing a stool. Claude knew enough to check the focus. Clever cop, he took a glass jar with a spoon in it from the darkroom and set it on the stool, went behind the camera and looked: a couple of gentle turns of the lens, the spoon protruding over the rim of the jar was perfectly seen. He left everything else as it was, reckoning Bonneau knew his business. Removing the jar and placing himself on the stool, Claude turned at an angle, just as they'd told him to do for his official portrait. He adjusted his stolen tennis hat and held the cable-release trigger down behind his hairy knee to keep it out of the shot. Raising his chin, Claude smiled a *Fuck you* smile and pressed the button.

A quiet pop was transformed into a crackly hissing sound, echoing behind his eyes.

Claude wanted to shut his eyes, the better to see this hissing in the dark.

To look at a sound? Claude's sense of sight and sound seemed to combine and merge with the feeling in his chest; he wondered for an instant if it was a pinprick hurting or a burning buzz that was piercing him to the core. But only for an instant. Then wondering stopped. He knew he needed something to fix on. His eyes were demanding it, his mind registering an anterior confusion it had never experienced, and that sound factor—continuing, indistinct, roiling, a whirlpool, drawing him in—it hurt. Stung. And there was this countervailing inability to take his eyes away from the strobing pulsations encircling him, keeping him there, inside a fence of light. But it did not occur to Claude Néon to be frightened.

Commissaire Claude Néon held himself rigid in front of the light. Flashing. Flash after flash after flash after flash after flash after flash...a series muffled explosions. And the sound: Was the sound purely imaginary? Not to Claude. 'God!' Like nothing he'd ever felt, lost in the green-white pulsing in his mind... Yes, but envy and jealousy are green, glory and enlightenment, white. Exclusive;

no logical connection. No time to understand it. The combined effect sent Claude Néon thrashing around Tommi Bonneau's studio, gasping, grasping, smashing into everything, whirling in a maelstrom of searing, burning, blind confusion. God, it hurt! Now he *was* scared.

And seduced? Fighting a malevolent urge to keep going deeper, plunging mind-wise into the relentless green/white halo, Claude Néon battled, thrashing through a field of unseen objects, bouncing off walls, desperate for control — then suddenly free of it as he threw himself at open air and crashed through the glass door in a shattering crescendo of chaotic force.

He staggered ten steps, felt his hands on a metal gate, pushed, pulled — was he howling? — and found himself in a grungy back lane. Not that he could see it. Claude fell against the fence, rabid fingers clasping for purchase, the inner halo fading enough for vague shapes to sketch outlines in corners of his mind. His heart was racing like a train, like nothing he'd ever felt, and he pounded at his heaving breast, ape-like, desperately willing breath to flow through in torrents. More! More! His senses told him breathing was the only thing that could give it a shape that he could hope to ride... He breathed, he breathed...Vomited once. And breathed.

But there were voices.

'I'm so sick of this.' A woman, nearby, very bitter.

'It's drugs!' proclaimed a man. 'You! You're a drug addict!'

Claude Néon believed he saw the shape of a fist, a face, another fence?

The woman said, 'I'm calling the police.'

'No!' Claude Néon took offense. He could not see himself reeling, shaking insanely, specks of blood from shattered glass flowering around his hairy knees and staining the skinny shoulders of his shirt, looking worse than stupid in a floppy tennis hat. 'I'm a cop!'

'Bullshit! It's drugs!' The man commanded, 'Hurry! Call the damn police!'

Claude refused to be reduced to a common B&E. Fathoming a semblance of direction, if not mental equilibrium, he ran. The tower in the distance, rising like a twinkling shadow behind persisting echoes of the green/white light, receding, receding and receding but not diminishing, *that* was his direction and he ran toward it. But where?... *Where*, Claude? A memory of an argument about *her* dream somehow surfaced in his boggled mind. Bonneau at the top of the world, bouncing on her board in moonlight? Still half-blinded, Claude Néon aimed himself at Pearl's building, twinkling in the distance. The highest point. And a figure spinning in the sky above it?

Whether that was his boggled eyes playing tricks, or indeed, his boggled mind, it *was* the logical place to head for on the logical path Claude was suddenly on. And running felt exactly right. It brought the rest of him in line with the out-of-control train pounding in his heart, pulling him through a seamless green-white plane, demanding that he move.

Logical? *B'en*, there is no logic in any of this, Monsieur Commissaire.

This is a wild, angry, alpha fantasy. Please don't get these elemental things confused. Mm?

All right, fuck it, an instinct then. It's where I'm headed. The highest point. *Point finale.*

'*On roule!*' screamed Claude, speeding through the evening streets, this manic energy expanding, building on itself, a heightened buzzing in his inner ear.

## - 43 -
## Feeling sage-like

In the sixth century, Chang Seng-yu was famous for his dragon paintings. He is said to have left the eyes of the dragon untouched up to the last moment because as soon as the eyes were painted, the dragons would fly away! Just so, the way to the heart is through the eyes. And Tommi Bonneau ran lightly, swiftly across Alsatian rooftops, etched against indigo and fading clouds. He leapt... effortless, feeling sage-like. How could he not be feeling sage-like with all that light pulsing through his heart?

Tommi knew he was just a gossip columnist. Fun, but non-essential. His words would always be nearer the back page than the front. His pictures too. He lived with that—bore the scorn of so-called serious people. Pearl was an ideal that had to be served. After all, Diderot said, *Only passions, great passions, can elevate the soul to great things.* Tommi did what he could to make the people see. His gentle readers. He would never know if they did. He hoped they did. In an instant, we see all. But the moment of perceiving is the most personal—the moment of truth found in the eyes' interaction with a flash of light. Tommi's pictures captured the moment in the eyes of Pearl Serein. Shopping. Dancing. Hitting a tennis ball. Tommi's camera captured the eternal thing, the light that lasted. It was there. Tommi's words were merely decoration. Like a gilded frame. His pictures of Pearl said all there was to say. The crux of it was light.

*The light of immense desire*, said Dante.

Control of light is key to how incisive an image can be. Cartier-Bresson pronounced a link from eye to heart, but he never used a flash; in fact the master was opposed. *Thrusting a subject in the limelight is a sure way to destroy it.* Well, the master lived in far less literal times. Electronic manipulation of light enables the photographic eye to delve deeper through surfaces and layers, to strike closer to the essence. Tommi's inquiries, his reading and painstaking experiments, everything told him he was getting close to the source: the juncture of the physical and the metaphorical in the light. The poetic link was electricity.

But does the heart have a surge protector?

Pearl fails at love. And then again. And the light of immense desire is refracted, grows vague.

*Perfect love casts out fear.* Tommi felt the temple he had built shake as one heart failed, then another. Heart after heart after heart, a daisy chain of failure, something essential in love's design gone wrong. Tommi goaded Pearl, teased and dared her to be braver, to follow her heart to the desired end. Searching for the source of imperfection, he challenged each of Pearl's failed men.

*What is shut out at the door comes in through the window.* Said Nietzsche.

Alighting in Georges Pugh's office window, Tommi had asked for the photo. 'Georges, having a picture of Pearl half-naked when she's got nothing to do with your life, this is a bit voyeuristic, no?' Georges whimpered his refusal. Tommi took a picture…then *took* the picture. Was that why Georges had died? Or any of them? Tommi had worked hard to find a moment alone with these pretenders. These straw men whose hearts weren't right. The moment of truth in a flash of light.

Raymond Tuche had run like a frightened rabbit. Till they had their moment 'Look, Ray! Look!' It's what artists are meant to do. Where's the heart transcendent? It seemed Ray, who'd always mocked Tommi and his camera back at the Lycée, almost understood the message in his lights. Almost. Poor old fucked-up Ray. But Duteil the banker—staring into it, silent and sullen as a pile of money when Tommi relieved him of his portrait of Pearl. He had no idea. Nor did Gagnon, alone in his bed with *Evolutionary Psychology,* baffled, trying to understand how his golden-throated voice had missed the highest mark. Pearl's heart. Wrong book, Jean-Guy. The poetics of Pearl is another story altogether. Smile, man! But he hadn't.

It had come down to a 'maybe' with Pierre Angulaire, a man who wanted to reduce Pearl to two hours of documentary. Two hours that could be re-cut and sold in smaller time-slots according to markets: When Tommi told Pierre that Pearl was a fiction beyond any commercial window, that his vision was never going to see the light and then demanded Pierre's collected images, Pierre had smiled. A smile is recognition of a truth, no? Yes. A smile is a lot like light.

Maybe Pierre had seen the light before departing.

But Bruno Martel? Cowering, blubbering, consumed by his own victim-slanted therapy and run to ground. (Easy: up a garden wall, through a bedroom window.) What bullshit, Bruno, Pearl's no victim. To approach love that way's just grotesque. Look at the light, Bruno.

And Didi Belfort had been embarrassing in his drugged-out tantrum, clawing the wall of the studio, pawing at Pearl's serene smile, choking on it, whining like the bitter spoiled boy he always was. 'Why was I born, Pearl? Why was I *born*!' Why, indeed, Didi?

One thing was clear: set in motion, failure was ouroboric, relentlessly self-consuming.

But their deaths were strictly their own. It was just a light. The worst a light might do was induce a man to kill himself. Like a mirror? Possible. A mirror will play hell on the face of failure. Having to confront the mediocre heart that can't measure up. That was *their* problem. Empty faith...*the great Faith is Love!* Proclaimed Rimbaud. Those seven failed hearts bore out the diamond-hard bottom-line truth of it. Tommi had pictures to prove it. How could you blame it on a light? Light is life, investigative, always *adding* to the story. Not subtracting, like the dark...

Tommi did not allow Remy Lorentz to cloud his reasoning; nor his sense of who he was.

No way. He ran on across the rooftops, stoked, exultant, till he descended along precarious fire stairs and creaky back steps, down from the beautiful gloaming into the darkened street.

The Rembrandt was empty. Willem van Hoogstraten was laying the next morning's tables before heading off to Georgette Duguay's drawing group when Tommi Bonneau entered through the kitchen door, insouciant, as if expected, camera bag slung over his shoulder. 'I enjoyed your letter, monsieur.' Willem bowed slightly, adjusted a knife. He stayed silent, as if he knew the best thing to do was act like a waiter. 'Really. It touched me.' Pulling a printed sheet from his bag, Tommi read aloud, affecting a sonorous basso that resonated in the pitched spaces of the empty room. *'Sir, If I could, I would send a violet to Pearl Serein, with a note asking humbly to be forgiven. But I fear it is too late.* Willem van Hoogstraten...A violet,' mused Tommi; 'that's so good. The tone of regret. Soulful guilt. In fact, it's beautiful.' Speaking as a man who knew, he told Willem, 'This is by far the best one we've received. My editor definitely agrees. The most heartfelt. And didn't I just see it in your eyes that day I came in?'

Willem's eyes were waiting.

Tommi said, 'They're going to run it. And Tommi will respond.'

Willem shifted a glass to a more symmetrical angle and considered it.

Tommi put two great hands on the waiter's spindly shoulders. 'Willem, this city will know that you were a tragic kind of man — one of the little people, but special, a big imagination, a true sense of romance.' Willem tried to free himself, jerking violently, in silence there in the lonely Rembrandt. But Tommi's grip was absolute. 'Don't worry, my readers will forgive you. I'll make sure of it. You're one of us, after all... You've proved it beyond any shadow. No?'

Willem was struggling to breathe as he confronted the ravaged eyes. 'Forgive me for what?'

'For killing them. All of them. Pearl's boys.' Tommi held the waiter tighter and recited from Guillaume Apollonaire: *'Pity us who fight always in the front lines/ Of the limitless and of the future/ Pity our errors, pity our sins...*Eh, Willem? That's you and me, surely it is.'

Willem gasped, 'Would you let me go, monsieur!'

Tommi shook his head. Can't do that. Not now. Lifting Willem like the lightest bride, he carried him up the apartment stairs and out to the small makeshift terrace on the back roof. 'Nice here.' It was: a fine place to be alone with the sun or the moon, some wine and a dream. You could see Pearl's building, monolithic, jutting into the sky. 'Willem, there's something you have to see, my friend — something that will make it all make sense.' Standing at the edge that evening, the captive was advised, 'Don't say a word or all you'll be is another wretch with a broken neck, robbed and killed and left in an alley. *D'accord,* my Willem? Better to go out big than small.'

Like Anne-Marie, Willem had to ask, 'But why?'

'Because you're right. It's too late. Pearl's dead. This thing can't go on. Tommi has to end it.'

Pure and spontaneous, Willem wept. He didn't know Tommi meant the story, not the lady.

But there wasn't time for tears. Dragging Willem by the wrist, Tommi led him down the fire stair and into the murky alley. 'Come on.' And they moved off.

Tommi loped, Willem was compelled to follow, clamped in a relentless grip, leaping to keep pace, up and down the alleys, from one street to the next. Emerging momentarily into the glow of a friendly street lamp, any passing citizen would smile to see two great pals, hurrying hand in hand.

The glow of a street lamp could not show Willem van Hoogstraten pushing the boundaries of fear's delirium as Tommi Bonneau pulled him onward, toward the highest place.

*Memories are hunting horns/ Whose sound dies out along the wind.*

Another pearl from Apollonaire. But a sad one…always sad as the beautiful thing recedes.

Long before Tommi Bonneau had taken to adventuring across the city's rooftops in dead of night, Tommi (the boy) had fastened on to quality ideas. He loved stories. He heard things that sounded right. *Perfect love casts out fear.* A priest read it, Tommi heard it, sitting at mass beside his mother. It sounded right and he believed it. He was happy to believe it. But: Perfect love. What *was* it? One clue: the way to find out was not to be afraid. If perfect love casts out fear, by not being afraid perhaps one would arrive at perfect love. Tommi was far from the brash self-conscious man the geeky camera-toting adolescent would become. He was only ten. That was when he learned to be unafraid to cross the rooftops. What a great time! And for part of it, Pearl (the girl) was happy to open her window and follow her friend. Together they moved along the rooftops of the quarter, unseen, discovering ways to go almost anywhere, never touching ground.

Pearl took the same precarious paths as Tommi. Tommi liked it that Pearl was brave.

It did not last long. Pearl soon found other things to do. One perfect day in May, a sunny Wednesday (no school on Wednesday afternoon is a tradition in France; we do Saturday mornings instead), Tommi sat perched above the neighbor's top room, signaling to Pearl. When she came to her window two floors below and signaled back, Sorry, I can't come today, he knew it was over. It was the end of the thing they'd shared.

But *not* the end, because they both still shared it, and always would. If they wanted to.

She knew it too, as perfectly as he did. It hurt. In a moment of innocent revelation Tommi Bonneau saw this most sweet and perfect thing beaming back from the eyes of Pearl Serein. He saw her awareness of that moment. It *was* shared, and this was signaled — Pearl instinctively knowing the importance of signaling to Tommi, all of her heart in that moment of moving on, and Tommi knowing enough to be grateful for her being there so he could see and know. It seemed the best possible thing to know. To feel. That was the thing of revelation, knowing and feeling combining as he sat up there above the city, signaling goodbye to Pearl. Even if he did not understand it, Tommi believed in that moment — because Pearl did too. He knew she did.

Pausing on the far side of the traffic circle, gazing at Pearl's diving tower up there beneath the moon, Tommi told Willem van Hoogstraten, 'I kept my revelation. I refused to let time dull it.'

Sure, he knew what the psychologists might say about that. Very boring. Tommi was more interested in how Dante would react. *As new trees are renewed when they bring forth new boughs, I was pure and prepared to climb unto the stars.* Tommi knew his moment on the roof had been a clear glimpse of the best part of being alive, and it was rare. He told Willem, 'If we're lucky, we're given glimpses of perfection when we're young because it's when we're able to see it clearly and believe it. After that, as this life gets so grim and gray, it's our duty to remember, to live by it if we can. Eh, Willem?' Could Willem understand how Tommi was a man shaped by a single moment when everything came together?

An original moment, you could say. Later, Tommi would see it in every view of Pearl:

Something full—full of life, yet incomplete. Forever waiting for completion. It bothered him, he felt a profound unease that no man seemed able to transform it, to move that gentle thing to where it seemed to want to go. So it was that Tommi chronicled the loves of Pearl Serein.

And Tommi told Willem, 'I never wanted her, not physically. I wouldn't know where to start. To have her body would ruin it. That's not my role. I only wanted her back in my story. But that *pute* Rose Saxe and the *connasse* cop who put her up to it are just so far from it, so completely wrong. It's not right.'

Not right that a cop playing a cheap game as an anonymous source would lower the quality by trying to insinuate Tommi into the frame as some frustrated lover incapable of letting a memory go. No! Exactly the opposite. It was pure inspired love. Something wordless. A history made from one moment of connection. *One moment*—as near as you can get to being out of time. Seen. Remembered. Cherished. Nurtured…against all odds, the odds that time will stack against you.

Willem managed to whisper, 'What cop?'

'Just some—'

'Aliette.' Desperate, Willem called, 'Alie—!'

'Please.' Draping a powerful arm, comrade-like, around his captive's quaking shoulder, Tommi placed a huge hand over Willem's pale white mouth. 'Or I'll pound your face till they won't know you.' Staring into Willem's frozen eyes. 'And they *have* to know you, Willem. So they can love you. That includes your sneaky friend, Aliette Nouvelle, damn her… No way, not right at all…You know Tommi gives his all for his gentle readers. Will you tell me that you do?'

Willem couldn't answer.

Tommi stood there, rueful, brooding on the flow of cars, the splaying roundabout of light. He finally said, 'But at the heart of it, the real Tommi is alone. And now it's too late. This story is running out of space. I know that.'

Then Tommi took away his hand. Willem couldn't speak. Tommi advised, 'Don't be afraid. Focus. Move past fear. This is what life is all about, Willem. Especially at the end of it. OK?'

Willem barely nodded.

Then there was gap in the flow and Tommi bolted, with Willem flying behind. In a blink they were past the door to Pearl's building, back in the shadows. Tommi held Willem's hand as he raised a long leg and smashed the door to the service stairs.

And so they continued, on and up to Pearl's.

## - 44 -
## GEORGETTE MAKES HER MOVE

Georgette Duguay did not believe Willem was not hiding Pearl Serein in his apartment. It was exactly the kind of thing a dreamer like Willem was prone to do. Georgette had been lurking, keeping an eye out, sipping more pastis in the seedy brasserie across the street from the Rembrandt. Not for a glimpse to confirm the lie. But because Anne-Marie was worried and somewhere in her cranky heart, Georgette cared for Willem's safety. That Tommi person was a monster. She'd seen it in an instant. Anne-Marie's love life was her own sordid business. But Willem was too much like a child at heart. When Georgette saw the monster come in, confront Willem, and then go upstairs with Willem in his arms, she left her vigil in a hurry and pounded on the Rembrandt door. But Willem did not come down. She hurried around back, arriving in time to see two men, hand in hand it appeared, disappear round the corner at the far end of the alley. She knew it must be them. But Pearl Serein? …The kitchen door was open. Georgette went in and rushed up the back stairs.

There was no Pearl. Had she fled from Tommi Bonneau? Was she making a run for home?

Standing baffled on Willem's tiny terrace, it occurred: they could only be headed for the shrine-like apartment in the sky where Pearl Serein was said to live. Georgette forgot to worry about being late for her drawing group as she hurried toward the park.

From the edge of the park she could see two figures, perched on the tower beneath the moon.

And then one of the figures did a backflip straight into the sky.

Georgette Duguay was experiencing fear. Fear for Willem! She had to get up there.

But the man in the ridiculous coat who guarded the entrance to Pearl's building was a problem. Running into the building with a breathless claim of two men in Pearl's penthouse garden wouldn't work. Nor would desperately trying to convince a flabby *flic* she might find on the street.

Georgette sweated freely as she stood on the edge of the park, fathoming her next move.

As Georgette waited, among the people she saw enter Pearl's building were Norbert Fauré with Rose Saxe on his arm. They were key to what would follow, but Georgette did not read newspapers and had no idea who they were. The only person who really mattered to Georgette's plan (to Georgette's fate) was Miriam, a low-rent junkie hooker, who happened to be passing by, having just earned some cash in a private spot behind the public washrooms farther up the park. One hundred francs *le pipe* (blow job) was Miriam's basic rate; about twelve euros now, depending on where the greenback stands. Whatever; it was enough to get Miriam more of what she needed and she was heading home…

The man who guarded the bridge to Pearl's castle was also a low-rent type, despite the fancy get-up. He saw Miriam. He was a man who spent his days watching the street pass by his door and he knew exactly what she had to offer. He stepped out of his elegant foyer, caught her eye, motioned her over, had a word. Georgette observed as he led the *pute* around to the back of the building. To the same place, in fact, where Didi Belfort was discovered—which discovery had opened a door for Pearl Serein. Which led her to Willem. Which now brought Georgette to this moment. It's incredible, the subtexts and synchronicities underlying a case like this. But Georgette had no idea of that either, and at the moment couldn't care much less. The *pute* was none of her business. What mattered was the lobby—now unguarded.

Georgette Duguay saw her chance and went.

There were keys behind the counter. She tried them, and finally one of them worked.

Stepping out of the lift into Pearl's domain, Georgette did not experience the quiet thrill almost every other visitor did. It was not in her nature to be impressed by high-end sound or Argentine leather.

Never having come anywhere near possessing things like these, how could she be? On the rare occasions she had money to spend, she would buy herself a decent pair of wool trousers. Or a sweater from Italy. That was about the extent of a poor artist's model's shopping. But as she passed through the place in search of a less direct entry onto the terrace than that afforded by the salon door, she paused in Pearl's bedroom. Georgette never read much either. She did her work, she walked, she sometimes stopped to drink pastis. But reading?... she took the book on the bedside table... Yes, it was open at the verse Willem had recited when he'd told his story of his night with Pearl Serein.

*From leaves of autumn flushed with love,*
*A pearl of dew shakes free*
*And falls to shatter on the earth beneath.*
*So too must I, to flee Love's stifling folds*
*Drop from the world.*

Georgette Duguay's world was limitless in the sense that a naked body is boundless and her naked body was her basic tool. And her world was compressed inside the tightest shell in the sense that, fifty years after the fact, Georgette remained obsessed with her mother — who had flown from a trestle bridge on the wings of wifely despair. This was at the core of everything. And the flying pose, to which the moody artist's model had been turning more and more in the dark aftermath of her estranged sister's sordid murder, was her soul's only way of resolving her life's choices — a puzzling figure flying away: it was all she knew, all she could see, all she could show.

The rest of life — money, library cards, people mainly, had been receding, as if down a widening whirlpool. As if into the mists of a bottomless gorge.

This Maid of Nagara, this book, this story: perhaps it might shed light.

Georgette put it in her pocket and stepped outside.

## – 45 –
## Tommi's mistakes

Judge Richand handed Inspector Nouvelle a signed mandate stating that in his opinion there was legitimate cause for a search on the place and person of Tomas Bonneau. She thanked him, she thanked them all, and went calmly but quickly out with Inspector Patrice Lebeau. Then, blue light swirling, they raced to the north end, to the home of Procureur Michel Souviron. Opening the gate, she navigated her way around two bikes, a soccer ball and a Marseilles team jersey, and three stray training shoes strewn across the paving. Where was the fourth? …Where? No time to spot it—her knock was answered almost immediately. '*Bonsoir*, Inspector.' Stepping inside, she found herself amid more kid-created clutter, balancing out but almost overpowering the tasteful bourgeois elegance. From above she heard a mother's voice snapping bedtime orders, a child's complaints, a door slamming. 'Come into the kitchen.' She followed Michel Souviron past yet more toys lying here and there—one of those remote-control robot things with tools for hands. Asking, she was informed, 'Some science-fiction cop. American movie.'

'Looks like fun.'

'It's good for about ten minutes, then they're on to the next thing,' He sat, opening his briefcase on the table. She took a seat opposite, in front of a cereal bowl displaying the brightly painted image of this same robot hero, and handed over the paper from Gérard Richand. After a minute's close perusal, Souviron said, 'All right, I'll sign this, but,' brandishing his pen, 'I'm amending it to make sure everyone knows it applies to him and him alone.'

'Fine.'

'You cannot go into his office—'

She understood Michel's concerns and helped: 'His office on the premises of *Le Cri du Matin*.'

'You cannot name *Le Cri du Matin*.'

'There's no need.'

'I mean it.' The proc crossed out one of the judge's lines, put a star beside it and scribbled something to replace it at the bottom. He initialed the correction, put his name beside Gérard's, then took out one of his own forms and filled it in. By way of closing the transaction, Michel Souviron said, 'Gets it away from institutions.'

'Good. I don't want there to be any chance of their shielding him.'

'Not with this.' Handing her the papers, noting with dry Proc candor, 'The same would apply to Néon. One man against one other man. Makes for a cleaner case, if need be.' To make it crystal clear, he added, 'The Republic will not take the part of Monsieur Néon if worst comes to worst.'

'I understand. Merci, monsieur.' Rising to leave.

'Any news on that front?'

'Not lately.' Unlike certain devious old cops, Michel would not ask if he already knew. Aliette felt safe in assuming the proc was assuming Claude was safe at home — about three blocks away.

He followed her out. 'Good luck!' Waving. Then locking his gate for the night.

Pulling away, Patrice relayed the news: Claude had suddenly skipped out of everyone's sight.

'Oh, *merde*. When?'

'Half an hour? No one's sure. Went to play tennis like he's been doing. Car's still in the lot. Somebody saw him jump the garden fence and take off. But they did not exactly run to report it.' Stopping at the corner, Patrice asked, 'Which way?'

She breathed. 'Bonneau's.' Whatever Claude was up to, she had to keep going.

The house at 33 Rue Pontbriand was dark but the front door was wide open. Did that have to do with a lover's quarrel? Or something more sinister? The Westfalia van was parked in front, a dim light shone inside it. Anne-Marie was sitting in the back, dully leafing through one of her fashion mags. When she noticed Aliette peering in at her, she nodded, with no hint of surprise, and gave the latch a kick. The side panel slid open. 'What are you reading?'

She held up the new issue of *Marie-Claire*. Listlessly turning a page… 'We had a fight.'

Voila. 'Serious?'

Anne-Marie shrugged in the hopeless blasé manner that was her life's only shield. 'About his bird, about you, about Willem, Pearl. Lots of things.' The inspector nodded, neutral, in the way she was trained to. Waiting. And so? Anne-Marie finally said, 'I'm not too good at picking them, am I? Men, I mean.'

'I don't think we have much choice,' responded Aliette, suddenly not a cop but just another woman, maybe a friend. 'The heart's a strange thing. It leads, we have to follow.'

'Must be something like that.' Flipping to the horoscopes. 'What are you, Virgo?'

'Mm…Georgette too.'

Anne-Marie consulted Virgo. 'Says you need less knowledge and more imagination, fewer hard facts and more dreamy truths.'

'What about you?'

'Oh, they never get me right.' She reached for her half-gone bottle of wine. 'Want some?'

Indicating no thanks, Aliette tried to keep it less than official. 'I have to talk to him and I think you know why. Is there anything you want to tell me? It would be better now than later.'

Moving on from the horoscopes, the errant street girl considered a perfect woman on the page in front of her. 'I guess I knew there'd be trouble when I saw the tennis racquet in with all his stuff.'

'You knew whose it was?'

'Monday I did… Not till then.'

'What did he say?'

'Nothing. I didn't ask.'

Aliette nodded: par for the course. 'I believe he killed him.'

'I heard something about another heart attack…You can't kill anyone with a camera.'

'How do you know that, Anne-Marie?'

It looked like she might cry. Her exquisite dark eyes appeared to swell. She controlled it. 'Tommi told me...He showed me. He's an expert. He's an interesting man.'

The inspector gestured toward the house. 'He's waiting for you. Left his door wide open. You want a word in private before I go in?'

'He's gone.' Whether for the night or forever wasn't clear as she leafed dully through another page or two of *Marie-Claire*, crying now, tears dropping on the fantasy images in front of her. Anne-Marie muttered, 'That was *your* guy.'

'*My* guy?'

'Your commissaire? Smashed his way in...' Fixing Aliette with a twinkle of sad street girl irony. 'They look so funny in their tennis clothes. Like little boys.'

Smashed his way in? 'Is he still in there?'

A shrug. She wiped a tear. 'Don't know. Lost track. Sorry... Please don't let him hurt Willem.'

'I won't.' Adding, 'Thanks.' And, 'Don't get too far away...and be careful.'

Standing at the open door, she called, 'Tomas Bonneau? I'm here to inform you...' et cetera, exactly according to the rules. No response. Then, more tentative, slowly entering with Patrice Lebeau, '... Claude?'

Tommi's studio was a smashed-up shambles with lights and stands knocked helter skelter; the entire pane on the back door was shattered, as if someone had been thrown through it, shards of glass everywhere. There was no blood immediately evident. But Pearl Serein's enlarged and dreamy B&W face was no longer on the wall. Shit and damn! She crouched for a closer look at the tennis racquet lying in the corner. It could be Belfort's. But not likely if Tommi'd thought to get rid of the picture, possibly ripped by the noble's hand. It had to be Claude's. The signs of a fight were recent; they fit with a kicked-in door. Inspector Nouvelle had to think Claude Néon had finally taken Tommi's bait.

Patrice beckoned from the darkroom.

She confronted herself—8x10, black and white, clipped to a string with a clothes peg.

A senior inspector did not take it upon herself to explain this picture to her assistant. It's that 'need to know' police mentality, and Patrice Lebeau did not ask. She began to go through Tommi's darkroom drawers. In the top: his shots of Pearl, which she had already had the pleasure of perusing; then his birds — many drastically over-exposed, solarized and otherwise drenched with light. Had they all been blinded in the process? Poor birds. And *why*?

From the bottom drawer she lifted a pile of more oddly bleached-out shots. Tommi's mistakes? These ruined photos appeared to be of faces; but it was hard to recognize characteristics. More like glyphs or carvings. Or those bogus images of spirits some people claim to have captured. Though almost void of facial character, the 'looks' in the eyes were haunting. Aliette's heart turned over and picked up speed. Forcing herself to slow down, stay calm, she spread the images on Tommi's table and, cop-like, began to go methodically from one face to the next.

'Looks like the tip of a tongue,' offered Patrice.

'Yes.' A tongue stuck between clamped teeth. Now the pained eyes in the ghostly face — over-exposure actually seemed to magnify it — showed the same helpless thing she had observed with horrified fascination amid chaos that night at the club. *My Pearl!* Raymond Touche struggling to understand why *his* Pearl, his all and everything, would dance away with another man. The inspector now knew Tommi had been at the club, with his camera, hiding under cover of the band's demonic light show.

This next shot showed a white swirly mass that could be Bruno Martel's ugly biblical beard.

These bent lips could be Pierre Angulaire's final grotesque rictus grin.

These were death masks. For the most part, they were thickly cloudy, white and indistinct. She hoped forensics had a technique for bringing out more clarity. Tommi's mistakes? The error was consistent, and — with the eyes at least, it seemed to convey a constant root quality, the same *non*-quality of a man utterly exposed and completely lost. A man disappearing from the core of himself.

Question: Were they intentional?

But you can't kill someone with a camera…

No? What about with a light?

Nonplussed, the inspector headed to the front of the house in response to Patrice's call.

Forcing the thought of Claude facing that same light to stay out of her mind so she could think straight, Aliette read a fax Patrice had found on Tommi's desk: a fax of a letter signed by Willem van Hoogstraten addressed to the editor of *Le Cri du Matin*, dated that day, forwarded from Christian Godchick, Ed., along with an effusive note: *This arrived with the evening post. If I have to pay to send someone to Paris for the weekend, this will be our man… You're doing brilliantly!*

Willem's voice came through all too clearly: *Sir, If I could, I would send a violet to Pearl Serein, with a note asking humbly to be forgiven. But I fear it is too late.* A Rembrandt menu was lying on the desk in plain view. As were several sheets, where Willem's baroque lettering had been copied with a wide nib several times. Tommi Bonneau had copied it out to the point of perfecting Willem's highly mannered hand.

Patrice retrieved several more attempts at it littering Tommi's floor.

Going through the drawers of Tommi's writing desk: here was a drugstore photo of a topless Pearl Serein on the sunny deck of a boat floating in perfect blue. A folder with Pierre Angulaire's production logo, packed to bursting with images of Pearl. A gilt-framed, rather formal portrait that would no doubt have a sad old banker's lonely fingerprints.

The two cops left in a hurry.

The old Westfalia van was no longer parked in front.

## – 46 –
### Convergence

'Do you have children, Willem?'
 No. Willem couldn't speak.
'But you were a child once?'
Yes. He tried...Tommi watched Willem trying to make a sound come to his lips.
'Of course. And I think you still are. It's in your eyes. You can't hide it, never in a million years. And that's what beautiful about you, Willem, what everyone will remember you for. Tommi's readers will be shocked and so sad. I believe each of Tommi's gentle readers is a child at heart. And full of love. Yes?' Tommi held him close like a mortified friend.

Perched at the end of the diving board extending from the top of Pearl's diving tower, a place so often dreamed of, Willem van Hoogstraten was numb with shock, traumatized from the dash through the the city's alleys and up eleven flights locked in step with a freewheeling, large-stepping Tommi Bonneau. Witnessing Tommi's show of diabolical talent on the wobbly board had almost stopped his heart. And now there was a rope tied in a noose round Willem's fragile neck. The hard foam lifebuoy from Pearl's cabana was looped around the board—making the board a makeshift scaffold. Willem was going to be hanged. It would appear as if Willem hanged himself.

Gazing into Willem's eyes, Tommi asked, 'Are you afraid?'
'Yes!' Barely a whisper.
Tommi was sympathetic. 'Fear's an intoxicating thing. Some people say fear focuses the mind. I think it's the opposite. Fear *floods* the mind, dominates the heart, drowns the soul. Not that I'd ever pretend to be an expert where it comes to psychology. Me, I'm more

a pure poetics type. I think you are too. Eh, Willem? My fellow traveler?...But how do we arrive at a place like this? Is it really for the love of Pearl? What else could it be?'

Willem couldn't answer.

Standing beneath the early stars and a storybook crescent moon, Tommi was feeling fateful, in a mood to talk. 'My devotion to perfection started early, Willem. I was shaped by it. My work, my story, all of *this* was shaped by that.' The mystery of Pearl's lovers. The fact that they had died. 'Now I've lost her, my story's over. Unfinished. Incomplete. It's sad: I don't know what she's become. She's never once since shown me what I need to see. What I saw. I believe it's still there, but...' Tommi watched a tear slide down his captive's cheek. 'Where *is* she, Willem?'

Eyes are amazing. Willem's understanding appeared to click on like a light. So Pearl wasn't dead and Tommi believed *he held the key*. Willem shook his head, defiantly. No way I'll ever tell.

Tommi was impressed. 'That's good. Be a hero, at least tonight...Did you know the ancients believed virtue resided in the heart? They were sure it was a real thing, like a gallstone or a tonsil, this little chunk of stuff called virtue that made a man what he was. Or wasn't.' Tommi stared far into the night. 'None of them had it. Eh, Willem? Pearl's boys... Have to have virtue if you want to have love. And if you want the love of the local goddess, then the bar has got to be raised, the stakes go up. Of course. But you and I, we knew that all along, didn't we?'

Willem looked away.

'All I ever wanted was to tell a beautiful story, bring it to my gentle readers because I know what a beautiful story can do to bridge the distance in the soul. I didn't want anyone to die. I was doing my job! I asked questions—tough questions, Willem, to get to the heart of it, and I took a picture to get a glimpse of the thing behind their eyes. For *you*, Willem, so you would know. Because you deserve to know. Pearl defines your life and you believe in Pearl. Your letter, Willem. It glows with virtue! *It* is beautiful and I hope that you, at least, won't be afraid.' He stared grimly at the man in the moon. 'How could a Tommi ever kill the likes of them? With a camera and a light? Sure, if you can get the strobe synced to the alpha waves, you can induce a seizure. That's basic RG, MI6, CIA, Stasi, KGB stuff. But it's top end, as in military, Willem. You can't just go and buy it at the corner. I never had anywhere near enough control to make it do something like that. They were petrified—but not of me. Of *themselves*. Do you know what I'm saying? Willem?'

Willem wasn't listening—you could see it in his eyes.

Tommi sniffed, 'I believe they just gave up and died.'

Tommi pulled an envelope from his pocket, waved it in front of Willem's nose. 'Here's a note for when they find you. You see, this cop, Néon, by now my readers agree, and some more than others, that the man is not only second-rate and nowhere near good enough for our Pearl, but he is also definitely the negative energy that sucked her out of our lives. All the letters we've been getting? We're going to do a special page in tomorrow's paper to support that view. And then there's yours, Willem, your heartfelt letter, pure poetry dedicated to *her*.'

In a choked-out whisper Willem pleaded, 'Then why kill me?'

'*B'en…*' Tommi slipped the note into Willem's breast pocket. He hoped it would stay dry; 'because of love. Anger. Then bitter hopelessness. And you're just a waiter. It's perfect. It's the only way out. They'll find you, and a note saying Tommi was right, Pearl deserved better, that you're sorry to act in such a heartless way, but you did what you had to do.' Tommi breathed. 'They'll find that cop in your café. I've got everything I need to lay all of it in his jerk-off lap, no problem, clean, clear, very solid.' Tommi took more deep breaths. *Control that anger; control it…* He breathed. He smiled at Willem. 'And you'll get full credit for getting rid of the cause of this sad thing. Tommi will do that for you. I'll bring my readers around. They'll be with you on this, I promise. Don't move now…' Checking the noose, Tommi left Willem balanced there. He pulled his camera and flash from his satchel and laid it on Pearl's board. Willem, balanced on the springy plank, did not dare budge. Tommi checked the hard foam ring…a nudge, a kick, he was satisfied it would hold a swinging waiter. Now he prepared to take a picture.

Adjusting focus, Tommi said, 'Really, Willem, this will be your finest moment.'

Willem jiggled, panicking…now he whimpered in despair.

Tommi reached, steadied him 'Wait. Have to get a picture first.' He aimed at Willem's eyes. 'It's the only way out for me, too,' confided Tommi, moving closer. 'It wouldn't even matter if you told me where she is. I don't want to know, not now, not anymore. Truth be told, it's better for the story if she's just gone.'

Then a voice enquired, 'But what will become of her?'

Tommi's breathing tripped over itself. There was an old woman with silver hair standing at the top of the ladder. With a book in her hand. Not the most threatening of opponents.

Tommi's breath restarted. He asked, 'Does it matter? I mean, who really cares?'

She raised an imperious nose toward the waiter. 'Willem is my friend. *He* cares.'

Willem gasped, 'Georgette!'

Georgette? 'Have I seen you before?' Then it clicked. Some kind of artist's model, sister of that seamstress who was killed at Mari Morgan's. He'd seen her observing the proceedings at the trial. That perpetually bleak face... But where else? More recently. Where? 'Another gentle reader?'

Georgette informed him, 'Everyone knows I don't go near your stupid column.'

Tommi smiled. 'Come up. A little closer. I need a picture.'

She slowly climbed the last two rungs, then took a careful step along the board.

Tommi had Georgette's ancient forest-green eyes squarely in his frame. He read contempt and something else. Pity? He adjusted his setting a touch to split the difference, and moved closer.

Taking one more step, Georgette reached out with the hand that held the book and swatted the camera away at the very instant Tommi pushed the button triggering the shutter and the light. Tommi's system fell, flashing up toward the stars...and it continued to flash after the brisk splash below, sending strange icy pulses through the water, layering the aqua depths of Pearl's pool with surreal dimension.

Now easing down the ladder, drawing him on with the driest smirk, Georgette Duguay repeated her question: 'What becomes of her—our Pearl? According to your story?'

Tommi advanced. 'The more interesting question is: Why did the waiter kill Georgette?'

Left bound and stranded at the end of Pearl Serein's much-talked-about 3-meter board, Willem moaned with terror as Tommi Bonneau stepped down the ladder, held by Georgette's eyes, considering it, teasing out his story line; '…and what was she even doing there? Maybe you were in love with this waiter. And you came after him on his tragic pilgrimage to the home of Pearl Serein, and you fought…yes, and then he threw you over the side of the terrace. Then hanged himself. That makes sense: an artist's model and a waiter, two of the little people, unknown, invisible, two gentle readers swept up in this larger thing. I think I like it.'

Georgette placed her feet on the deck. 'Everyone knows I don't love the waiter.'

'Maybe you loved the cop who's taking all the heat. They're going to find him in the morning on the floor of your friend's café. Yes, that works…I think it's you who you found him, put it together, followed the murderous trail. If you're here, you must have been there. No?'

'That would be impossible.' Georgette meant loving Claude Néon.

Tommi shrugged that away. 'No one really knows anything about love, madame.'

Georgette ran for the cabana…that spear thing hanging there!

Tommi leapt with a quick dexterity, landed squarely, grabbed her by the arm and threw her hard against the cabana wall. It shook. The impact stunned the seventy-one-year-old. She crumpled.

Tommi approached and bent to gather her up in his stringy arms, too calmly, an almost tender look, a hunter picking up a felled hare — this is how nature works, but he was a man with compassion at his core — and no clue how insulting this sympathy could be to a woman like this one. Seeing it, Georgette writhed and kicked. And kicked again. Her legs were powered by her fury, her outrage at the machinations of this absurd, this ugly man. Georgette was a large woman, a head higher than Willem, and nothing like passive. 'Cretin!' Ripping at his face when he tried to lift her in his arms.

'Oh–là-là…' Tommi realized he would have to fight. He kicked and sent her sprawling.

From overhead, Willem forced out a cry. 'Georgette!'

Eleven stories below, Claude Néon exploded into the foyer. Suddenly stopped dead.

A half-dozen residents were gathered there waiting for the lift. One woman was waiting at the reception desk, looking edgy, while the puffy concierge, back on duty after a sordid break with Miriam in the garage, faced the panel controlling the second lift, stolidly going through a massive key ring, testing each key against the top floor button which contained a lock: the lock to Pearl Serein's front door. All the residents turned as one — looked askance at the chaotic, bloodied tennis player. Except the one woman at the concierge's station, none too patient, waiting to be served. 'Where's Arthur? Can't he do that?' she demanded. 'I just want—'

The concierge was growing irritated. 'Arthur is at home, madame. Do you really think Arthur lives in the engine room twenty-four hours a day?'

'While you fiddle, I am missing my show!'

'You could come and see me in the morning.'

'I will complain,' said the woman. 'I did not pay for this kind of disrespectful service.'

'Police!' announced Claude.

But no one believed him. The other lift opened. Five people came out, everyone else got on, including the vexed woman who was missing her show.

The door closed. Claude was alone with the concierge, who informed him, 'You'll have to use the stairs. Someone got up there and jammed it.' Smiling. 'The police are on their way.' He left the riddle of the key ring and took Claude around a corner and opened a door. Pulling yet another key from his pocket, presenting it. 'I hope this is the one. Should take you right into her laundry room…' Pausing, the concierge added, 'I thought you were in the dog house.'

Claude did not have time to explain his life. He snatched the key from the white-gloved hand.

Heart leading, he sprinted up the service stairs.

Georgette Duguay kicked, scratched and flailed at the side of Tommi Bonneau's head with the hard edge of the book she still clutched. 'What the hell book is this?' muttered her attacker as he maneuvered her toward the fence enclosing Pearl's garden...He grabbed her wrist. 'Japanese? Never heard of it.' Georgette broke away, running blindly. He chased, caught her, threw her down. Another flurry of long-legged kicking. He stood back, she found her feet again and ran. He caught her from behind, they recommenced their brawling pas de deux toward Pearl's fence. With a groan and an elbow to his mouth, Georgette again broke free.

But perhaps Georgette sensed she was losing ground. Because suddenly she turned and threw the book she'd found on her way through Pearl's apartment. It seemed she paused to watch *The Three-Cornered World* go flying out over the barrier, then fall.

Then Tommi had her, pummeling her around the mouth, edging her toward the barrier.

Willem van Hoogstraten could only watch, afraid to breathe, heart seized up tight.

Far below and a world away, Aliette Nouvelle arrived with Patrice Lebeau.

The inspector paused for a split second to note Pearl's book lying on the lawn.

Poetry. Novels. Non-fiction best-sellers. The NEWS... Headlines and columns. The never-ending flow of work–related materials: Memos. Briefs. Files. Directives...Don't forget *Marie-Claire* and *Paris-Match*. All this stuff to read if one hopes to stay on top of what is going on. Page by page. A city full of gentle readers. So many hearts' desires. At a moment like this, one wishes for the cinematic, the better to convey the converging of these hearts' movement toward a common highest point: No sense of time, simply engaged, all body in its collective form, pure adrenaline flowing from every direction. And if this *were* a movie, this would be *the* scene — the money scene, production values flowing free, all artifice directed here, a prolonged heroic moment, sublime, extended, deepened, for every solitary heart to observe from a darkness akin to sleep; to see and deeply feel. To own! Chief Judge of Instruction

Gérard Richand is not wrong: there is this need to possess it, to hold it close in the most personal of ways.

Picture it: Georgette Duguay, flung like a giant rag doll, cracks her head, loses her breath, she can't fight this man any longer, his eyes are remorseless, she's only fighting to breathe as Tommi whispers, 'Shhh,' a finger to his lips like a father to his child before lights out. Another fist, in terrible close-up, and she can't think, there's no time to think, but she knows it's over, everything finished, it's silent now save for the wind. She believes Tommi has already pushed her into the sky and all that's left is a woman flying, a reflection in a window — there! — feeling nothing like the bird she has always imagined when imagining her mama, a mother who had flown away from a broken heart when Georgette was still a girl. Why be afraid? It's as if Georgette Duguay sees a woman with nothing to be afraid of and *no time to think at all*. The feeling lasts an eternity.

But is it time enough for Claude Néon to get there? The exiled cop was climbing, deep inside his body, controlling pain, feinting past exhausted focal points, rechanneling dwindling energy streams... Hurry, Claude! Keep it moving, this leg, now the other.

Because Georgette is dropping through a hole in time, a lifetime, time transformed, while Claude is ramping upward, a machine that will *Make* it, you *Know* he *Will MAKE* it, ex*UR*rtion fragmented to essential units, a man, bare bones (metaphorical) set against the spiritual wonder (symbolic) of Georgette as she falls (inside her mind), breathless but alive in one suspended moment within her long-gone mama's heart — as breathless as the breathless man who bursts into the scene, reaches out an arm, catches her, holds her, two of them tumbling away from Tommi Bonneau, Claude's body doing everything it needs to, every instinct in each movement being fulfilled, so natural, a natural man: Claude Néon. Yes!

These reports of people on roofs, on towers. People flying? There are always reports and you have to read them closely. Because they're random, some near the scene, others miles away, still others, simply dreaming. Commissaire Duque's City force will follow up, to be sure, but let's be real: those reports will most likely sit in drawers.

Bottom line: Claude Néon was alone with it, no credible witness (Willem's eyes still frozen) when he got to the top, almost dead from running up eleven flights because Georgette Duguay didn't know enough to disengage Pearl's lift key, smashed through an already severely busted laundry room door and onto the terrace, entered the struggle and successfully, if not gracefully, prevented Tommi Bonneau from following through on his horrible scenario.

Heroic? Claude found himself in a tangled heap in the shrubbery. He knew, with the last bits of sense that could send this information, that he was fast approaching delirium. The woman, whom he'd recognized as Aliette's bitchy old friend, appeared to have fainted in his arms. Maybe it was more serious than that. But Claude shoved her away and let her collapse as Tommi Bonneau attacked. The camera had been traded for a pole, the one Pearl used to fish bugs out of her pool. It had a spike with a hook on the other end. Ugly… Bonneau's face was turning ugly, the way a man's will when he's about to strike. Claude Néon rolled one way as he pushed Georgette the other. Bonneau's stab went between them and punched through the webbing of Pearl's chain-link fence. When Claude looked, his attacker was trying to pull his weapon free, but the hook had caught. It gave him time to find his delirious feet.

Tommi Bonneau gave up on the spear. He came at Claude with his own brute force.

A fight to the death is essentially crude, pure adrenaline, a perfect color. Bonneau's force turned out to be something the training machines in his dining room had barely hinted at. Claude could match the man for height, but that's where it ended. Some blows to the face and the cop was near helpless. With a bearish grunt, Tommi corralled him and lifted—easy, no more than an inconsequential featherweight bundle to be carried to the edge and tossed back into the night. 'Reputation belongs to the one who lives the longest,' sang Tommi Bonneau. Claude had a moment of feeling he'd heard that line somewhere, when? how? but all he could do was clutch the chain-link fence. Moments before, powered by the adrenaline fantasy, this cop's fingers had been veritable steel clamps—now they were bloody, soggy butcher's string, shredding, about to break. Claude Néon held onto the chain link and tried to kick with feet that had no purchase…with a knee…or…

Bite the fucker's nose. 'Ah!' Tommi reeled away in pain.

Not the most manly of moves, but it gave him another moment to regroup. Claude ran to the other side of Pearl's pool. Grabbing a folded deck chair, he wielded it.

'*Connard*,' sneered Tommi. He leapt across Pearl's pool, no problem, far too fast, grabbed the chair when Claude moved to strike, ripping it away and smashing him with it. 'Stupid, weakling cop!' Tommi Bonneau hammered Claude Néon —

— who went back-pedaling, tipping chairs, warm blood leaking down the side of his head, badly needing an angle, an advantage, desperately needing help.

Aliette found the concierge still working on the problem of the stranded lift. Someone had not thought to disengage the key (which he'd left carelessly unguarded) upon their arrival at the top-most floor. His only explanation was that Arthur, who ran the building's engines, did not work nights. Madame Inspector would have to proceed on foot. He showed her to the back stairs. Presumably her colleague had succeeded in gaining access.

My colleague? Right, merci...

A heavy frustrated train of uphill thinking hitched itself to the inspector's already over-extended sense of duty. She, logically, thought it must be Pearl up there *with my colleague* as she frantically climbed eleven flights with Inspector Patrice Lebeau. Stupid woman, Aliette. Only the 7th? Please! ...these never-ending steps, each and every one weighed down by an overwhelming sense of futility. Why in God's name did she bother? When they arrived in Pearl's laundry room and moved with caution into the darkened apartment, she was sweating like a pig.

'Careful...' sending Patrice creeping down the hall toward Pearl's bedroom, pistol at the ready.

Then, stepping onto the terrace, she sprinted to Claude's aid, kicking at Tommi Bonneau —

— who turned and punched her in the face.

Stars. Aliette Nouvelle saw stars...first time in her career...in her life! and went sprawling.

Then she heard Patrice yell, '*Arretez!*' and a moment later the blunt report of his gun.

## – 47 –

### Face in a pool of light

Norbert ('you can call me Norrie') Fauré had been gazing down from a 7$^{th}$ floor window as Rose Saxe had fussed in her *salle de bain*. He was not undercover (as they say). He'd shown his ID card to the man guarding the club gate, and had shown it again as he walked through the front door. Not hiding at all. He made sure Gaston knew exactly who he was: Commissaire Néon's guest.

'Of course, monsieur.' Fauré was shown into the bar, where he could wait for the commissaire, who was 'out on the practice court, I believe.' Fine. Nice service at this place. 'What are you drinking, monsieur?' Suze and soda. 'Very good.'

But the man who brought it refused to take his money and Gaston appeared again to explain:

'No, no, monsieur, one does not pay with cash or a card. It has to go on a chit.'

A chit? But whose? 'I mean I'm not a—'

'*B'en*, Monsieur Néon's…' Shrugging; obviously.

Norbert Fauré balked. Having a word is one thing; having a drink that would be on the record is something else again. Then a woman walked in, in a tennis skirt, showing legs which were still quite fine. She approached Gaston, exasperated, looking for the very man he was watching. And she recognized him. 'Aren't you the divisionnaire? What was your name again?' He admitted that he was and told her his name. She had taken his hand. 'Rose Saxe…of *Le Soir*?'

In reply to her offer, he asked, 'But how could we ever help each other?'

She told him. It was logical, and all the more so when it was confirmed (phone brought to the table by Gaston) that Néon had made a run for it. Well, you have to be ready to improvise. She'd put his drink on *her* chit and gone to change while he made a call instructing his men to blockade the house in the north end. Then Rose Saxe returned, now in smart gold buttons. Her car was in the lot. She smiled a quiet smile, 'I'll shower at my place.'

Fauré followed her out. A shower? She smelled fine enough to him.

They had passed the time in this apartment—a friend's, she said—four floors below the place where that fool Néon had made his big mistake. A logical destination. A perfect place from which to watch the door while getting to know each other.

They did like each other, didn't they? Norrie?

He felt they really did…oh, yes, very enjoyable.

So his vigil had been pleasantly distracted. But when Norbert Fauré saw the car screech to a halt below and Inspector Nouvelle and her assistant race into the building, he knew it was time to pull his pants back on and get going. How! Where! Why! demanded Rose, emerging from the bathroom. She was naked. She was feeling deceived.

'Calm down, get dressed.' What they were on the verge of doing would have to wait.

Rose acquiesced. She sensed an exclusive story. That could be just as good.

The lift was out; they took the service stairs. Being sixtyish, Norbert Fauré took them at a measured pace, emerging in Pearl Serein's laundry room, feeling his gun as he moved toward the opened door, Rose Saxe right behind him, such a breathless woman, but that was part of their deal. And she *was* well made. And manageable for a man of his age and point of view. Not a righteous girl like that Inspector Nouvelle. But she had to keep quiet. '…and stay! well! down!'

'What?…what is going on out there?'

'Shh!' Because no one needs to speak in this kind of situation, which is not unlike an auction, where the most subtle of motions—movement of an eye, a deflating breath indicating *I give up* (too often false) will indicate intentions. The divisionnaire assessed the situation: Néon was severely bloodied. Inspector

Nouvelle had taken a blow. Her assistant had Bonneau lined up, but looked unsteady. Bonneau had a hostage on a precarious edge. There was a body over by the fence.

Norbert Fauré watched Inspector Nouvelle struggle to her feet.

—◦—

The inspector picked herself up slowly. The pain was searing, spreading around her eyes. She dabbed tears with her shirt cuff. Tommi Bonneau came in and out of focus, a shadowy, blurry rim where Patrice held him in his sights at the top of the tower, one step onto the board. Her nose felt strangely cold. There was a throbbing. She took deep breaths and took stock: Claude had taken a beating. Was that *Georgette* sprawled in the bushes? Blinking, wiping her nose on her sleeve, telling Patrice with a gesture to stay cool. Her vision clearing somewhat. Tommi was gazing down at her with that smirk. Be gentle. Any pronounced movement and Willem will fall and be hung. *Don't dare him...*He's waiting to be dared. 'It's time to come down, Tommi.'

'I didn't kill anyone.'

'Please come down...very slowly.'

'A camera never killed anyone.'

'Then your problems will be less than they appear.'

'I was looking for the limits of the heart.'

'Tell this to the court.'

'Don't you patronize me.' Tommi stood up there, defiant. 'People need to know!'

'What if it can't be told? What if there are no words?'

'I have my camera. My lights. My lights see everything...But they don't kill.'

'We'll see.'

'They don't. How could they?'

Wiping more tears, too aware of the dull stabbing between her eyes, too weary of men and their excuses. 'She didn't love them. Her reasons are her own. This won't do, Tommi. Be realistic.'

'No!'

'Please. For Pearl. You've caused a lot of pain. If nothing else, show some compassion for Pearl.' That confused him—she could see his eyes react.

Almost prayerful, Tommi whispered, '*Eternal woman draws us upward.*'

Aliette heard it through the night wind. Beside her, Patrice Lebeau muttered, 'Goethe.'

Georgette, clearly struggling, beaten, choking, called, 'It's garbage! What you do is garbage!'

'*Ta gueule!*' (Shut up!) Angry, Tommi moved, the board bent, Willem wavered…moaned.

'Georgette!' commanded Aliette, 'Please!'

Too late: A popping sound outside the wind, hardly audible (Norbert Fauré favored silencers), a bullet through Tommi's brain, all circuits instantly shorted, Tommi dropped into the glowing pool.

Willem teetered… He didn't topple, but it appeared he was going to faint.

Patrice Lebeau scrambled up the ladder and secured him. Aliette allowed herself to breathe.

Tommi Bonneau floated to the surface of Pearl's pool, face up. Tommi's face in the greenish water was frightening in its heartless emptiness. The inspector, delicate nose swelling grossly, subtle eyes puffing black and blue, turned away to attend to the living.

Claude was incoherent, babbling about a wall. 'Which wall, Claude?'

'This wall…She was flying away…Me! I caught her!' He meant Georgette.

Aliette ignored it. Claude had suffered some serious blows.

As for Georgette, she'd collapsed again. Badly beaten. It wasn't looking good.

To Patrice Lebeau: 'Is she in there?' Meaning Pearl.

Patrice indicated negative. No, no one.

## - 48 -

### Pearl's recurring dream

It's not that hard to hide in a mid-sized city. Or somewhere near it. Two days later, when she gave herself up to the police, Pearl Serein refused to say. But wherever she was at the penultimate moment on her much talked-about terrace, Pearl was safe in a bed, fast asleep. And dreaming.

She dreamed her usual dream of Tommi Bonneau, balanced at the end of her diving board, rocking lightly, testing its spring, gazing up at the stars. Watch: With no fear at all, Tommi pushes hard and is launched into the night sky where he does a perfect-ten, straight-bodied backflip, alights, boom, then another…spinning up into the darkness, landing lightly, arms outspread, elated, shining like a daring *saltimbanque* who knows he controls the hearts of all attending.

But Pearl is the only one attending, always, and he always bows toward her window, smiling.

And she always has to clap, soundless, from the depths of her sleep, marveling…

Yes, this was the dream Pearl Serein told Claude Néon, more or less. Pearl had roused herself and gone to him. She had traded access to her body for another ear to hear her dream. There was always slight relief in the arms of some imperfect man, leaving Tommi alone with his tricks and his smiling. Until it came again. She told the dream to Willem van Hoogstraten. Of course she had told it to her seven lovers. And to Remy Lorentz before them. What Pearl did *not* tell Claude, or Willem, or any of them, was the fact of herself, enthralled by Tommi's every nerveless movement. How she watched with affection and deepest admiration. How she loved to see him — Tommi, the bravest man on earth! spinning in the air for *her*.

Pearl knew it was a love that was unreal, foreign to the waking world, and it made her ache with dream-borne longing. You feel the dream within your body, poignant joy, tactile sadness. She always felt her heart was trapped. I want reality.

But Pearl's eyes were always fast on Tommi. The real Tommi?... The true Pearl?

Pearl told Claude Néon it was a dream that would not go away. She feared it for this reason, and couldn't understand why it would be such a constant part of her life. Which was true. Totally true. We mustn't lie to the police. Pearl had given Claude the scene but not the context:

One moment, years ago, one vital thing passing from Tommi's eyes to hers, never to be repeated, always to be sought. The moment was reciprocal. A flash of lasting beauty. From one heart to the other, light is never just one-way. She could never understand it—how it shaped her. But it had. Was she linked forever to the man in the moon who'd been a beautiful boy in the sun?

So confusing, so deep-seated. You can't tell *that* to another man. Especially not a cop.

Each man has his own context. Pearl Serein knew that. Any woman does.

This time when she awoke, Pearl was free of Tommi, if not the dream, because a dream crosses lines of death. She made her way back to the light of day. Put herself at the mercy of the police. During the follow-up interrogation, Pearl Serein spoke freely with Inspector Aliette Nouvelle. She sensed they shared a lot where it came to men. And books. Pearl was happy to find another soul who understood her kinship to the conflicted Maid at the crux of *The Three-Cornered World*. And she made no attempt to conceal her friendship with the youthful Tommi. She even tried to describe that moment on the roof. Or part of it. Tommi's part. Pearl tried to provide as much insight as she could that might be useful in the reconstruction of the crimes. If they were crimes.

But the inspector was not a man and Pearl kept her dream to herself. She sensed this Aliette Nouvelle might have understood completely, and so she did not tell her of the dream.

It was *her* dream. And Pearl couldn't bear to give it up.

# Epilogue

All initial police communications focused on the abduction of Willem van Hoogstraten and the concise action on the part of Divisionnaire Norbert Fauré which likely saved his life. When the inevitable search through Tommi Bonneau's residence uncovered the body of tennis professional Remy Lorentz in a hastily made grave in his yard, the authorities were happy to shift away from problematic heart attacks. The murder weapon — Didier Belfort's tennis racquet — was found with the body. The fact of Claude Néon's tennis racquet in Bonneau's studio coupled with the published photograph of Claude Néon watching Remy Lorentz hit tennis balls was vaguely circumstantial, but only briefly. Forensics quickly left Claude Néon far from the circumstances attached to that gory discovery. The large fingernail-shredded photograph of Pearl Serein also found with the body proved Belfort's presence in Bonneau's studio, nothing more. A series of ghostly 8x10 black-and-white faces were intriguing. But you didn't need an expensive expert from the capital to explain how Remy Lorentz had been dispatched. The office of the *procureur* saw no need for any follow-up to establish criminal links from Bonneau to the seven deceased lovers — heart attacks would remain the accepted version. A somewhat arcane photographic lighting set-up in Bonneau's studio was left unexplored.

    Inspector Nouvelle considered hauling Anne-Marie back in. But finally didn't. There was no need. Nor any demand on the part of the court. Apart from Georgette, who even knew of Anne-Marie's latest romantic misadventure? She had slipped from view — no sign of the old Westfalia van anywhere. Aliette would never see Anne-Marie again. She would hear from sources on the street that she had gone back to Switzerland. But it was never verified, and she would never go to look. It was a fact of life that street people, even beautiful ones, often disappeared.

The inspector wondered if Anne-Marie ever knew about Georgette.

Aliette brought the book Georgette had stolen from Pearl's bedside table and put it on her pillow. She sat there as a faltering Georgette contemplated those five simple but evocative lines left behind by a despairing Maid trapped in *The Three-Cornered World*. It was impossible to tell what the old artist's model made of it. Georgette Duguay, badly battered, died in a hospital bed three weeks after the fact. Aliette Nouvelle was not there for the end, but the nurses said Georgette had been serene. Although Aliette and Pearl discussed the book in the interview process, it was the *missing* book — Aliette never did return that book to Pearl Serein.

Despite Pearl's expansive, too often meandering confessions, Aliette realized she did not like this woman much. She sensed she was hiding something very important. A cop can feel it.

No, Aliette did not trust her much at all.

Reinstated Commissaire Claude Néon withheld comment. He was quickly given to understand that no one wanted to hear about his heroics, much less his experience in front of Tommi's lights.

Willem van Hoogstraten was still in shock, doubting his own words. Willem's version of Tommi's deranged confession was patchy at best. And while he (too) eagerly confirmed the fantastical reports of a man demonstrating flips on the tower under the moonlight, none of it helped bring closure to the matter. Chief Magistrate Richand strongly advised Monsieur van Hoogstraten to resist media blandishments. Closure applied to all involved and Willem would surely regret it if he blabbed. In a word: They wanted it over and done.

Inspector Nouvelle did not argue this result. When asked, she held to the official line.

Absent Tommi, absent Rose — who'd gone to the more exciting regional capital to pursue a career in investigative journalism (and a love affair with Norrie), the popular spin wound down. When Cakeface put her mic in front of Pearl Serein, Pearl told her, 'We follow our vocation. It's the calling of the heart.' Thus Pearl announced the opening of an exclusive kindergarten for boys, which would be located on the premises of her magnificent home in the sky—an excellent vantage point from which a young man could develop a crucial overview of how life really worked. Places were limited, the selection process would be rigorous, Pearl Serein was deeply excited.

Cake smiled earnestly, then took her camera elsewhere. Kindergarten didn't cut it.

But thanks to Cake's investigations, the *parkour* phenomenon quickly grew within our town beyond the smattering of disaffected adolescents, much to their displeasure. Such is the nature of the next new thing. Each night the city skyline was dotted with bodies in marvelous motion. This helped us keep a sense of being plugged in to the zeitgeist in the absence of our Pearl.

Apart from a small group of bourgeois parents clustered in the north end who claimed she worked magic with 'her boys,' the city soon forgot Pearl's name. Because (let's be honest) although fundamental to cultural cohesion, a schoolteacher just isn't very interesting.

Privately, Aliette Nouvelle still had many questions.

'Knowing what you know, would you trust her with your child?'

Claude said, 'I want to be believed, but if I'm not, it doesn't matter. All I know is that I never felt more alive than that night.'

Aliette asked, 'Why does it have to be just boys? What does she have against girls?'

Claude said, 'Maybe I experienced something like it when I was kid. When every street was huge, you know? A little bit of freedom. Invincible. A sense of immortality.'

Aliette mused, 'But just boys? It seems less than evolved. You know? It goes against that tough, independent streak I thought I saw. No?'

'Never felt more like a man...never felt more alive,' said Claude.

'All the parents say she tells them stories—her boys, I mean,' said Aliette.

Claude told Aliette, 'I felt I couldn't die!'

Aliette told Claude, 'I felt she was hiding something from me. I wonder what she tells *them*.'

Claude insisted, 'I've told you everything. There's nothing more.'

'There was something not quite right about this woman,' Aliette insisted.

'I agree,' Claude murmured. But he never again mentioned her name.

'I should not have been so quick to give her the benefit of the doubt...but I'm not perfect.'

Claude laughed, of course she was perfect! And he dared her to try a run.

With him. *Un petit parkour?* Come on! They would go together.

But the inspector said she was happy enough with her feet on solid ground.

Yes, Aliette and Claude were sometimes off on different trains of thought. But lovers can do this because the bed they share creates abiding context. The only power game is love. Claude was hers again and (almost) everyone was none the wiser. *She* listened when he tried to explain his version of that night. She listened and, trained as she was to sort through lies, realized it was something he believed. She sensed he believed it because it tapped intrinsic levels, a deep vein of imagination, the self in embryo (Claude's self, at any rate), never clearly known, transported by pure energy, or the dream of it, via the heart to an image formed in the core of his brain.

Perhaps not the story of what actually occurred, but certainly the story of Claude.

*Bon.* So Aliette and Claude had survived their first *crise d'amour*. Hadn't they? And they shared a secret. Yes, he could agree they had survived the crisis. And they did share a secret.

So now? What next? How much further could they take it?

But men hate that kind of question. Try a different tack, Inspector.

She ran a finger down his belly...going, going...Claude's heart was beating!

'*On roule?*' whispered Aliette Nouvelle.

– *fin* –

John Brooke became fascinated by criminality and police work listening to the courtroom stories and observations of his father, a long-serving judge. Although he lives in Montreal, John makes frequent trips to France for both pleasure and research. He earns a living as a freelance writer and translator, has also worked as a film and video editor as well as directed four films on modern dance. His poetry and short stories have been widely published, and in 1998 his story "The Finer Points of Apples" won him the Journey Prize. Brooke's first Inspector Aliette mystery, *The Voice of Aliette Nouvelle*, was published in 1999, followed by *All Pure Souls* in 2001. He took a break from Aliette with the publication of the novel *Last Days of Montreal* in 2004, but returns with her in *Stifling Folds of Love*.

Eco-Audit
*Printing this book using Rolland 55 Enviro White
instead of virgin fibres paper saved the following resources:*

| Trees | Solid Waste | Water | Air Emissions |
|---|---|---|---|
| 3 | 162 kg | 10,719 L | 422 kg |